THE UNREPENTANT

HELL'S REDEMPTION: BOOK 2

GRACE MCGINTY

ALSO BY GRACE MCGINTY

Hell's Redemption Series

The Redeemable: The Complete Novel

The Unrepentant: The Complete Novel

The Fallen: The Complete Novel

The Azar Nazemi Trilogy

Smoke and Smolder

Burn and Blaze

Rage and Ruin

Dark River Days Series

Newly Undead In Dark River

Stand Alone Novels and Novellas

Bright Lights From A Hurricane

The Last Note

Hunting Isla (Coming Soon)

Castle of Carnal Desires

Treasure

For my Family

THE UNREPENTANT

PART I

PROLOGUE

I t wasn't often that I got to mix work and pleasure, but today was one of those days. I stood at the back of the large auditorium, invisible to the world leaders that filled its seats, but not to the woman on stage. She saw me all too well, and her smile lit up my heart like a Christmas tree. She looked beautiful on the stage, her deep red hair ethereal under the lights pointing at the lectern. Hope. That tiny baby had turned into this beautiful, strong, intelligent woman, and I couldn't be prouder.

I gave her a thumbs up as she began to speak.

"Ladies and gentlemen, esteemed leaders of the world, I thank you for inviting me to speak at the World Humanitarian Summit. I know that you wished for my father to speak here tonight, but unfortunately they are caught up in Hurricane Katherine in Polynesia, where they have been building clinics and schools in the poorer island nations. But as the Director of the NRH foundation for the United States, I can assure you I am more than qualified to speak in his place.

"As many of you know, NRH started as eight people with an idealistic idea to use their wealth to better the lives of others by dressing up as ninjas. Hence the Ninja Robin Hood name." There was a muted laugh from around the room. "Since then, NRH has spread across the globe, teams of people working on the ground to better the services and facilities available to all. My parents were the first team and they will continue to do so until they can do no more. Luckily, between them all, they make quite the team." There was another small chuckle from those who knew the story, who'd read the tabloids that had 'exposed' them as a polyamorous group. Hope continued.

"Our mission is to globally raise the level of health-care and education to a standardized level, so everyone can have an equal opportunity to survive and thrive. And whilst we are doing that on the ground, we also want to do that on a much larger scale. We want to eradicate viral diseases that can cripple whole countries. The pharmaceutical wing of NRH has purchased half a dozen patents for vaccines to crippling diseases such as AIDS, hepatitis and the omega virus. We have also purchased the patents for the new cancer cure for 27 billion dollars and intend to distribute it at cost price plus 1%. Our working model is that if the patent pays itself off before the its exclusivity lapses, which is unlikely, we will make the patent public for free use by other companies. We do not want to make money, we want to eradicate needless deaths."

Hope continued, and I dragged my eyes away as I felt a presence beside me. I almost startled when I realized it was Michael. I nodded my head in respect. "Archangel. What brings you here?"

He smiled at me, in that beatific way, but his eyes stayed on the stage. "She speaks beautifully, does she not?"

I nodded warily. Michael laughed. "Don't look so worried, Acerezeal. I am just touching base? That's the human phrase, no?"

I nodded again. "How are they doing? Your Arcadia and her redeemed Sins?"

"They are bettering humanity, as Hope said. Banging like monkeys in their down time. Seriously, if they don't cut it out, one of them will have a heart attack."

Michael frowned at me disapprovingly, but he couldn't hide the shine of amusement in his eyes.

"I am glad it all worked out in the end. There has been too much animosity through the ages and it has led to attitudes like Uriel and Azriel's, though I think Azriel may be tested soon." He looked back at the stage, and I didn't blame him. Hope looked magnetic. Michael continued. "Lucifer, for all his faults, fell because he cared too much not to question the Father. There is so much heart in him, more than he gives himself credit for. But there's a faction that believes in following the Father's word to the letter, twisting it to go down the path of near cruelty." Michael sighed.

"Uriel is an asshole," I agreed. Being the top Archangel had to suck. "You'll bring him to heel,

Archangel. Without more of us falling. Though, if they do fall, I promise that Lucifer will squash the cruelty right out of them. Fire meeting fire, and all that."

We watched the crowd, but their attention transfixed on the stage. Hope definitely had a little extra oomph that wasn't entirely human. Her eyes glanced our way and she too startled slightly at the sight of Michael. He smiled and gave her a wave and she raised her hand back, before continuing her speech, the consummate professional.

"I fear she'll be tested too, soon enough," he murmured. "And the other twin? Estrella?"

"She joined the Boston Police Department," I smiled, still remembering the Mulligans horror that she was going to become a cop. Hilarious.

"Aiding humanity too," Michael nodded. He placed a hand on my shoulder. "You did a good thing all those years ago."

"I know."

CHAPTER ONE

ESTRELLA

The force of Hope's scream in my head knocked my legs out from under me. My 'World's #1 Cop' mug slipped from my hands and fell to the ground, shattering. My head cracked against the old linoleum floors, and the world went grey.

Hope! I screamed back, but all I got was complete silence. I mentally scrambled around for my bond with my twin, but although I could feel she was still alive, I was getting nothing back. I jumped to my feet, slipping into the supply closet at the back of the precinct, thankful that no one else had arrived this early. Being an overachiever had its perks.

Luc! I shouted. *Luc, I need you! I'm at work, supply closet in the back of the building near my desk, fourth door on the right.* I could feel my call connect with Luc, and an instant later, the door to the supply closet was yanked open by no one; at least that's how it would appear to normal humans. But I was not normal. I saw the two huge Fallen Angels that stood there. One was Lucifer, Lord of

Hell, and the other was one of the Princes of Hell, Mephistopheles. They jammed their way into the supply closet with me, and I was soon crushed in by a solid wall of muscle and massive wings.

"What is wrong, Estrella?" Luc's voice held a sense of urgency.

"Something is wrong with Hope. She screamed and our connection went dead." Luc's body tensed against mine.

"Last location?"

"UN offices in Geneva." Luc grabbed my arm and we sifted, and that rollercoaster feeling swirled up in my guts like always.

Sifting was like teleporting, but with a greater chance that all your parts won't mesh back together properly at the end. It was the worst and left me incapacitated for about ten seconds after we landed. Didn't sound like much time, but I'd learned even seconds counted.

We landed on the footpath beside the conference center, and I sucked in a gasp, cold dread settling over my body. Hope's bodyguard, JJ, lay dead on the pavement, two shots in his chest and one between his eyes. He'd been professionally executed. I scrambled for my connection to Hope again, but it was still blank. My fear threatened to choke me.

Luc looked down at me. "Be calm. You would know if she were dead." I nodded stiffly and tried to slip back into cop mode. I looked at the scene with cool professionalism.

JJ's gun was still holstered, which told me that it was

a surprise attack. Hope's tote bag lay beside him, contents spread across the ground, as well as her purse and the latest model cellphone. She was a bit of a tech geek, not that she would admit it. The fact that it was all still here told me that it hadn't been a random act of violence. As if JJ's wounds hadn't been enough. The fact the stuff was still here and the place wasn't crawling with cops told me that it hadn't happened that long ago. Skid marks led away from curb.

"Luc," Memphis called. I turned to where he stood beside a small row of box hedges. I looked over, holding my breath, prepared for it to be Hope's dead body despite Luc's confidence that she was alive.

I felt like an asshole when I was overcome with relief that the bodies of two valet's lay crumpled there, like discarded trash blown into the shrub.

"They masqueraded as valets," I whispered to myself, though Luc was nodding in agreement.

I pulled my phone from my pocket, scanning through my messages to the group chat we had with our parents. Hope had sent a picture of her rental Prius to taunt Tolliver. He hated her Prius at home, and she loved to tease him about his car snobbery. I clicked #3 on my speed dial but there was no answer. Dammit. Stupid Hurricane. I needed my Dad right now. I called #4 on my speed dial instead. It answered on the second ring.

"Charlie speaking," a bored voice said on the other line.

"Charlie, it's me. I need your help. I need you to track Hope's rental Prius, license plate number VK-96-

KT. It should have a LoJack. She's been taken." I cursed myself when my voice wavered, but Charlie wouldn't care.

"Fuck. Fuck. Hang on, Rella." I could hear his fingers flying across his keyboard. Charlie was a Mulligan, of the Mulligan mob, and he was their resident tech expert. Everything he knew though, he learned from Oz, my dad. Mom was not amused when she found out, though the Mulligan's had been over the moon. "It's on a stretch of road about three miles away; sending you the coordinates now. Looks like it's been dumped." He hesitated. "Rella, can you, you know?"

We'd grown up with Charlie. He knew Hope and I had a bond; that we could communicate telepathically and feel the twin bond no matter where we were in the world. It defied explanation, but it was hard to hide as a kid.

"She's not dead, Charlie. I can't reach her, but she's not dead." With that I hung up. I showed Luc the coordinates, and he sifted us there. My heart pounded as we walked toward the car. I knew how Schrödinger's cat felt now. If I didn't look in there, I could hold onto the belief that she may still be alive. Luc strode ahead and looked into the backseat. He pulled open the boot using brute force.

"She's not here." I let out the breath that was burning my lungs. I looked through the car, careful to not touch anything for the lab guys. Did Geneva have lab guys? Fuck it, I didn't care. There was blood on the backseat, and my heart lurched. She was injured, but I knew that. She'd have to be unconscious for me not to be able to feel her.

"You guys getting anything?" The Fallen had abilities, especially Luc. I didn't know what they were really, other than being piss-your-pants scary. Memphis looked at me, his eyes swirling with anger.

"They left an imprint of evil. Death. Bloodlust."

"Can you tell where they were going?" Memphis shook his head, and Luc just stared at the car intently. Any more intently and the Prius would set on fire.

"Nothing," Luc growled out.

I looked at my watch. Thirty-seven minutes from her abduction. The golden hour was winding up fast, and we had nothing.

Wake up, Hope. Goddammit, wake the fuck up! I shouted down our link. I yelled it over and over, until I felt her stutter awake. And then I let out a scream and fell to my knees. She was in so much pain. Luc was beside me, dragging me to my feet.

"North, about five miles. Warehouse." I sent him a mental image. Luc's face got even scarier, and he sifted us to the location that only I could feel.

Three sifts in quick succession had left me disorientated, and I barely held my feet and my lunch when we landed

"Azriel, no!" Memphis yelled, and I spun, my vision whirling with me like I was drunk. I saw an angel sift out of the room, taking all my oxygen with him.

Hope was chained to a pipe, her body naked and severely beaten. She made a wracking, gasping noise, and blood pooled on her lips. I moved inhumanly fast to her side. I whispered reassurances, though I didn't comprehend what was coming out of my mouth. I tugged at her chains, but then Luc was there, pulling them apart like string, and Memphis was catching her frail body in his arms as if she were made of the finest porcelain. Then Memphis disappeared. "What the fuck? Luc, where did they go? She needs a hospital!" Luc looked pissed, but he managed to mutter. "Memphis will not let her die. Let's go see if there's anyone here that knows death stalks them."

I followed behind him as he strode out of the basement, and up into the main room of what appeared to be mechanic workshop. A man leaned against the wall beside the door, and all the color left his face as he took in the Devil.

"Who are you?" Luc roared, and the guy legit pissed himself. I got it. I was tempted to do the same, lucky I did my Kegels. "Answer me!"

"Paul-l-o Varucci," the guy stuttered out.

"Why did you take the girl?"

"I didn't." Tears were beginning to stream down his face.

"Do not lie to me." Luc's voice went whisper soft, and it was even scarier than his yell.

"I just get paid to guard the door," the man cried, as blood began to trickle from his ears. "By the Estonians." The last word was a whisper.

Luc leaned forward, putting his hands on both sides of the guy's head, and it looked almost loving. He leaned real close, and I thought he might give him the kiss of Judas. Instead he whispered, "You will know no rest in my domain," and ripped the man's head from his shoulders.

I struggled to stop myself from throwing up, but I didn't want to leave any evidence that I'd been at the crime scene. It was a close-run thing though.

Luc cocked his head. "There's no one else here. Let's go."

He wrapped an arm around my waist, and I stared up at him. "I'm going to kill them all, you know."

He nodded, and there was a glint in his eye that may have been pride. He sifted us one more time, and I clung to his shirt until my land legs came back. Then I gaped. I stood in the presence of an Archangel. I couldn't be sure which one, but there was no doubt in my mind *what* he was. Luc smiled and wrapped his arms around the Archangel. "Hello, old friend."

I was more shocked by Luc hugging someone than I was about him ripping the head of that guy. I was so mesmerized by the brilliant light coming from the Archangel that I missed all the conversation, unable to drag my eyes from his face.

Memphis handed Hope to Luc, and Hope looked less like death. They sifted away, and I looked back at the Archangel. He smiled at me, and cupped a hand around my temple, his warmth flooding my mind.

"Don't let it consume you, sweet one," he said, and I resisted the urge to turn my face into his hand. I couldn't make my tongue work, and Memphis just rolled his eyes and sifted us away, the Archangel's laughter trailing us.

We were back in Hope's Manhattan apartment, and she connected with me straight away.

I could read Raphael.

I jolted with shock. So that was who the Archangel was. Still, I gave her the same warning I always did. Keep it quiet, don't tell anyone. It was more important than ever now. Her empath abilities were our lifelong secret, though I suspected everyone knew, and kept it a very close secret. We never spoke about it. It was too much of a threat.

After Luc laid her on the bed, I wrapped the sheet around her and then I laid down beside her, wrapping my body around her small broken one.

I'm okay now, she whispered in my mind. I let the tension leave my body. When Mom and Eli turned up with Ace, I knew that it would all be okay.

But I knew what I had to do.

CHAPTER TWO

I downed another glass of whiskey and caught Mike the Barman's attention. I pointed to my glass, and Mike raised his eyebrows. I scowled at him. I was good. He just laughed and came over to pour another one.

"You putting my kids through college, Jones?"

"As long as they don't wanna become cops, Mike."

"Sip this one, Jones, or I'm gonna have to cut you off." I rolled my eyes but nodded.

Someone settled onto the stool beside me. "I got her, Mike."

I looked at Charlie, and then back at Mike accusingly. "Traitor." Mike just laughed and walked to the other end of the bar.

"Getting messy, Rella?" he asked quietly.

I looked over at him, his sharp jaw pressing against pale Irish skin, a few freckles across his nose highlighting his boyish good looks. The sparkling green eyes and dimples made him an adorable lady killer. But I knew that he blushed when he was embarrassed, and he didn't have his first kiss until he was seventeen and had a growth spurt. We were best friends.

He just happened to be the Mulligan Gang's tech guy.

I just happened to be a Boston cop.

Well, I used to be.

"Bernie at the precinct told me you quit."

I glared at Mike and downed my drink. Take that, Mike. "Is Bernie a Mulligan informer now?"

Charlie grinned. "Nah, Bernie's banging Aunt Clary."

I tried not to imagine that. Bernie was gross, and Clary was like a second mother to me. She'd adopted Adnan and Nazir after they'd been rescued from the rubble in Aleppo and raised them in the brownstone next to ours. I still didn't know the entire story there, but the whole lot of us were close. Well, except Nazir. I didn't really remember him. He'd gone to military school before I was five and hadn't really been home since. But Adnan was like the third musketeer to Hope and I. Add in a couple of the Mulligan cousins including Charlie and we had raised hell in our Boston neighborhood.

"I'm doing what I need to do, Charlie. I thought you of all people would understand that. They put her in hospital. If you had seen her..." I trailed off and wished there was more whiskey in my glass. Or maybe I just needed the bottle. I couldn't chase away the images fast enough.

Charlie put his hand on my knee and squeezed. His

touch was a comfort. He was my best friend. He knew me as well as I knew myself. Well, almost. There were secrets we all had to keep.

"I understand, Rella. I do. But whatever you are planning, you aren't doing it without me."

I tensed my jaw and turned to look at him, his brilliant green eyes like sparkling like gems. Such a weird shade on a man, but I had found them mesmerizing as a child. Hell, they were still mesmerizing to this day. His look told me he was with me, no matter what, until the very end. I sighed and leaned my head on his shoulder.

"I'm gonna find them all, Charlie. And I'm gonna make them pay."

He kissed the top of my head and wrapped an arm around my shoulder. "Okay, Rella Rua. We will make them hurt for what they did for Hope. Just don't cut me out okay. I've got your back." I smiled at his use of his childhood nickname for me. Apparently, it's an Irish thing, adding rua to the end of the names of people who had red hair. Rua meant red.

I sighed, my head churning over with hundreds of possibilities, where to start, what my end game was, everything.

Eventually, Charlie peeled me off the barstool and took me home. I lived in a converted warehouse apartment, with barely any furniture and a fridge basically just for beer and ketchup. Not that I was trying to live up to a stereotype or anything. Sam, one of my Dads, called it Cop Chic. Usually with his nose screwed up.

But it was close to the precinct and Mike's bar, so I didn't mind. I didn't inherit any of Sam or Tolliver's aesthetic tastes. If the bed was warm and the pillow was fluffy, I was good. I wasn't here often enough for the rest of it to matter.

Charlie walked me home, unlocking the door with his spare key. The whole place was open plan, except the bathroom. My bed was a four poster, with gauzy white curtains. It looked like a princess bed in the middle of a frat house. Swords were poised on the wall, looking like decoration, but I knew how to swing those bad boys like Joan of Arc, thanks to Lux. My only other luxury was the kitchen. I loved to bake cupcakes, so my kitchen was state of the art. I smiled at the thought. My love of baking was intertwined with my love for Valery, my other father. Yeah, I have seven Dads, so what?

"I know that, Rella. We grew up together, remember?" Charlie laughed at my drunk ass, and I realized I must have been speaking out loud.

I muttered something and staggered toward my bed. Maybe I was still getting vertigo from all the sifting I did a week ago. Or maybe it was the bottle of whiskey? Nah, definitely the sifting.

I sat down on my bed and tried to untie my boots, but all the blood kept going to my head and made me want to puke. They could just stay on. I flopped back on to the satin comforter and squinted. If I closed my left eye just right, the room didn't spin as much.

Charlie was still laughing as he undid my boots and pulled them off. Then my socks.

I pulled my shirt over my head, and Charlie let out a choked gasp.

I rolled my eyes, or I thought I did anyway. "They're just boobs, Charlie. Nice boobs too, I think."

Charlie looked at the floor. "Sure, Rella. Let me just get you a shirt."

He rummaged through my drawer and pulled out an old cotton tee.

I stood and undid my bra and giggled at Charlie's bright red face. He threw the shirt at me.

I fiddled with the button of my jeans, but they refused to come undone. I stamped my bare foot.

"Charlie, help me take my pants off?"

Charlie's eyes snapped to mine, dipped to my now naked breasts, then back to my face and stayed glued there.

"Am I interrupting something?" A dark voice asked, its growl somewhere between amused and threatening.

Charlie went pale.

I whipped around too fast and lost my balance, landing on my face at Luc's feet.

"Sup, Luc?" I looked at his shiny black shoes. He seemed more like a brogues kinda guy. Or those combat boots next to his. I counted his feet. One, two, four... "Did you know you have six feet right now?" I asked, my cheek pressed against the polished cement floor that was currently freezing my nipples. There was a small wave of laughter in the room. He clicked, and I was clothed.

"God, I wish I had that trick," Charlie muttered from somewhere behind me.

I was in fluffy pyjamas patterned with pink elephants in tutus. I think I had a pair exactly like it when I was four. Luc reached down, and I grabbed his hand, resisting the urge to grab my head as he pulled me to my feet.

"Uh, Luc, I take it back. You only have two feet."

Because the other two sets belonged to two scary ass guys who made my nonexistent panties go up like a Roman candle.

"Yes, I only have the two, Estrella. It is good to see you again, Charles Mulligan."

Charlie came up behind me, placing his hand on my back. I didn't know if he was trying to be supportive or thought that Luc wouldn't eviscerate him for seeing me naked if he was somehow attached to me. He needn't have worried. Luc was cool. If it'd been Lux in my apartment, he'd have been in way more trouble. That Dad had been a Spartan and had made dating in my teens a nightmare.

"Hello, Sir."

The Devil scared the shit out of the Mulligans; although they weren't certain of who he was, they were Catholic enough to guess. Pretty sure they had their own little section of hell reserved, so they were right to fear him.

I took in the men with Luc. They weren't Fallen, I knew that much. They were big and dark, their olive skin hinting at something Mediterranean, or Spanish perhaps. They were nearly identical, but there were a couple of subtle differences. The least subtle was that they both had different colored eyes. The slightly bigger one on the left had one emerald green eye and one that was sapphire blue. The one on the right had one that was a deep chocolate brown, almost the color of his hair, and the other one was the color of liquid gold. Their eyes were captivating. They stood well over 6"5 and they were hard. That was the only description I could think of. Their eyes were hard, their expressions were hard, and their bodies were like stone. I took another moment just to appreciate every defined muscle.

"Who are your friends?" I really didn't mean to purr the question out, but the whiskey was loosening my tongue.

"Romanus and Rouen. They are *Gargoille.*"

"They're what?"

"Demons," the one on the left growled.

"Gargoyles," the one the right clarified, still a growl but a little less inhuman.

"Gargoyles," I repeated. "Fuck me."

The big one's nostrils flared, and Golden Eye quirked an eyebrow.

"I wouldn't go throwing around offers like that, Estrella, Child of my Beloved," Luc said, his tone bland but something in his words wiped the expression from their faces.

"Did you just Rock Block me?" I asked Luc. "Get it? Rock Block, because they are gargoyles and turn to stone?" I began to giggle again. Dammit.

"I get the pun. Unfortunately, that is really not how it works. They have a light sensitivity that meant they had to seek shelter from the sun in the early days, hence the myth that they turned into statues. But now they have polarized glasses. Welcome to the twenty-first century."

"Such a killjoy." I sighed and sat down on the bed,

picking fluff off my pink elephant pajamas. "To what do I owe this super awkward visit with your demon entourage?"

Luc's lip quirked. He may have been amused or pissed. One of those things was extremely bad for your health.

"I have heard you have quit the human police force and you have plans to become some kind of red-headed vigilante."

I stiffened. Shit. If Luc knew, then Ace knew. They didn't keep anything from each other. If Ace knew, then she would totally tell either Hope or Mom, depending on who would amuse her most at the time.

"Who'd Ace tell?"

Luc just smiled at me enigmatically. Asshole. But I grinned back. Somehow, I think I got all the rebellious genes. Hope, well she was something else. Pretty sure she was as close to angelic as you could get while being related to me.

I tried to work it through. If Ace told Mom, Mom would tell all my Dads. Which meant she would tell Lux, which meant that I'd be grounded for the foreseeable future. You wouldn't think it possible to be grounded at twenty-two, while living in your own apartment, but Lux would just rock up on my doorstep and keep an eye on me. May as well as be fifteen and grounded again.

That wouldn't suit Ace at all. She was a rabble rouser, a bad influence and she liked nothing better than some brutal revenge. So, she'd tell Hope, who'd keep my secret but still chew me out.

I sighed. "Dammit, Ace."

Whatever.

I looked between Tall, Dark and Scary One and Two. "What's with the lawn ornaments then?"

The big one, I think his name was Romanus, growled again. They did that growly thing a lot. "Demon."

Another sigh overtook me. "Yeah, I know, Big Guy. Gargoyles. I was making a joke. Me Tarzan, you Jane."

The little one laughed. I had to stop calling him the little one though. He was still, like, six feet six or something.

"Wouldn't you be Jane, and Romanus Tarzan? I've seen him naked. He's definitely got the vine to swing on, if you know what I'm saying?"

I blinked, stunned to muteness. They spoke more than single syllables? Good, I was beginning to wonder if the rocks were just in their heads. Unwillingly, my eyes dropped to the tight leather pants the big guy wore. He was indeed packing.

"Stop staring at my dick," Romanus growled again. I was beginning to think it was the natural timbre of his voice.

I smirked and looked back at Luc, my eyebrow raised in question. Luc didn't look half as amused as I felt.

"They are here to help you. The Gargoyles are my best hunters. Hell, they are my best killers. And they will watch your back. Not that I doubt the proficiency of the Mulligan over there." His tone insinuated that Charlie would be as useful as a snowball in hell.

I looked between them again. "You know, most

parents get their kids a pony for their birthday, not a matching set of bloodthirsty demons."

Luc cleared his throat, uncomfortable. "I am not your parent."

An uncomfortable Luc was the best kind of Luc in my opinion. If you can fuck with the Devil and get away with it, well, that was the best feeling ever. I couldn't stop.

"Well, you're not my Daddy either, so I don't know why you are giving me the statue of David over there." I pointed at the shorter one, Rouen.

"I can assure you, I am better hung than David," Rouen said, and winked. Actually winked. And it went straight to my pussy like a heatwave. Luc's mouth tightened into an unamused line.

"I do not trust you not to get yourself killed. I can't track you, and I can't hear your thoughts, and I do not have time to babysit you while you seek your petty revenge. Consider these two your babysitters-slash-junkyard dogs."

"What am I supposed to do with them? What do I even feed them?"

"I like to eat mouthy redheads," Romanus said threateningly.

"Not right now, big guy, we barely know each other," I gave him a saucy wink, and Rouen laughed.

Luc threw his hands in the air. "Ace had way too much effect on you!" He looked at the gargoyles. "Don't let her die, or I will personally flay you alive and stake you in the demoness pit with a permanent hard on."

With that, he disappeared in a puff of smoke. Showoff.

I looked over at Charlie, who was doing a pretty good impression of a statue. Charlie was tall for an Irishman, and had broad, muscular shoulders that tapered down into a narrow waist, and a cheeky grin that told a girl that it probably wouldn't be permanent, but damn it would be fun. He wasn't cover boy handsome, but still managed to take the V-card of more than one girl in our neighborhood.

Next to Romanus and Rouen however, he looked like a daisy next to one of those huge man-eating plants that lived in the jungle. Bad analogy. Still, I took a step back, so I was standing side by side with Charlie.

"Are you guys gonna murder me in my sleep?" I asked Romanus.

He grinned, and it was fucking scary as hell. "Not today."

Rouen leaned over and punched him in the arm. "Don't be a jerk. Besides, I really don't wanna be staked in the demoness pit. They wear it down to a nub." He shuddered. "Don't worry, we were made to protect the innocent and destroy wrongdoers."

"Like unicorns with virgins? Sorry guys, I haven't been innocent in a long time."

Rouen laughed. "I like you. No, not like unicorns, though I do have something long and hard if you wanna see it?"

I grinned. "Not tonight, Killer. Raincheck. I'm way overdue for monster hangover." I walked back to the bed, and climbed beneath the covers, careful to keep my butt covered. I was a smartass, but I wasn't about to waive a red flag at a minotaur. Charlie climbed in the other side of my bed, still fully clothed.

"No way I'm leaving you here alone with those two, I don't care what they say," he muttered, and I snuggled into him. We'd shared a bed so many times over the years that it was basically second nature, even though we'd never been more than friends. His smell was comforting, like soap, and man, and too much cherry cola. I loved that he thought he would be anything more than cannon fodder for the two gargoyles.

"Thanks, Charlie," I said and kissed his cheek.

He sighed. "Anytime, Rella. Now go to sleep. I'll keep watch."

CHAPTER THREE

The hangover was everything Mike had promised it would be. My mouth felt like it had been wrapped around a blow dryer all night. I dragged my sorry butt out of bed, trying hard not to wake Charlie. He was snoring away softly, the blankets tucked around his waist. He must have lost his shirt at some point during the night.

It might have been the hangover, or the fact my libido has been hit with a two by four in the shape of a gargoyle, but I took a moment to appreciate Charlie the man, and not Charlie, my best friend. His shoulders were wide and strong, although he was so pale he may as well be translucent. Reddish curls spread across his chest, trailing down a pretty decent set of abs for a computer nerd and thickened where the V of his hips met the thick waistband of his denim jeans. I blinked. When had Charlie got hot? I mean, I remembered him as the scrawny teenager who couldn't even grow a half decent moustache. Now, strawberry blonde stubble glinted across his jaw.

I turned away and ignored the weird fact that my body was turned on by the sight of him. It was Charlie, for fucks sake. We'd shared a bath when we were four. I'd fallen off his bike and broken my arm when I was eight. He was not someone I should even consider taking to bed.

I walked into the kitchen, gravitating toward the coffee machine like a moth to a flame. But first I chugged three bottles of water.

I almost choked on my last gulp when I saw my two hellish housemates. Both were sitting in front of my large arched windows, the sun shining across hard muscles that gleamed as if oiled. And they were perfectly still with their eyes closed. Like statues.

"Uh, good morning?"

With creepy synchronization, they turned to look at me. They both slid on sunglasses.

Rouen smiled. "Mornin'," his voice boomed, and I winced as the noise speared through my brain. His grin told me he'd done it on purposes and I scowled.

Romanus grunted.

Probably not a morning person then. Me either.

"Coffee?" I asked him. Maybe he'd be more personable with some caffeine in his system.

He nodded. "Black."

"Like your soul?" I laughed, though he just scowled again.

"My soul is much blacker."

I rolled my eyes and pressed the appropriate buttons

on my machine. It was the true love of my life, bringer of caffeinated goodness. I let the silence stand. I couldn't deal with demons until I'd had at least two espressos.

I downed the first one, feeling a lot more human as the artificial happiness rushed through my veins.

"So, what was with the statue impression over there?"

Rouen shrugged and set my coffee machine to latte. "When you spend centuries avoiding the sun, it's nice to get it where you can. Besides, it gives us energy. So does moonlight, but the sun is more potent."

"Like Superman?" I teased.

"Better," Romanus answered. I wondered if he could say more than one-word sentences.

I waggled my eyebrows at him, and he scowled. I handed him my second espresso, and he drank it in one gulp. I stared at him expectantly.

"What?"

"I was just hoping coffee would lighten you up a little. I'm disappointed."

I walked to the white fluffy rug that sat in front of the large arch windows where the gargoyles had been doing their best impressions of rocks. I called it my hangover safe space. Laying down and pressing my cheek into the soft tufts of carpet, I let out a contented sigh. I loved this spot in the morning, with the sun coming in and warming me on cold winter days. I closed my eyes and let the warmth spread along my skin. Now, to sleep.

I could feel someone's eyes on me. I opened one eye

and let out a startled yip. Rouen lay on his stomach right next to me, his face inches from my nose.

"What the hell are you doing? And how did you move so quietly? You know what, don't answer that, just make some noise next time, or I'm getting you a cat bell." His dual colored eyes were so close, looking intently into mine. He didn't even blink. If I wasn't so caught up in their depths, it might have been weird.

"You look like an angel," he whispered.

I scoffed. "I can promise you I'm not."

But he didn't seem to be listening. "I wonder if you taste like an angel?" He whispered it reverently, but now I was getting freaked. Romanus was suddenly there, hauling Rouen to his feet.

And then he bit him on the shoulder. Hard. The fuck?

He murmured something in a guttural language, and Rouen seemed to snap out of it. I jumped to my feet and backed away from them both. "Dude. What the hell was that?"

Romanus just stared at Rouen, who hung his head. Then he turned his blue and green eyes to me.

"We feed from the sun's light. But that's because it is just a concentration of energy. Of life. Angels possess that very life energy in their veins, which means the blood of angels is very...potent to us. Hard to resist."

"I'm not angelic, and neither is my blood," I protested weakly. It was the longest sentence I'd ever heard him speak, and I found myself a little lost in the very cadence of his voice.

He stepped closer to me, this huge mountain of a

man, uh gargoyle, and I resisted the urge to reach out and touch his slightly luminescent skin. How hadn't I realized last night that it had a faint shimmer to the golden tone, like it was dusted with flecks of gold.

He leaned down, so his face was close to mine. My hindbrain was yelling to run, because that was what normal humans did in the face of terrifying demons that could crush you in an instant. But I wanted to lean forward and capture his full lips with my teeth. God, no one was ever going to accuse me of being normal.

"But you aren't completely human, are you Red?" His growling voice came out as almost a purr this time, and it thrummed down to my core, making me wet.

"Human enough to know I don't taste good," I protested weakly.

Romanus inhaled deeply, his pupils dilating until there was barely a ring of color around them. "I'm gonna have to reserve the right to disagree until I taste for myself."

I had a sneaking suspicion he wasn't talking about my blood. My heart thumped wildly in my chest, making me short of breath, and a wave of excitement rolled over me. My eyes darted to Rouen, who stood slightly behind Romanus, but his pupils were equally as dilated. I wonder if they shared, then I chastised myself for the stupidity of the consideration.

"Rella, are you okay?"

Charlie's voice snapped me out of my lust induced trance, and I threw him a thankful look. Whatever they made me feel couldn't be natural.

Romanus snarled, and I blanched.

"I'm good, Charlie. Actually, I was hoping you could take me to see the family."

"Your family or..."

"No, Charlie. The Family. Capital F."

Charlie groaned. "Aw, man." He pulled his shirt over his head and ran a hand through his tousled hair. He did bedhead well.

"Can you set it up or what? I need to know what they know. None of my police contacts will be any good for the kind of information I'm after. Please, Charlie?"

When I'd become a cop, we'd drawn a big, thick line in the sand. Anything work related, for either the Mulligans, or me, was completely off limits. If I wanted to talk to them about anything nefarious, I had to make an appointment through Charlie and they'd treat me like any other cop. It stopped family functions from being tense.

"Fine. But you are so gonna owe me. This means I have to sit on the other side of the table to you and pretend I'm tough, and you know I hate all that macho posturing bullshit."

I walked over to him and wrapped my arms around his chest.

"I owe you more than one, Charlie Bear."

His big hands spread across my back as he hugged me in return, and I took a huge breath in. How anyone could smell so nice after just rolling out of bed was beyond me, but something about Charlie's scent had always made me feel fuzzy, even when I was a kid.

"Okay, you go get your tough face on and call me

with the meet details? I need a shower, like ASAP. I stink."

Rouen let out a laugh, the intense look gone from his eye. "I think you smell kinda good."

My eyes flicked to Romanus, but his face was impassive.

Charlie leaned down and murmured in my ear. "I don't like leaving you here with those two. They are dangerous. They make the hairs on my arms stand on end."

Someone scoffed. "We have good hearing, kid. You should be scared of us. In this form we are a nightmare, but shifted we are your very worst nightmare made real. The only thing scarier than us is Lucifer in a bad mood. She's safer with us than she would ever be with you."

I whirled around, the urge to protect Charlie making me narrow my eyes. "Back off. I don't need your protection. I'm more than capable of kicking your ass myself." Romanus raised a brow. "Fine, probably not, but I can call Luc quicker than you can say grrr, so stay out of my personal space and we'll get along fine." I turned back to Charlie. "Luc trusts them, and you know Ace would stake him with the demonesses if they murdered me in the shower, so it'll be all good. Go. I'll be fine."

I pushed him towards the door, because I kind of did believe what I was saying. Hope always said that Luc loved us, and she'd know, being an empath and all. It was hard to hide your feelings with resting bitch face when you had an empath as a pseudo-child.

Charlie turned at the doorway and opened his mouth to say something.

"Love you!" I said and shut the door in his face.

I turned back to the gargoyles in my living area. Rouen was smiling, perfect white teeth glinting in the sun, and I noticed his incisors were longer than a human. As were the bottom ones. They were some serious chompers.

Romanus just scowled.

I ignored them and headed straight for the bathroom. I would feel better behind the flimsy lock. I grabbed my gun from the locked nightstand and took it into the bathroom with me. "Stay out of the bathroom, or I will shoot you in the head first and ask questions later. Got it?"

Rouen gave me a grin and a snappy salute, and Romanus just grunted something that sounded like an affirmation.

It had been a hell of a week.

I SAT across from Uncle Joe, Uncle Colin, Cousin Marty and Cousin Paulie inside the Hammer and Pinwheel bar, which was in the shadiest district in Boston. The bar was the base of the Mulligan Family operations, and it lived up to every mob cliché you could conjure.

"Where's Johnnie?" I asked as I sat down. They usually had five at these kind of meetings in case they needed to vote.

"Johnnie is escorting Granny Mulligan, Mam and Aunt Clary to Manhattan to see Hope in the hospital. They're taking her a gift." Paulie's shit eating grin made me instantly suspicious. Paulie was a couple of years older than Charlie and me, and he used to pick on us terribly, in the way only an older brother/cousin could. I didn't bother asking why the female Mulligans taking Hope a present was so amusing, because he wouldn't tell me. That wasn't why we were having this meeting.

Uncle Joe looked at Romanus and Rouen over my shoulder, and if he was fazed by the big gargoyles behind me, he didn't show it.

"What's with the muscle?"

I shrugged. "New bodyguards slash pains in my ass. Everyone's been a little on edge since the thing with Hope…" I trailed off, and anger crossed every one of their faces. They were old school mob. Women and children were off limits. No innocent bystanders. Plus, they loved Hope. While they'd been disappointed with my choice of career, in their eyes Hope was the epitome of the Blessed Virgin herself. The fact that someone had hurt her got their good Catholic misogynistic pride all riled up. I didn't tell them that the gargoyles were demons. They didn't know Ace and Luc were Fallen, though Luc gave them knowing looks at all the family functions. I'd only ever seen the Uncles uncomfortable once or twice in my life, and each time Luc was the cause.

"What can we do for you, Estrella?" Uncle Colin asked, straight to the point as always.

"I need to know who traffics people in Boston."

They looked like I'd slapped them with a fish. "We don't deal in that kind of thing, you know that Rella," Marty chastised. "Besides, I heard you quit the PD."

Seriously, cops gossiped more than old ladies. "Bernie needs to learn to keep his mouth shut. This question is of a more personal nature. Luc and I found that Hope was meant to be sold by traffickers from Estonia. I want to know if anyone here would have a name I could track down. It can't be that big of a community that no one knows nothing. People talk, there's chatter on the market, someone knows something. I just want to know what. I just need a start, so I can make the bastards pay," I implored.

For the first time ever, I'd shocked them to silence. "And what do you intend to do with them once you find them, Officer Jones?" Uncle Joe asked, his head cocked, making the cigar in his mouth slip to the left.

"I'm going to make the hurt, Uncle Joe, and then I'm gonna make 'em die. No one fucks with my family. No one."

When mobsters look proud, you know your life has taken a wrong turn somewhere. "We know who handles the go between in Boston. Usually it's forced labor in this area, but they'll know. They all dabble. Once you've sunk that low, there ain't no filth you aren't willing to wallow in," Joe said, scribbling on a piece of paper.

"Do you need an army?" Uncle Colin asked, and his eyes flicked back to Romanus and Rouen.

I shook my head, smiling fondly at them. Sure, I didn't agree with most of their actions, but they offered me back up without question, just because that's what family did. They had your back.

"Nah, Uncle Colin. A small group is better for

tracking and infiltration. I'd like to borrow Charlie for a while though, if I could? I need a computer guy."

Uncle Joe waived away the request. "Of course. If you need any clean weapons, let me know. I know a guy with some quality product."

I stood, smiling, and they slid out of their chairs. I went around and hugged each one.

"Thanks guys. I'll take you up on that before I leave."

Joe patted my cheek. "Be safe, Estrella." He slipped me a piece of paper with the name and address I needed.

I just nodded, because I could make no promises on that front.

They all turned to Charlie and gave him a pointed look. He sighed. "I'll catch you up in a sec, Rella."

I knew they were making sure he knew to protect me. While they might approve of my bloodthirsty actions, their natural misogyny made it hard for them to send a woman out to do a man's job. Especially when that job included killing.

According the Mulligans, the men were sinners and the women were martyrs. Little did they know I was more than comfortable with the denizens of Hell.

The Gargoyles escorted me out of the Hammer and Pinwheel. They took up the same formation as we walked in. One in the lead, and one bringing up the rear, me wedged in the middle like a sandwich. My mind wandered down a dangerous path, wondered if they did anything else in pairs, a woman sandwiched in between. I let out a little huff, as electricity shot straight to all my happy places.

We stood on the footpath, the cool early spring sun warming my face, and I was suddenly the focus of two very intense gazes.

"Uh, you guys can't read minds, can you?"

Romanus narrowed his eyes. "No."

Rouen grinned like the Cheshire Cat. "But we have acute senses. We can smell tiny changes in human physiology. We can hear a heart rate accelerate before a man strikes, or the smell of a lie." He leaned in close. "The sweet scent when a woman is aroused," he purred next to my ear, and my pussy tingled. His nose flared. "Yeah, that scent right there. Fucking delicious. The way your heart is pounding right now, I think you might like it if I took you down that alley and showed you just what I can do with my tongue. What do you say?"

HELL YEAH! My pussy yelled, fighting the part of my brain that cared about self-preservation. I panted a little with the effort, but I took a step back and out of his intoxicating personal space. I blinked to get my brain cells back online.

"Uh, so apart from good senses, what else do you guys do? If you don't turn into rock monuments that hang out on churches."

"We turn into dragons," Romanus said it as if his answer was as mundane as scrapbooking and crocheting stuffies.

I blinked.

"Small dragons," Rouen clarified. "Like the size of a sports car maybe."

"Oh, just turn into car sized dragons. That's all." My tone was flat because, holy crap! "Well, okay then."

Charlie, with his impeccable timing as always, pushed through the bar door. He looked at me and rolled his eyes.

"Let's go."

We walked to the parking lot at the back of the bar, and all piled into Charlie's SUV. I slid into the back, because I'd already argued with Romanus this morning about calling shotgun. Apparently, I was easier to protect in the back seat. Whatever. It wasn't worth the grief.

"What did the Family say?" I asked Charlie as we pulled into traffic, fiddling with my seatbelt around my jacket. Rouen's hands wrapped around mine and guided the seatbelt into the clip.

"You know the usual stuff. If she is harmed, don't bother coming home, she's worth a hundred of me, the role of a man, all that macho shit. You know the Uncles. Old school."

My fingers buzzed where Rouen had touched my hand, and I was only half concentrating on Charlie's words.

"Do you wanna stop at home and grab your gear? Your gun at least?"

I laughed at the ridiculousness of it all. "Don't need a weapon. These guys turn into dragons."

Charlie swerved, and a taxi laid on its horn. Charlie flipped him the bird out the window.

"Say what?" He stared at me in the rearview mirror. "Seriously?" He flicked a look at Romanus, who just gave a single nod. "Rella, don't take this the wrong way, but your family makes mine look like the fucking Brady Bunch."

Preach.

"I think we should still go and get something a little more human to threaten people with. Probably wait to unleash the dragons on Boston until it's absolutely necessary."

Yeah, that was probably a good point. "Okay, weapons first, then we are gonna pay," I looked down at the paper clutched in my hand, "Alonso Alverez a quick visit."

HOLLYWOOD ALWAYS PORTRAYED the bad guys as being the same. Cold, living in dingy rooms and tenement buildings, twitchy and trigger happy. As a cop, I knew that wasn't true. Sometimes the worst monsters look completely normal.

As I sat in front of Alonso Alverez's house in the suburbs, this truth had never hit me harder. He had a beautiful whitewashed house, with a wraparound porch and a tire swing in the front yard. Kid's bikes laid abandoned beside balls and barbies on the front lawn. There was even a white picket fence.

Alonso Alverez was living the American Dream. All financed by selling people into slavery. I was going to throat punch that guy as soon as he told me what I wanted to know. And then I might let Romanus eat him in his dragon form.

I turned to Charlie. "No name dropping. Keep the

Mulligans out of this." I slipped out of the car and stood on the sidewalk. "No violence unless we are defending ourselves, okay?" Rouen shrugged, and Romanus stared me down. "I'm serious. We will get our fill of bloodshed, but this guy is just a middle man. We'll scare the shit out of him, but that's it."

I walked through the sweet little waist high gate, down the path past the standard roses, and up to the solid oak door with stained glass panels. I wanted to put my fist through it.

I pressed the doorbell, and the sound of little feet running towards the door made me tense.

A little girl, about five, with curly brown hair haloing her cherubic face, answered the door.

"Hello." Her voice was friendly and completely without fear. Anger riled in my gut, but I pasted a smile on my face.

"Hi, is your Dad home?"

"Sure," she said, shutting the door in our faces, but I could hear her yell for her father behind the solid wood.

When it opened again, I was looking at a handsome man in his mid-forties. He had an expensive haircut, a brand name polo shirt, and an artfully trimmed goatee.

When he saw us, his face shut down into an impenetrable mask. We probably made quite an impression as a group.

"Can I help you?"

"You let a child answer the door? Do you have no fucking common sense?" I whisper-yelled at him, in case the girl was still in earshot. I couldn't contain my disgust.

He stepped out of the house, shutting the door and

placing his body between it and us. Like one man would be able to stop us if we'd been someone more nefarious.

"Who the hell are you to come here, to my house? How did you find this address?"

I'd been slightly worried we'd got the wrong guy when we'd pulled up, but his words chased away any lingering doubts.

"You should know better than anyone, Alonso, that shit has a way of following you home and dirtying your nest. You're lucky really, that it was me and not someone less concerned with innocent life. Someone who decided that trafficking your daughter would be a worthy way to punish their competition."

Alonso turned a little grey, but I felt no sympathy.

"I don't traffic kids."

I gave him a sarcastic round of applause. "Someone get him a humanitarian award. You just traffic the desperate, which is so much better."

I was done with this piece of shit. I pulled my gun from my waistband and held it to his gut, angling myself so I blocked the view from the picture window, where any little eyes could be watching. To them I'd look like I was telling him a secret, which I was.

"I need to know who is in charge of the Estonian ring, either their branch here, because I know they'd have one, or their one in Europe. I need names and locations, otherwise I'm gonna let my friends here paint your pretty white fucking fence bright red. I have zero problem with wiping a piece of shit like you from the planet, and they'd enjoy it too," I said the whole thing with a scary smile on my face, and I found I meant it.

Anger warred with fear in Alonso's eyes, and I
shoved the muzzle of my gun a little harder into his gut.
He heaved out a sigh.

"I don't have much to do with the Eastern Euro-
peans. They are scary fuckers, way scarier than you," he
flicked his eyes to Romanus's hard face, and I knew that
no one was scarier than the Gargoyles.

"The Estonians work out of the Gulf, their leader
here is an unstable bastard called Volchek. They ship the
cargo over with normal trade containers, and then
unload them in international waters and move them to
some private cove." His eyes darted between us. "That's
all I know. I don't know where their home base is, or any
of that shit, I swear. I don't know who heads the family,
or anything like that. I'm a middle man, nothing more
than a go-between. I don't know shit."

"Do you have a contact number for this Volchek?"
He shook his head, but I didn't believe him. Rouen
growled. Apparently, he didn't believe him either. "That
scary bastard will seriously eat you, right here on the
lawn, in front of your kids and neighbors. I'd probably
let him too. So, let's rethink your answer? Do you know
how I can contact this Volchek?"

Alonso's eyes were glued to Rouen, who was still
growling inhumanly.

"He operates out of a penthouse in New York, so no
one can connect the Gulf shit to him. He'll kill me if he
knows I ratted him out."

My ability to care was almost non-existent. "Write
down the address and pray he never finds out. But, if I
were you, I'd be working on an exit strategy right about

now. I hear Australia is nice this time of the year. If I come back and you are still in the game? I'll make sure there's not enough left of you to bury. Go straight, Alonso. This is my only warning. Because I found you once, and I will find you again."

He finished scrawling the address and handed the notepad back to Charlie.

Rouen shifted forward so fast that I couldn't even track him with my eyes. He had Alonso around the neck and pressed to the door. Alonso clawed at his muscular forearm futilely. Rouen leaned forward, inhaled deeply then licked the man from jaw to temple.

"I love the smell of your fear," he growled. I grabbed his shoulder and yanked him back. "Hands to yourself," I chastised, but damn if he didn't make my point. Romanus let out a little huffing noise and I turned, staring at his face in shock. He was laughing.

That was probably our cue to go before shit got out of hand. I wrapped my hand around Rouen's other wrist and tugged him toward the road. I took in Charlie's slightly pale face, and the curl of Romanus' amused smile. I waved them all toward the car with a mental groan. I had a sneaking suspicion that the Gargoyles were going to be a handful.

CHAPTER FOUR

B ack in my apartment, we had come up with a
plan. Well, we had part of a plan, and the rest
was up to Lady Luck. It'd been tough to find a
course of action we all agreed on.

Romanus just wanted to walk into the place and
start hacking off limbs until this Volchek talked. Charlie
wanted to do a bit of reconnaissance first, so that we
weren't wasting our element of surprise.

I was more inclined to go with a stealthier approach.
Get in, snoop through some things, and hope that no
one caught us going in and out. No muss, no fuss.

Rouen just demolished the better part of the
Chinese takeout menu and let us all argue.

"If we can get in there, find something useful and
get back out, the whole organization won't go into lock-
down, like they would if the head of the US branch was
found eaten alive."

This was the third time I'd explained it, but they
were ganging up on me. Charlie thought we should get

his routine down pat then torture the answers out of him before making it look like a rival gang hit. Or an accident. Maybe a heart attack. He knew a way.

Rouen held out a dumpling clutched between chopsticks to me, and I leaned forward, eating the dumpling in one bite.

"There's too much room for error, and if we were caught..." I let the words trail off. If we were caught, we'd be screwed no matter how you looked at it.

I caught Rouen's intense face out of the corner of my eye. "What?" He bowed his head low. "What's with him?" I asked Romanus.

Romanus's face was unreadable, well, more unreadable than usual. He was purposefully keeping himself locked down tight. "You let him feed you."

"So?" These Gargoyles were damn hard to figure out. "Did me eating a dumpling break him or something?"

Romanus sighed, letting go of his mask a little. For the first time, I saw tiredness around his eyes. "It's a sign of respect in our culture. Well, what was our culture. We are the last. The shrunken heads of our ancestors' litter buildings around Europe to protect against evil spirits." He gave a laugh, though it wasn't from amusement. "It's like thinking oysters are an aphrodisiac. Superstition. We are demons. Getting a demon to guard against other demons? Ridiculous."

"And he's bowing his head because?"

Rouen's head snapped back up, but he remained silent as Romania explained.

"We are matriarchal. The females kept whole

harems of mates, for protection, to care for her needs, to protect her young. She fed from our hand. You honored him by doing the same."

Charlie scooted a little closer to me, though the Gargoyles weren't giving off any threatening vibes. He rested a hand on my thigh, almost proprietorial, and scowled at the two demons opposite us. Was he staking a claim?

Geez, this shit was getting insane. I leaned over and kissed his cheek, to soften my next words.

"Go home, Charlie. Get some sleep. I need you to go get some clean weapons from Uncle Joe and let them know you will be out of touch for a month or so. Pack some crap. Tomorrow we will head to New York. I can't wait to see Hope." The urge to hug my twin was getting intense. I'd almost lost her, and my bond was still floundering. She was still in hospital, so she'd probably be glad to see us too. She didn't do well with forced inactivity.

"No, Rella. I'm not leaving you here alone with them." He was trying for firm and immovable, but I could hear the hint of desperation in his tone.

"They won't harm me," I protested gently.

"That's not what I'm worried about," he said, his face as stern as I'd ever seen it, not a dimple in sight.

"What? You're worried I'll sleep with one of them?" I scoffed, but all humor left me when his jaw clenched tightly. "Seriously? It's none of your business who I sleep with, Charlie. If I decide to screw both of them, it still wouldn't be any of your concern. That's not how we roll. Leave that misogynistic crap for your cousins, because that ain't you."

Charlie stared at me long and hard, his eyes searching mine for something. He shook his head and stood from the couch.

"Whatever, Estrella. I'll see you in the morning." He strode out of the apartment, closing the door with a careful snick. I kinda wished he'd slammed it.

Romanus looked at the door with what appeared to be a faint hint of respect. Rouen just shook his head. "Humans."

Suddenly, I was overwhelmingly mad with the both of them. "Shut it. I don't want to hear another word from either of you. I've had about enough alpha male posturing for one day." I stood and started collecting Chinese containers. I threw them in the trash with more force than necessary. "Go out and find some willing chick to bang, because I've had it up to here with the weird sex vibes you guys give off. Turn that shit off already."

Romanus stood, taking plates into the kitchen and loading them into the dishwasher. There was something attractive about a man doing household chores.

Rouen just stood across the room, trying hard not to look at me. "We don't fuck humans."

"What?" I said for the hundredth time today. My life had taken a sharp left turn into some dark alleyways. I'm not sure I'd like myself when I made it to the light at the other end.

"Romanus and I, we're connected. Part of the remaining pack. For us to have sex with outsiders, we must both agree on the person, both feel lust and some-thing more, something like respect, for the woman we are sleeping with. Romanus hates humans."

"I thought you guys were related. So, who do you sleep with? Demonesses?"

Rouen shuddered. "Romanus and I aren't even a little bit related. All Gargoyle have similar features, but we are different in a lot of ways if you care to look hard enough. Plus, demonesses are not the kind of being you'd trust enough to put your dick in their mouth." Hell no. Ace hated the Demonesses, and she would be happy to list all the reasons why if you gave her half the opportunity. It was a long list.

"You guys have been celibate for all these years?" I looked at his wide chest, the faint outline of muscles beneath his tight shirt. That didn't seem right.

Rouen laughed. "God no. We have quite a healthy sex life."

"How…" I started, and then I looked between them. Rouen. Then Romanus. Then back again. "Oh, you, uh, together?" I was making weird involuntary pointy actions with my fingers, and I curled my fists to stop it.

Rouen grinned, and Romanus's scowl dared me to say anything. He needn't have worried. My brain had conjured an image of Romanus fucking Rouen, his big hands wrapped around a well-muscled hip, Rouen's face twisted in pleasure, and then my fragile little brain had stuttered to stop. Frozen on that image. I remembered Romanus biting Rouen this morning, and that was it. It felt like lightning had scorched along my nerve endings and touched down in my clit.

Rouen sucked in a breath, and I knew they could smell that my panties were suddenly damp. I wanted more than anything to insert myself in that image. I hadn't even realized that was something I'd want until I was presented with it, wrapped in a bow.

Rouen took a step closer to me, then another, until his huge chest was the only thing I could see. He leaned down until his lips were close to my cheek. "Do you want to play with us, Estrella?"

"But I'm human," I protested weakly. Ugh, why did I say that? I wanted to have sex with them, not give them reasons to change their mind. I looked over my shoulder at Romanus, who was still scowling in my direction. "Romanus-"

"Has a massive fucking hard on right now. He wants you too, he's just a growly old bastard."

My eyes dropped to his dick again, and I sucked in a breath. Holy shit. I could see the outline of what I assumed was a Louisville Slugger in his dark leather pants.

"You're staring at my dick again, Red," Romanus growled. I knew how I must have looked, biting my lip, my eyes wide, my breaths coming out in hard gasps. Desperate and wild. Rouen hadn't even touched me yet. He was throwing out some serious sex juju though, making me so needy that I just wanted to peel off my clothes and climb up his big mountain body until I could impale myself on his rock-hard cock.

Romanus was up in my personal space in the blink of an eye, so fast that he actually blurred. I'm pretty sure he was lying about not being able to read my thoughts.

His sex vibes mixed with Rouen's and my knees threatened to drop me.

"You guys have sex magic?" I gasped out, not that I cared at this stage. My body had begun to burn with the need to have one of them in me.

Romanus pressed against my back, his hard dick searing into me. "No, just pheromones. If we find a mate, we release pheromones that increase her pleasure." He leaned down, and nipped my neck, in the hollow beneath my ear. I shuddered and moaned. "If you said no right now, we would stop. Your wish is our command, even if my dick exploded with the need to be inside your tight little pussy."

I stared up into Rouen's burning brown and gold eyes, and something inside me snapped. I jumped, wrapping my legs around his waist and my hands coming up to curl in his hair, pulling his mouth roughly to mine.

It was like someone had fired a starting gun, and we were a flurry of mouths and hands. I could hear the tearing of clothes as Rouen's mouth pressed hard against mine, his tongue thrusting into my mouth, tasting me, owning me. Romanus's hard torso was pressed against my back, his hands moving over my body as he tore off our clothes. His teeth scraped down my neck, nipping gently, not breaking skin but sending shivers down my spine. Somehow, he was suddenly naked, and I could feel his cock pressing against the crease of my ass.

His hands travelled down my sides, sliding over Rouen's hands under my ass, and then down my thighs, all the time he licked and nipped at my bare skin.

Rouen growled and turned, walking toward my bed. When he was standing at the foot, he placed me on the ground and Romanus's hands were freeing me from my jeans roughly. Then Romanus lifted me into his arms, and my legs were wrapped around the hard muscles of his torso, his dick pressed between us. All he needed to do was slide me up a little, and he could be inside me. I whimpered, begging wordlessly. He kissed me bruisingly hard, before backing off a little until he was barely sipping at my lips.

"Not yet, Red. We haven't even started yet."

A light chuckle had me looking over my shoulder. Rouen was lying on my satin comforter, his head right at the foot of bed. He grinned and winked, the raw lust in his eyes making my juices coat Romanus.

The man in question growled in response. He peeled me from his torso and placed me so I sat on Rouen's chest. "This is what's going to happen, Red," Romanus purred. "Rouen is gonna eat your pussy until you scream. Then, I'm going to fuck you until you beg to come. Then, Rou is going to have a turn, and while he is fucking you with his big dick, I'm going to fuck him, nice and hard. You okay with all that, Princess?"

His tone was a challenge, but I couldn't be more okay with that. Already, I could feel my orgasm rising. I wanted to be on Rouen's face already. I moved up his body, my core poised over his face, and Rouen let out a shuddering groan. But Romanus halted me. "I asked you a question, Red. Are you okay with that?"

"Yes," I moaned. "Hell yes." With that, I lowered myself onto Rouen's mouth and shuddered as his hot tongue slid along my slit. He wrapped his hands around my hips and ground my core against his face, his nose bumping my clit and I let out a little yell. He pulled me back and his lips gently sucked on my clit, then he growled.

Holy fuckballs.

A shout tore from my lips as I came, creaming all over his face. But he wasn't done. He continued to lap at my juices, and then started again, this time pushing his tongue deep into me. That was when I discovered that Gargoyles had abnormally long and dexterous tongues. My moans turned into yells, which devolved into screams. Romanus wrapped a hand around the back of my head and caught my screams in his mouth, as his tongue worked my mouth in time with Rouen's in my pussy. His hands cupped my breasts, his thumbs teasing the hard points of my nipples. He leaned forward, taking one nipple into his mouth and caught it gently between his teeth. His sharp canines ran over it, gently scraping and I lost it. I was writhing against Rouen's face, and he loved it, holding my hips hard against this mouth. I hope Gargoyles didn't need to breathe. I was so fucking close.

"Enough, Rouen."

I'll be damned if the man beneath me didn't just stop dead, his deliciously talented tongue darting back into his mouth. He did lean over and bite my thigh though, and I moaned. Rouen sat up, and I slid down his washboard abs, the delicious friction making me whimper. I sat on his lap, his hard cock so close to where

I wanted it, and I wiggled a little, trying to get closer. He groaned, but held my hips still.

"Soon," he whispered against my lips, kissing me, and I could taste myself on his tongue. He broke away. "Romanus is going to take care of you, babe. Trust me." With that, he flipped me onto my hands and knees, moving around to my front so he could kiss me again. I felt Romanus's big body settle behind me, that hard length of his cock teasing my slit. He ran a hand down my back, his hand squeezing my ass and he gave a little groan of appreciation. I grinned, happy that my body could get pleasure from the growly gargoyle. He curled his body over mine, his lips kissing my shoulder.

"Ready?" I nodded and moaned as he slid his massive cock into me slowly, waiting for my body to accommodate him. It stretched me wide, almost painfully, until I was sure I was too full to even feel good. But then he hit that sweet spot deep inside me and I let out a long, tortured moan. Then he began to slide out again.

"Ohmmyfuck." My eyes rolled in my head as he did the whole motion again. And then again, faster and faster, his rhythm smooth and strong, and my climax hit me like a sledgehammer to the side of the head. I saw stars, and then I was on my back, and Romanus was gone. In his place was Rouen, and he slid into me in one hard thrust, and I screamed. He caught my lips and kissed me so hard I tasted a little blood. So did Rouen, because he let out an inhuman noise and devoured my lips. Romanus was there, pulling him away from my mouth although his cock still hammered into me. Then

Rouen let out his own guttural moan as Romanus slid a finger into his ass, then another, stretching him.

I knew when he replaced his fingers with his cock because Rouen went deeper, the heaviness of their combined bodies pressing me into the bed. Rouen grabbed one of my legs and pulled it wider, settling himself deeper in me with every thrust, though he was no longer in control. I watched Rouen's face, his eyes closed, and his lips parted in a wordless moan, as Romanus fucked us both. I looked over his shoulder at Romanus, and his hot gaze burned me.

I clawed at Rouen's shoulder as I fucking came again, my inner muscles clenching hard around Rouen, milking him with the power of my release.

Rouen came on a roar, deep inside me, and collapsed against me. But Romanus wasn't done. He wrapped a hand around Rouen's throat, leaning down to fuck him harder, pounding him and me deep into the mattress. His thrusts got ragged and uncontrolled, and then he let out a roar that rattled the windows, one last thrust hammering deep into Rouen.

He withdrew and flopped down onto the bed next to us, and then Rouen rolled off me onto my other side.

My brain stopped trying to comprehend what the hell just happened and slid into blissful blackness of exhaustion.

I woke briefly to Romanus with a warm washcloth, cleaning the stickiness between my thighs, then cleaning up Rouen too.

"Hush. Sleep," he whispered over Rouen's soft snores. I gave him a half grin and did as I was told, snuggling back into his body as he slid back beneath the blankets.

Pressed between the two warm bodies, I sighed contentedly. I could definitely get used to this. At least until I had to examine my decisions in the cold light of day.

Romanus wrapped a big hand around my thigh, and Rouen flung an arm over my stomach, and I slid back into the contented blackness of dreamless sleep.

MY BODY FELT achy and sore, but in the fun way. I cracked open an eye and pouted a little that my bed was empty. I'd had them again and again last night, every time one of them woke, they'd roll over and be between my thighs in seconds. I barely got any sleep, but my grin hurt my face because it was so big.

Oh well. It was probably for the best. The curtains were still drawn around my four poster, and I tilted my head at the sound of angry whispers. My hearing was better than average. Actually, I didn't want to sound too full of myself, but physically, I was superior to normal run-of-the-mill humans. You know, the type that weren't conceived by zombies resurrected by the Devil and protected in the womb by a fallen angel. You know, that old story. I was just more. I had better hearing, better eyesight, better strength. I could still be injured but I healed with a swiftness that defied modern medicine . It only took me two weeks to heal my broken arm when I fell off Charlie's bike. I always joked that when Ace was handing out Angelic gifts, Hope got all the Angelic qualities and I got all the Fallen qualities. I was meaner, more brutal than my softer twin. But together, we were a pretty awesome team.

Until someone tried to break her. Now they'll see just how Fallen I am.

The whispers got angrier and I tuned in.

"What's the problem with you humans? I thought it was dragons who wanted to hoard things, but you are worse. You want to take something beautiful and wild, and cage it always. You say she's yours, but you won't fight for her. You'd rather have none of her than let her take what she needs from all of us. You want to tie her down. We would make her soar," Rouen's gruff voice sounded angry and frustrated.

"You don't even know her," Charlie let out his own Gargoyle worthy growl. "You don't know me."

Rouen laughed then. "I know everything I need to know. I can smell your longing, your lust. I can see how much you love her, but you do nothing. You can't hide this from us. Like I know that you are scared despite your bravado."

Woah. What? Rouen was wrong. Sure, Charlie loved me, like I loved him. It wasn't a lusty kind of love. Was it? I remembered gazing at his bare torso yesterday in bed, and how much I wanted to curl my fingers in his chest hair.

No. Fucking Gargoyles and their sex pheromones were still messing with my brain. I shimmied into some pjs and a tank that was in a pile beside my bed. I slipped out of the curtains, and when I walked out into the open living room, they were standing side by side, as if nothing was amiss. Except the red ring on the pale column of Charlie's neck, and the fact the Rouen was completely, buck ass naked.

I squinted at them both, but kept my mouth shut. I walked to the coffee machine and pressed the buttons. When I had my java in my hands, I turned back towards them.

"Uh, morning?"

I looked for Romanus, and found him on my fluffy rug, sitting perfectly still in the sun again. At least he was wearing tight black boxers. I went and sat beside him, resisting the urge to lean into him.

Apparently, I didn't hide my desire well enough, because he picked me up and placed me on his lap, his face still turned to the sun, his eyes still closed. I sunk in against the warmth of his chest, and realized that it felt a little like heated stone. Like lying on a sun warmed rock beside a river. I purred a little and snuggled back against him. It was nice.

I let out a long sigh. "What's going on?" I asked Romanus.

"Your human-"

"Charlie.'

"Yes, Charlie, has a key. He came in early this morning and saw all of us in bed. He did not take it well." His chest tensed beneath my head. "This is my fault. I should have been guarding you better but I was otherwise… preoccupied."

I let out a little hum of appreciation. Me too.

"Charlie?" I called, my voice soft. I couldn't forget what I'd heard. When Charlie came to stand in front of me, I looked at him with all my senses. The tightness in his body, as if it was practically vibrating with tension, his heart thumping in his chest, the desperation in his eyes that he was trying, and failing, to hide behind anger. Charlie was my best friend, but if I was honest, there was always hints that he felt something more. A touch that lingered too long, the fact he went above and beyond for me every time. Looks that I wasn't supposed to see. I usually shut those hints away in my mind. Outside of my family, Charlie was the most important person in my life. The thought of losing that over something as stupid as a lover's quarrel sank a barb into my heart.

But looking at him now, I knew that if I didn't open myself to the possibility, I might lose him anyway. If I didn't open that locked door where I kept the feelings that were outside of my life's master plan, then he might just walk away.

I reached a hand out to him, and he stared at it. With a shuddering breath, he reached out and wrapped his hand in mine, pulling me out of Romanus' lap, until I stood in front of him, inches from his face. Instead of listening to that scared part of me, I listened to what my heart was whispering.

I reached out and cupped his cheek. "Me too. But I don't want to ruin this. Slow okay? I can't lose you, Charlie. I need you."

He sucked in a breath. "Your goddamn super hearing. I forgot about that. Rella, the Gargoyles are-"

"Completely right. Don't start lying to me now," I interrupted.

He leaned forward and rested his forehead on mine. "I've been lying to you for years."

"Years? "I squeaked.

"Since you were seventeen and punched Paulie in the mouth for talking about Hope's boobs. Fuck, you were beautiful. Are beautiful." The admission whooshed out of him.

When the hell did the careful structure of my life start to crumble?

"Charlie, I-" He plastered a hand over my mouth.

"I know, it's not the same for you. I know. Let's just forget about it until after we do this thing for Hope. Either way, you'll never lose me. I might drink the bar dry and ball every woman that moves until I get you out of my system, but you won't lose me. And I know you have a thing with these two," he pointed to Romanus and Rouen, "and I'm gonna be okay with that. Because, despite what Asshole Number Two over there says, I only want whatever makes you happy, and if that's them? I'll deal with it."

His grin was brittle, but its presence was reassuring.

I leaned forward and kissed his cheek, and when his arms came around me, I laid my head on his shoulder and pressed my nose into his neck like I'd done a million times before. But for the first time, I analyzed the instinctual action. Why was his scent so comforting to me? Why did I always find such peace in his arms? Was it because we were best friends and knew each other like we knew ourselves? Or something more?

"I like Romanus and Rouen, I feel a connection to them that seems important. But, you know my background, Charlie, my family. It doesn't have to be all or nothing, you know."

He tensed against me again. Our families couldn't be more different, supernatural aspects aside. His strict Catholic mob family, and my family which were the poster family for a happy polygamist relationship. We couldn't come from two more different lifestyles. But I wouldn't force him into anything. I wasn't going to make ultimatums. Not with Charlie.

He just nodded, his cheek against my hair. He let out another long sigh and straightened. "I came with gifts."

Charlie pointed to a duffle that had been discarded by the door. He unwrapped his arms from me and walked over to get it, hefting its weight across the shiny cement floors. When he unzipped it, I let out a little whistle between my teeth.

"Uncle Joe said to tell you they are all clean, and to go and get 'em." Underneath several handguns was one sawn off shotgun and box after box of ammo. Merry Christmas to me, love the Mulligans.

SIX HOURS LATER, we were loaded into Charlie's SUV. I'd fed my goldfish, cancelled my cable, and prepared for the fact I may never come home. But I always felt that way before a big operation, even when I was still in the BPD.

Rouen and Romanus had retrieved their packs, which they'd stored in the basement of my building before they'd even poofed in with Luc. Cocky bastards. Well, pack might have been a bit of a misnomer. It was a backpack with a single change of clothes and more knives than a celebrity cooking show. My own pack was similarly stuffed, but with a few wads of cash and guns. Charlie had the most gear, bringing all the tech gear he would need to track down our prey.

I leaned against the window, watching the lines on the road fly pass in a blur. Romanus was in the back with me, Charlie driving and Rouen singing along to a Rolling Stones song in the front. Sympathy for the Devil. I chuckled beneath my breath at the irony.

For the first time in forever, I felt confused and almost… alone. I was floundering, but I was too stubborn to admit it to even myself. Denial was my middle name.

Warm fingers wrapped around mine. Romanus was still looking out his window, assessing for threats, his eyes never still, but his fingers twined in mine, and for some reason it made me feel better. Which was a bad, bad thing. I knew that logically. Being emotionally codependent on a demon was the opposite of healthy. But no matter how hard I rationalized it, I couldn't move my hand away. So instead I compartmentalized it, pretended my arm ended at the elbow on that side and that I didn't feel the rough callouses of his hands or the warmth that spread through my veins, warming the chill of my fear. I desperately tried to block the memories that rolled through my head of those hands last night, running over my body.

Rouen let out a strangled noise in the front of the car, and Charlie's eyes shot to the gargoyle then to the back seat. I kept my face completely neutral. I didn't want to talk to Charlie about this. I needed Hope. She would know how to help. She always knew what I was feeling better than I did.

Charlie broke the silence. "So, tell me more about this whole Gargoyle pack thing? Where is your, uh, subspecies from?" Apparently, Charlie had been reading the Demon etiquette book I got him for Christmas. Not.

Rouen cleared his throat. "It's not all that different to most pack dynamics, except a female is Queen, and we rank below her by order of dominance. She'll have a harem of however many she likes. The women have a ranking as well, to decide which female is leader of the whole clan. Well, we did, when there were more than two of us. We were most concentrated in Europe. My pack is, uh was, from France."

I didn't need Hope's empath abilities to feel the wave of sadness pour off the both of them. I squeezed Romanus's hand. I turned toward him and met his blue and green eyes. They were perfect, deep and glinting in the sunlight, and I found it hard to look away from the resounding sadness that churned in them. I wanted to soothe his hurt. But he pulled his gaze from mine, staring straight ahead, his other hand reaching up to squeeze Rouen's shoulder in support.

"Who is the more dominant between you and Romanus?" Charlie asked, apparently missing the memo on not asking impolite questions when the people you are talking to could pop your head off your shoulder like a child picks a dandelion.

"Romanus. That's why he's always top."

"Top?" Charlie asked, and I grinned. Oh, this was

going to be funny. "Of the ladder? You mean first?"

It was Rou's turn to laugh now. "Oh, he rarely comes first. He's too much of a control freak for that. No. I mean, he's Alpha and I'm Beta. He's top, I'm bottom. In bed," he clarified slowly, like Charlie was a little dim.

I saw the moment that Charlie got it, because his face turned the brightest shade of red I'd ever seen on him, right to the tips of his ears.

"So you and he…?" He did the same pointy thing with his fingers that I did last night, and I couldn't help the laugh that burst from my chest.

Romanus' lips quirked, though I thought he might be smiling at my laughter rather than the actual joke. Rouen huffed out a sigh. "Humans. Yes, Charlie Mulligan, we have sex. A lot. We don't do humans or other demons and there are no other gargoyles left, let alone females. I don't know about you, but I find the idea of two centuries of celibacy really unappealing. Besides, in our society, it is not as taboo. There is only one Queen, and some harems had up to fourteen mates. We were all close. As close as you could get to another being, and the bond ensured that we had each others backs. Pleasing each other pleased the Queen. A well fucked Gargoyle is a happy Gargoyle. Take my word for that."

Charlie was frowning. "You don't do humans? I thought you and Rella-"

"She's different," Romanus said gruffly, and Rouen murmured an agreement, meeting my eyes in side mirror. It was my turn to blush bright red, and it was not an attractive color with the fiery auburn of my hair.

Embarrassment made me try to tug my hand away from Romanus', but he held fast.

"You will not regret what happened between us," he declared. Declared! Like he could just choose my emotions for me. He pinned me with his gaze. "What we did was…" He struggled for a word.

"Beautiful?" Rouen supplied.

"A mistake?" Charlie countered, and the car swerved when Rouen let out an ominous growled.

Romanus shook his head. "Fate."

Fate had always been the original four-letter F word in my family. They resisted the preordained and made their own rules. But I could acknowledge that I felt a crazy amount of attraction for the both of them, like someone had a instruction manual of all my happy buttons, and manufactured Rouen and Romanus with the ability to push them all.

Instead of answering the unspoken question that thickened the air inside the SUV, I ignored it completely and played dumb. I wasn't ready for this conversation. Actually, I wasn't ready for any conversation that involved my love life at the moment. I just wanted to kill the people who hurt my family.

I probably needed to see a shrink, when murdering people smugglers was more appealing than having a conversation about my feelings.

Catching the hint finally, silence fell over the car. This trip couldn't end fast enough. I closed my eyes and pretended I was asleep, until I dozed off for real.

I woke as Charlie slowed the car, pulling into a car space. In front of me, the hospital stretched toward the sky. I felt a tug on my bond and knew that Hope was close by. We were in Manhattan.

I was out of the car door as soon as the vehicle slowed. "I'll be back in an hour. Stay here. We don't need to give the nurses spontaneous orgasms."

I ignored Romanus' shout, and sprinted through the doors. I dodged the line at the reception desk and skipped the elevator to sprint up the stairs. I didn't need directions to Hope. She pulled at our twin bond like she was reeling in a fish. I just knew where she was. I knew when I was at the right floor, and when I was standing in front of the right door, skipping the nurses station altogether. I pushed open the door and launched myself across the room and into her arms.

God, it was awful, being apart from her when she was injured. Every part of my body was always on high alert, ready to protect her from school yard bullies or criminals who wanted to harm her. She didn't get my physical enhancements. She still healed average-joe slow. She hugged me tight against her, whispering soothing things that eased that ache I felt in my soul, stitched back the shredded pieces of my fragmented conscience. Her warmth pulled me back from the darkness. I sucked in a deep breath and let my body relax, moving away a little. She looked better. Her body was still patchworked with bruises and cut skin, her torso strapped to support her ribs, but she was no longer the sallow white of death.

Oh fuck, her ribs. I jumped away, and she smiled. "Don't worry, they don't hurt too bad anymore. Besides, I needed that too."

I'd had to leave, when we first got her back after the abduction. As much as I had wanted to wrap myself around her fragile body and snap at anyone who came close, I couldn't. I'd felt the darkness rising in me, this suffocating burning in my soul, and I knew she would have worried about me too much to concentrate on healing herself. She would have tried to soothe my emotions like she'd done just a moment before. But I needed that anger, that thirst for retribution.

I caught sight of movement to my left, and I had a gun out and pointed to the corner of the room in a blur of motion.

When I saw who sat there, I didn't know if I should lower my weapon or not. I kept my hand tense but pointed my gun at the floor.

The man sitting on the hard hospital visitor chair looked relaxed, as if he'd just been lounging there for fun. He wasn't tall, or physically imposing, although he was still built with a lean kind of muscle that spoke of ways to take down an opponent with merely a touch in the right place. No, he wasn't at all scary until you reached his eyes. Those eyes chilled a person to the bone. They were an icy blue, sparkling with a dangerous glint that promised death.

"Hope? Why is Blue Halloran sitting at your bedside?"

Hope let out an amused sigh. "He's a gift, from the Mulligans. It seems they were less than enamored by the effectiveness of my last bodyguard." We both paused to think about JJ. He'd deserved so much better than the end he'd gotten. Hope sucked in a shuddering breath.

"So, they have given me Blue, like he's some kind of indentured servant."

"They gave you the Mulligan's most brutal enforcer as a babysitter? Apparently, man flesh must be the hot new Christmas trend this year."

As if on cue, the Gargoyles walked through the door, and Blue was on his feet with his gun pointed at them almost as quick as me. The Gargoyles tensed, brutally long knives unsheathed and in front of them in an instant. The violence in the room was an almost physical force. We were one wrong move away from a massacre.

"Well, isn't this fun? Hope, meet my very own matching set of extremely inappropriate gifts, compliments of Luc. Romanus, Rouen, this is my sister Hope. That is her, uh, bodyguard, Blue."

Everyone stared, and no one lowered their weapons. I took a deep breath for strength. "Seriously, stop measuring dicks and put your weapons away."

There was a knock at the door, and every single one of us whirled toward the door with weapons raised. When Adnan, adopted Syrian orphan and now bad ass ballet dancer with the New York City Ballet company, poked his head inside. He looked amused rather than scared.

"Did someone say dick, because I brought one of my very own," he said dramatically. Framed by the doorway was Nazir.

I dropped my gun. "Fuck."

Adnan laughed, his eyes roaming all over my Gargoyles. "Oh, Relly, you can say that again."

CHAPTER FIVE

Nazir Ashear was basically a ghost. A name that my parents smiled over when they talked about old times, when we were younger. A name that made Clary tear up a little, but she'd always smile as she said it. Adnan was the only one who knew Nazir at all.

He'd join military school when I'd been four. I barely recognized him except as this glorious big kid that Adnan absolutely worshipped. Living through the Syrian war had changed Nazir, even as a boy.

After military school he'd gone on to join the army, then became SAS, then covert ops, and then he'd dropped it all to join some renegade offshoot of the Legion and became a mercenary. Or at least that's what Lux said, his voice filled with something that sounded like worried pride.

I barely knew him. I'd seen him once when I was sixteen, at Adnan's debut performance as lead dancer for the Ballet Company. He'd come home to see his baby brother achieve his dreams. Even though Adnan's left leg was amputated from the knee down, the best prosthetics that money could buy ensured Adnan could do whatever his heart desired. Nazir had sat at the back of the theater, his back to the wall, with Lux. The rest of us sat down the front row, cheering so loud that I thought they'd kick us out.

I remembered Hope's face when she'd read him, though. She'd flinched, a barely perceptible expression, but I'd seen it and so had Nazir. Hope hugged the Devil with joy on her face. Whatever she read in Nazir that was enough to make her flinch had put me on guard and I'd remained that way, even after he'd disappeared into the night, never to be seen again. Until now.

He was tall, over six feet, and strong. Strength poured off him in waves, his forearms and biceps huge, tattoos running up and down their length, except for his hands. He was dressed as a civilian, but he didn't do a very good job of it. Even in worn Levi's and a t-shirt, he looked like a mercenary. Wraparound sunglasses were on top of his head, and a gun was in his hand. He looked unflustered as he took in the other three armed men in the room, positioning himself in front of Adnan.

I sent Hope an accusing look. "Seriously?"

She shrugged. "I'm your twin, Rella. I know what you are going to do. I don't want you to die doing it. So I called in a favor."

"Not a favor if it's family," Nazir muttered, but his eyes didn't leave the threats in the room.

"Ace told you, didn't she?" Hope just grinned. I scowled at the men in the room. "Let's just all put our guns and stupidly big knives away, okay? Seriously, Rouen, where the fuck were you keeping that thing?"

Rouen just waggled his eyebrows at me, but he made the knife disappear. The other three didn't make a move to disarm.

"Simmer down guys, we are all friends here."

I pointed at Blue. "Murdering mob enforcer." Then at Romanus and Rouen. "Murdering Demons."Then at Nazir. "Mercenary." The murderer part was implied.

"Seriously, there's so much machoness in this room, I think I'm getting a hard on," Adnan stage-whispered to us from where he'd perched on the side of Hope's bed. We grinned, and Blue flicked an eye to him, the good Catholic killer that he was. Nazir eyed them all for any sign of disgust at Adnan's sexuality. Pretty sure he'd put a bullet in them to teach them to be more tolerant.

Rouen threw Adnan a wink and a grin.

Adnan clutched his chest. "Gay?"

I shook my head. "Kinda, but not really. Besides, he's mine."

Now Adnan and Hope were staring at me. It had just slipped out. "Fuck it." I leaned over Hope and kissed her cheek. "Get better soon, Hope. I love you."

She wrapped her arms around my back and squeezed me hard. "Be safe, Rella."

I gave Adnan a kiss on the cheek. He patted my butt. "Give them hell, but come back, you hear?" I turned to the other men in the room, most still hold in their weapons.

I gave Blue my best hard stare. "Keep her safe, or so

help me god, I will find a way to make you hurt." Blue just nodded once.

I pointed to Romanus, pushing down his knife hand. "Come on, Boulder Boy. Let's go."

I walked past Nazir and tried not to flinch at the intensity of his gaze. "You too, if you're joining us. We have a hotel to settle into and a human trafficker to torture."

His eyes widened a little, the most expression I'd ever seen on his face. I leaned close and whispered next to his ear.

"I'm not the good twin."

Then I walked out the door. Damn, it was good to make a dramatic exit.

CHARLIE HAD BEEN SECURING us a hotel room in a divey little place that paid its employees to forget faces and you paid by the hour. Pretty sure I got fleas from walking through the doors. No one else seemed to care, and I didn't want to seem girly, but I hated bugs. Roaches were the worst and I'm pretty sure they were the only thing keeping this place standing.

When Charlie saw Nazir walk in behind me, well behind Rouen but in front of Romanus because the Gargoyles didn't trust him, his eyes nearly bugged out of his head.

"Naz?"

Nazir surprised me and pulled Charlie into a hug, an actual smile on his face.

"Hey, Charlie. Look at you!"

I looked between the two of them. "Well, you two look cozy. Wanna share with the rest of the class?"

Charlie got his best 'busted' look on his face. The same one he got when he snuck hot cookies from Mammy Mulligans oven, or when Debra Depetra's dad caught them making out in the back seat of his beat up 'Stang.

"Charlie links me in to Adnan through secure channels. I haven't seen his face, though, in what? Five, six years?"

"Since Adnan's debut." Charlie smiled at Naz, and a wave of jealousy crawled through my gut. I just didn't know who I was jealous of right now. The fact Charlie gave someone the smile that he usually reserved for me? Or that he'd gotten to know Naz the Ghost all these years and shut me out? I'd thought we'd shared everything, but maybe I was wrong.

I didn't know dammit, and I didn't care. I walked past them both, and towards the only door in the dingy little room. I needed a shower, a break from all the goddamn testosterone surrounding me, and a fresh pair of panties.

I undressed and tried not to stare at any part of the bathroom too long. I hopped into the shower cubicle and pulled the moldy shower curtain. At least the mold kind of made it a more opaque. But the water was scalding, and that's what I wanted right now.

The door to the bathroom opened and closed, and I somehow instinctively knew that it was Charlie. I also knew, in my gut, that none of the men in the other room would ever hurt me. Even Nazir, who I'd barely even met.

"Rella, you okay?"

I sighed and wished I could rest my head on the tiles without the risk of contracting botulism. "Yeah, I'm fine Charlie."

"Is Hope alright?"

This time I stuck my head out of the curtain, because I wanted to see Charlie's face. "Yeah, Hope is fine. The Mulligan's gave her Blue as a bodyguard."

Charlie's jaw dropped like one of those cartoon characters. I chuckled and put my head back under the scalding spray. "Blue Halloran?"

"Uh huh. Guess they really love Hope."

I heard the toilet creak ominously as Charlie sat on in. "They love you too, Rella. Just differently." I poked my head back out and smiled at my friend. So much angst in the last 24 hours, but he still soothed my wounded feelings.

"I know, Charlie. I know Hope and I are different. Hope inspires that kind of loyalty in people, even in me. Hell, especially in me. She's beautiful and fragile and people want to protect her. I know that all that sweetness is wrapped around a core of steel too, but it doesn't matter. Hope and I are twins, but we are different, and I'm okay with that." I leaned back in and just let the water wash away the tension in my muscles. "Can you go out there and make sure they don't kill each other?"

"Sure thing."

I heard the creak of the toilet again, "Charlie?" I poked my head out of the shower one last time, my hair dripping on the floor. "I, uh, I just… Thank you, I guess. I couldn't do this without you."

Charlie stopped and just stared. Then he leaned forward and kissed me softly on the lips, barely a touch, but it was filled with emotion.

"Anytime, Rella." He opened the door and walked out, closing it softly behind him. I leaned my head against the tiles, no longer bothered about the mold.

It had been a hell of a week.

CHARLIE HAD LEFT clean clothes on the counter, because I'd stormed into the bathroom with no thought to towels or clothes. Slipping into yoga pants and a large black hoodie, I walked out of the bathroom, not sure if I was cleaner than when I went in.

Someone had ordered pizza, and an impressive stack of boxes sat on one of the beds. There was only one single bed, a double and a chair that had a suspicious stain in the corner. Honeymoon suite, my ass.

Rouen held out a piece of pizza to me but pulled it away when I went to grab it. He gave me an intense look, and I sighed. I opened my mouth and he placed it on my lips, and I took a bite. Nothing like a good pizza pie. Once I'd taken the bite, Rouen let me hold the rest. Naz just watched us, his face giving nothing away.

"It's a gargoyle thing," I said and shrugged.

"Gargoyle?"

I nodded. "It's their demon subspecies." If the guys wanted to give Naz a crash course in gargoyle history, that was up to them.

"I thought you called them demons metaphorically."

I gave him an intense look. "Have you forgotten already, Naz? Ace and Luc?" It would be easy to rationalize away as the delusions of a traumatized child. If he had chosen to forget, then I'd let him have that. Probably wouldn't last though. My world had always been steeped in the paranormal. When Fallen angels came to your tenth birthday, you began to normalize it. Even Charlie knew, or at least heavily suspected he was the Devil. He did know he was something paranormal, but no one talked about the particulars.

But Nazir had been gone a long time. Naz held my eyes a little longer, and then ducked his head.

I moved on. "Did anyone catch Naz up on the plan?" I stuffed half a slice of pizza in my mouth and desperately tried to chew around it.

"Yes. And it's a weak plan."

I crossed my arms over my chest and scowled. "Oh?"

"The apartment is on the twenty-seventh floor. One way in, one way out if you exclude the elevator. He'll have security, all armed with semi-automatic weapons. You have no exit strategy whatsoever from the twenty-seventh floor and I'm sure that even if the Gods smile on your little crusade and you find Volchek alone and actually manage to secure him, you won't have the stomach to get the information from him. He's not going to roll over and rat out his bosses. You don't seem like the torturing type, despite the badass persona you are trying to portray. Have you ever killed a man, Estrella?"

I narrowed my eyes at him, and ground my teeth.

"I didn't think so. And torturing a man is infinitely worse." He looked from Rouen to Romanus. "Maybe the big guys will do it for you, but it takes some serious stones to stand by while a man screams in pain. You are a liability in this operation."

I growled, and launched myself over the bed at him, but Rouen caught me around the waist and pulled me back down, settling me into his lap. "Easy, Tiger. Fuck you are sexy when you growl." I could feel the evidence of just how hot he found my growling growing beneath my ass.

"You underestimate her. If she wants to be there, then she will be there," Romanus stated, staring Naz in the eyes. They stared at each other for so long, neither prepared to be the first to drop their eyes. Eventually Naz cursed, blinking as he looked away. A small smile curled Romanus' lips, but it was gone in a second.

"We had an exit strategy," Rouen said, catching Naz's eye, but dropping them quickly. "It's a last resort, but it is pretty bulletproof."

"Was that a rock joke?" I asked. I leaned my head back against his shoulder.

Rouen just smirked down at me, but looked back at Nazir. "We shift, and we can fly."

"You shift and fly?" Naz repeated back.

Rouen grinned. He enjoyed this way too much. "Uh huh. Into dragons. Bulletproof flying dragons. But only little ones, though."

I scoffed. "Yeah, basically pocket sized."

"So, if it went bad, you guys planned to turn into

dragons, bust out the window and fly away?" Naz repeated. Kinda sounded crazy when you put it like that, but this was New York. No one would blink at a small flying dragon.

"I also planned to eat this Volchek," Romanus said. "Anyone who sells women like meat deserves to be a meal."

Naz flicked his eyes to me, then back to Romanus. "Agreed."

As much as Naz pissed me off, with his cool expression and stupidly muscular thighs, Naz probably had the most experience at this kind of thing. I was just a normal beat cop who had plans to make detective one day. Charlie was more used to hacking bank accounts. The Gargoyles were a battering ram, not made for stealthy infiltration. I sighed.

"Do you have any suggestions on how to make the plan better, or are you just here to be a Debbie Downer?"

Naz grinned, and it thumped the air out of my chest. When he didn't control his features like a mask, he was beautiful. Or sexy. Or some other thing that defied definition in a single word.

Rouen leaned close to my ear. "Better breathe there, Tiger," he whispered quiet enough that it was for my ears only. "Don't want to have to give you mouth to mouth." His words were purred, and arousal made my skin feel tight. I wiggled my ass a little to even the playing field. I grinned at his near silent groan.

"Are you and he a couple?" Naz asked, and tension spread through the room like a wildfire, like everyone was holding their breath, waiting for my answer. I guess it better be the right one. I didn't meet anyone's eyes, lowering mine to stare at the floor as I worked out my thoughts. I liked Rouen, with his easy laugh and cheekiness. I loved how safe Romanus made me feel, and the things they made me feel in bed together was out of this world. Then there was Charlie. Screw it.

"We aren't a couple, but we are definitely a thing. Him too," I pointed to Romanus. "And Charlie and I-"

"Are none of his damn business," Charlie interrupted, but he was smiling. He'd known I was about to claim him as mine. "This isn't the time or the place, Rella Rua."

I smiled at Charlie, then turned back to Naz. I had a funny feeling that he was taking our measure, and he'd found us wanting.

"So, you are starting your own harem?"

"Do you have a problem with that?" My eyes dared him to say anything.

He surprised me again with another smile. "No. I've seen firsthand that when it works, it works." He turned to Charlie, his face shutting down again to his mercenary mask. "Charlie, can you get me schematics for the building and the surrounding block? We'll have to do surveillance. If he's a professional, he won't have the same pattern every day. If not, it's hard to eradicate all routine from your day." He crossed his arms across his broad chest. "We work out who his guards are, when there are shift changes, when he brushes his teeth, what his favorite restaurant is, whether he cried at the beginning of Bambi. We find the chink in the routine, and we exploit it. We strike when he's most vulnerable, we get what we need, and we leave no loose ends. Do you get what I am saying?"

My lip curled. "Did you expect me to cry over the death of a criminal? Wrong girl, Naz."

I ignored the appreciation that flashed across his face. I had ninety-nine problems and boys were at least three!

"Okay, here's the new plan."

BY THE TIME we had every tiny detail worked out, contingency plans A through to Z, one of which was riding a dragon out the penthouse window, we all fell into bed. Well, I fell into bed beside Rouen, who had insisted with a lot of growling that I took the bed, and that he would protect my back. Naz had taken the stained armchair for first watch, and Charlie was in the bed beside me. Charlie had tried to protest that he could sleep on the floor, but I'm pretty sure once the fleas had finished snacking on him all night, he'd be nothing but a husk. Romanus had taken the single bed so he could relieve Naz in the middle of the night, so everyone had a chance to rest.

I woke in the middle of the night, and I couldn't see who sat in the chair keeping watch. The lights carpark were blown or shot out, so there was no external light in the room. I realized a hand tracing over my body was what had woken me. I was pressed into the curve of Rouen's body, and I could feel the hard length of him against my ass. Again.

"Shh," he whispered against my ear, his hand wrapping around my thigh, shifting me a little to hook a leg back over his, making way for his hand to travel up the inside my thigh, and press against my core through my yoga pants. I let out a little moan, but the hand that was under my face wrapped around to cover my mouth.

"Hush, Tiger, people are still asleep. I just wanted to hear you purr. If you make too much noise, I'll have to stop." It was barely a whisper, but it made heat rush to my center. His fingers brushed against me again, and I bit my lip.

His hand ran up my body, under my hoodie, his big rough hand cupping my breast, rolling my nipple between his thumb and forefinger. I sucked in a breath but kept quiet against his hand. When he squeezed my nipple roughly, I let out an involuntary moan, and I could feel his sexy chuckle vibrate against my back. His hand roamed back down my body, beneath the waistband of both my yoga pants and my panties, until he slid his fingers through my already wet folds. Oh god.

He stroked me gently, his thumb brushing over my clit, making me buck back against him. His thumb rubbed little circles, and I pressed against his hand. He slid one finger into my pussy, then two and I moaned again. I couldn't help it, as his fingers stroked inside me just right, finding my G-spot with unerring accuracy. I closed my eyes and threw my head back, consumed by his hands stroking me higher and higher. He added another of his big, rough fingers, and I desperately tried to hold back the moan, but it was no use. I let out the moan, and it was caught by soft lips on mine. My eyes flew open, and I saw Charlie kissing me, his eyes open, watching my face.

I kissed him back, all the feverish energy in my body trying to escape from my body into his. I kissed him harder as the orgasm built in my body, swelling, and my moans escaped between us. Charlie's hands came up under my hoodie, pushing it up under my chin, tracing the lines of my body with his strong fingers. He cupped my breasts and lowered his mouth to my nipple, sucking it between his lips.

I wrapped my hands in Charlie's soft, gold curls, and moaned. His mouth switched to the other nipple, and Rouen's fingers began to pound me hard, the heel of his hand rubbing my clit mercilessly. I was going to come, and I wasn't sure I could be quiet about it. Rouen's hand wrapped around my mouth again, muffling my cries against his palm as Charlie scraped his teeth along my aching nipple. In a rush, I came all over Rouen's fingers, squeezing tight around him and he groaned against my hair. I panted against Rouen's hand, and Charlie popped my nipple from his mouth.

As Rouen moved his hand away, Charlie leaned forward, his eyes running all over my face like he was memorizing this moment. Then he looked at me, so much emotion in his eyes, and kissed me tenderly. That kiss said so many things, and my heart thumped so hard in my chest that I was sure he could feel it against his own. He gave me a lopsided grin, his dimple winking at me, then rolled over and pretended to go back to sleep.

Rouen took his hand from my pants and pulled my hoodie back down over my body. He licked my juices from his fingers, his body rumbling in a low, almost inaudible way that shook the bed.

He kissed the back of my neck, his arm banding across my stomach, pulling me tight against his chest.

"You taste like heaven," he whispered. "Go back to sleep, my Queen."

My eyes had adjusted to the darkness, and I could see Romanus sitting across from us, keeping watch. The hard bulge in his pants was visible in the darkness.

I tilted my head toward the single bed, where Nazir slept. Hopefully slept.

"Asleep?" I mouthed. I knew he could see me in the dark. Gargoyles were naturally nocturnal creatures and had the night vision to match.

Romanus shook his head, and a breath whooshed out of me. Fuck. Naz had seen my little pleasure party with Rouen and Charlie. Tomorrow was going to be a whole new level of awkward.

CHAPTER SIX

S urveillance sucked. We'd been sitting here so long my ass was numb. Luckily, Volchek had bought a penthouse apartment across from Central Park, so our cover was easy to maintain. We were dressed casually, pretending to be tourists sitting in the park. I was with Romanus, and we were cuddled together like a couple honeymooning in the bright lights of NYC. My bright red hair was pushed up under a cap and oversized sunglasses protected my eyes.

Rouen had the back of the building, and Naz had the employee entrance. Charlie was back at our hotel, his fingers flying across the keyboards of his computer, doing whatever it was that Charlie did.

This morning Naz had just ordered to watch and remember. We noted who came and went, times, if we saw Volchek, that kind thing. Charlie had found us his mugshot from an assault and battery case from a few years ago that had been mysteriously dropped when the girl just disappeared. The guy's face was burned in to my brain now. I'd be able to pick him in a crowd easily.

No one had spoken about what had happened in the darkness last night, not even Charlie. I'd think the whole thing had just been an amazing, dirty dream, except for Rouen's smug grin.

"We've got movement," Romanus said, his voice pitched low.

The huge double doors opened, and a powerfully built man with close shaved head and a face that looked like it'd been hacked with an icepick, stepped from the building. Following him was an older man, equally as tall with light gray hair and a handsome face. Volchek. The first guy must be his guard.

"Selfie!" I said to Romanus, my voice perky and my smile genuine. Romanus turned and smiled, showing way too much fang, and we took a picture. I made sure to get Volchek and Ugly in the background. A black SUV pulled up, and our prey hopped in.

"Getting into a black Range Rover, plates Alpha Delta Zulu Six Three Nine."

"Can you get him on the traffic cameras, Charlie?" Naz's voice came over the earpiece.

Charlie let out a disgusted noise. "Child's play."

"Okay, keep an eye where he goes. Even a direction will help. The rest of you, regroup at the hotel. Leave subtly."

Rouen agreed, and Romanus confirmed.

Then there was silence.

I sat against Romanus' side, his arm curled around

my shoulders. It was a beautiful day, and I wasn't in a hurry to get back to our roach motel.

"Rouen called me Queen last night," I said casually. "Does that mean something?"

Romanus looked down at me, but his face betrayed nothing. "Everything means something."

I rolled my eyes. "Get that from a fortune cookie? I meant to you, to Gargoyles."

Romanus sucked in a breath. "Yes. It means he's bonding to you, we're bonding to you, the way we would to a female mate. Like a Queen. If that isn't something you want, you better say so quickly. Mating isn't something that can be taken back easily."

I was silent for a bit, watching two little girls chase a big yellow dog through the park. "That's a big decision to make about two people who were strangers less than a week ago. Humans don't rush headlong into things like that."

Romanus didn't say anything, just inclined his head.

"Plus, there is Charlie. He already holds a piece of my heart; I'm just figuring out how big of a piece. It complicates things, you know? I didn't necessarily want to follow in my family's footsteps. I thought I'd settle down, probably with another cop, and maybe get a dog. Make Detective and try not to burn out too young. And when I was done, I'd go work with Hope. This," I pointed between the two of us, "wasn't in my grand plan."

Romanus made a sympathetic noise, which just seemed totally abnormal coming from a large scowling demon. "In our culture, it was said that some Queens just had too much emotion, and the only way for them to survive was to give it as many willing hearts as she needed to hold it. Probably romanticized bullshit to explain an evolutionary need. But I understand it's different for humans. It is more complicated for you with your conservative mating rituals. You will get no pressure from us. I will make sure Rouen knows."

"No." The word was out before I could swallow it back down. "I'm not saying no. I'm just saying let's take it slow. The most I've ever committed to anyone that wasn't family was my goldfish, and I've killed two this year. I'm not good at this whole feelings thing. That's Hope's deal." I tried to read his face but got nothing. "What about you, Rom? Do you want whatever it is that Rouen wants?"

This time, he looked away. He was silent, and I couldn't deny the disappointment that felt like lead in my stomach. Finally, he turned to me and caught my eye, holding it. I couldn't have looked away if I tried.

"I do. We weren't always demons, you know? Once, we were just a well-hidden race of people who hid in the shadows and lived the happiest lives we could. But when our pack died, my former queen as well, it broke us. They were slaughtered by humans in their sleep, and Rouen and I only escaped because we weren't in camp. The pain of losing my whole pack was..." he trailed off. "And we went feral. For a long time, we were completely without remorse. We tore through towns and left nothing but fire and blood in our wake. When we were finally killed, we went straight to hell, to Luc, who saw our thirst for vengeance and used it as a tool. It took

Rouen a long time to get over it, he'd been so young when it happened, and seeing him smile again makes me happy too. And you, Rella, you smell like everything we should no longer hope for, and that makes you dangerous to us. To Rouen, who I would kill for. If Luc doesn't kill us for sleeping with his precious offspring, then you yourself are a danger to our very souls. But I can't deny that I want you so much that my dick aches and my heart longs for things that I can no longer have."

I'd never heard him string so many words together, or speak with such emotion. I didn't know what to say. I just reached over and twined my fingers in his. I needed to think, but I had to put it off until we'd dealt with Volchek. I needed my head in that game. I would deal with my heart later.

"Let's go home, Romanus. Rouen is waiting for us."

I heard a faint click in my earpiece and realized that comms had been open that whole time. Shit. I can only hope that no one was listening, but I wouldn't bet my trust fund on it.

THAT NIGHT, I was on night watch, as was Rouen, which meant that I got the single bed and Naz, Romanus and Charlie were in the big bed. It was a tight fit and watching them try not to touch each other in a double bed was hilarious. Someone was going to be on the floor by the end of the night, and my money was on Naz. He did not look comfortable. Everyone was trying to do their best to sleep, and Charlie's snores told me that he could probably sleep through the apocalypse. But apparently not me getting fingerbanged by a badass gargoyle.

I yawned and looked at my watch. Three more hours. I was not made for night watch. I was a solid eight hours kind of girl, and I hadn't gotten even close to that last night.

"Would you like me to take over?" Naz asked, and I felt bad that I got caught yawning.

"No, I'm good. You should sleep. I'm pretty sure no one is going to bust in here, even if I fall asleep. We should be good."

Naz slid out of bed and came over to sit on the coffee table beside me. "I don't need much sleep. Hazard of the profession. Go lay down if you want. I know your sleep was interrupted last night."

He said it completely without inflection, and I couldn't tell if he was reprimanding me or teasing me. I narrowed my eyes. I wish I could smell like Romanus, so I could get a hint on what was going on behind that mask.

"I'm going to pull my weight," I said, ignoring the innuendo. "I'm not a burden."

We sat in the darkness, the silence hanging between us. I took the opportunity to study him in the dark, while he couldn't see my blatant perusal. He didn't have a shirt on, and I noticed that the dark tattoos moved up his arm and down his shoulder and left pec, but they covered the entirety of his back. I couldn't make out what they were, I hadn't seen him without his shirt on in the daylight, but I could tell that a lot of time and pain went into inking that much of his skin. I couldn't help but admire his body, the solid curve of his muscles, the hard lines of his abs, one long scar puckering over his gut.

"That looked like it could have been bad," I said inanely, pointing at the scar.

"Very nearly a permanent trip to the sands. An extraction gone bad in Egypt."

"Must have been scary."

He shrugged. "Another hazard of the job. They become a little like a resume. Proof you've done something good and lived to tell nosey redheads the tale in dingy hotel rooms."

A shock laugh burst from my chest, and I smothered it down before I woke any of the other guys. I catalogued the puckered scars on his body, testaments to a life lived hard. "Managed to keep the pretty face though," I joked back.

He leaned in closer, so I could see his eyes, even though they just looked like an abyss you could drown in. "Do you think I'm pretty, Estrella?" His voice was low, husky in a way that made my nerves tingle, though I didn't know if it was arousal or some kind of acknowledgement that he was a predator just as much as the Gargoyles.

"Yes," I breathed out.

His lip curled, and then he straightened, his eyes scanning the room lazily. "Don't worry, kid. There's only one more day of surveillance, and then you can have your blood." My mind spun trying to keep up with the conversation shifts.

"It's not all about revenge, you know. How many women have they hurt like that? How many just end up dead in the ocean on the way to wherever they are shipping them? How many die once sold, their deaths covered up? I can't end it, but maybe I can make a little difference while I claim retribution." He said nothing, and we fell into silence again.

"What are you going to do about your demons?" he asked finally.

"You were listening?"

I saw his teeth glint in the moonlight as he smiled. "Everyone heard, Estrella. Both times. You aren't very stealthy. You wouldn't make much of a spy."

I buried my face in my hands. Maybe I should just join a convent or something. I'm sure Luc would get my retribution and my life would be way less embarrassing.

"So?" he asked again.

"Why do you want to know?" I looked at him through narrowed eyes.

"Human curiosity? Because I care about Charlie?"

I sucked in a deep breath, letting it whistle out through my teeth. "I don't know. It's all too much, too soon. I'll figure it out later. After this op. After Hope is back on her feet. After I work out where I went wrong and why my life has become a cross between the Bourne Identity and Jerry Springer." He let out a little chuckle, and I liked how it sounded. "What do you think I should do?"

"Are you asking my opinion, or do you want me to tell you what to do?" He raised an eyebrow.

I grinned back this time. "Both? Or either. I'll take what I can get."

He turned so his body was facing mine, and stared down at me in the chair of grossness. "I can't tell you what to do, but I can tell you what I'd do. I've seen so many things, terrible things. But I saw how Charlie looked at you when you were a kid, and how he looks at you now. You are buried under that kid's skin deep, and he loves you in a way people can only dream of being loved. I'm not even going to pretend to understand what is going with the other two, but they seem pretty intense. I'd wanna make really sure that I knew exactly how I felt before I did anything drastic, because heartbreak hurts way more than this." He pointed to the scar on his stomach.

I frowned at him. "Real helpful."

He held up a hand. "Not finished. But, don't wait too long. Because despite what the movies tell you, happiness doesn't happen for everyone, and for some it never appears. Take it where you can get it and if it feels right, grab on with both hands and don't let go. Doesn't matter what that happiness looks like, or how other people will perceive it. Trust your gut. It will rarely lead you down the wrong path."

He gave me an intense look, then thumped me on the back. "Go sleep. I'll take your shift. I need you on your A-Game."

Sick of fighting the yawns, I nodded and walked over to the bed. I slid in beside Charlie, who curled his body around mine in his sleep. I smiled and breathed in the scent of him, the steady thump of his heart lulling me to sleep.

SURVEILLANCE the next day went much the same as the day before, although we swapped positions. Romanus and I were watching the employee door, which led to the kitchens of a ground floor cafe. It smelled like garbage and grease, and the scent was making me queasy as hell. We sat in the shadow of the dumpster, but so far all was quiet. Not nearly as interesting as the park yesterday.

We sat on two crates, dirty aprons wrapped around our waists so we looked like a waitress and kitchen hand sneaking out for a cigarette. It was boring.

I started out counting rats, but I was just grossing myself out. So I switched to counting muscle bulges that showed under Romanus' tight black shirt. I was up to twenty-five and beginning to think I was just torturing myself, because goddamn that man, uh demon, was built. He definitely wasn't made for stealth missions, because beside his height and his golden skin, the guy looked like he'd be able to bench press a Buick. His shoulders were broad and muscular, tapering down into a slim waist and an ass that was basically sculpted by gods. He looked like heaven in leather.

"You gotta stop, Red."

"Stop what?"

"Smelling like that. Seriously, I'm moments away from pushing you up against the dirty wall and fucking you senseless in this disgusting back alley." His words were gruff, his voice so deep it sounded like those few moments before an avalanche and it made my pussy throb. I was turning into a sex addict in the middle of staking out a human trafficker. That was all sorts of messed up. He took a deep breath and growled.

"Fuck it."

He picked me up and pressed me against the wall as if I weighed nothing. His heavy body pinned me as his mouth found mine, and he kissed me punishingly hard. I wrapped my legs around his waist, my hands clinging to his shoulders. His hands slid under my ass and squeezed.

He let out a happy little hum as he deepened our kiss, our tongues intertwining.

He pushed my skirt up until it was around my upper thighs and his hard dick ground against my lace covered pussy, giving me delicious friction. I moaned as his hand reached between us, and he pushed my panties aside, dipping his fingers into my already soaked core.

"So wet. You ready for me, Red? God, not being inside you has been torture. Watching Rouen make you cum almost sent me crazy."

I kissed his jaw, moving down the column of his neck and biting gently. He let out a long moan. "Like that, huh?" I said, grinning with feminine satisfaction.

He growled. "Harder." He was stroking my pussy, making me slick. He unbuttoned his fly and freed his massive cock, and I did what I was told and bit hard into the tendon of his neck. He groaned and buried his dick deep in me with one hard thrust, making us both shout. He was huge, and my pussy burned as it stretched around him. He held me still, his big fingers biting into my hips, waiting for me to adjust. I didn't want time to adjust.

"Move," I growled out, and that was all he needed. He pounded into me hard, and I no longer cared that anyone could walk down the alley at any second, or that my tank was riding up and the rough bricks were scraping my back raw. All that mattered was how it felt as he pounded into me over and over again. I buried my face in his neck, muffling my moans as he pushed me higher and higher. My orgasm shuddered across my body and I bit down on his neck, hard, tasting a little blood, and he roared his own release, pinning me back against the wall and burying himself so far inside me we were practically one person.

I panted, allowing him to hold my weight because I was pretty sure that I wouldn't be able to stand. He leaned back and stared at me, his eyes telling me all sorts of things that I wasn't ready to hear out loud. Suddenly, his nose flared.

"You're bleeding."

He placed me on my feet and turned me around, pulling up my tank to see where the rough bricks had grazed my back. I looked over.

"It's fine. It'll be gone by tonight. I'm a pretty fast healer."

But Romanus wasn't listening. His pupils had gone wide, and he was staring down at the little dots of blood. He squatted down, and he sniffed again.

"Romanus?" He leaned forward and licked the graze with one long swipe. Then another, harder than the first. He kept lapping at it until the blood was gone and the wound had started to sting.

"Hey, Rom? Snap out of it, dude." I tried to move away, but his hands held me tight. He wasn't hurting me, but he was seriously weirding me out.

Rouen came tearing down the alleyway. He skidded to a stop in front of us and wrapped an arm around Romanus' shoulders, yanking him back. Romanus snarled at his packmate, but Rouen just raised both hands placatingly. He dropped his gaze. "Hey there, Alpha. It's all good. But you are freaking her out, okay? Take a deep breath."

Romanus blinked a couple of times, then shook his head. He looked between Rouen and I, his face shutting down. He stormed out of the alleyway and I watched him go, completely bewildered.

"I guess surveillance is over?"

Rouen grinned. "Yeah, Volchek left ten minutes ago, exact same time, exact same bodyguard. Naz told us over comms, but I think you were probably a little preoccupied."

I looked at the ground and kicked a piece of cardboard that had the audacity to be close to my foot. "I turned my earpiece off so everyone didn't hear...that." Rouen just grinned as I connected the dots, his eyes glinting. "Which probably means you shouldn't have been able to hear Romanus losing his shit back there unless-"

"Rom didn't turn his off. Bad practice, in case you were jumped, you know."

I groaned and slapped a hand to my forehead. "Seriously? Again? Is there ever going to be a time that everyone isn't a participant in my fucked up sex life?"

Rouen just laughed, the asshole. "Probably not. Small group, harder to keep secrets."

He straightened my clothes and took my hand, leading me from the alley.

A flush made its way to my cheeks and I wondered how I was ever going to look at them again. All four of them heard me come. Rouen didn't seem to care, but he didn't have human sensibilities.

"Is your comm turned off now?" I asked Rouen. I wasn't going to make the same mistake for the hundredth time.

Rouen nodded. "It's just you and me, Tiger."

"What the hell was that back there with Romanus?" We walked down the steep stairs of the nearest subway station to get back to the hotel. Always separate, although I was never alone.

"From what I heard, I think he fucked you against a wall." I punched him in the arm, hard, and felt my knuckles crack. He didn't even flinch, just chuckling at his own joke.

"You know what I mean, dickhead."

He shook his head. "Just an evolutionary throwback, nothing to worry about. Our saliva has healing qualities. Nature designed it so that when our Queen is injured, we are instinctively compelled to heal her wounds, or heal her enough that we can get her to a proper healer or she heals herself. To achieve that, they made the scent of our mate's blood like the best thing you can imagine. It smells like cookies and summer and everything good, but times a thousand, and tastes even better."

"I'm not your mate," I stated firmly.

"No, you aren't," he said quietly. He didn't look at me though. I'd hurt his feelings, dammit. "So, it was probably just because you'd fucked right beforehand."

He didn't meet my gaze again, his eyes roaming the train carriage for threats and looking everywhere except in my direction. We walked back to the hotel in silence.

What I would have given for a drink right then. A little dutch courage before I had to walk into a room that currently held a guy I just fucked, his gargoyle boyfriend, my best friend who wanted to be more and a killer who seemed to know all my secrets. And they all knew I'd just had dirty sex in some back alley like a prostitute.

I straightened my shoulders and raised my chin. It was none of their damn business. I was here for one reason only. I'd keep it professional, at least until the awkwardness was gone. Burying my head in the sand was one of my go-to avoidance techniques.

I pushed open the door. Three sets of eyes looked at me, and two slid away immediately. Charlie went back to staring at his computer screen, and Romanus was staring at paper plans on the bed. Only Naz held my gaze, but they gave nothing away. Perfectly blank. He nodded towards the end of the bed.

"We were just going over the footage from the CCTV outside the Starbucks across the street. I was right, his routine is never completely the same, but it's not random either. They change the pick up and drop off times every three days, and it's always the big guy with the ugly mug with him every time. Which means tomorrow, we'll have a pretty good idea when he will leave, if you want to get up into his apartment to look around. Romanus thinks the best way to get you up there is to fly you up under the cover of night, but you'd have to sit out there until he leaves. The Gargoyle assures me that he can carry you up there with no problems."

"You want me to ride a dragon to the top of the building?" It sounded even more ridiculous coming out of my mouth.

"I didn't think you would have any problems riding a dragon."

I squinted, trying to work out if he was fucking with me, or alluding to what he heard earlier. I sighed. "It'll be fine. You know, I could always get Ace or one of the other Fallen to sift me in?"

Nazir nodded. "Sure, you could, but we might want to save calling in the big guns for when shit gets pear shaped. I also happen to know for a fact that Memphis is occupied right now." His tone had zero inflection, like usual, but something like mirth danced across his eyes. Hmm.

"Fine, if the guys don't mind me using them like a pony."

Rouen seemed the only one who was oblivious to the underlying tension in the room. Or maybe he just didn't care. He wrapped an arm around my shoulder and hugged me close to his body.

"Babe, I'd let you ride me however you liked for the

rest of my immortal life. You only have to say the word." He was teasing me, that I knew, but I couldn't help but think that there was probably some underlying truth in there.

Charlie stood. "I'm gonna go shower." He walked to his duffle, pulling out some stuff before striding into the bathroom and slamming the door. I flinched.

Rouen sighed. "Humans."

I sat down and listened as Nazir went over the rest of the plan. I was going to try and find out any information about why they tried to snatch Hope, of all people. It didn't fit their MO of taking the vulnerable and the desperate. Hope was neither of those things and the attack was way too coordinated. They were after her in particular, and it didn't make sense.

If that wasn't as fruitful as we'd like, Charlie had placed a tiny little DotBot, a magnetic droid the size of a bug that used magnetic energy to move, as a tracker under his car to see where Volchek went every day. While I was rummaging through his apartment, Charlie and Naz would be tracking where he went, and do a little reconnoitering on the location.

Rouen and Romanus would be with me.

The shower was still running, and I walked into the bathroom without knocking. I didn't want to go to bed with bad feelings between us. If growing up in my family had taught me anything, it was that communication was the key to any happy relationship, be it familial, lover or friend. The other thing it taught me was to never go to bed angry, because life can shift dramatically in a single rotation of the sun.

"Charlie?" Silence. "I'm sorry."

I heard a sigh, and the thunk of flesh against the tiles. "What are you sorry for, Rella?"

It was my turn to sit on the lopsided toilet this time. "Everything? For screwing this up so bad? For taking so long to recognize…"

His head poked out from the shower curtain. "To recognize what?"

"That what I feel for you isn't just normal friendship. That it's something more. But you've always been there, and it was easier than trying to make it more and messing everything up. But I did it anyway."

Charlie pulled his head back into the shower cubicle. The shower curtain hid a lot of things, but I could see the silhouette of his body just fine. The long curve of his back, the firm muscle of his ass, his long strong legs he got from running every morning almost religiously.

"It's fine, Rella. I will always be here for you, you know that. Plus, the Gargoyles are probably a better fit for you. They want to devote their life to you, and how can any guy compete with that? They look like Vin Diesel had sex with the goddamn Oscar statue."

I laughed at the visual, remember the actor from all those old car chase movies Charlie had made me watch as a teenager.

"You're perfect as you, Charlie. I don't need muscle-bound; I need my best friend."

"Don't lie to me, Rella. I have eyes. I can see how you all are together. You move in perfect synchroniza-tion, even though you don't realize it. If you have a need, they seem to be able to preempt it, and they're there. I can't compete with that, and it's unfair to ask you to choose."

"Do I have to choose?"

"I need you to choose," he murmured, more to himself than to me.

"Need or want, Charlie?"

"Does it matter?"

"Yeah it matters. You seemed okay with the whole sharing the other night."

Even as I said it, I knew it was the wrong thing. "The fact you think my problem is sharing you for sex, means you know nothing of how I feel, Rella." His angry tone told me that that was the end of the conversation, but I felt worse than when I walked in here.

I stood and moved closer to the shower. "I hate this, Charlie. I love you. I don't want all this angst between us."

He flicked the shower curtain aside, exposing one side of his body, though hiding all the fun bits. "I love you, too. No matter how this all pans out, nothing will change that. How about we just table it until later, okay? Can you pass me a towel?" He turned off the shower, and I watched the little droplets of water cling to his chest hair, and rivulets run down his bare skin. "But you're gonna have to stop looking at me like that right now."

I handed him the towel and averted my eyes. "Don't pretend you weren't perving on me through the shower curtain the other day, Charles Mulligan. I know exactly how see-through that curtain is now!"

He wrapped the towel around his waist and stepped

out. "Off you go, Rella. We are okay for now. We'll figure the rest out later." He leaned over and kissed the side of my head like he'd done hundreds of times before.

I smiled at him and slipped out of the bathroom. Only Naz was in the main room.

"They've gone to grab food. I think they needed to talk. Seems to be the flavor of the day."

I flopped down on the bed and flung an arm across my eyes. "Sorry about earlier."

Naz laughed, and the sound made me look at his face. I was struck again about how handsome he was when he smiled.

"Hey, don't be. I'm living vicariously through you, I think. Though I'm going to have a serious case of blue balls soon."

My face flared red and I groaned. Now I knew he was teasing me. "I'm glad this is so amusing for you."

"Don't stress it, kid. There's worse things than having men fighting over you."

"Yeah, like what?" I taunted.

"Like being alone." My eyes traced over his face, searching for a hint of emotion behind those words, but there was nothing. He'd locked his emotions behind an impenetrable wall, and no matter how I searched, I couldn't find a crack.

I nodded. "You're right. Don't worry, I know how lucky I am, no matter how it feels right now."

He nodded, and we were silent, each lost in our own thoughts.

CHAPTER SEVEN

We'd all woken in the middle of the night, dressed in black and armed ourselves. We drove to Central Park, eerie in the darkness. Rouen and Romanus got out of the car, Rouen holding my elbow as I slipped out of the back seat.

"Who's changing?" I asked.

In answer, Romanus shifted. It happened between one blink and the next, and all I caught was a shimmer and a few grunts. When I opened my eyes, a large slate grey dragon stood in front of me. He was about the length of a pickup truck, and about as wide. He had four powerful legs the size of tree trunks and large ridges down his back. His body was patterned with alternating muted green and blue vee's down his spine, interspersed with the grey. The same blue and green of Rom's eyes. He was beautiful.

I let out the little gasp I'd been holding in and walked towards him. So beautiful. I reached forward and ran a hand down his side. It felt a little like his human skin, like sun warmed rocks. I walked down his side, awed by the sheer power of his body.

"Aw, no fair. I want her to stroke me like that," Rouen pouted.

"Yeah, but I have to carry your heavy ass to the top of the building, so we are even," a voice rumbled, and I realized it was Romanus. Well, Romanus the Dragon. It was like his ordinary voice, but more. It was deeper, louder and you felt it right in the marrow of your bones. A roar from Romanus would make a human mess himself.

"You like my ass," Rouen said, winking. The dragon chuffed out a laugh.

"Let's do this before we give some night-time jogger a heart attack," Naz said, apparently completely unfazed by the freaking dragon in his midst.

Rouen was beside me in a second and boosted me up. "Settle at the base of his neck, between his shoulder blades." I shifted into the spot and then Rouen was bounding up the side of Romanus's body to settle behind me. He leaned forward and nuzzled my neck. "This shit is going to blow your mind," he whispered, and Romanus' wings spread wide.

They were as beautiful as his hide but better. One wing had sapphire blue spots and the other one emerald green. Spots was probably the wrong word. It was like someone had jammed the actual gems into his skin and they glowed with otherworldly beauty. Like stars across his wings.

With a few powerful beats of those glorious wings, we were airborne. He pushed higher and higher, and weirdly, I felt perfectly safe. Rouen had his arms wrapped around me, and I was pressed securely into his chest. When we were a fair way off the ground, high enough that pedestrians wouldn't notice us, he circled back to Volchek's building.

"How does no one see his wings from the ground?" I asked. They shone like stars.

"The underside of his wings are dark grey. It would be very difficult for human eyes to see him in the darkness." We glided down and landed on the roof of the apartment building with a barely audible thump. He tucked his wings back in, and Rouen slid down off his shoulder.

I ran my hands up and down his neck, and he rumbled a purr. It sounded like thunder in the distance.

"I don't want to hop down yet," I pouted.

"I promise one day you can lay all over me for hours, but a dragon on the roof of a building is a little conspicuous for a stealth mission." He shifted, and I was falling, but human arms caught me before I even hit the ground.

"That happens so fast," I said, sounding breathless as he held me in his arms, cradled protectively against his chest. He put my feet on the ground and took a big step away from me.

"It's a skill I have. It takes Rouen a little longer."

Rouen shrugged. "Women like a man who takes his time." He gave me a saucy wink and I laughed. We settled in beside the air conditioning unit, hiding us from the view of surrounding buildings. It was a tight fit, but they were both conscious not to get into my space. Eventually, Rouen growled. "Nothing sexual, but I need to touch you."

Romanus gave him a hard look, but Rouen lifted his chin. I was missing something, but I didn't want to try and figure it out now. I just settled back into the comfort of Rouen's chest and yawned.

"Sleep, Red. We'll keep watch and wake you when it's time."

"Okay," I said. I didn't want to second guess it, to mine is tone for nuance and ulterior meanings. I wanted to rest, so I curled in his arms and dozed off. All this emotional angst was exhausting.

"WAKE UP, TIGER."

A warm cheek rubbed against mine. I blinked my eyes open, and noticed the sun just peeking over the tops of the skyscrapers. The left side of my body felt like I was sleeping on a hard hot-water bottle. I shifted in Rouen's arms and looked up into his pretty gold and brown eyes. I'd been dreaming of dragons, and sex. Luckily not at the same time. Dragon sex was probably a little wild even for me.

"Is your dragon as pretty as Rom's?" I asked sleepily.

"Nah. Everything is a lot more subtle unless I'm in the sun. He's more vivid because he's an Alpha. Better to attract the ladies," he said.

Romanus laughed. "And the Beta males."

I swallowed. If I spent too long thinking about them having sex with each other, I'd smell horny all over again and everyone would be distracted. Besides, it sounded like they'd come to some kind of agreement last night during their little chat.

"So, you guys are kind of like peacocks? The females go for the prettiest plumage?"

Romanus screwed up his face. "I am nothing like a peacock."

Rouen laughed quietly. "I don't know dude. All that green and blue? And there was that one time 300 years ago with that bird shifter…"

Romanus's eyes turned into daggers and Rouen laughed, and I laughed along with him. Together, just the three of us, it was kind of nice.

"Volchek has left the building." Nazir's voice came through our earpieces. "Make it quick and thorough, but be stealthy. We don't want to blow our element of surprise for nothing."

"Ten-Four," Romanus said as he stood. "Let's go."

We walked to the edge of the building, keeping low. Romanus looked down onto the balcony below. It had a six-foot tall glass railing, but it was quite wide. Romanus hopped over the side and made the fifteen-foot drop like it was child's play. Like he was jumping over a puddle or something.

"You're turn, Rella," Rouen said, helping me up onto the edge.

"You want me to fall fifteen feet? I'll die?"

"How'd you think we were getting down there?" he said, his arms around my waist.

"A ladder?"

Rouen laughed. "Don't worry, we wouldn't let anything happen to you."

"Because Luc would feed you to the demonesses?"

"Uh, yeah. Exactly. Okay, close your eyes, it'll make it easier. On the count of three. One-" Then he dropped me. I freefell for what seemed like an hour and landed with an 'oomph' into Romanus' arms. He put me on my feet as Rouen landed beside us.

"See? Easy."

My thumping heart would disagree.

I scowled at him, but walked to the sliding door, opening it quietly. It wasn't locked. Who was going to get in twenty-seven stories from the ground?

Romanus stepped in first. "There's someone in the bedroom. Rouen, go."

Rouen moved like a shadow through the light filled apartment. He appeared moments later. His face was livid.

"It's a woman. She chained to his bed, and she's covered in bruises and cuts. I put her out, but we'll have to be quick."

"We can't leave her here," I whispered furiously.

"We'll have to, but we'll come back for her, Rella. I promise. She's an unknown variable. People who have been prisoners too long, well, sometimes their minds are all screwed up. We can't take the chance. We'll take out Volchek and then let her go, but if we try now, she might turn on us."

I sighed. I knew they were right, but the thought of leaving her chained here made my blood boil.

We moved through the apartment silently, finding his office easily enough. A laptop was on the desk, and I picked it up, putting it in my pack.

"Naz said stealth."

"Volchek isn't going to live to come back here." My voice trembled with cold fury. Romanus' jaw tightened, but he didn't disagree. I would deal with Naz when we got back to the hotel, but it wouldn't matter by then. I turned back to my search. Moving aside a picture, we saw a safe.

"How very Hollywood of him. A safe behind a painting," Rouen sounded amused. "Well, if we aren't covering our tracks." He put his fist through the safe door. We emptied the contents of the safe into the backpack, including a couple of hundred grand in cash, several key drives and some old-fashioned ledger books. Probably a good idea to keep things off the networks where hackers could get them.

Romanus growled. "Better hope that wasn't alarmed. Let's go before the cavalry arrives."

We moved back out of the room, but I handed Rouen my pack and moved toward the bedroom. We walked quietly, but the girl was still out to it. Rouen hadn't been kidding. The girl looked like someone had taken a whip to her.

"Snap the chains. Then it's up to her," I whispered.

Romanus inclined his head and snapped the chain like it was nothing more than thread. That was some seriously impressive strength.

Rouen was waiting for us on the balcony. He handed me back my pack, and I strapped it tight to my body. He leapt to the top of the railing, balancing like a cat, then sprang up to grab the edge of the roof. He must have jumped eight feet straight up. He pulled himself over the ledge, and his torso dangled over the edge.

"Throw her up."

I turned to Romanus. "He's kidding, right?"

"Nope."

"Can't you just fly us up?"

He shook his head. "It's the middle of the day."

He put his hands around my waist. "Arms up. Ready. Set-"

Then he tossed me up to Rouen, who grabbed my outstretched hands and dragged me up over the edge. Seconds later, Romanus was up there beside us.

"Okay, we are going to climb down the ladder on the other side. That should lead us to a service balcony, then down the elevator and out the front doors. Easy. Why was I even worried?" I grinned.

Famous last words.

"We've been made," Nazir's voice came over our comms. "Fuck." There was the sound of metal crunching, the screech of tires, then silence.

"Naz? Nazir? Charlie?" I screamed down the comms. No, no, no. I looked at Romanus. "Shift. Both of you. We need to go."

Neither of them protested, bowing their heads in time. Romanus shift was instantaneous again, but Rouen's was slower, his body stretching in the haze that surrounded him, like a mirror reflecting reality back at me. Eventually, a slightly smaller dragon stood before me, slate grey as well, though there was a hint of gold running in stripes down his spine.

I climbed onto Romanus' back. "I need to drop this

pack on the roof of Hope's apartment. Someone needs to have this information, just in case…" I didn't finish the sentence. "Then we need to go to the address where the DotBot pinpointed Volchek." I opened my phone and looked at the address the DotBot had messaged through to me. "Let's go."

The heavy flap of wings lifted us into the air, and I was kind of glad that this was the highest apartment building in the area. Hopefully their natural camouflage would hide them from people on the ground. We flew high, and it was bitterly cold without Rouen wrapped around me, but I laid along Romanus' neck and tried not to look down. We circled down low to the roof of Hope's apartment building. I lowered both mine and Rouen's packs down gently but quickly with a rope from Rouen's bag, and then let the rope go. As Romanus took off, I reached out to Hope.

I'm leaving a backpack on the roof of your building. I need you to get someone to go and get it immediately. If I don't contact you by tonight, I need you to give it to Lux or the cops. Bernie maybe, or someone here in the NYPD that you trust implicitly. It's important Hope.

Hope's startled mind connected with mine. *Rella, what's going on? Are you okay?*

I didn't say more. *I love you, Hope.*

I cut the connection. I couldn't block her completely, but I could make the connection weaker.

I knew we were travelling faster than any car could, but the slow beat of their wings drove me insane.

"Faster," I shouted over the wind.

"If we go any faster, you will fall off. We are minutes out, Estrella. Hold strong."

We circled a decommissioned dock, just down the coast from Jersey. Huge warehouse buildings crowded the docks, and the dragons' dead dropped into one of the narrow pathways between them. I slid off and pulled my gun. Romanus changed instantly, his huge knife in his hands and Rouen was beside me moments later with his own knife. "Can you smell anything?" I whispered.

"Fresh scents. The smell of terror is coming from that building, but it's old, stale terror."

A shout of pain tore through the silence, and we all turned in the opposite direction.

"Charlie."

I ran down the rows towards the scream, until someone caught me around the waist. "Slow, Tiger. We will get them back." I took a deep breath and tried to remember my training.

Romanus took lead, and Rouen brought up the rear, and we crept through the docks. Every so often, a very male cry of agony would echo around the buildings and make me flinch, but I tried to block it out. They needed me on my A-Game.

Eventually, Romanus narrowed it down to the right building. We looked through the windows at the rear. Naz and Charlie were tied to chairs, and a man was twisting a knife sticking out of Naz's thigh. Volchek.

Volchek was talking to Charlie, whose face was battered and swollen, but I couldn't make out the words. When Charlie just shook his head, Volchek reached over and twisted the knife in Nazir's thigh. His scream rattled the windows and then his head slumped forward. He'd passed out. Thank god.

I was going to throw up. Naz had been right all along. I didn't have the stomach to watch a man being tortured. Especially not one of mine.

Romanus turned from the window. "There's twelve in there including Volchek. Rouen, take the left, I'll take the right. Red, you must stay covered or behind one of us at all times. Our hides are like Kevlar. Ordinary bullets can't pierce it. Can you do that?"

When I didn't agree quickly enough, he grabbed hold of my shoulders and lifted me up to eye height. "Can you do that? Because if not, I'm leaving you outside tied to a tree. I need to know you're safe, Estrella."

I nodded. "Fine, I get it. Hide behind you guys. Let's just get them the hell out of there now!"

He nodded. "Good. Try and keep up." He walked to the door, and kicked it hard, making it slam open with a thud and every man in the warehouse turned at the sound.

But it was already too late for them. The Gargoyles moved like death, their movements too fast to track with a gun, which meant bullets just went flying around the room. I took cover behind a crate, not even close to being able to keep up to the demons as they whirled and sliced their way through the warehouse. I leaned around and shot at a guy who'd circled around, and another who was trying to run. Fuck that shit. No one was leaving here alive.

When it fell silent, I looked cautiously around the

crate I was using for cover and saw a blood bath. But the Gargoyles were both standing proud in the center, covered in blood and chunks of things I didn't want to think about too hard.

I ran down the battlefield, jumping over body parts, until I reached Charlie. Naz was still thankfully passed out.

I dropped to my knees in front of Naz, but my eyes were on Charlie. "Are you okay?"

It was a stupid question, of course he wasn't okay, but he nodded anyway. I searched his body for any sign of serious injury, but nothing was oozing blood, which is less than I could say for Naz. I could only assume that the last twist of the knife nicked his femoral artery because blood was oozing out around the edges of the blade. "Shit, shit, shit," I chanted as I took off my shirt to pack it around the wound. If we shifted him, or the knife, he'd bleed out in minutes.

Volchek was down, unconscious on the ground but still alive. I assumed he was still alive anyway. Rouen was watching him. Romanus stood behind me. "That is not a good wound. It has hit the muscle and severed the tendons. If he makes it to hospital, he will never have full use of it again."

His words hit me like a sledgehammer to the gut. So many missions as a mercenary and he's going to die because of me.

"Can you fix it? With your healing saliva or whatever? Can you heal the wound?"

Romanus reared back in shock. "It doesn't work like

that, Estrella. It only works on the Queen or pack. Otherwise we'd heal things as we ate them."

I stood. "Then make him pack!"

"It's not that easy. I can't bind another member to the pack. We have no Queen."

I pushed into his space. "Then make me Queen and him pack and we'll heal him together. I can't let him die, Rom."

Romanus sighed, looking at Rouen, whose face was unreadable for once. But he gave a single nod.

"I don't think you understand what you are getting into, this isn't something you can take back when the heat of the moment dies down. You are making the decision for him, too."

"It's better than dead," I whispered. "Please, Romanus."

He sighed, rolling up his sleeves. Rouen came over and untied Charlie, taking my gun from me and handing it to him. He bent down and looked Charlie in the eye. "You did good, human. Watch him. This might get messy."

I looked over at Charlie and silently begged him to understand. He just stared out at me through swollen eyes, blood still dripping into one and nodded. I let out the breath that I'd been holding.

Rouen and Romanus knelt before me. "With our blood, we pledge to you our lives as our Queen." Then Rouen sliced both their wrists and they held them out to me. "You have to taste our blood to cement the bond."

I should have told them that blood kinda made me woozy, but I steeled my spine. I leaned forward and lapped at the gash on first on Romanus's wrist, proud that I didn't gag. "My Alpha."

"My Queen."

Then I licked the blood from Rouen's wrist. He bowed his head.

"My Queen." He looked up into my eyes. "This is not how I wanted this to be," he murmured, and I stroked his dark hair.

"I know."

Romanus held out his hand for mine, and I gave it willingly. He placed the tiniest cut along my wrist, and I winced at the sting. "We take your blood to tie us to you forever." He put emphasis on forever, but I just nodded. I got it. Still wasn't much of a choice in my opinion. He lifted my wrist to his mouth and sucked, and boy, it tugged all the way to my center, shooting pleasure through me. Rouen cut my other wrist, and sucked as well, and I knew I was going to cum. I let out a long moan that echoed across the warehouse, as an orgasm swept over me like a wave.

Woah.

I could feel them in my head now, a new bond pressed close to the one I had with Hope, separate and different but just as strong.

"We have to hurry," I said, shaking myself from my fugue.

Romanus stood and went around to Naz's head. He gently tried to wake him, but he'd lost too much blood. Rouen moved to beside his leg, ready to heal him as soon as he was pack.

"I can tie him to the pack for both Rouen and I, but

you have to claim him first." He nicked my wrist again, and I held it to Naz's lips which had turned a grey color.

"Sorry, Naz, but it's better than dead." I dripped some of my blood into his mouth, and he swallowed reflexively, and Romanus chased my blood with his own.

"Now some of his," Romanus instructed, his hand over the knife. "As soon as the bond is in place, we can begin to heal him."

I swiped at the blood on his leg with a finger and placed the red liquid in my mouth. I felt a golden thread snap against my bond with the guys, making it thicker, stronger.

"It's done."

As I said the words, Romanus pulled the blade and blood started pouring from the wound. Rouen pressed his mouth against the wound, catching the blood, and I assumed began to work his magic.

Then I felt a presence behind us. I whirled around, Romanus's blade suddenly in my hand. Azriel, Angel of Death, stood behind us, his own dagger hanging loosely at my side.

I took a step forward, raising my knife. "No. This one is mine. You can't have him."

He looked past me to the Gargoyles, one of whom was healing Nazir more by the second. He gave me a disgusted look.

"The other twin. I should have known. Your family is the bane of my immortal existence." And then he disappeared.

I turned around and nearly fell over when I saw the wound in Nazir's leg had almost healed completely.

Naz was still passed out, but he wasn't the grey of death.

I wanted this done, and I wanted it done now. I turned toward Volchek.

"Rom, can you shift for me please?"

He shifted mid step. I kicked Volchek in the side, and he came awake with a start. He looked from me, to Romanus, who was glaring down at him with sharp teeth and eyes like death.

"Answer my questions or I'll let the dragon eat you piece by piece. Got it?"

Volchek just stared at Romanus, until he growled low, and then he was nodding furiously.

"Why did your organization abduct Hope Jones from Geneva?"

"I don't know."

"I don't believe you. Rom, eat a foot." Rom opened his mouth wide, and perfect sharp, serrated teeth glinted in the fluorescent lights.

"Okay, okay. We were paid to abduct the girl. $30 million dollars, and we got to keep her as long as she disappeared for good. A big pay day and we got to keep the merchandise? It was too good to say no." His accent got thicker as he stumbled over his words.

"Who paid you?" I sounded way too calm. Calmer than I felt.

"I don't know. It came from the top. I had nothing to do with the actual grab. I just kept an eye on her here, I swear."

"I don't believe you."

Volchek tried to scoot away, switching to his native

language as he begged. Begging sounds the same in every language.

"Who's the head of your organization?"

"No."

"Who runs your organization?" I said again, laying a kick into his ribs. Still silence. "Fuck it. Eat him."

"No, no. Vladimir Rousevik. Vladimir Rousevik!"

The name rang a bell, but I didn't know why. "Thank you." I refused to turn away as he died. I cemented his face in my memory. Romanus swiped one of those steak knife sized claws across his throat, separating his head from his body.

I walked over to Charlie, who was eyeing me warily.

"Are you okay?"

He just nodded, but he wouldn't look at me. I reached up and grabbed his face, lowering his eyes to mine.

"You know I had to, right?" He nodded, but there was so much sadness in his expression that I felt my heart crack.

Rouen was lifting Nazir into his arms. "He's stirring."

I ran over, stroking his face. I could feel his pain and his confusion. "It's okay. We've got you now. It's gonna be fine."

Naz's eyelashes fluttered against his cheeks, and then they slid open. I held back my gasp, but Charlie didn't.

One eye was his normal dark brown, the other a swirling mercury silver.

What had we done?

PART II

CHAPTER EIGHT

Naz looked around the room, his mercury silver eye darting from Romanus and Rouen, to the floor which was painted red with blood and littered with body parts. When his gaze settled on me, my heart stuttered to a stop. I could feel him. I could feel them all, but Naz's emotions were like this bright flare of pain that burned like acid in my veins. He was so confused, scared even, although his outer demeanor looked in control.

"Hey, Naz. Are you okay?" My voice was gentle, like I was talking to a wounded predator. The feral look in his eye was making my heart pound. "It's alright now. I've got you, okay?"

Praying that the bond worked similar to the one I had with Hope, I sent reassuring feelings down the golden thread. I always imagined it like one of those tin can phones you made as a kid.

He sucked in a breath, and if anything, looked more outwardly panicked. He stepped toward me, but

Romanus was suddenly there, his body partially blocking mine. Naz raised his lip in a silent snarl that was almost animalistic.

I rested my hand on Romanus' back. "It's alright."

Romanus didn't turn to look at me but Rouen crept around my other side, one hand resting on my arm.

"Charlie," Rouen said pleasantly. "Could you do me a favor and take Rella out through the back door? Things are about to get bloody. Again. It will be worse if they have to fight over her like a dog with a bone."

Charlie was beside me before Rouen had even finished his request, wrapping his fingers around my wrist, tugging me away.

"Come on," he urged, sounding desperate. I looked at him quickly, noticing that his face was pale and his hand was trembling where it was gripping my wrist. I'd been a cop for long enough to recognize the signs of shock. I was torn.

"What are they doing?" I asked Rouen, letting Charlie tug me a few steps.

"They are going to fight it out to see who is more dominant," Rouen said casually, but he reached out a hand and cupped my cheek. "It'll be fine, Rella. I prom-ise. They just have to establish each other's strength, and then everyone will be happy. Rom won't hurt him too much. You have my word. He's pack."

I jolted like I'd been hit. I'd changed him. I'd made Naz something else. He was going to hate me.

Rouen wrapped his arms around me. He pressed his lips against my temple. "It'll be fine, my Queen. Just go."

I finally let Charlie pull me away, and I was careful not to step in any of the rapidly congealing blood. We needed to get out here. We didn't have time for this shit, when anyone could turn up at any moment and find us in a room full of dead bodies.

We got to the kicked-in door, and I pulled out of Charlie's grasp. I needed to watch this. I'd stay out of the way, but I couldn't leave. He might need me. I didn't know which *he* I was referring to, but I couldn't leave when everything was so tense. The new bonds were already fucking with my head.

"Stand down, Soldier," Romanus growled, maintaining eye contact. Surely, one of them had to blink, or look at Rouen, or for me, or something. They wouldn't stand there in a room full of body parts forever, right?

"No," Naz growled. Actually growled, like a lion or a tiger or some other predator that was basically prowling death.

"So be it," Romanus growled back, and handed his knives to Rouen, never looking away. "Let's do this, but make it quick. Our Queen needs us."

Naz's eyes shot away then, searching for me in the falling darkness of the warehouse. His eyes locked with mine, and oxygen seemed to turn to lead in my chest. So much darkness in him. So much pain. I felt like I was having a heart attack.

He tore his gaze away and rolled his shoulders, his feet apart, his balance centered. They sized each other up, and then Naz attacked.

He was inhumanly quick. He whirled in with two quick left jabs that Romanus ducked, but a low kick got the gargoyle in the knee. But Rom's reflexes were equally as fast, and he kept his feet, using his forward momentum to get inside Naz's reach, throwing a hard left that Naz dodged, but following it with a quick right and an uppercut that connected with a jaw cracking thud.

I stepped forward. I knew that a blow that hard would break a man's jaw.

But apparently Naz was no longer simply a man. He shook his head, and then swept out with his legs again. He couldn't reach Romanus' head for a clean knockout blow, because Rom stood a good half a foot taller, but he was slower than Naz. The low kick connected hard and Romanus stumbled backwards. Naz was on him in a second, taking the gargoyle to the ground, laying brutal blows to Rom's face with his elbows. But he had no chance of keeping him there. Rom rolled over until he was under Naz's back, pinning his arm around his throat, Naz's other arm locked in a brutal hold that I was sure would pop his shoulder right out.

"Submit."

Naz just shook his head. He couldn't get enough air to speak.

"Submit, you fucker. We don't have time for this bullshit," Romanus' voice echoed around the warehouse.

Naz just continued to struggle. With a snarl, Romanus flipped them both over, and in a move so fast my eyes couldn't even track it, had Naz pinned to the ground on his back, his huge body lying over the top of the smaller man's and his fangs on his neck.

Naz stilled. His eyes met mine, and I saw him tilt his head a little to the left, baring his throat. It wasn't a submission by any stretch of the imagination, his eyes still held fiery anger, but it was the end of the fight. Romanus reared back a little, and hammered a fist into Naz's temple, and the body beneath him went limp.

I ran over to them. "Romanus, what the fuck? He submitted."

Rom stood, and wiped the blood from his mouth. "Hardly. We don't have time for his posturing bullshit, and we need to get the hell out of here before the cavalry arrives. We'll figure the rest out when we get back to the hotel. Don't worry, Red, a hit like that won't kill him anymore." He turned to Rouen. "The human got our strength. Hits like a sledgehammer and takes injury like a tank."

Rouen bent down and picked Naz up like a ragdoll, cradling him almost gently against his chest. "Think he'll get the dragon?"

I sucked in a breath. Holy shit. Would he? Would I? Fuck, why couldn't I breathe?

Both of the Gargoyles turned in unison. Their concern pulsed in down our bonds. They could sense my panic too.

Romanus came over and wrapped his arms around me. "Don't panic. We will figure it out. Maybe we can find a way to undo it."

I felt a wave of Rouen's anguish as Romanus spoke. He might not have chosen to become a pack this way, but he didn't want to take it back.

I looked around at the carnage. I slipped out of

Romanus' arms, and tried to think. We needed to burn this whole place down. "Do your dragons have fire?"

Romanus shook his head. "No."

That was disappointing. I looked around. In the movies there was always an extremely convenient form of accelerant just lying around. Best I had was Volchek's Range Rover. I walked over to the back and prayed that someone was a boy scout. While I didn't find a convenient can of gas, I did find a small case of vodka. I couldn't read the label, but it was definitely Russian. I raised my eyes at the alcohol percentage. We might just have to confiscate one of these.

Hmm. "Romanus, can I have your shirt?" He didn't even question me, just peeled off his shirt. I openly appreciated the ripple of his muscles as he pulled it over his head. I popped open the gas tank, took a bottle of vodka and poured it over the fabric in my hands. "Tear it please?" Romanus tore the vodka drenched shirt like it was tissue paper, a smug grin on his face.

I stuffed one end in the gas tank and used the vodka to make a trail to the closest body part. "Grab a bottle and start pouring it over the bodies. Especially over Naz's blood." I looked at Charlie, who was staring at me as if I'd grown horns. I touched the top of my head, just in case I had. I wasn't about to dismiss anything as crazy anymore.

"I know, Charlie. Let's just do this and go home, okay?" I held out the vodka to him. His jaw tensed, but he took a long hard pull at the bottle, but then started coating the decapitated heads. We made short work of the whole thing. Charlie pulled out an old-fashioned

Zippo lighters, the type that flipped open with a click. He'd gotten it for his sixteenth birthday from Uncle Joe. It had the Mulligan family crest on it. He carried it everywhere, even though he didn't smoke, like some kind of security blanket. Plus, he used it to pick up women, the suave bastard.

I lit the end of the alcohol that now puddled around Naz's chair, so I was sure it would burn.

Then we all ran for the door.

"Where is your car?" I panted, and Charlie pointed to the back side of the next warehouse.

"They ran us off the road, zipped tied us while we were out and then drove the car back here. Guess they wanted to be thorough. Hopefully, the keys are still in it."

It wouldn't matter either way. We could both hotwire a car. Misspent youth and all that, but it would be a bitch to get the spare key.

I jumped as the car exploded in the warehouse. Romanus put a steadying hand on my back, and I could feel his calm confidence flowing down our bond. Our fucking bond. I still hadn't wrapped my mind around the whole thing.

We found Charlie's car easy enough, and the keys were still in it, thank fuck. Rouen slid Naz, who was still unconscious in his arms, into the cargo area. I don't know how hard Romanus hit him, but it must have been a punishing blow if even the car exploding hadn't woken him. I knew it would be enough to kill a normal man.

I slid in the cargo area beside him, despite Romanus' disapproving glare. Rouen stretched across the back seat. No one argued about seating arrangements. I needed to be with Naz. He was gonna have a killer headache at the very least, and the last thing we needed was a special forces trained mercenary freaking out while we were driving. Romanus drove, and Charlie sat in the back beside Rouen, his head in his hands.

Romanus sped out of the docks, and I looked out the back windscreen fire licked out the windows of the wooden warehouse. Good. I hope the whole thing burnt to the ground before anyone noticed.

I laid down beside Naz and just watched his face, focusing on our connection. I knew why Hope flinched when she met him now. It wasn't because he was bad or evil, but because he emitted wave after wave of guilt, pain, and darkness. That would have been like a physical slap to sweet little sixteen year old Hope.

But I wasn't a sixteen year old empath. His darkness called to my own. I rolled onto my back as the car bounced over uneven road. That little part of my soul that revelled in bringing pain to those who had harmed my own, the part that wanted to drink and fuck and do every terrible, sinful thing I could think of, clung to my new links. The part of me that knew that Hell was the best I would ever obtain, so I was going to make my time here worth it. Besides, I was almost unofficially the Princess of Hell, so why not?

I sensed when Naz came awake, and now that I could brace myself for his pain, it wasn't so suffocating. I turned and met his eyes, trying not to focus on his left eye, with its shining silver iris. My body tensed, waiting for him to go full kamikaze on me.

Instead, he just stared at me. Maybe we'd broken him. "Do you feel okay? Physically?" I asked quietly.

He just nodded. I let out a little sigh of relief. At least it hadn't been all for nothing.

"For what it's worth, I'm sorry. But I couldn't let you die."

He nodded but still didn't speak. Despite what he said, I was worried we had done some serious damage. I felt fine, but I wasn't all that human to start with. Nazir had been one hundred percent Grade-A human. Who knew what effect it would have, making him part of a gargoyle pack.

Physically, he'd changed almost completely. I didn't mean his aesthetics. He still looked like Naz. Hard, tattooed body, sexy square jaw, the scar I could see that started on his hip where his shirt had ridden up a little. But he could survive a temple blow from Romanus, and that was no easy feat. He'd gotten their nearly impenetrable hide. If the heat warming my own shocked system was anything to go by, he'd gotten their inner warmth as well.

"Are you okay, you know, up here?" I tapped my temple.

"It hurts."

I let out the breath I hadn't even realized I was holding when he spoke. "That's probably because Romanus hit you in the side of the head like a steam train."

He shook his head again, and winced. "No. It's you. Your pain. It hurts."

Oh shit. I took several deep breaths and locked away

everything but my concern for the people in this car. I could deal with my own crazy emotions later. I sent my reassurance down our bond again. Hopefully it would help this time.

"I need to touch you. I'm compelled to do it. I can't help it," he forced the words out through gritted teeth, fighting the impulse. I held back the sob that clogged my throat. He was going to hate this, having his autonomy stripped from him.

"It'll get better, Naz. I know it, okay? I just couldn't let you die," I repeated. It was a plea for understanding.

"I know. Thank you. I'm alive because of you." His words were sincere, I knew that. What I couldn't understand was why the thought of being alive caused him so much pain. I let out a shuddering breath, and that was as much as Naz could take. He reached out and wrapped an arm around my waist, pulling me close so he could spoon his body around mine.

I held still, letting him take a few shuddery breaths as he sniffed my hair deeply. He was working on instinct. He was no longer in control.

"We will try and fix it. Romanus said we could. I didn't want you to die, but I don't want you to live trapped by this bond either. I'll find a way to take you out of the bond without hurting the other two."

Naz didn't say anything, just dipping his head so his nose was buried in my neck. There was nothing sexual in the act, even though we fit together like two pieces of a whole. He just needed an instinctual comfort, and I would give it to him if it eased some of the tangled, dark emotions that were sliding through the bond between us.

We stayed like that the rest of the way to the motel, everyone in the car trapped by the uneasy silence. When Romanus finally pulled up in front of the tiny little crap shack we'd been calling home for the last few days, I nearly cried with relief. I put on a brave face but realized that would never work again because most of the rooms occupants now had their own plug into my emotional hotline.

For the first time since Charlie rented the room, I didn't give a damn about bugs, or dirt or suspicious stains. We were battered and bruised, physically and emotionally. I just wanted to sleep for a month.

But we couldn't sleep. Not really. We just committed murder on US soil. What if the cops linked it back to us? I straightened my spine. I'd committed to this and now was not the time to get assassins remorse.

Naz walked through the room, heading straight into the bathroom. Moments later I heard the shower running. I flopped face down on to the big bed.

There was so much I still had to do. We needed to set alerts to ensure that the local cops had no idea it was us. We needed to research this Vladimir Rousevik guy. We needed to be in Geneva ASAP before the trail ran any colder.

But all I wanted to do was lie in bed in a massive puppy pile of bodies and reassure myself that we were all okay. Different, but okay.

And I needed Charlie.

"Charlie." He hadn't looked me in the eye since we set the warehouse on fire. But I needed my best friend right then.

My eyes found him standing at the foot of the bed, staring down at me with something that looked like anguish on his face. "Please."

I wasn't above begging sometimes. I need his familiarity, because my world had gone completely crazy.

His face folded. He kicked off his shoes and hopped into bed beside me, stiff. I wasn't going to let that happen. I refused to let things be weird. I burrowed against his body, tucking my head on his chest, and wrapped my arm around his middle. I breathed in deeply, allowing the fear for his safety, the horror show at the warehouse and all the other shit that played on my mind, just drift away. His body eventually relaxed minutely, and he stroked my hair.

"What have you done, Rella? This changes everything," he whispered so softly that I wasn't sure I was meant to hear. So, I didn't answer because I didn't know either. I'd saved a life and taken a dozen more. My soul wasn't as light as a feather any more, if it ever was.

I shook my head minutely. It changed nothing, not really. I still loved Charlie, and I wished he had a bond with me so he could feel that. Then he could feel my heartbreak that he was pulling away. I could feel the distance increasing between us, deep in a part of my heart that belonged only to Charlie.

I couldn't see or hear Romanus and Rouen, but I knew they were around. They would take the night watch. Naz stepped out of the bathroom in a cloud of steam, and he made his way to me. I rolled over to face him, my body still pressed against the length of Charlie's. Naz didn't speak, just climbed beneath the covers in nothing but tight boxer shorts. His hair smelled like cheap hotel soap. As he slipped in, I could see the brand new pink scar on his thigh. The gargoyle healing gift was truly amazing.

Naz turned his back to me, and I felt the sting of his rejection. I sucked in a breath and tried to calm my emotions by staring at his tattoos. It was the first time I'd ever seen them in the light. They were huge black wings, glinting like midnight darkness, deep blues and hints of silver making them look almost real. I recognized them, of course. They were Luc's wings.

I didn't understand what that meant. Why would he tattoo Lucifer's wings on his back?

It physically pained me not to reach out and touch him, but I held back, giving him his space. I moved closer to Charlie, seeking his comfort.

Naz shot out a leg and hooked it around mine. It was only a little contact, but I instantly felt better. I couldn't distinguish whose emotions were whose anymore.

Charlie wrapped an arm around my waist, his hand tucked beneath my side. "Sleep, Estrella," he whispered against my hair. Sandwiched between the two of them, I slept and dreamed of blood and scales.

CHAPTER NINE

When I woke up, I was alone in bed and light was just beginning to pierce the curtains. Charlie sat across the room, his laptop in front of him, a frown on his face. He chewed on his bottom lip as he concentrated, his fingers moving quickly across the keys.

No one else was here.

"Where is everyone?"

Charlie startled at the sound of my voice. "They went out. Secret pack business, I guess."

I didn't like the tone of his voice.

I stood up, and realized that at some point during the night, someone had peeled me out of my jeans. I strode over to Charlie and put my hands on my hips. I gave him my scariest look.

"Right, Charles Mulligan. We have talked about anything and everything since we were six, and we aren't going to start being passive aggressive now. Get it all out in the open, because I know you are pissed. I don't need a special magical bond to see that."

Charlie stood, a scowl on his face. For the first time in his life, Charlie looked almost scary. "What do you want to talk about, Rella? The fact that, despite literally telling me two days ago that you had feelings for me, you went and tied yourself to not one, but three other men? That you turned a member of my family into a weird hybrid creature? That you might have turned yourself into some kind of hybrid? The Gargoyles are fucking demons, Rella. Can they even die? What does that mean for you? For them? Hell, can Naz even die now? You just don't think. You barrel into everything with barely a thought for anyone, even yourself, because you have some weird belief that you are damned or bad. But you aren't."

He lurched toward me, and I almost flinched back, but it was Charlie. He held my face in his large, warm hands. "You aren't. You are beautiful and kind. You have the emotional range of a frat boy, but you go above and beyond for anyone who you think is the underdog. You've collected broken animals, broken things, broken people all your life, and you glue them all back together, and when they get emotionally attached to you, you freak out and send them to Hope. Or set them free. But you can't set your new toys free now, Rella. This is permanent. And it means that this dream I've had since I was a boy, where you love me so much it hurts, that you actually *lean* on me, is gone and now I don't know what the fuck to do."

He was panting like he'd run a one-minute mile, his

cheeks were red and his eyes were glassy. I'd fucked up so bad somewhere along the way, I'd hurt so many people, and I felt like this big sinkhole of guilt was about to swallow me up. If only I could pinpoint where I went wrong. Why couldn't I be Hope, just for a moment, so I could just *know* what would make him feel better, to just know the right words to say to soothe the pain that was ravaging his expression?

He was right. I did have the emotional range of a frat boy, but not with Charlie. Charlie I loved without reservation.

I stepped into his space and looked him in the eye. I gave him all the silent warnings I could about my next move, giving him the chance to run, to preserve whatever it was we had now. But he didn't. So when I went to kiss him, it was like two steam trains colliding on a rickety bridge. I wasn't sure either of us would survive.

Charlie's mouth slammed against mine as he kissed me angrily. His hand fisted in my hair and he held it tight, not letting me move an inch. That was okay. I didn't want to move. Our teeth clacked as he forced his tongue between them, his lips branding mine. I made an angry noise and bit his lower lip, then sucked it between my own. My hands clung to his shoulders, my nails digging into the muscles beneath his t-shirt. I didn't want to let him go.

He pulled my head back by my hair and turned it to the side so he could kiss and nip down my neck. I sucked in a breath.

"Charlie." My whisper was rough, choked out around the weird tumult of emotions that clogged my throat. He stiffened at the sound of his name and pulled away.

"No," he ground out, stepping back. "No. Not like this."

He turned around and strode out the door.

And then I was truly alone. A sob escaped my lips, and I startled at the sound. How weird is that? Then I sobbed again, and again, and soon tears were trailing down my face, hot streaks that cooled on my skin. I never cried like this. Not even when I broke my arm. Or when I thought Hope was dead.

Rella? Hope's mental voice was like a balm, as always. Never alone. I had her. No one would take her from me again. The anger and darkness swelled back up, replacing the pain.

I've fucked up, Sis. I fucked up big time. And I don't even have the decency to feel bad about it. If I had my chance again, I don't think I'd change anything, except the fact that I've hurt so many people.

A massive push of love and reassurance came down my bond. Bonds. I could feel Romanus and Rouen giving me the same warm feelings as Hope.

It just made me cry harder.

Come see me, Rella. You're still in New York? It wasn't a real question. She knew exactly where I was.

Yeah. I'll fly to Europe tomorrow if I can get the jet. I cleared my throat and wiped my eyes on my forearm. I straightened my shoulders. I needed to get my shit together. We needed to sort this out, but first, I needed my sister. *I'll be there in an hour?*

They released me yesterday, so I'm home. Bring bagels. I let out a little laugh. Hope had an addiction to starchy carbs, yet somehow it never went to her ass. Or mine. Maybe we had supernatural metabolisms?

As if I'd summoned them by my will, Romanus and Rouen were standing outside the motel doors when I walked out. They fell into step beside me. I didn't protest, being with them made me feel better.

"Charlie?" I asked Rouen, who seemed fonder of my Charlie than Romanus.

But it was Romanus who answered. "Naz has him."

I didn't even want to know what that meant, but Naz liked Charlie too. They were both satellites spinning around the shit show of my life.

We walked a couple of blocks over and hailed a cab. I could afford the fare and I didn't feel like sitting in the stinking underground for an hour. The cabbie pulled over, smiling at me. Quite frankly, a smiling New York City cab driver was harder to believe than two gargoyles. His smile crumbled when Rouen and Romanus slid in either side of me. It was understandable. They looked like scary walls of muscle. He didn't know that Rouen had a wicked sense of humor that was so far beyond dirty it may as well be pornographic. He didn't know that Romanus had a quiet intensity that hid an ancient soul, or that he loved Rouen ferociously.

Despite the turmoil, the heartache and the uncertainty, I knew I hadn't been lying to Hope. I wouldn't change anything. I might not have wanted to be Romanus and Rouen's Queen, but it felt right. I reached for each of their hands and threaded my smaller fingers through theirs and pulled them both onto my lap.

The smile Rouen gave me threatened to explode my heart. Romanus' face didn't change, and he didn't turn to look at me, but I could feel the happy hum along his bond. No one said anything, but the silence wasn't uncomfortable. Well, except for the glares that cabbie kept giving us in the rear-view mirror. He looked at me like I was the Devil incarnate. Little did he know. I gave him an exaggerated wink and tried not to laugh at his indignant grunt.

We pulled up at Hope's apartment, and I threw some cash at the cabbie. He didn't even wait until Rou was out of the cab completely before he peeled away from the curb. Rude.

"You guys don't have to come up, you know. I'm safe in there with Hope and Adnan."

Romanus frowned. "I don't trust her new bodyguard."

I laughed. "Good instincts, but I can handle Blue." I knew his mother. Tootsie Halloran may be second or third cousin to the Mulligans, but the blood still ran strong. She took no shit, not even from her son and she was one of the few Mulligan aunts who liked me just as much as she liked Hope. "I mean it guys, I'll be fine."

Romanus gave me a hard stare, and then nodded once.

"We will walk you to her door." It wasn't a suggestion. I just rolled my eyes and strode into the building. I waved to Henry the Doorman. Henry gave the guys a cursory glance, but if there was anyone who was the very epitome of a New Yorker, it was Henry. He was used to the strange people who came and went from

Hope and Adnan's apartment. Actually, next to some of Adnan's artsy friends, the Gargoyles were downright average joe.

We rode the lift up to Hope's apartment. The air of awkwardness between us was almost as bad as the elevators music.

"We'll have to talk tonight. All of us," I told them as the doors closed, and Romanus nodded. Rouen moved with supernatural speed until he was in front of me.

He lifted me up and pressed me against the elevator wall. He kissed me fervently, his hands under my ass and his whole body pressed tightly against mine. I kissed him back, of course. The man had hundreds of years of experience. He kissed like a freaking god. Who was I to resist? I swirled my tongue against his and he moaned, pulling away.

"Rouen," Romanus growled. "We talked about this."

Rouen grinned, completely unrepentant. "I don't have your self control. Besides, I just needed one for the road."

He eased me down, but I was still pressed hard against his body. Best slide of my life. "Am I missing something?"

Romanus shook his head. "We'll talk about it later."

I frowned at him. "Maybe I want to talk about it-" The elevator chimed and the doors slid open on my floor. I scowled and Romanus just smiled, the bossy jerk. The corners of my lips tugged up but I refused to give him the satisfaction.

"Call us through the bond when you are ready to leave."

I raised my eyebrows. "How?"

"You just reach out, grab it tightly and give it a firm tug. We'll come," Rouen said, grinning. I ignored the innuendo and flipped him the bird. This time I couldn't resist the smile as the doors closed.

I walked to Hope's door, but I didn't need to knock. Adnan was there, pulling open the door, grinning. "I was watching you through the peephole like a dirty voyeur," he announced, pulling me into a tight hug.

"Hey Ads," I said and hugged him back. Like Hope, he was pretty universally loved. Even the conservative Mulligans loved Adnan, despite his sexual orientation. They didn't have much choice. Clary, his adopted Mom and my Mom's bestie, would kick their Irish asses if they disrespected her baby. And she did treat him like her flesh and blood and spoiled him terribly when he was a kid. But Ads turned out alright.

"Hope's in the living room binge watching old 80's rom coms. Says it's medicinal. I say it's just sad."

I walked down the short entry hall and into the wide living room. It somehow looked expensive, yet cozy. Hope had gotten all the artistic genes from my family. The fact that Adnan had an addiction to interior decorating magazines also helped.

Hope was curled up on an overstuffed dove grey sofa, a white fluffy afghan draped around her waist and a bag of M&M's in her hand. The fact she was eating candy at ten in the morning never mattered to my twin.

"No bagels?" She looked crestfallen, and I mentally slapped my forehead. I'd forgotten completely.

"Sorry, Sis."

She gave me that brilliant smile, the one that made it feel like the sun had come out just for you, and waved me over. "Don't worry. Come here."

She lifted the soft blanket and I sat down beside her, toeing off my boots so I could curl my legs under me. She passed me the bag of M&M's.

"I left you the red ones," she said as she paused Sixteen Candles.

I could feel the tears well, but I couldn't stop it. I wondered if Charlie was right, would I be immortal now? Would I have to bury my twin? I couldn't live in a world where she wasn't with me. She wrapped me in her arms and stared at me with a face so like my own, but still so different. "Aw, Honey. What's wrong?"

"I became the Queen of the Gargoyles and now I am not sure I can even die." It came out like one long wail, and she pulled away.

"What? You aren't making any sense."

"I tied myself to Romanus and Rouen so I could save Nazir's life, because he was tortured by an Estonian people smuggler."

I didn't see Adnan coming in from the kitchen, or I would have said it to Hope through our mental link. Adnan dropped the teacup he was holding, his face going pale. "What?"

CHAPTER TEN

I stood and went over to him, holding out my hands placatingly.

"He's fine."

Kinda, I clarified mentally to Hope. *I think I might have made him some kind of gargoyle hybrid.*

Adnan gripped my shoulders. "Where is he?"

I shrugged out of his grasp. "He's with Charlie. He's perfectly fine, as healthy as he's ever been, I promise you that."

Pretty sure he could be hit by a car now and not get a scratch, I said to Hope. *How am I going to tell Adnan that I changed his brother irrevocably? Oh, and that I made him part of my gargoyle harem? Did I mention Charlie has had a crush on me since, well, forever and now he hates my guts?*

I bent down and started picking up shards of teacup.

Everyone knew Charlie had a crush on you, except you. I'm sure he doesn't hate you. He probably just needs time to adjust to your, uh, situation. He'll come around, Hope said soothingly.

I sniffed. "He said I'd crushed his dream," I said out

loud, my tone furious. "He said he won't share me, and basically insinuated that I didn't give a shit about him for even asking."

"What?" Adnan's impeccable eyebrows pulled together then his jaw tensed angrily. "You guys are having one of those telepathic conversations again, aren't you? It's just rude," he huffed and then stormed out of the room.

I clenched my fist and realized belatedly that I was still holding the shards of the china teacup in my hand. I felt the slice along my palm, sucked in a breath at the sting.

I felt the alarm along my bond, and then they were moving towards me.

"Huh, so that's what that was. I felt presences on the periphery of our bond but couldn't work out what it was. You've bonded them. Naz too?"

I threw the bloody teacup in the trash can and sighed. "Yep. Just wait. They're all coming because I cut myself."

Hope frowned, and I wrapped my hand in a towel so I didn't bleed all over her pretty afghan blanket when I climbed back in beside her.

"Be gentle. It's a biological imperative."

She gave me a questioning glance, but I shook my head. She'd find out soon enough.

Within minutes, two large bodies were dwarfing Hope's living room. They didn't even bother to knock.

Rouen was on his knees in front of me in seconds, unwrapping the towel from my hand. "Sorry, but I can't…" he trailed off, and I stroked my good hand over his hair.

"I know. Do what you need to do. This isn't even close to the weirdest thing that's happened this week."

Rouen's tongue lapped at the cut on my hand, the slight sting telling me it was healing. The warm glide was oddly erotic, and I snuck a look at Hope from the corner of my eye. Her nose was scrunched up in disgust, but I knew it was because she was squeamish about blood. She wouldn't judge my guys.

Romanus looked on, his expression intense. I resisted the urge to beckon him to me. I wanted to touch him, but it could wait. It was enough to have him here, protecting me from invisible foes.

Speaking of which…

"Why don't you have any bodyguards, Hope? Where's Blue?"

Hope's face went blank and she jammed our bond. Interesting.

"He's gone back to Boston for a while."

I narrowed my eyes at my twin. She wasn't a good liar. I didn't need the bond to tell me she was fibbing.

"Oh?" I said, raising an eyebrow. Luckily, she was saved by the arrival of Charlie and Naz.

Charlie barrelled into the room and into the arms of my twin.

"Damn it's good to see you," he said, holding her tight against his chest. He should have fallen for Hope. She was perfect for him. Sweet, loving. She never got into fights and his family adored her. She wouldn't have dragged him into some harebrained plan that almost got him tortured.

"You too, Charlie. You feel like shit though." She sounded disapproving. Hope's disapproval made you feel two inches tall.

He just lowered his head and mumbled something to her under his breath. Apparently, he remembered my super-hearing this time. Whatever he said made her laugh, and he grinned back at her. Jealousy stabbed me in the heart and I turned away. Unfortunately, that meant I was looking straight at Naz.

"I let it slip to Adnan about your leg. You might want to talk to him? Or I can, if that's easier?" I hedged, hoping to God he'd say no.

Naz just nodded and walked down the hall toward the bedrooms like he'd been here a hundred times. Maybe he had. Still so much of his life was a mystery to me.

Rouen still sat at my feet, one of his huge hands wrapped around my calf. He'd let go of my hand and all that remained of my cut was a slight pink line.

Hope grabbed my hand and stared. "Holy hell, Rella. That's amazing."

A wide smile stretched my face. It really was. "The power of gargoyle cooties."

Charlie sat on the coffee table, silent. I guess if we were all here.

"Does the name Vladimir Rousevik mean anything to you?" I asked Hope, because it rang a bunch of bells for me, but I couldn't quite put my finger on why.

"You mean the founder of the Shine Foundation?"

All the pieces snapped together in my brain and I reared back in shock. No fucking way. That's why it sounded familiar.

Son of a bitch.

He ran an aid foundation that helped relocate refugees from war-torn or environmentally impoverished countries. Apparently, he helped relocate them right into slavery.

"Have you ever met this Rousevik?" I asked, but Hope just shook her head, frown lines creasing the otherwise smooth beauty of her face.

"No, he's a bit of a recluse from what I've heard. Came from Bosnia or somewhere and got horribly disfigured so he never leaves his mansion. That's just a rumor though. I've met his public relations rep a few times. She's a nice woman, late forties, kinda matronly looking. Why the interest in Shine?"

I sighed. I hated smearing her bright, shiny world with the filth of society's dregs. "Not sure if it's connected to Shine, really. It might just be a good way to launder his money for all I know. But Rousevik has been linked as the head of the people smuggling ring that snatched you."

She looked like I'd slapped her. I felt her confusion, her disbelief, and the fear crawl up her bond like an insidious leech.

"Hey. They won't get you again. I swear it on my life. Don't you worry about Rousevik or Shine or any of that other shit. I've got you." I wrapped my arms around her and hugged her close, sending her all my reassurance. I felt another set of arms wrap around me, squishing me between a hard chest and my sister. Hands patted Hope's back.

I looked over my shoulder at Rouen, who had his face buried in my hair. He shrugged. "Her distress is your distress."

I could feel Hope's body tremble as she held back a laugh, but it bubbled through the bond anyway.

"You are in so much trouble, Rella," she said, pulling back and giving Rouen her radiant smile. I expected to feel that rush of adoration through my bond with Rouen, the rush that everyone got when Hope smiled at them, or laughed at their jokes, or just listened to them speak in that way she had, where it felt like what you were saying really mattered to her. But all I got was a general feeling of polite respect, and he nuzzled my hair a little more.

Charlie was looking between us all strangely, but when I tried to catch his eye he looked away. I choked back the sigh that wanted to escape, squeezed Rouen's hand and stood. We needed to go.

I kissed the top of Hope's head. "We head out to Geneva as soon as possible, but when this is over, we are going to the diner near Time Square, you know the one? And we are gonna ice skate and get our nails done and go shopping, just like old times. I need girl time. The testosterone overload of the last few weeks is killing me, and I grew up in a household with seven dads!" I gave the guys a smile so the knew I wasn't being serious. I gave Charlie a fake stink eye and hoped that he knew I was joking too.

Naz still hadn't reemerged from Adnan's room, so I

wandered down the hall to let him know we were going. He could stay. I wasn't his keeper.

I could hear the raised voices from a couple of doors away and contemplated turning around. I'd leave a note with Hope.

"How can you defend it? Defend her? She fucking made you into a demon, Naz. I don't know if I believe in heaven, but I'm pretty sure you can't get there as a fucking abomination." Adnan's voice had reached a higher octave, which meant they'd probably been arguing for awhile.

"Would you rather I be dead?" Naz growled out, and I paused, unable to step closer, but unable to move away either. "She saved me."

"She made you her slave for all eternity!"

"There's worse things to be than the slave to a beautiful woman, Ads. You don't know the things I've done, the places I've been. You should be kneeling down and kissing her goddamn feet, because she's saved me in more ways than one. In ways you will never understand."

I heard Adnan's bed springs squeak, and I guessed he was sitting down. "I have a purpose. For the first time in my life, I have a reason to wake up in the morning other than to kill some bad dude that some richer, not-so-bad dude pays me to kill. It might not have been a purpose that I willingly chose, but I'm going to work with it, to come to terms with this situation, and I suggest you do too."

The door to Adnan's room opened and he strode

out, only to stop at the sight of me standing like an idiot in the hall.

Adnan stormed out after him. "Is that even you talking or has she…" Adnan stopped when he saw me too, shock and guilt making his eyes go round.

"Rella-" Naz started, but I waved him away.

"It's okay, Adnan is right. I've had those exact same thoughts myself in the last twenty-four hours." I looked at Adnan. "I'm sorry. I wouldn't have chosen it if there was any other way."

Adnan screwed his face up like a petulant child. "He should never have been there."

I raised my eyebrows. "I didn't ask him to be. If I remember correctly, that was you."

With that, I turned and walked back down the hall, blowing Hope a kiss and heading to the door.

Romanus and Rouen fell into step beside me, but when I reached the elevator I was surprised to see Naz right behind them. I was even more surprised to see Charlie as well.

He just shrugged and gave me a watered-down version of his famous Charlie grin. "I brought my car. No point catching the subway."

The doors slid open, and we all piled in. There wasn't a whole lot of room in the tiny little lift, and the four guys took up more than their fair share of space. Romanus and Rouen crowded me just out of principle. The tension was almost suffocating. I leaned around Naz and hit the stop button. The elevator lurched to a shuddering halt.

We needed to get this all out in the open. Why not here, in an elevator where no one could escape?

Just last week, I would be doubting my sanity for voluntarily being stuck in an elevator with two demons, a mobster and a mercenary. Oh my.

"Let's just talk about the elephant in the room."

"You mean the Gargoyle in the Elevator, right?" Rouen corrected.

I rolled my eyes at him. "I know that none of us exactly planned on this happening, me becoming a Gargoyle Queen and turning Naz into whatever he is now. I didn't mean to somehow acquire a pack and hurt my best friend in the process." I stared at Charlie, who just stared back, his face impassive. "But it happened. It can't be undone, and I wouldn't want to undo it. But I am not forcing anyone to stay either. If you want to leave and go back to wherever it is you came from," I looked between the Gargoyles and Naz, "then you have my blessings and no hard feelings. You've all paid enough for my vendetta."

Rouen scoffed. "Like you could get rid of us that easy, Tiger. Sorry, but you are stuck with us." His laughing face lost all its mirth. "If you want to be. We can't ditch you, but it is possible for you to ditch us." He didn't say anything more, but I got the feeling that if I left it would be catastrophic for them, maybe even deadly.

"I'm happy right here," I said, smiling. I was. I didn't feel trapped, which was how I usually felt if I committed to anything more permanent than a cellphone plan. It felt right. Charlie was the only sour note to my potential happiness.

Naz shrugged. "I meant what I said."

"Charlie?" There was a fragile part of my heart riding on his answer.

He sucked in a deep breath, and his shoulders sagged. "I don't know. But I'm not about to abandon you now. I've got your back until the end. As for the rest… let's just take it one day at a time."

Relief swelled in me, probably prematurely, but I couldn't help it. It wasn't a no. "That's all I ask. Charlie isn't pack. Does anyone have a problem with that?"

All of the other guys shook their heads.

"Good, because Charlie is mine, regardless of whether he is officially pack or not."

Romanus shrugged. "I like the human. If he pulled his head out of his ass and just fucked you already, you'd be happy, we'd be happy and we wouldn't have to have these touchy-feely conversations."

My cheeks turned as bright red as Charlie's. I leaned around and restarted the elevator. Rouen leaned into me. "I happen to like all the touchy, and definitely all the feely."

The flush spread right down my body, and someone cleared their throat. I gave Rouen a stern look. "Not the time."

He just winked. If I didn't have an invested interest in his lower appendages, I would have junk-punched him.

CHAPTER ELEVEN

The plane hit turbulence for the tenth time, and I contemplated throwing up. I wasn't a good flyer, which was funny considering I sometimes sifted from place to place with Fallen angels, which had a far higher fatality rate than a normal plane.

Charlie grumbled under his breath in the plush leather seats, and I leaned forward to stare at his screen. I shouldn't have bothered. None of the lines of numbers and letters on his screen made any sense to me anyway.

"What's wrong?" I said, unclipping myself and walking unsteadily to the table where he had set up his mile-high tech hub.

"I can't find anything on this Rousevik guy beyond PR spin released by his own company. Not a picture holding a baby, or a social security number or even a record of his birth. It's like he appeared out of thin air."

I chewed my lip. "Could it be an alias to protect his real identity?"

Charlie shrugged and scowled at his screen, as if it

was being recalcitrant and not giving up the information we needed. "Maybe. But normally there's a paper trail of some kind, or more likely a money trail that would lead back to the guy. But nothing. It's just like an eternal babushka doll of shell companies that lead nowhere. Shine Foundation is very upfront with their financials, but it's only on the surface." He sighed and gripped the edges of the table. "Either he doesn't exist, or he's got a really good hacker who went in and deleted him from everything. No social media, no drivers license, no reference to him whatsoever outside of Shine."

I could hear his frustration. Charlie prided himself on his abilities, and even Dad was proud of him. This would be a serious blow to his ego. I squeezed his shoulder. "Cast the net wider and see what fish we catch. You can do this."

I walked up the aisle to the bedroom. The NRH, my parent's charitable foundation, had a seriously fancy private plane. It had a full bedroom, bathroom and bar. Pretty much all you'd need on a flight to Europe and all privately paid for by Tolliver. We'd used it to ferry more than one group of people from nature ravaged areas.

I was exhausted, and the idea of lying in a bed that wasn't infested with fleas sounded like bliss. I could sleep for a week, but I'd settle for sleeping through this flight.

I kicked off my shoes and peeled off my jeans and weapons holsters. I slid beneath the plush down quilt and sighed.

The door opened, and Naz walked in. He jumped a little when he saw me on the bed.

"I'm sorry. I thought you were in the bathroom. I

was just going to catch an hour nap, but I'll do it back in the seats." He was already turning before he finished.

"It's all good, Naz. There's plenty of room for two."

He gave me a hot look that had me swallowing my words.

"I think it's best to go back out to the cabin."

He was probably right, and I should just wave him goodbye. Instead I said, "Is that what you want to do?" And it came out all raspy. I was turned on just by him standing in the goddamn doorway.

"No."

My stomach fluttered. "What do you want?"

"I want to go over there, flip you over, push those fucking sexy red lace panties to the side and fuck you slow and hard until you are nothing more than a trembling mess beneath me."

I swallowed hard as heat rushed to my pussy. "How do you know the color of my underwear?" I asked as I watched him stalk toward the bed. There was no other name for the way he moved; slow, deliberate, graceful.

"They teased me by riding up above your jeans when you were stowing your weapons in the overhead lockers. As well as a section of that creamy skin that I just want to mark up."

He was beside the bed now, his eyes roaming over my body with naked hunger, but he made no move to join me. I pushed down the quilt so it bunched at my hips, exposing just a hint of red lace. His eyes ran over my breasts, my nipples hard and begging for his lips. My tank had ridden up, gathering at the bottom of my ribs, exposing the flat expanse of my stomach. He growled as his eyes moved lower and ran into the barricade of the quilt.

His swirling mercury eye caught mine, and guilt hit me. Did he really find me desirable, or was it the bond at work? Would the other guys feel my pleasure under Naz's gaze, and would they care?

"Is it the bond making you feel this?" I asked. I had to know. It felt wrong otherwise.

"Yes and no. I thought you were the fucking sexiest thing alive before you made me into this," he pointed to his eye. "But I would never have acted on it without the bond. People like me, we don't form attachments. And you weren't some chick that I could love and leave. But now, for better or worse, we are tied together. So being able to do this," he reached out and ran a finger down my stomach, over my pubic bone and beneath my panties, stroking his finger in wet folds of my pussy, "is the fucking best silver lining ever."

He pushed his finger inside me, kneeling next to me on the bed, and I let out a long moan. He slipped between my knees and kissed me, his thumb finding my clit and rubbing it with the perfect amount of pressure to make me writhe against his hand. He leaned in and kissed me, his soft lips pressing hard into mine. The bond between us lit up and I gasped. I felt his pleasure at tasting me, at how I felt riding his hand, how desperate he was to replace his fingers with his dick. I felt all those sensations through the bond on top of my own and it was almost an overload. Double the pleasure, but it was hard to filter his from mine.

He tore his mouth away and kissed his way down my

chest to my lace covered breast. Freeing one, he sucked my nipple into his mouth so hard I felt the sensation pull deep inside me. I moaned again, grinding against his hand. I didn't know if it was his urge or mine, but I wanted him inside me. Now.

I grabbed at his shoulders. "Please, Naz." I reached for his jeans, tugging at his belt, but he grabbed my hands, and held them above my head, manacling them with one of his own.

"Uh uh, I wanted to do this slow. I wanted to drive you to the brink so many times that you beg me to let you come, so slow that I get to taste every inch of you before I fuck you." He let out a frustrated groan. "But I don't think we have time and I don't have the willpower. You're just so sexy and it's been too long." He liberated my hands so he could kick out of his jeans and I tore at his shirt. I wanted to trace those tattoos with my fingers, then with my tongue.

I let out a disappointed moan when he flipped me onto my stomach, but it was short lived as his whole body pressed along mine, the hard bulge of his cock against my ass making me moan. He grabbed my hands again, raising them back over my head. I could feel the head of his cock pressed against my entrance, the lace of my underwear the only barrier between us.

"Don't move these," he whispered against my ear, and I sucked in a breath, complying as his hand ran down my body, and wrapping around one of my thighs. He spread my legs wider, settling his big body between them. His fingers slid up my thigh and hooked around the soaking wet fabric of my panties. I shuddered out a moan at the feel of his calloused finger against the aching flesh. He dipped a finger into my juices and my pussy clenched.

He groaned. "I want to tease you so bad, but I'd just be making myself crazy. I need to be inside you." With that, he replaced his finger with the head of his cock, his body pressed right along mine. As he slid his way slowly inside me, his hand slipped under my hips, lifting them higher to go deeper. His pace was so slow, driving himself into me with complete control and hitting every sensitive spot on the way, until I thought I was going to go insane if he didn't move faster. I pushed back, urging him to move, but his heavy body pinned mine to the mattress.

"Naz, faster. More," I whispered on a moan, and he laughed. He drew back and slammed himself home, fast and hard, and a shout escaped me. I need more of that, more hard, fast fucking. I clenched my pussy tight around him, flexing my inner muscles and he sucked in a breath.

"Naughty. Alright, Princess, you get your wish." He pulled back and pounded back into me. He had both hands on my hips, thrusting deep into me, the dull slapping of our bodies almost drowning out the sound of my moans that I was trying to muffle with my palm.

My orgasm burst out of me on a scream, but Naz wasn't done, a small hitch to his breath the only way I knew he was even affected by my screams. He pulled out, flipping me over onto my back and hooking my legs over his shoulders, sliding back inside me with a grunt of satisfaction. He bent forward and kissed me, the angle hitting my g-spot and sending me back under a tidal wave of pleasure.

I slipped my legs from his shoulders and gripped his short dark hair. Pulling his head to the side, I bit the muscle in his neck softly, just like I'd done with Romanus days ago. Naz roared as he came, burying himself inside me.

He collapsed down on top of me, and I wrapped my arms around his torso. He was huge and heavy, but I loved the feel of the weight of him right along my body. He was resting some of it on his forearms, but I could feel the slight shake in his muscles. I stroked my nails up and down his back, and he let out a contented sigh.

He rolled away, curling me against his side and wrapping his body around mine.

"Wow," I breathed, and he huffed out a laugh.

"Yeah." He smoothed my hair from my neck and kissed the spot between my shoulder blades.

His tattooed arm looked like burnished gold against the paleness of my skin, and I took a moment to appreciate the art that adorned his forearms. There were words in his native language that I couldn't read, but there were also pictures of anguish and death. A crying woman, her hands pressed to her face as she wailed, beside the grim reaper walking through streets that were nothing but rubble. It was all black and white, and told a terrible story. I pressed my finger over the tears on the woman's face.

"This is so sad."

He made a small hum of agreement, and I looked over my shoulder, and met his hooded gaze. The deep brown of his right eye was the color of bitter chocolate, and in this light, his silver eye glinted like liquid metal. I couldn't look away, so I turned in his arms and reached up to cup his cheek, the stubble scraping my palm.

"Do you feel different?" I didn't really, despite the extra bonds. I didn't feel any stronger, or more immortal. I was used to having a bond in my head.

"Well, the sex was pretty mind blowing," he said, his face serious but his eyes giving him away. Their sparkle said he was teasing me.

I leaned forward and bit his nipple lightly. He groaned and wrapped his hands in my hair.

"You know that's not what I meant," I said sternly.

He turned my face up, and moved down, kissing the corner of my mouth gently. "I feel like a whole other being, Rella. Physically and mentally. I feel like I'm invincible, but at the same time my whole happiness rests in these tiny hands." He entwined his fingers in mine and lifted my hand to his mouth. "So, to answer your question, Estrella; yes, I feel different because you remade me."

There wasn't any anger or regret in his tone, and I mined our bond for any darker emotions. Oh, I found darkness alright, but it was old, as cemented to his soul as tar to a road.

"What was your life like before I came in and took a wrecking ball to it? Where were you when Hope and Adnan called you home?"

"It's classified," he said, kissing my lips softly.

"Were you the good guy, or the bad guy?" I whispered. He looked down at me, his face serious.

"Even when I was doing good things, I was the bad guy, Rella. Men like me are necessary, but not because we did good. We did what needed to be done. We were like a forest fire. Sometimes old establishments need to burn down before something new and better can grow in its place. That's what we did." He pulled away, but I wrapped my arms around his torso and held him close.

"No one knows that better than me, Naz. It doesn't change my opinion. I know your heart now, through this bond. You don't have to hide from me, ever."

He pulled me hard against his chest and tucked my head under his chin, holding me so tight that it was almost hard to breathe. I stayed quiet and let him anchor himself to me, until I slipped into sleep.

CHAPTER TWELVE

nother bout of rough turbulence bounced me awake. Naz was gone, but I wasn't surprised. He didn't seem like the kind of guy who woke up next to a woman very often. I didn't take it to heart.

I stood, contemplating a shower when we hit more turbulence. I wasn't sure if being clean was worth dying naked in a fiery plane crash. On the flip side, I smelled like sex, and god only knew when I'd get another chance to shower. Decision made.

I stripped off quickly and jumped in. If you've never showered at thirty thousand feet in turbulence, you've probably never lived. Let's just say, it's hard to hang on to those tiny soaps when the plane is rocking like a RV at a music festival.

I dressed back in my clothes sans underwear, which I stuffed into the back pocket of my jeans. I'd put them in my pack later, when four sets of eyes weren't watching my every move. As it was, I doubted my shower would fool the gargoyle sense of smell.

My cheeks flushed red at the thought of them scenting me. This was going to be awkward.

I opened the door and walked out as if nothing was amiss. As if I hadn't just joined the mile-high club with the sexiest goddamn merc on the planet.

Naz was talking to Charlie, who seemed oblivious to what went on behind closed doors. I don't know how Naz managed that, but I was glad I didn't have to have another Charlie guilt trip to ruin my post-coitus glow. Charlie was talking animatedly, pointing at his screen, and I was beginning to see how he could miss the whole thing. When Charlie got on the trail of something big, nothing and no one else mattered.

Once, about three years ago, he'd figured out a way to bypass the security of a rival gang, and slowly syphoned small amounts of money from every member over the course of a month, through hundreds of accounts until it ended up in the Cayman Islands. He had barely eaten or slept during that month, but he had the stupidest grin on his face the whole time. I'd taken him Chinese food, made sure he slept every second day and then stayed the hell out of it. I'd walked a fine line as a cop.

Naz turned around and winked at me over Charlie's shoulder. But Charlie was still talking so fast I could barely keep up.

"That's why I know that Vladimir Rousevik doesn't exist. He's a straw man, a front!"

I stilled. "What are you saying?"

Charlie turned, excitement at solving a puzzle lighting up his handsome face, and I sucked in a breath.

How had I missed how alive he was? How that smile made him look so deliciously handsome?

Seemingly oblivious to my stunned look, he turned his computer toward me, showing me raw data on a screen.

"I couldn't find any information on him because he didn't exist. I hacked the Shine Foundations financial records and traced the initial transaction from Rousevik to an account in Switzerland, before the entries for Rousevik were ever added to any other databases. They tried to backdate them, but there's still a trail. Anyway, that first transaction was made by a shell corporation that was created and then dissolved in the space of a year, as was the previous to shell companies that housed it…"

Charlie went on, but my forte wasn't financial forensics.

"Bottom line me, Charlie. You lost me."

He smiled. "The initial funds were used to create Rousevik. He doesn't exist."

I sat down opposite him. "Then who runs the whole thing? Both the legitimate Shine operations and the people trafficking?"

Charlie's smile fell, and I felt like I'd kicked a puppy. "I don't know."

I put my had over his. "You unraveled their secret in a day. You'll find out the rest before they know what hit them."

I leaned over and kissed his cheek.

"Where's Romanus and Rouen?"

Charlie shrugged, as did Naz. "They weren't here

when I got back from my shower." Naz's eyes crinkled at the corners, and he gave me a hot look. I cleared my throat, turning away before Charlie saw my heated cheeks.

"I better go and find them in case they've eaten the pilot." I moved back down the plane towards the rear. There was a separate kitchen and washroom back there. Seriously, this plane was better decked out than my apartment.

They weren't in the kitchen. I pushed against the door to the bathroom. It wasn't locked, and I was about to turn away when I heard a noise. Pushing open the door more, what I saw made me suck in a surprised breath.

My first thought was how did two guys as big as my Gargoyles fit together inside such a tiny bathroom stall. The second thought was apparently it wasn't just Naz and I who'd decided to join the Mile-High Club.

Romanus had Rouen bent over the sink, which looked miniscule beneath his huge hands. Both of their jeans were around their ankles, and Romanus' body was pressed tightly against Rouen's back, his cock buried deep in Rouen, his hand around his dick and his teeth buried into the meaty bit of his shoulder.

Holy fuckballs.

I must have squeaked out a noise because Romanus' eyes snapped to mine, though he didn't slow his punishing pace. He removed his teeth from Rouen, and wrapped a fist in his hair, pulling back his head and turning it toward me. The action was so brutal, but given the guttural moan Rou released, I didn't think he minded.

"Our Queen is watching, my Beta. I think she likes it when I fuck you like this," he gripped Rouen's hip and slowly slid out of him, until just the head of his cock was still hidden, and then slammed home, the sound of their bodies crashing together a dull thud that mixed with Rouen's grunts. "I think she likes to know that I'm the Alpha, and that my body can make a strong man like you beg. What do you think, Rou?" Another deep thrust. "Should we make sure our Queen knows that we were made for her pleasure? Should we put on a show?"

"Yessss," Rouen hissed out, his eyelids hooded and his muscles shining with sweat. "Fuck me, Romanus."

Heat rushed to my pussy, and I was moments from coming just standing there in the doorway. Romanus looked satisfied. "Watch our Queen, Rou. Don't take your eyes off her," Romanus ordered and released the hand he had twisted in his hair. That hand wandered down Rouen's body, over the twitching muscles of his back, the sweat making them glisten even more golden. Rouen caught my eye, and I was momentarily transfixed by the swirling gold and brown of his irises. That was until Romanus kicked his feet apart and bent him over further, their bodies now distinct and I could see every inch of Romanus' cock as it worked Rouen's body. He picked up his pace, moving with demonic speed.

"Touch yourself, Beta. But do not come until I say you can, you hear me? And do not take you eyes off our Queen for a second."

Rouen fisted his hand around his cock and pumped

ferociously, his moans and grunts getting louder, Romanus finally losing a little control and growling with every thrust.

I was starting to pant, and Rouen did something that shocked the hell out of me, though it shouldn't have. He stopped fisting his cock, instead reaching out a hand and pulling me closer, jamming me into the tiny bathroom with them. He leaned in and kissed me, his hand snaking between our bodies and into my jeans. He moaned when he met no extra layers.

"Rom, she's not wearing underwear."

Romanus' gaze lit me on fire, promising me pleasure even though he wasn't touching me.

Rouen's fingers slid between my folds, and although I was still a little sensitive from my moment with Naz, I pushed against his hand. I wanted to be a part of this.

Shifting his body, Romanus changed his pace, and Rouen let out a whimper. "Make her cum all over you hand, then you can cum too."

His eyes still on mine, not defying his Alpha's orders, Rouen slid his fingers inside me, moving them in and out of me in time with Rom's thrusts. I knew Rouen wouldn't have to wait long, I was primed and halfway there already. When his fingers brushed against my clit, I let out a scream, kissing him punishingly hard to muffle the sound. Without conscience thought, I tore my mouth away and moved down, burying my teeth in the hard muscle of his pec.

He let out raw, pained noise as hot streams of cum spurted all over the basin in front of him.

A few more ragged thrusts, and Romanus bit down

into Rouen's shoulder as he came hard, balls deep inside his lover. He pulled out, licking the small points of blood from the bite mark.

Rouen lifted his fingers, the ones still glistening with my wetness, and Romanus took them into his mouth, sucking them and tasting me.

I let out a shuddering breath. "You guys should come with a warning label. That was…indescribable."

Rouen kissed me quickly, a contented grin on his face.

"Yep, it definitely was." He pulled up his jeans, and found his tee, pulling it over his head and hiding the delicious planes of his muscles. "We felt all the fun you were having with our new pack member. It's exciting to ride the wave."

I swear my left eye twitched a little. "What?"

Romanus rolled his eyes at Rouen, buckling his belt but not bothering with a shirt. "We feel your connection to things. Pain, anger, fear. Desire. Lust."

"Mind blowing orgasms," Rouen interjected with a grin.

I gave him a little smile. Couldn't argue with that.

"Your pleasure gets layered onto ours, making the whole thing twice as mind blowing. Making you cum makes the whole thing more intense for us," Romanus continued.

"I would have you on your back all day every day, giving you orgasm after orgasm if Romanus wasn't such a spoilsport," Rouen said as he gave Rom a mischievous smile.

For some reason I'd thought they'd stop having sex

with each other, now that they'd found a Queen. I wanted to slap my head at my own hubris. They had centuries of love and companionship between them. It hadn't just been a Band-Aid measure while they'd waited for me to come along.

Rouen rolled up his t-shirt and appreciated the tiny little teeth marks where I'd bit him when I came.

"Ugh, why can't I help but bite you guys? I swear I have never been a biter. Now you guys come along, and I'm basically part vampire." It was a compulsion that I couldn't deny, especially when I was about to orgasm.

We walked into the kitchen, and Romanus made coffee in the French press.

"It's just another evolutionary throwback. You're Queen now, so you're claiming us and asserting your dominance over us at the same time," he explained.

Rouen pulled down two mugs. "I like having your marks on me." He gave me another hot look that seemed to explain all the different ways he'd like to fuck me on the kitchen counter.

I picked up Romanus' shirt and resisted the urge to smell it. I couldn't believe I was about to say this but… "you should put a shirt on. We are going to land soon and we should get back to our seats."

What I really wanted to do was run my hand over his hard, defined abs, and memorize every single one. And the V of his hips that was currently being framed by the low rise of his black jeans.

I hadn't touched them much over the last couple of days, and I was beginning to feel the longing to just curl up in their arms and let them make love to me for days.

Romanus finished making coffee and handed one to me, exactly how I liked it. Strong and a little sweet. How he'd found the time to learn how I liked my coffee was a mystery. He handed the other cup to Rouen, and they shared a small, intimate smile. He took the shirt from my other hand, and leaned forward, whispering a kiss across my lips.

He made a happy humming noise, then left the kitchenette.

Rouen nudged me after him, his hand slipping down to pat my butt. "After you."

The Captain's voice came over the intercom. "Please be seated for landing."

I walked past Naz, who gave me a sultry look. Yep, there goes any chance of having sex on the sly ever again. Or touching myself in the shower, not that I would need to. I was pretty sure I wasn't going to be short on shower buddies anytime soon.

CHAPTER THIRTEEN

O ur hotel room this time was a suite. There were two bedrooms, which I thought was a little disappointing, and a large open plan living room/kitchen area. Both Naz and Romanus appraised the building for entry and exit points. Romanus had growled when Naz had insisted on doing it too.

Rouen whistled low between his teeth. I shot him a sharp look and he gave me an innocent smile. I didn't trust that smile as far as I could throw him. Which is not far at all considering they seemed to be a more solid mass than humans. Rouen weighed about the same amount as a smart car.

"What?" I snapped, my eyes narrowed.

"They are going to have to figure it out soon, once and for all. Neither of them has conceded Alpha."

I remembered their first fight, back at the warehouse. "Naz conceded." Kinda. Even though at the time it seemed kind of half-hearted.

Rouen scoffed as he unpacked his duffle, pulling long knives wrapped in worn leather sheaths out by the dozens. Where would he put all those? When he pulled out two swords, I drooled.

Lux had taught me how to fight with short swords when I was five, much to Mom's disgust. But he'd busted me trying to steal his sword one too many times and argued it would be better to teach me to use it rather than cut my arm off on his deadly broadswords. He was the reason I was so quick on my feet, that I could think with a clear head during stressful situations. Running on raw emotion will get you dead quick. Your mind is your greatest weapon. Lux had drilled those lessons into me over and over again. Those short swords were still mounted on the wall of my apartment.

Rouen saw my adoring look, and handed me the blades, hilt first. I pulled them from the elaborately tooled sheathes. They fit perfectly in my hand, balanced evenly in my grip. I frowned.

"These are wrong for you. You need something longer, weighted for your increased strength."

I felt stupid lecturing a couple of hundred year old Gargoyle on swords. I guess, with his strength, he could make a toothpick a deadly weapon, but still. Lux had taught me you were only as good as your sword.

"I know." He gave me a grin, the warmth reaching right up through his mismatched eyes and into my chest. He tilted his head to the weapons. "They aren't mine."

"Who's are… ? Oh, they are for me?" I held one of the swords in my hand, the flat edge of the blade resting on my palm. They were beautiful. There was intricate scrollwork for about three inches up the blade from the simple pearl inlaid cross guard. The grip was wrapped in a deep red leather. As a pair, they were gorgeous.

"How did you find a matching pair in New York? Or a swordsmith anywhere at all. These are beautiful, Rouen." I placed the sword down and wrapped my arms around his waist, pressing tight against his chest. I blinked back girly tears that threatened to pool in my eyes. He reached down and tilted up my chin.

"Not half as beautiful as you. Consider them a welcome present. It's customary to give a new Queen gifts. Romanus said we shouldn't overwhelm you with our customs, but I can't tell you how happy I am to have you as my Queen."

He kissed me then, his tongue gently slipping between my lips, running over the edge of my teeth. I kissed him back, stroking his tongue with mine as they danced. Rouen reached down and placed his hands under my ass, lifting me until we were face to face. I wrapped my legs around his waist and kissed him back with a desperation.

A throat cleared. "Are we interrupting?" Romanus sounded amused.

"Yes," Rouen growled. I tore my lips away from his and looked over his shoulder. All the other guys stood there, Naz and Romanus looking amused, and Charlie looking exasperated, but not angry. That was a step up, right?

"No, it's fine." I wiggled out of Rouen's arms, and he mumbled out a complaint. I stroked his chest and smiled. "Raincheck," I whispered for his ears only.

I stepped around him to the guys. "Rouen was just giving me my gift."

Romanus raised an eyebrow at Rouen, and he looked sheepish. "She saw me taking them out of my bag. They are from Romanus, too."

Romanus shook his head. "You just wanted all the appreciation. I'm no fool, Rouen." He looked down at me. "Were they a good fit?"

I nodded and grinned. "Perfect. Like they were made for me."

He winked. "Good. I thought we could take this opportunity to go over what Charlie found and come up with a plan on how to track down the real power behind Shine."

I picked up my swords and slipped the harness loosely over my shoulders. I didn't need to strap them on inside the hotel room. But I wanted my new toys with me all the same.

The living room had large leather couches, and a huge flat screen tv. A chrome and glass table currently held all of Charlie's tech gear. He grabbed his laptop and brought it over to the matching coffee table.

"First-"

"We should-"

Both Naz and Romanus spoke at the same time, and I winced. They scowled at each other, and I saw what Rouen had meant. This had the potential to go very, very bad. We needed to sort this out soon.

"We need to pick an Alpha. Shit turns pear-shaped when there aren't clear lines of authority," I said softly.

Naz scowled. "I agree."

Romanus just made an extremely inhuman noise in the back of his throat.

"Can I just appoint an Alpha?" I asked.

Both of their eyes snapped to me, but Rouen put his hand over mine to still my tongue. "That would be bad. They need to work it out themselves, through force. One needs to submit, or they will never be content."

I sighed. I knew it wouldn't be that easy. "Can we just appoint a leader of this operation, and leave the pack stuff until after we are done? A month at the most. Can you guys keep your shit together that long? Consider it a compromise."

They both eyed me suspiciously. "What did you have in mind?" Romanus growled.

I thought about it. I'd have to phrase this so that both man and beast were appeased. Despite what their mouths said, I had a feeling that their gargoyle nature had a lot more control than anyone wanted to admit, even in Nazir. Hell, especially in the newly made Nazir.

"Nazir can have control of the mission because he has more expertise in these kinds of human operations." Romanus went to interrupt, but I held up a hand to stop him. "But Romanus gets total control over my protection."

They gave me wary glances, working through the idea, like it was some kind of trap. I rolled my eyes. The testosterone in the room was so thick I could probably light it with a match.

It was the best I could do. Romanus would have taken control of my safety whether I wanted him to or not. This way I made it sound like my idea. I was telling him that as Queen, I trusted him as Alpha with my safety.

Giving Nazir the mission let him maintain some control of his life, which would have chafed under Romanus' orders. We had to ease into our pack roles, me especially.

Rouen leaned into me. "Well played, my Queen," he said from the corner of his mouth. I nudged him with my elbow.

"Agreed?" I asked again.

Both of my Alphas nodded. It was a quick fix at most, but it would have to do. I was pretty sure this hotel didn't have an arena floor, filled with gladiator sand and reinforced walls. Though it did have a really nice pool that I was desperate to try out sometime this century. Time to dazzle and distract.

I pulled off my hooded jumper, so I was just in my tight tank top. I stretched my arms above my head and yawned. Four sets of eyes dropped to my boobs and the mood in the room changed. Hooray for boobies.

"Tell me your plan, Naz."

Naz gave me an intense look, like he hadn't thought I would actually side with him. I think I was going to have to get used to the whole testosterone overload thing, because it wasn't going to lessen any time soon.

"We should make some subtle enquiries here, check out where they were holding Hope. Try and determine if they have a cell in Geneva, or if they were just in town to grab your sister." He drummed his fingers against the arm of his chair. "Charlie should continue to find out who is the real power behind the ring, and whether the whole organization is in on it, or just a few shit people."

Sounded solid to me, so I nodded.

"We have another problem," Charlie interjected. "If they were informed enough to snatch Hope, they'd have to know what she looks like, right? That means her exact replica is going to stand out when she is running around asking questions, no matter how subtle she is."

He made a good point. I only had to walk past someone who'd been involved, and we'd be screwed.

I knew what Charlie was suggesting. "Can't I just wear a hat?" I whined.

He grinned and shook his head. "Oh yeah, spy movie style makeover time!"

Crap.

TURNS out that Romanus was actually pretty good at cutting hair. I'd seen him wield knives, so I guess that wasn't super surprising, but I didn't think cutting off hair and cutting off heads were transferable skills. He gave me an edgy pixie cut, and I don't know who was sadder watching my hair fall to the ground, me or Rouen. He'd refused to cut it at all. We'd dyed my hair a dark brown that looked like burnt coffee. It completely changed my look, I'd give them that. I looked paler, almost sickly, my green eyes looking huge in my face with the shorter style.

When it was done, I sat in the middle of the guys, feeling oddly self conscious. Four sets of eyes appraised me.

Rouen ran a hand over my new, feathered tresses. "Still beautiful."

Romanus smacked him on the back of the head. "She could look like a garden gnome and still be beautiful."

Rouen pulled a face, like that was obvious, but the whole interaction made me smile. And perhaps feel a little better about it. I mean, it wasn't like it wouldn't grow back, right?

"Oh, here's the final touch," Charlie said, placing a pair of square rimmed hipster glasses on my face. I raised my eyebrows and he just grinned back. "What? It worked for Superman!"

I'd gone from badass vigilante to hipster nerd in the space of an hour.

Despite my plane nap, I felt like I could still sleep for a week. I yawned deeply, but I was going to hold out to avoid jet lag.

Naz shrugged on his own hooded jumper and pulled a dark leather jacket over the top. He looked sexy and as dangerous as a switchblade.

"I'm going to check in with some people from an old job. Maybe they'll know what's going on in the underground."

I gripped his arm. "Take Rouen to watch your six." I squeezed his forearm, both as a silent plea to say yes, and because I liked the feel of his muscles beneath my fingers. Hey, I'm a multitasker.

He nodded and Rouen stood, dipping down to kiss the top of my head.

"Stay out of trouble, Tiger." His look said he'd

punish me if I didn't, and I'd probably like it. Hated for them to leave, but damn it was nice to watch them go. I was definitely an ass girl.

After they left, Charlie stood. "Let's get some food, then I have a couple of people I want to speak to on the dark web."

I nodded. "Dumplings!" I yelled to his retreating back. Charlie wouldn't be back tonight. He'd be lost in the blue glow of his computer screen until sleep, or me, pulled him away.

Romanus made no move to stand, so I cuddled into his side. He stroked a large hand over my hair, and down the nape of my neck, sending little shivers down my spine.

"Sleep, Rella. I'll wake you when the food gets here."

I couldn't argue with that logic, so I closed my eyes, resting my cheek against the hard warmth of his chest and nodded off.

A DEEP RUMBLE against my cheek woke me. And the smell of Chinese food.

"Doesn't it bother you? Naz joining the pack, I mean?"

It was Charlie's hushed voice asking the question, and I kept my eyes closed.

"No, not at all. We will sort out the dominance issue eventually, and either I will remain Alpha, or I won't."

"No offence, but you aren't that easy going. You won't be the first person she turns to anymore, the one who protects her even when she doesn't know it. It will be someone else's job."

Romanus made a low noise in the back of his throat. "Huma-" he corrected himself, "Charlie. You've known Estrella for her entire life. Do you doubt her capacity to love us all? That she can only give her heart and trust to one person? I have known her barely a blink in comparison, but I can tell that she has a willingness to love us all with everything she possesses. Just because she loves another, does not mean she will love you less. By fixating on the way things were, am I not just denying myself the happiness of now?"

Charlie was silent, and I decided that now was as good a time as any to "wake up".

I shifted on Romanus' lap, and made a show of blinking and rubbing my eyes. I let out a tiny yawn. Someone give me an Oscar.

I locked eyes with Charlie. "Dumplings?" I said hopefully.

He laughed. "Three different kinds."

I sat up as he handed me the first box, and I peeled open the container. The waft of spice laden steam made my mouth water.

Charlie used chopsticks to grab one of the dumplings from in front of me and hold it to my lips. Like a gargoyle. What did that mean? I looked at him, trying to decipher the expression on his face.

I wrapped my lips around the offered dumpling and ate it slowly, chewing thoughtfully. Before today, I thought only reality cooking show hosts and people who Instagram their food could eat thoughtfully, but I stood corrected. Charlie watched me eat intensely until I swallowed, and then dug into his own food like nothing out of the ordinary had happened. I looked at Romanus who seemed almost proud.

Men were weird. I took my bowl of dumplings, put it in the crook of my elbow and ate it quickly. I couldn't take anymore food related overtures today.

I didn't want Romanus to feel slighted, in case he was about to feed me an eggroll or something, so I settled back close to his side. Charlie flicked on the tv, and we watched an old Kung Fu movie in companionable silence. I expected it to be weird, or for Charlie to look at me cuddled into the crook of Romanus' arm and storm off. But they just laughed together at the bad dubbing, made appreciative noises as the lead actor did gravity defying martial arts moves and we waited for the other members of our pack to return.

I'd fallen asleep by the time they came home, and the sound of the front door slamming made me jump to my feet, heart pounding out of my chest.

When they made it to the living room, they came in a stink cloud of cheap perfume and expensive whiskey. Big, stupid grins were stretched across their faces. I felt my brows draw together. Romanus looked equally as unimpressed. I glanced at my watch. 3:36 a.m. Charlie was at the dining table, his features illuminated in the glow of his screen. He hadn't even looked up when Naz and Rouen had stumbled in.

I crossed my arms over my chest. "You smell like you've been bathing with hookers in a whiskey still."

"Uh oh, Mom and Dad look pissed," Naz joked drunkenly.

Rouen punched Naz in the arm and it sent him flying across the room. "Dude, that's gross. I've fucked both of them. That's just weird," he laughed and my lips twitched, but I got it under control.

Naz was shaking with laughter, laying like he had no bones over an armchair. Within seconds, low snores echoed through the room. Passed out cold.

"You got drunk on assignment." Romanus' voice was hard.

Rouen came over and wrapped his arms around me, planting a huge kiss on my lips and then burying his face in my neck and making nom-nom-nom noises. I couldn't hold it in anymore. I laughed, lifting my shoulder because it tickled, dammit!

"Relax, Rom. It takes more than a little dirty water to make intoxicated. Nazir's informants are mostly Russians. They are more forthcoming when they are well lubricated, and even more so when everyone else is drunk as well. Naz didn't have a choice, and I was there to watch his back."

I pulled back and gave him my best stern librarian look. "And the cheap perfume?"

"Strip club."

I put my nose to his neck and inhaled deeply. The perfume was stronger there. Someone had been putting their hands on my Beta. "And why is another woman's scent so strong here?" I whispered against his skin.

"Uh, lap dance?"

For a reason I didn't want to overanalyze, I leaned in

and bit his neck, hard. Harder than I usually did when we made love, harder than I would have ever contemplated if it wasn't nearly four in the morning and jealousy wasn't coursing through my blood.

"Mine," I growled around the flesh between my teeth. Fucking growled. It was definitely a gargoyle thing, and apparently I was turning a little more Gargoyle Queen then I first suspected. I began to freak out, but I felt Rouen's long, low moan beneath my lips.

Then there were hands under my ass and Rouen was carrying me to the bedroom. He threw me on the bed and was between my thighs, his hard body pressed right along the length of me.

"Seriously, what is with you guys? Are you a race of nymphomaniacs or something?" The last word might have been a moan, totally ruining my mock disapproval.

He kissed my neck, his lips tender over my flesh as he stripped my clothes off with supernatural prowess. The heavy weight of his body grinding against the apex of my thighs.

I kept waiting for Romanus to appear, but the door never opened. I didn't mind. They weren't always going to be a package deal, and although watching them together soaked my panties at the speed of light, I was attracted to both of them separately. The threesomes were just the royal icing on the cake.

Somehow, magically, my pants were gone and the rough fabric of his jeans was scraping over my clit, making me arch against him.

He flicked open my bra and wrapped his lips around

my nipple, humming happily against my breast like he couldn't believe his luck. It made me smile.

Then he caught the hard nub between his teeth and bit down gently. I sucked in a loud breath.

He looked up at me, meeting my eyes as he sucked and nipped at my breasts. He pulled back until my nipple slid out of his mouth with a wet pop.

"My Queen."

My body felt simultaneously languid and filled with electric need, and the sensation was threatening to tear me apart.

"Clothes off. Now."

He gave me a sexy grin. "Whatever you wish."

He moved away, shedding his clothes and moving back to his place between my thighs before my body had even cooled slightly. His hot skin pressed against mine, and he looked down at me, barely a breath between our lips.

"You're so beautiful. We got so lucky."

Feelings that I didn't want to name swelled in my chest, and I kissed him hard, pouring my emotions into the embrace.

He pulled back, panting softly. "What do you want, my Queen?"

I wanted so many things that I was scared to name, futures that I had thought would be improbable, if not downright impossible. Happiness that I wasn't sure I deserved. So, I decided to hedge my bets.

"I want you to fuck me, Rouen."

His knowing look told me that he knew that's not what I wanted to say, but he stayed silent, giving me one long kiss, wrapping his arms around my waist and rolling us over. I sat astride his body, the massive length of his hard cock deliciously pressed against my center. I reached a hand between us and made a fist around his dick. He was huge and my fingers only just touched.

His big hands held my hips tightly, and lifted me up, as I guided him into me on one long moan. I wasn't sure if the sound was mine, or his, or a beautiful combination of us both.

He controlled our pace, lowering me down inch by tantalizing inch, letting me accommodate the delicious girth of him until he was buried deep. He looked at me reverently, his brown and gold eyes running over me like I was a goddess come to life. It made me feel powerful, worshipped even, and I loved it.

He crooked a finger. "Kiss me," he said, his voice rough.

I leaned forward, my nipples brushing the smooth, hairless expanse of his chest and kissed him deeply.

He took my hips again, drawing himself out and then thrusting hard back inside me. I squealed as the pleasure spread through me. Then he did it again, and I was lost. He banded both arms around my back and held me still as he slammed himself inside me again and again, his sexy abs rippling beneath me with each upward thrust.

He shifted me down a little, his strokes still even and powerful, and I found myself nose to nipple on his chest. I ran the flat of my tongue over the peaked flesh and sucked it into my mouth. He moaned, thrusting harder, getting deeper and making me whimper between moans.

I might have said something about coming, or maybe it was just the crescendo of my moans, but he sped up even faster. Inhumanly fast. Gargoyle fast, pounding into me until I was screaming so loudly that it was a wonder I didn't shatter the windows.

"Bite me," he panted. "Hard. I want my blood on your lips."

My hindbrain knew I would be grossed out by the request later, but now, having his flesh between my teeth sounded like the best suggestion ever.

I bit the muscle of his pec firmly, opposite the one from the plane, and a muffled pop echoed in my head as the tips of my teeth pierced his flesh. He threw his head back and roared like an injured animal. Ragged thrusts matched ragged breaths, and then he was coming too, grinding his hips against mine.

I lifted up a little and looked at the wound on his chest, the perfect crescents of my teeth marking his flesh. They could have matched my dental records to it, the bite was that clean. I felt a little swell of pride at the mark, but it was closely followed by guilt that I'd made him bleed.

I licked the wound almost subconsciously. Rouen's hand under my chin stopped me. He shook his head.

"Leave it. I don't want it to heal. I like it there."

I was about to argue that I wouldn't be able to heal it, but the blood had stopped dripping and the open wounds had healed over a little. It would still bruise, but it was definitely partially healed.

I had done that.

I could feel the freak out surging up from my chest, but Rouen just pulled me up his body, his semi soft cock sliding out of me, making me give an involuntary hum of pleasure.

He didn't stop until we were cheek to cheek. "It will be okay. You are still you, just with a few extras. You are everything now."

He kissed me gently, then tucked my head under his chin. The steady thumping of his heart calmed my bubbling hysteria.

In the haze between wakefulness and sleep, it occurred to me that Hope and I probably weren't identical twins anymore. We'd always been emotionally different, but physically the same. I wasn't sure that was the case now.

CHAPTER FOURTEEN

I studied the exterior of the worn-down mechanics shop. The sign was in French, its swirling font almost too elegant for such a manly shopfront. And for the horror that went on behind its rusting roller door.

I'd never seen the outside of the shop, only the basement where Hope had been held, and the top of the stairs where Luc decapitated the door guard. My heart thundered in my chest. I didn't want to go in, but it wasn't a rational emotion. There was no one in there. The doors were covered in police tape, Hope was safe at home in Manhattan, and I was surrounded by some of the meanest beings to ever walk the mortal plane. But PTSD wasn't a rational beast.

"We'll split up, just in case someone has decided to come back to visit their old haunts. Rouen is with me," Naz said, his eyes covered with dark shades. His hangover must be a real bitch. I bit my lip so I didn't grin.

Obviously, Rouen was with him. He'd have to pry

Romanus off my ass with a crowbar. I had my swords crisscrossed in a double holster over my back, and I stroked the chest strap. It was so beautiful.

"We'll take the back," Romanus said, stepping in front of me and assuming the lead. I could tell he didn't like leaving my back unprotected by the stiff way he held his head, trying to keep his eyes on what was in front of him, but an ear for sneak attacks at the rear. He seemed to be feeling the loss of Rouen in our little ménage.

He halted us at the padlocked backdoor, listening for Naz and Rouen's confirmation that they were in position.

I drew my sword and held it loosely at my side. It was perfectly balanced to my hand, and I wondered again how they could get it so right without having me there with the swordsmith. Romanus raised a brow at me, probably because I was making goo goo eyes at my swords. He must have guessed my thoughts. "He makes them himself."

"What?"

"Rouen. He makes the blades himself. I helped him source the material for the hilt, but the blade is all him."

I shook my head at the impossibility of the statement. The swords must have taken days to create, let alone all the fancy swirls and decoration.

"Not impossible when you have superhuman strength and claws that can pierce medieval armor like a tin can. He saw the swords on your wall and wanted to make you a set. He knows how you hold yourself, how you move, your grip, just from watching you do day to day things. He's pretty good at the art, even though we've no need for swords personally." He gave a soft smile, one I realized was almost exclusively reserved for the other gargoyle. "He's a little taken with you."

I let out an embarrassed laugh, my cheeks reddening. I was a little smitten with Rouen, too.

"In position." Naz's voice came over the comm. "Three. Two. One. Go, go."

Romanus pulled back a foot and kicked the bottom of the door. It crumpled like an origami swan. We weren't even pretending to be stealthy today.

The interior of the mechanics shop was dark, the hulls of car bodies lying abandoned around the wide, empty space. An office in the rear corner was also dark.

Romanus cocked an ear to the side. "All clear. No one here."

We stood next to a heavy metal door. I recognized that door. I looked at the ground, at the large stain that could have been rust in a mechanics workshop, but I knew it wasn't.

Naz and Rouen peeled out of the shadows at our backs. "All clear at the front too." Naz looked at the door, and then at my face. "You okay?"

I nodded and schooled my features. "I'm good."

He rested a hand on the center of my back. "All three of us can feel your fear and pain, Estrella. You don't need to lie. No one will stop you from doing what you need to do."

"As long as it doesn't put her in the path of actual harm," Romanus clarified quickly.

Naz nodded. "Of course."

I sucked in a deep, calming breath. I was fine. I repeated it out loud for the guys, and none of them contradicted me despite the swirling mess of my thoughts.

Naz opened the doors and went down into the darkened basement first. A small torch clutched in his offhand, his weapon raised. Neither Rouen nor Romanus needed a torch, their night vision was perfect. I didn't even think to bring a torch. Rouen went after Naz, but not before turning to me.

"You won't need light," he murmured. "But put a hand on my back if it will make you feel better." We stepped into the darkened stairway, and I sucked in a breath, my hand clutching the back of Rouen's shirt like a scared girl in a haunted house.

The light of Naz's flashlight flicked off halfway down, and as I looked around, I understood why.

My night vision was exceptional. I could see every step beneath my feet and every groove in the rough rock walls around us. I still held onto Rouen's shirt though. The contact calmed the thudding of my heart, so I'd pretend it was because I couldn't see for a little bit longer. I felt the vibration of Romanus' steps on the stairs, although his movements were almost silent, impressive considering both he and Rouen were huge.

For a moment no one moved toward the light switch on the wall as we looked for threats in the dark.

"All clear," Romanus said again. I didn't scrabble around for the light switch like I would have done a month ago. I saw it with perfect clarity.

"Close your eyes first. The light can hurt a little,"

Rouen said loud enough that I wasn't sure if it was directed at Naz or me. I did what he said, and then flipped the switch.

Squinting, I let a little light in one eye, and then the other. Not too bad at all. Sure, pain from the light speared my brain, but no worse than staring at the sun when you're hungover. Not that I would do anything that dumb.

Lux had been liaising with the police in Geneva after Hope's abduction, trying to track down the culprits through the proper channels while I snuck around the shadows. One look at the basement told me my way was going to be more productive.

I'd expected the basement to be cleared out, dust from the CSI guys coating the room, and every loose thing bagged, tagged and in an evidence locker somewhere.

What I found just told me that the traffickers had a cop, or maybe a whole team, on the payroll.

The place was basically untouched. Papers were strewn across the floor as if someone had grabbed armloads in a hurry. A metal waste paper basket held ashes in the center of the room. Hope's blood still stained the cement and I resisted the urge to throw up. In the light of day, when my whole focus wasn't on Hope's broken body, the basement told a horror story.

Dirty mattresses were pushed against the back wall and rings and chains were drilled deep into the stone above them.

They hadn't even bothered to clear out the place,

they had been so sure that it wouldn't come back to bite them. It stunk of system deep corruption.

Naz must have been making the same deductions. "Spread out. Get everything you think looks even a little relevant. And someone clean up Hope's blood from the floor. I want no trace of her in this place."

No one argued. I walked to the burnt papers in the bin. I sifted through it with my fingers, most of it charred beyond redemption. The edge of a flyer caught my attention. It was a hand-written time and address, for what I don't know. It looked photocopied. Charlie would be able to track down the address. Everything else in the bin was toast, including what appeared to be some kind of ledger book. I picked up the remains of the heavy leather book and lamented that none of it was salvageable. Not a single name.

Romanus was pouring bleach over the dried pool of blood. He stopped, sniffed, and walked a foot to the left, pouring more bleach over what appeared to be unmarked concrete.

Feeling my gaze, he turned. "There was a drop over here. None of it should remain." He seemed just as adamant as Nazir had been, although he didn't have the same personal connection to Hope. Well, except through me. He was being thorough because he was just a decent, uh, gargoyle being.

Naz held a Ziploc bag that he'd pulled from the same place as the torch I guess and held it out for my burned flyer. There were a few other bits and pieces in that bag, but not as much as I would have liked.

We worked down there for an hour, gathering what

we could, looking under every upended crate, and even testing for loose stones. I avoided the dirty mattresses, and the guys went through the evidence over there. Rouen's eyes were hard, like polished stones, and his face promised hellish vengeance. It was the first time he'd ever truly looked like a demon to me.

When Naz was happy we'd gotten everything we could from the room, we switched off the light and climbed back up the stairs.

When I stood in front of the workshop again, I had the overwhelming urge to burn it down too.

I was going to burn their whole world down.

I NEVER THOUGHT I'd say this, and it almost felt un-American, but I was sick of pizza. I would seriously maul one of Papa's ratatouilles. My mouth literally watered at the thought, and my chest ached.

I missed my family. I hadn't seen any of my parents in months, with the exception of Mom and Eli, since they'd been on a six-month Aid Tour of the Pacific Islands. I missed Sunday night family dinners, with everyone there, when Valery would make something delicious and ridiculously complicated, and Oz would put on his themed music playlist for the night. Lux would talk to me about work, and Ri would ask me about who I was dating. Hope, Sam and Tolli would talk work until Mom would put her foot down about shop talk at the table.

Sometimes Clary and Adnan, or even Ace and Luc, would be there, and we'd laugh, talk and drink wine.

The whole thing was almost wholesome and idyllic. Well, as wholesome as you could be when you were the child of polyamorous parents and kind of pseudo-children to the Devil and his Fallen Angel consort. Okay, so we weren't ever going to be a Norman Rockwell painting, but we were happy.

I inserted my guys into the picture in my mind. I had no worries about Naz and Charlie; they already had a place at our table. It wasn't a struggle to see Romanus talking about old times with Lux, or Rouen talking weird eighties pop culture references with Oz.

Telling my parents that I accidentally got Naz semi-executed and then became a Gargoyle Queen to save his life was going to be an interesting conversation to say the least. Not that they had any right to judge, considering they'd all been the immortal embodiments of the seven deadly sins, and Mom had been their 'Redeemer' once upon a time, before Hope and I came along.

I felt eyes on me, and I looked up to see Naz staring at me from across the table, his head slightly cocked to the side.

"Okay?"

I smiled and ran my foot up the inside of his leg under the table. He gave me a hot look and a half grin but chased the expression away with a mock stern scowl.

He held up a crumpled-up piece of paper, with a scrawled name and time. It wasn't like the burnt flyer I'd found. It said "Lucy, 1:45."

"A mark?"

He stared at the paper as if it might whisper to him

its secrets. "Maybe. Charlie, any luck with the burnt paper?"

Charlie made a non-committal noise, his fingers still working the keyboard. "I might have something."

He pulled up what appeared to be a message board on one of the social media platforms. There was a post that looked like it was designed by a My Little Pony on a bad LSD trip. It advertised a secret rave at a place in an industrial district. Why would they have this? Why would they bother to burn it?

"Hunting ground," Romanus murmured as he came back into the room. I hadn't even noticed he'd left the table. He placed chicken salad in front of me, with a whole bunch of roasted vegetables mixed through. It looked amazing, and it was exactly what I had felt like.

I beamed up at him. The corners of his mouth turned up in a smile, and he leaned down until his lips were close to my ear. "Eat, my Queen." He kissed my cheek and went over to look at the rave poster on Charlie's screen.

Romanus never called me Queen outside of the bedroom, unlike Rouen, who I think had forgotten my real name. I ate a cube of roasted squash and didn't bother to hide the moan. It was delicious.

Four sets of eyes shifted to me, and I shrugged. It was too damn good.

Romanus cleared his throat. "It's a hunting ground for young, inebriated humans. Easy pickings. Crowded like that, no one will notice if you separate the weaker ones from the herd."

He was right. Normal nightclubs were a hotspot for

crime. Secret, underground rave parties were basically a criminal playground.

"Are there anymore? Any coming up?" I asked Charlie.

He looked back through the message board. "It looks like they have them once every three weeks. There's another one in two days. Makes sense. They wouldn't be able to take too many at once otherwise it would be suspicious as hell and the police would be all over it, so better to have them frequently."

Naz growled. "I don't think they are too worried about the cops."

"Even so, in this day and age, it would be easy to make the connection between people going missing and the parties. So, do they take them from there, or just wait and snatch them later? Or a bit of both?"

We all stared at the screen in silence. The whole idea of kids being led to a meat market for human traffickers made my stomach sour. But we were going to fix it, one blood-drenched way or another.

"I guess there's only one way to find out. Get out your glow sticks and put on your dancing shoes. We're going to a rave."

CHAPTER FIFTEEN

The steady thump of trance music pushed against my chest like another heartbeat. The warehouse was so packed that it smelled overwhelmingly of sweat, cigarette smoke and fish. The fish smell was because we were in the currently closed fish market building. It wasn't a pleasant.

The other rave goers didn't seem to mind. The flashing lights and electric music seemed to have them in a fugue, their bodies bouncing and writhing almost as one.

We walked in separately, because together we stood out. Surrounded by my guys, I looked like a royal princess surrounded by her bodyguards. Interesting idea, but stealth was what we needed.

Though, even by himself, Romanus stood out. He looked like sex. Golden, hot sex. You couldn't even see his dual colored eyes in here, but I'd taken one look at him before we left and felt my panties dampen beneath my too short skirt.

Actually, they'd all looked sexy, dressed in varying black clothes, mostly dark tight jeans and tight shirts. I'd almost abandoned my vendetta and suggested we stay home for an orgy. The idea of having all four guys at once made my brain fuzz over, so I shook my head. I needed my mind in the game, not imagining Charlie's head between my thighs.

I was dressed for temptation tonight. I was in a short, black leather skirt that showed off my long smooth legs, and my tiny top left nothing to the imagination. I'd bought it at some little boutique in a rush yesterday. I'd asked for the most tempting, slutty thing they had in stock. They had not disappointed. It was basically a small strip of slinky gold fabric held together by loose chains. I may as well have gone out with a sign saying, "pick me, I'm premium merchandise".

I moved through the crowd, only a little worried that one of the chains would get caught on something and break, leaving my breasts hanging in the wind. Anonymous hands took advantage of the forced closeness to pet my skin or squeeze my ass. Normally I would junk punch someone for having the audacity to take something not freely offered, but I had a bigger fish to catch than some horny dude-bro who'd had too much tequila.

I got to the bar and casually looked around. I could see Romanus, who stood a foot over most people in the crowd, and he was standing near the rear exit, his back to the wall. Between one blink and the next, he seemed to fade into the shadows of the room. Well, that was a neat trick.

Rouen wasn't trying to hide. He was on the floor

dancing with some serious skill. People crept closer to him as he danced, his feet moving at a speed I couldn't even fathom and his head thrown back in pure joy. Seemed like my Beta loved to dance. I wasn't surprised. From what I could tell, Rouen just loved to live. Soon, so many people swamped him that I lost sight of him, but not before he held my gaze and winked. He was partying, but he was watching my back too. I couldn't see Naz anywhere, but I wasn't worried.

Someone leaned on the temporary bar beside me, and I gave him a coy smile. Charlie smiled back.

We'd decided it was best if Charlie pretended to pick me up at the rave, so someone was close enough to have my back. And Charlie was the least physically terrifying.

He grinned and gave me a conspiratorial wink. "Can I get you a drink?" he asked uncertain, his eyes running slowly over my body. The heated look was not an act.

I gave him a seductive look from beneath my lashes. "I'd like that. Vodka and juice."

Charlie ordered it from the bar, and I took the opportunity to appreciate the perfect proportions of his muscular back beneath the tight tank. I wanted to dig my fingers into those shoulders, to run my hands up and down the long lines of muscle on either side of his spine.

Charlie turned to hand me my drink and froze. He must have seen the heat on my face, because his own eyes hooded. He stepped into my space and gave me my screwdriver. I took a sip and set it on the bar. I wasn't really drinking tonight, I needed my wits about me.

"Do you want to dance?" Charlie's voice was a husky tickle close to my ear.

I just nodded, and he downed his drink and led me to the dance floor.

We were pushed close together, but I didn't mind. That was exactly where I wanted to be. My body involuntarily swayed to the beat, and Charlie closed the remaining space between us. His hard body was pressed right along mine, his hands on my hips, moving in perfect synchronization with mine. My ass brushed the front of his jeans as he swayed and his fingers dug harder into my hips. I turned and hooked my arms around his neck, not leaving an inch of space between us. He stared down at me, such raw need on his face.

"Rella." It was a desperate sound. God, I wanted to kiss him. This was not the time or the place, but I couldn't resist. I leaned up and brushed my lips over his. He kissed me back with the same desperation. His lips were hard and demanding, but I wasn't resisting. I wanted to give him everything right here on the dance floor.

Somehow, we were still dancing perfectly to the beat, our bodies moving sinuously against each other. I sipped at his lips greedily. I wanted more, right now. His hands slid down to my ass and pulled me tighter against him, and I could feel the outline of his own need. I rolled my hips, creating delicious friction between our bodies and he moaned low against my lips.

"Rella," he repeated, and my name was a plea. I just didn't know what he wanted. Did he want to take me here on the dance floor? At this moment, I would have said yes. Or did he want to stop, because he didn't want our first time to be on a sweaty dance floor surrounded by a thousand people? That sounded more like Charlie. He'd want it to be special.

Still uncertain, I just kissed him again, and he groaned against my lips, his fingertips stroking the bare skin of my back.

We kissed like that on the dance floor for hours, or maybe only minutes, I couldn't be sure. Eventually we pulled away, panting.

My body screamed with desire. I had this crazy need to make my best friend something more. I needed to make love to him, to make him my fourth. I felt incomplete, which was such an odd sensation, given that two weeks ago we'd been nothing more than lifelong friends. I'd been happy that way, too. Now my soul ached with the need to tie him to me, to my pack.

"Not here," he murmured against my lips. "I've waited too long to rush it. I've wanted to see your face as I made love to you for so, so long." He kissed me again, two magnets that refused to be apart.

I nodded. "I can wait. But Charlie…" I didn't know what to say. I couldn't promise him what he wanted. Monogamy was no longer an option. I would do almost anything for Charlie, give up almost anything, but I couldn't give up the others. They needed me, and although I would never have guessed it, I needed them.

"I know, Rella and it's okay." Then the need for words disappeared beneath the soft warmth of his lips. We stayed like that for a while, kissing tenderly in the center of a writhing mass of dancers.

I pulled away and sighed. "We should get back to work."

We walked off the dance floor. I'd lost sight of all my other guys. Logically, I knew they were probably fine, but I'd feel better if I could just catch a glimpse of them.

"Let's go check out the bathrooms," Charlie suggested.

The toilets were in a small portable building out the back area of the warehouse. A long line led from the doors, and I groaned. The line to the men's block was two people long at most, with the excess taking a pee in the dark alley that ran alongside the building. Men.

I ignored the disgruntled shouts as I jumped the queue, walking up the steps. The stalls were all occupied, and a woman dressed in fluro pink faux fur grinned and swayed drunkenly in front of the mirror as she tried to apply lipstick. Her friend came out, and I ducked into her cubicle. I desperately had to pee.

I finished up quickly and walked to the sink, ignoring the death glare of the girl who'd been the next person in line. Fluro girl was gripping the sink now. She was definitely going to puke. Her friend got a shoulder under her arms.

"Come on, sweetie, we'll take you out the back way," Fluro's friend cooed.

I looked around. I hadn't noticed the door at the rear of the building, next to another bank of sinks. I followed along behind fluro and her friend, reopening the door when it swung shut on their retreating backs. I wondered if this was how they were getting their prey?

I soon answered my own question when I saw

Fluro's friend pass off a now completely unconscious Fluro to a guy, who stuffed her unceremoniously into the back of a van.

"Hey," I shouted on instinct, and all eyes shot to me.

Something pricked me, and my vision went blurry. I looked over my shoulder at another woman, with lipstick that was way too pink to be flattering, and my world went fuzzy. I stared at the number plate on the van as they dragged me toward it.

Hope, I murmured groggily, *ZH547912.* That was it. Lights out.

THE ROCKING of the van made my stomach roll. My first thought when I resurfaced was that I was going to puke all over Fluro. I forced my eyes to open and look around. We were in the back of a normal van, which looked like millions of other utility vans. White. Unremarkable.

I glanced at Fluro again, but she was still out of it. Her body bounced around as if it had no bones. Or as if she were dead.

I slowly shuffled closer to her prone body. I didn't want to alert the men in the front I was awake. I lifted my fingers to her pulse. Still strong and steady. I moved my arm slowly back to my side.

Whatever they jabbed us with was obviously meant to keep us unconscious for a lot longer. Apparently burning through drug cocktails was another perk of my newfound Queendom.

I sent a reassurance to my guys and felt a huge wave

of anger and relief pour back to me. The Gargoyles had been all but rabid.

I reached out to Hope. *I'm fine. Just a minor kidnapping. Can you let the guys know for me? I'll stay with it, maybe get some intel.*

Hope's relieved voice answered right away. *Thank goodness. Do you need an extraction? I can send Memphis.*

Could she now? When did she get a Fallen Angel as a golden retriever?

I'm fine. There's another girl here, and I want to see where this van goes. The guys will get me out if things get too out of control. I had complete faith in my guys.

I could feel Hope's indecision. She didn't like this at all, but I was normally the one doing the saving. If I said I was alright, I probably meant it.

Finally, she sighed audibly in my head. *Fine, but be safe. I love you, Rella. Call me if you need me!*

Love you too, Sis.

I closed my eyes and opened my ears, picking up what the guys in the front of the van were saying. My already enhanced hearing had become supernatural when I bonded with the guys. Perk #673. There were only two people that I could hear. Given how powerful those drugs were, I wasn't surprised.

"He's going to be happy," the driver said as the van sped up. We were going straight, and fast. The freeway maybe?

"The brunette will bring in some good coin with a body like that," the passenger said, make a gross noise like a grunt. "I bet he puts her in the auction."

It took me a bit to figure out they were talking about

me. I still wasn't used to having my dishwater brown locks.

"It's too late for that. It's only two nights away. The catalogue has gone out. Maybe he'll save her for the next one?"

"He'll put her in the auction as a surprise lot, you wait. She'll start a bidding war. It's too good an opportunity to pass up, and she won't look as fresh in a month as she does now. Bet she's got a bit of fight in her," the passenger said, making another lewd noise.

Oh, they were going to see how much fight I had as soon as we stopped.

The two men upfront moved on to comparing my ass to some Hollywood starlet's and I tried to formulate a plan. I could go through the auction and hope I got a good look at the man behind the curtain. Maybe I could get a good look at the customers too and put them on my shit list.

As much as I needed that intel, my sense of self-preservation rebelled at the idea of putting myself in such a vulnerable situation. The drugs wore off quick, but they worked for a little while, and being unconscious in the presence of human traffickers was not an ideal situation. That would definitely be Plan B.

Plan A relied on me getting the hell out of this van before we arrived at our destination and possible reinforcements. I needed to get a look where we were, but that would involve spoiling my element of surprise.

The van slowed and veered left. Maybe we were taking an exit? If we got somewhere open, I might be able to take the chance of disabling them while the van was moving. It'd be rough, but it was doable.

I laid back and formulated a plan. I had no weapons, only my hands. I would have killed for my short swords right now. But Lux had made sure I could fight with nothing but my body and my mind from a young age. You didn't have an ancient Spartan for a father without learning a thing or two.

"What the..." the passenger yelled as the driver slammed on the brakes too late. The van went airborne, flipping, and I grabbed hold of Fluro with subhuman speed, wrapping my body around hers to protect her head and neck as gravity flung us into the air.

Time slowed, making it feel like one of those zero gravity chambers astronauts used to acclimatize to space. The van flipped over, and I finally got a look out the windscreen. Two big dragons stood in the middle of the road, and unmovable roadblock with snarling faces.

Then the van crashed down to earth on its roof, and I hit the ground with a bone cracking thud. I still held Fluro tight in my arms, and she was still blissfully unaware of what was going on around her.

I rolled her off me and tried to breathe. Definitely winded. The back doors of the van were wrenched open, and Naz and Charlie were there. My heart flip flopped at the sight of their concerned faces. Claws reached in and plucked the male occupants of the van from their seats. They dragged them to the middle of the road, one was still alive because he was screaming.

At least until my Gargoyles ate his head.

My stomach rolled again. "I'm gonna throw up."

Naz was beside me in a second. "Anything broken?"

"No." I hurt like a bitch, but nothing had cracked. Naz half carried, half dragged me from the van. He looked at Charlie. "Get the other girl."

As soon as I was free from the crumpled wreckage, Naz picked me up in his arms and carried me to the other side of the road, where our rental sat on the graveled shoulder. I snuggled close to Naz's chest, sucking in a lungful of his scent, reassuring myself that they were really here. I could see Charlie carefully carrying Fluro toward our car too, and past him to where Romanus and Rouen flung the bodies of the drivers around like a dog with a rabbit, whipping them violently back and forwards, claws shredding delicate flesh..

I buried my face in Naz's neck and pretended that the dragons before me, and the men that had made love to me, were two entirely different beings.

We stopped outside the rear passenger door. "Can you stand?" Naz asked, his jaw so tense I could almost hear the grinding of his teeth.

I nodded, and he placed me on my feet. My body ached, and I was probably going to have a pretty good abstract artwork of bruises tomorrow, but I was alive and whole. That had to have something to do with my newer gargoyle traits.

Naz helped Charlie get the still completely unconscious girl in the car. I hoped she stayed that way. I hoped she could wake up tomorrow and never know she was almost sold into slavery, and that she was saved by two big ass dragon like creatures who ate her captors. I hope she woke up tomorrow and thought the effects of the drugs were just an epic hangover.

I didn't know how we were going to get her home, though. It would look extremely suspicious if we dropped a drugged girl off at the hospital, or the closest police station.

"Does she have any ID?" I asked the guys, and both of them looked down at the girl. Because now that I could see her up close, she couldn't have been more than eighteen or nineteen.

"Where the hell would she keep it?" Charlie grumbled. He had a point. She was wearing what I could only call Flintstones in Fluro. Kind of a hot pink fluffy bikini combo. The fluffy skirt couldn't have been more than six inches wide, and the fluffy boobtube thing barely covered anything. The boots however were fluro yellow and came up to just above her knee. They were also, you guessed it, fluffy. Nothing had anything as practical as pockets. "Boots?" Naz suggested, and Charlie slipped off one boot, then the other. Nothing.

I sighed. I'd been to enough nightclubs to know where most girls kept their cards and cash. "Look out of the way."

I reached up and poked at her fur boobtube cautiously with one finger, like whatever stuffed toy she made it from was going to come back to life and bite off my finger for touching an unconscious woman's boob.

"Sorry, Fluro," I said, as I found what I was looking for. I pulled twenty bucks, a cellphone, a small flask and her driver's license out of her bra. Ah, the humble brassiere. A pocket for when you have no pockets. The guys were staring at me as if I'd just discovered Mary Poppins magical carpet bag. I rolled my eyes and read the license.

"Sadie Ridge. She's nineteen in a week."

Charlie and Naz's serious faces told me they were thinking the same thing as me. If we hadn't been here, looking for Hope's abductors, Sadie Ridge would have had a very different birthday.

Naz stuffed everything but her ID back in her long boots, then held my arm and maneuvered me in beside her. Before he could shut the door, he was yanked out of the way by a very intense looking Romanus. Rouen was only slightly behind him, looking just as wild-eyed.

Romanus pulled me from the car and wrapped me in his arms. He crushed me to his chest, and I tried to suck in air as he held me close. I could feel the hammering of his heart, the hot gush of his breath against my cheek. I could sense his panic through our bond.

"I'm okay," I reassured him as I tried to draw breath. "I'm okay."

He relaxed his grip and I sucked in a huge gulp of air. It didn't last long as Rouen pulled me from his grasp. Romanus was reluctant, and I briefly worried that they might play tug'o'war with me, but eventually Romanus let me.

"I was so worried," Rouen whispered between pressing kisses to my face. "I thought we would lose you." He didn't hug me as tight as Romanus had, but he only stopped kissing me long enough to bury his nose in my hair.

Rouen hopped into the back of the car, still holding me tight against him, and nestled me into his lap. He banded two arms around my waist, unprepared to let me go. Naz stared daggers at Romanus as he got into the driver's seat, and Romanus' face showed nothing. Charlie climbed into the rear of the SUV. He hadn't said a word.

The silence was deafening the entire drive back into Geneva. The only noise were the tiny sounds of Rouen's lips pressing against my skin. I thought he was handling it better than Romanus, but now I wasn't so sure. He seemed to *need* to have his face pressed against me, and there was a hint of desperation to his movements. I just let him go, let him soothe us both with his tenderness.

Still, no one had spoken by the time we had pulled up in front of Sadie Ridge's apartment. Rouen volunteered to carry her up to her floor, and I accompanied him. There was something less suspect about a man carrying an unconscious woman if there was another female there too. Which was so wrong. Our little altercation with the woman in the bathroom had shown that evil was both genders. We found her apartment, and then stopped.

We hadn't found a key on her, and I wasn't willing to do a more thorough search of her bra pockets.

We'd have to knock.

"Can we just dump her on the ground and run?" Rouen asked, and I shook my head.

"She isn't' a flaming bag of dog poo, Rouen. Besides, what if no ones home?"

Rouen nodded reluctantly and shifted the girl in his arms.

I knocked. It must have been close to 3 a.m. and there was no movement inside. Eventually, I heard shuffling from the other side. An elderly woman opened the door, which showed a stupid amount of trust given the time and the fact we were complete strangers. Probably the girl's grandmother. She stood in a fluffy pink robe, apparently the love of fluffy things was hereditary, and her hair was salt and pepper grey.

She frowned, the wrinkles on her face deepening, as she said something to us in rapid French, her eyes darting between the unconscious Sadie and the large scary man holding her.

I hoped the old woman spoke English, or this was going to be very hard to explain.

"She was at a party. We found her passed out in the corner." I waved a hand at Sadie, and mimicked drinking.

"*Oui.*" The woman's frown deepened, if that were possible. "She told me she was at her, err, friends house. Uh, looking at the books, err, learning." Her English wasn't great, and was very stilted, but I got the idea. Sadie had told her grandmother she was going to study at a friend's house. Man, that excuse never gets old.

Rouen said something to her in perfect French, and my eyes shot to him. The old woman smiled at him and motioned us in. She led us down a short hall to Sadie's room. It was the room of someone who still hadn't fully grown out of their teen years. Her comforter was hot pink, the same color as her Wilma Flintstone on Acid getup, and the rest of the room was decorated by posters, photos and school ribbons.

Rouen placed the girl gently on the bed and left the room. The woman spoke to him again, and he shook his head, giving her his warmest smile. He totally wooed the old woman, and I grinned to myself.

She thanked us profusely, even my terrible grasp on French recognized that, and we left. We walked back down the stairs, and Rouen wrapped his hand around mine.

"I didn't know you spoke French."

He gave me a mock disapproving side-eye. "Our pack was from France. My dialect is a little outdated, but I told her I was French-Canadian. I was worried that she'd call the cops if we couldn't get our story across properly."

I grinned at him. "Don't have to justify it to me. Just whisper dirty things to me in French next time we are in bed," I purred, giving him a saucy wink.

He turned and had me in his arms and pressed up against the wall in seconds. "I can whisper whatever you like right now," he said, and kissed me. I kissed him back ravenously, trying to consume him right here in the stairwell. I wanted so bad to let him make love to me right now, responsibilities be fucking damned. But I could feel the pulsing anger from the bond. Something was going wrong in the car, and we needed to be there.

I pulled away and wiggled out of Rouen's arms. "I wish I could, but the Pack needs us."

Rouen sighed, and grumbled something that sounded like all the ways he wanted to castrate the guys, but he followed along behind me as I continued down the stairs.

When we reached the car, the tension had rocketed up to nuclear. Rouen opened the drivers door and muscled Nazir out of the seat. Nazir snarled, and Rouen tilted his head to the side exposing his neck.

"We both know you are more Alpha than me, so cut that shit out. You can't drive. I don't want our fucking Queen to die because you and Rom went at it in the middle of peak hour fucking traffic. Now get in the fucking car. It's been a long bitch of a night, I have blue balls, and I'm not in the fucking mood."

He said all this with his throat bared, a sign of submission, but it didn't seem very submissive to me. Naz seemed content with the gesture though, and walked around to the back of the car, climbing in beside Charlie. I got the whole backseat to myself and gladly laid along the plush leather seats.

Rouen drove us out of the city, and despite the crazy tension in the car, I slept.

The sound of gravel crunching beneath the tires woke me. I hadn't been asleep long, as the sky was still dark, just the edges of the horizon lightening with the rise of the sun. The absolute darkness surrounding the car told me we weren't in Geneva anymore.

The car rolled to a stop and everyone exploded out of it like a pipe bomb.

"Did I miss something?" I asked Charlie, as we stood next to the car. Romanus and Naz circled each other in what looked like a small clearing in a pine forest. How the hell had Rouen found this?

Rouen was watching the guys warily, standing in between me and what I knew was going to be an epic fight.

"Are they fighting for Alpha?" I sounded breathless. I wasn't sure if it was from shock, or from the Alpha magic that seemed to permeate the clearing so thickly I was choking on it.

"Yes," Rouen said, not turning from the two large men who were growling inhumanly.

"Will they hurt each other?"

Rouen did look at me then, and gave me a 'what the hell kind of question is that?' look

"I mean, will they kill each other," I clarified.

Rouen turned away. "I don't know."

"Will you stop it if it goes too far?"

He shook his head. "I can't. I couldn't beat them, but I can protect you against them. My loyalty is to you first, and foremost. Then to my Alpha." He meant Romanus, but whether he was still his Alpha at the end of the night, or even alive, was now uncertain.

My heart started to pound. Naz and Romanus had started to yell at each other, though it was muffled by the low growls.

"You went against orders." Naz's voice had a scary note to it, something disconnected. The voice of a killer.

"She is my priority. I'll tear your head from your shoulders and stuff it up your ass if it means protecting her. When it comes to my Queen, your orders mean nothing. You wanted to leave her there, with people who wanted to sell her, harm her!"

Romanus' yell made me wince. He was losing control.

"You *ate* our only source of information. Against orders. She would have been fine. I'd never let her be harmed."

Romanus launched himself at Nazir, the thud of their bodies colliding making me cringe. He had Naz pinned beneath him, and his fist cracked into his face, once and then again. "You have never lost a Queen. Felt their pain as they died screaming and you were helpless to defend her. To comfort her. You've never had to hold your Queen's body in your arms and weep knowing you will never have another. You've never walked for centuries alone and missing a vital piece of your soul. You don't know!" he screamed in his face.

I thought it was going to be over, that Naz would submit beneath the weight of Romanus' body, and his words. But Naz was no longer a newly made gargoyle, weakened by blood loss. He bucked Romanus off, rolling away from the smashing fist that hurtled toward his face. They were like lions fighting, each blow as punishing as a hammer to an anvil.

They were both on their feet lightning fast, back to circling each other. Romanus was big, and his reach was massive, but Naz was fast. His gargoyle boosts had only made him faster, his movements barely a blur. Romanus didn't seem to have any problem following the new gargoyle's movements though, his arms blocking the brutal kicks that Naz was trying to hammer against his thighs. Naz feinted a left hook, and instead kicked out at Romanus' knee, making red hot waves of pain spear into my head.

I knew Rom could block me, so Naz must have really caused some serious hurt for the pain to leak through to me. The big Gargoyle fell to the ground and Naz was on top of him in an instant, pounding punishing blows into the side of his head with his elbow. The sound crunching bone echoed in the silence making me feel ill. Any wildlife that had been here had left as soon as they recognized the predators in their midst.

I was going to throw up. Blood poured from Romanus' nose, and he couldn't get his arms high enough to protect his face.

This was it. Naz would be Alpha.

I should have known better. Gargoyle hides were as tough as stone, and it was never going to end that quickly. Romanus stopped trying to protect his face, letting blow after blow land, and instead moved both of his arms between their two bodies. With a stunning feat of strength, he pushed making Naz flip backwards and slide across the pine needle covered ground.

Romanus rolled onto his feet with dexterity that spoke of centuries of training and prowled toward Naz, who was back on his feet too. I couldn't see how this was going to end. Would they always clash? Did one have to die? Could I look into the face of the other knowing he'd killed someone I cared for?

Romanus shook his head. There had to be some kind of internal bleeding or swelling or something in there. Could gargoyles die from internal injuries? What about half-gargoyle hybrids?

All these questions swirled in my brain as I watched them circle each other warily again. One would feint forward and then retreat. They did this for a few more moments, both of them heaving in air.

Romanus grinned. His face covered in blood, his lip split, and he smiled at Naz. I couldn't work out if it was sweet or unnerving as hell.

"You are a great fighter. A worthy addition to the pack," he said, though he remained tensed to defend.

Was he conceding Alpha?

He answered my question in the next move. With more dexterity, and defiance of gravity itself, he did a hard turning kick to the side of Naz's temple. Naz's head snapped to the left and I sucked in a hard breath. That had to have broken his neck. I was running toward them before my brain even comprehended what my feet were doing.

Naz was on the ground, and Romanus was over him, sharp canines pressed so hard into the column of Naz's neck that rivulets of blood pooled on the ground underneath him.

"Do you submit?" Romanus growled, and the sound was not even remotely human. It was the voice of something primordial. Alpha power pushed Rouen to his knees. Even Charlie looked shaken, and he wasn't even gargoyle. While the alpha power crawled against my skin, I didn't feel the need to submit. I continued to run toward them, but I skidded to a stop a few feet away.

"Submit," Romanus growled again. Naz didn't answer. Fuck, fuck, fuck. He was dead. This couldn't be happening.

A huge shudder ran through Naz's body, and he tipped his head to the side.

"I submit, Alpha." The words were a choked out growl, but they were sincere. Thank god. My Alpha took Naz's throat between his teeth and bit hard.

Romanus pulled back and ran his tongue over the puncture marks on Naz's neck, and they healed before my eyes. I hesitantly walked the remaining steps, falling to my knees beside them.

I cried. I couldn't tell if it was the rush of adrenaline from my fear, the reverberation of Rouen's worry, or the lingering pain from both Naz and Romanus' injuries, but the whole thing was suddenly just too much. I sobbed my black little heart out and hated every second of it. I hated showing weakness. I hated being a fucking damsel.

Rouen barreled into us, the weight of his body knocking me into the guys until we were one huge puppy pile. The breath left my lungs in a whoosh, though Romanus was doing his best to take the brunt of his Beta's weight.

Rouen hugged us all, his huge arms made to encompass his pack. I could feel his overwhelming relief as if it were my own. Eventually, we all extracted ourselves and Rouen moved back a few feet. He took off his shirt, slowly exposing his gold dusted skin.

"Uh, Rouen, what are you doing? Put your clothes back on." Or not. I enjoyed the view but I had no idea why he'd be stripping in the middle of a forest. He leaned over and kissed me, and I reveled in the feel of his lips against mine.

"There's not some kind of ceremonial orgy that's about to happen, right?" I shot a look at Charlie, who was watching our little group like a starving man. His eyes were big and brimming with longing, his normally smiling mouth turned down at the edges.

"Normally, yes. It cements everyone's position in the pack, strengthens bonds and doubles as a celebration at the completion of the pack." Rouen followed my gaze. "But our pack still has one member to go."

He turned toward Romanus and Naz. He crawled toward Romanus first. "Alpha." He pressed his cheek to the ground, his neck bared, but he looked up at his Alpha, grinning.

Romanus hauled him up onto his feet. "Beta." Then he kissed him hard on the lips, before taking the vulnerable neck gently between his teeth. Rouen shuddered, and Romanus released him.

Then Rouen turned to Naz, and did the same submissive gesture, cheek to the ground. "Second."

Naz raised both eyebrows. "I'm not gonna kiss you, man."

Rouen laughed, but didn't rise from his position. "I wouldn't want you too. You're not my type."

I coughed. "Liar."

He smiled at me wickedly. Naz ignored the expression, leaning in to bite hard on the back of Rouen's neck. And that was that. Weird dominance ritual complete.

Romanus turned toward me, his expression one of love, his body brimming with power. "Do you accept me as Alpha, my Queen?" I nodded as words failed to get past the swelling lump of emotions in my heart.

"Always."

Romanus raised his eyes and looked behind me. Charlie stood staring down at me, his expression even more shattering up close. I stood awkwardly, uncomfortable like I'd been caught doing something intimate. Which I guess we had been. I hated excluding Charlie.

"Turn me." His voice was rough, as he held back the emotion that was displayed so openly on his face.

I reared back in shock. "What? No! We aren't vampires. I'm not turning you."

Charlie grabbed my shoulders. "I want to be part of the pack. I want to know if you've been stolen away right under my nose and I don't even notice because I'm just standing there with my thumb up my ass waiting for you to come out of the bathroom. I want to know when you are hurt, or happy, or angry. I want to be almost indestructible so I can protect you."

I was shaking my head before he'd even finished. I could feel the intensity of the eyes behind me. None of them spoke, a silent statement that it was up to me.

I reached up and pressed a hand to his cheek. "Charlie…"

"It was the worst feeling ever, Rella. I thought you were going to die, or worse, and it would have been my fault."

I tried to wrap my arms around him, but he pulled away, stepping around me to stand in front of my Alpha. He looked down at Romanus. "Change me like you changed Nazir."

Romanus stood, coming to stand behind me. He towered over me, but his body language was clear. He was second to me. My decision would be final.

"I want you to be Pack, Charlie. It's an ache in my soul, a loose connection where you should be. But not like this. Not with your head all messed up about tonight. Not because you feel guilty, or hurt, or left out or whatever is going on in that sexy head of yours. I want you to join us because you want to be with us forever. Because you seem to forget it is forever, Charlie. No take backs. And it's not just with me, it's with all of us. That's a lot of people to have in your head. A really long time to be with another person, another four people, no matter what you might feel for me now." I grabbed his hands, squeezing them tight and imploring him to understand with my eyes.

Watching Charlie's face as he processed my rejection was like watching the seven stages of grief in time-lapse, his face contorting rapidly with so many emotions. Rejection, despair, anger, sadness. I was waiting for acceptance, but all I got was a dismissal as he wrenched his hands from mine and walked back to the car.

Nazir came to stand on my other side. "You made the right choice." He wrapped his hand around mine, but it was still tacky with blood. Charlie didn't understand now, and I could only hope that when the events of tonight weren't quite as fresh, he'd forgive me.

CHAPTER SIXTEEN

For the first time in a few weeks, I slept alone. I kicked the guys out of my room and snuggled down in the blankets by myself. I didn't want to pour salt in Charlie's wounds, although he'd disappeared as soon as stopped outside the hotel. Nazir had followed along behind him, melting into the bustling crowds.

I laid long ways across the bed. I stuck my head under the pillow. I laid on my stomach, my back, the freaking downward facing dog position, but nothing was comfortable. I missed them. I'd gotten used to sleeping wrapped in a cocoon of hard muscle.

I tiptoed out of the room, moving on silent feet. I walked toward the sound of voices, and I knew the guys would be in front of the windows, letting the sun heal their wounds and restore their energy.

What I didn't expect was for them to be completely naked. They looked like lizards in the sun; a comparison I wasn't sure they'd appreciate. The sun shimmered off their skin, making it look like it was oiled, but I knew their skin was smooth and soft. They didn't move from their positions, lying on their stomachs, perfectly muscled asses on display like beautiful sculptures. I wanted to run my hands over the hard lines of their body about as much as I wanted my next breath. Maybe more.

They both slid their eyes to me but didn't say a word. Romanus crooked a finger, beckoning me forward. I sat down between them.

"The sun will help," Rouen said from the corner of his mouth. "It works better if it can touch your skin." He didn't clarify what it would help, but I trusted Rouen.

I was only in one of Naz's shirts and my panties on anyway, so I peeled the shirt off. I left on my sports bra and underwear, not quite game to go as naked as my gargoyle lovers. They looked at my body appreciatively, but neither one of them looked lascivious. Now was not the time for sex.

I laid between them, my head on Romanus' back and my thighs draped over Rouen and let the sun soak into my skin. I sighed at the blissful feeling. I could almost feel every cell of my body vibrating with renewal, bursting with life. No wonder Romanus and Rouen spent so much time just lying like statues. I could feel my body restore itself one cell at a time. The newly minted nymphomaniac inside me wondered what it would be like to make love to them in a field, the sun shining down on us all, a light breeze cooling kisses over bare skin.

I smiled at the thought as the warmth of the sun,

and the comfort of my guys, lulled me into an exhausted sleep.

A SHADOW BLOCKING out my light woke me. I looked up to see Naz smiling down at me, his head silhouetted by the setting sun.

I blinked, lifting a hand to wipe the crud from my eyes. "What?"

He shook his head, making the tattoos that crept up his neck dance. "Nothing. I was thinking about this whole… situation. Just looking at this beautiful woman that stole my life and somehow transformed it into something better, that I'd made love to only days ago. Now here you are, draped over two naked guys, and I feel nothing but contentment. If I'd tried to explain how things would turn out to eight year old me, the boy that lived in a city torn apart by war but didn't know any other life, he would never believe me." He let out a soft warm laugh. "Or even ten year old me that walked over the corpses of his dead family to have his little brother healed by an archangel. That boy didn't believe I would live to see another day, let alone another twenty years" He reached down and lifted me up, pulling me into his arms. "Even thirteen year old me who was now loved, but I still had such raw pain in my heart the I could never shake. Hell, if you'd told me last year, when I'd put a gun in my mouth in a bid to hold back the darkness, that less than a year later I would be here, immortal, oddly happy and half in love with a Gargoyle Queen… well, I probably would have pulled the trigger because I would have thought I was crazy."

I stiffened at his words, holding him tighter to me. The idea of a world without Naz was an antithesis to me. I needed him just as much as I needed Romanus and Rouen. He was mine, and I refused to let anyone, even himself, take him from me.

"Your monsters can play with mine, because there is no way I'm letting you go." He ran light fingers up and down my spine, and I shivered at the touch. "You are mine now, Nazir. Your darkness, and your light."

He kissed me lightly, our lips barely touching. "Yes, my Queen."

A hand curled around my ankle. "I'm not ready to wake up yet," Rouen groaned. "Take off your clothes and come lie with us," he said to Naz, and there was nothing sexual in the offer. He really did just want us to all lie together in a gargoyle pile. He was so damn cute for a giant, head-rending, people eating, demon.

"Not today, Rou. I need to borrow our girl."

Our girl. The warm glow of pleasure lit me up from the inside out, although I was trying not to show it. Rouen's lip curled and I mentally slapped my forehead. Emotions. They can read me like a children's book. I knew I was never going to win a poker game with these assholes ever.

Romanus cracked open an eye. I wondered if he was going to protest me leaving with Naz, but he just looked between us and closed his eyes again.

"Keep her safe." The *or else* was implied.

Naz nodded. "Yes, Alpha."

I blinked a couple of times. Given all their bickering, they'd settled into their new dynamic with ease.

Naz ran a hand down my bare spine, and I curved my body towards him. He made a satisfied hum as his hand slid over the slope of my butt. Then he sighed and took a step back.

"I'm going to kick Charlie's ass for this tomorrow, but we gotta go."

I nodded, heading for the bedroom as I pulled Naz's shirt back on. I shimmied into my jeans and boots and was standing back in front of Naz in minutes. I still had bed hair. Was it still called bed hair if I was technically lying on someone's chest? Naz reached out and fingered the hem of my shirt. His shirt. Whatever. "Looks good on you."

I threw a look at my gargoyle statues in front of the window. They were both still feigning sleep, and Rouen was letting out small theatrical snores. I'd slept beside him. He didn't snore. I rolled my eyes at his ridiculousness, but I had to admit that perhaps that bubbly feeling in my chest might be something like love.

I followed Naz into the elevator, and he hit the ground floor button. "Where are we going?" I asked, resting my body against his as the lift sped downwards.

"The hotel bar." Naz tightened his arms around my waist and kissed the top of my head.

"Like, on a date?" There was a pathetic amount of hope in the question, and I kicked myself instantly. I didn't need dates. I didn't have time for dates.

Naz's chest vibrated against my cheek, his small chuckle disturbing my already wild hair.

"Not today, Babe. Today, we have to go peel a pouty Irishman off a barstool. When we get Stateside again, though, I'll take you on a hundred dates." He leaned forward and kissed me softly. I was beginning to associate those soft, yearning kisses with Naz. They were always so gentle, but they set me on fire.

"I'm going to hold you to that."

The doors slid open and we walked through the lobby to the bar. Luckily, it wasn't overly crowded at mid-afternoon, so spotting Charlie was easy.

He was a mess. He was leaning on his hand, his elbow pressed to the polished wooden bar top. So polished that Charlie's elbow kept slipping, and his head would drop so fast I was worried he was going to give himself whiplash. The bartender, a pretty girl about my age who was made up just enough that horny businessmen would give her big tips but not think she was a hooker, was giving Charlie a look that was halfway between amused and annoyed, but she relaxed when she spotted Naz stride up. She more than relaxed actually, she preened like a goddamn chicken, her eyes watching Naz hungrily.

I resisted the urge to stake my claim. I was a bigger person than that. I wasn't threatened by some random bartender that looked like a Victoria Secret model.

I ignored her and sat beside Charlie. I leaned forward until I could catch his eye. He reared back like I'd somehow appeared by magic, a huge drunken grin on his face. "Rella Rua!"

Charlie had always been a jovial drunk, which was great given his family's love for whiskey and machismo.

"Hey, Charlie Bear. Ready to head home?"

He threw the stink eye over his shoulder at Naz. "I told you I didn't wanna leave," he pouted. "The nights just getting started."

"It's four in the afternoon," Naz corrected, resisting the urge to smile.

"Bringing Relly here was a low blow, dude. I thought we were friends." He downed his whiskey, and I wondered how much he'd been tipping that the bargirl if she was still serving him while he was this messy. I scowled in her direction, but she didn't notice. She was too busy eyefucking Naz.

A growl rose in my throat, and I swallowed it down. But the noise caught the girl's attention. I tried to choke back the words, but I couldn't fight the instinct.

"Mine," I growled out. "Eyes off." It sounded primal, the threat implied. Apparently, I wasn't the bigger person. Whatever the girl saw in my expression made her all but run to the other end of the bar.

I looked at Naz and he raised his eyebrows. I just scowled. I hated feeling like I wasn't in control of my own basic instincts.

I turned back to Charlie, who was looking between us all like he was a spectator at Wimbledon.

"Come on, Charlie. It's time to go."

This time, Charlie came without a fuss. He wobbled precariously on his feet but righted himself enough to walk on his own. I still stood close enough to steady him when he banged into tables and people.

He flung an arm over my shoulders, and we walked the short distance back to the elevator.

"If she'd been looking at me like that, would you have sexy growled at her?" Charlie asked, and I willed the lift to descend a bit faster.

"Yes."

He sighed. "No, you wouldn't. That was the Queen who growled, not my Rella."

The shiny gold doors slid open and I walked in, my arms still supporting Charlie.

He continued. "No, you wouldn't. You don't love me the way you love them. You love me because I've been here forever. It's not the same."

I sighed. That was it.

I grabbed Charlie's chin. "Now you listen to me, Charles Fucking Mulligan. I love you with every fiber of my being, right down to the darkest corner of my fucking soul. One day, the Gargoyle Queen will make you hers, and I'll have an eternity to show you how much I want you. But know this, even before all this, before the mystical vigilante bullshit, simple, ordinary Estrella Jones loved Charlie Mulligan, and I will until I take my last breath. So pull your fucking head out of your ass already, you big baby."

I was shouting at him, inches from his face, his eyes staring into mine unblinkingly. He dove for my mouth in a rather haphazard way, kissing me with the abandon of a person who has lost all their inhibitions to malt whiskey. What he lacked in coordination, he made up for in raw passion. He picked me up and pressed me a little too hard into the wall of the elevator, his body grinding between my thighs as I kissed him back. He tasted like whiskey and longing.

He pulled back, sucking in air. "I love you so much, Rella. So much that it fucking hurts and the thought of not spending my life with you makes me feel like my heart is gonna explode." He made an exploding fist action, complete with sound effects, which caused me to slide down the wall a bit more. "And I don't even care that you love the other guys, or if you never love me back, or if the idea of watching you touch them, or letting them touch me makes me hard as fuck even though I don't know why, and I..." he stopped and cocked his head to the side adorably. "Where was I going with this?"

I looked over his shoulder and raised my eyebrows in shock at Naz.

"You were telling her how much she means to you, buddy," Naz said in a completely neutral tone even though his shoulders were shaking with contained laughter.

"Oh, yeah! I love you, Rella and I want to marry you and make love to you and cook you breakfast and have babies with your red hair that won't ever have to become criminals and we'll live in a nice house... oh this is our floor." He stepped through the elevator doors and I shuffled out after him. Naz put his hand on my back as we watched Charlie pinball his way down the hallway to the wrong door. "He's not gonna remember any of this, is he?" I asked. Naz shook his head, and I sighed. "This one, Charlie Bear," I shouted down the hall.

He looked at me, then at the offending door, then back at me. "Oh."

He walked over and banged loudly. Rouen appeared

almost immediately. He was still naked. Charlie looked him over, one eye closed to keep everything in focus. "Why do you fuckers have to look so good naked? Doesn't matter, I'm gonna marry Rella and we'll be sister-husbands." He stumbled forward, tripped over the edge of the mat, landed on his face on the ground and just stayed there. "I'm good. I'm just gonna stay here, okay?"

He was asleep in seconds, soft snores echoing around the room.

Rouen was holding his stomach as he wheezed out a laugh. "Holy hell, that was the funniest thing ever. I love that kid." He leaned down, scooping up the passed out Charlie into his arms, carrying him gently to the couch. He pulled the soft blanket over his lap, tucking him in.

Romanus came up behind me, still naked too. We all looked down at our wayward fifth. "He's going to be hurting tomorrow." A small smile played at the corners of his mouth.

Naz cleared his throat. "If you guys could put some clothes on, that'd be great. I don't want to look at your ancient dicks for the rest of my days."

Rouen sniffed. "I'll have you know that my dick is as young and nubile as a twenty-one year old. Ask Rella."

I raised both hands. "Leave me out of it," I laughed, walking to the kitchenette to get Charlie a glass of water, and the bottle of aspirin from my purse.

The guys went and pulled some pants on, and Naz ordered dinner from room service. I pulled a beer from the mini fridge and cracked it open. I'd earned a stupidly expensive beer today.

I boosted myself up onto the granite bench top and took a long swallow of the cold brew. Naz came and stood in front of me, nestling his body between my thighs. Rouen walked over, now clad in pants which was a pity, and pulled another beer from the mini fridge. He handed one to Naz, who took it gratefully.

Romanus was the last to appear, fully clothed, and he leaned on the bench. He looked at Naz. "What should we do?"

The simple question hung in the air. It was a white flag, an understanding between the Alpha and his Second.

"I think we should attend this auction. My connection might be able to get us at least an address. If I pay him enough, he might be able to get us an invite. He's… connected."

Well, that sounded cagey.

Rouen scoffed. "He's an arms dealer. Yeah, he's connected."

I raised both my eyebrows at Naz. His source was an arms dealer? "What kind of merc were you?"

Naz just shook his head, his body tensing between my thighs. "That's classified."

"It wasn't for the government like I thought, was it?"

He met my gaze, the silver of eye that marked him as gargoyle swirling. "No"

I ran my eyes over his face, the straight autocratic nose, to the slight scar on his cheek. There was still so much I didn't know about all of them, these men I'd tied my life to for all eternity. I just had to trust my instincts that it was right. The rest I could learn later. I bit my lip, repeating to myself that I wasn't a cop anymore. My idea of right and wrong had become one large grey area in the last two weeks. I had no room to judge.

"Money's no object. Pay him what he wants to get us an invite. I'd like to see what is going on from the inside." I took another long pull from my beer bottle. His body was still rigid, and I reached out to stroke his cheek. "Will you go back? After this is all over?"

He shook his head. "My life has a different purpose now." He stared unblinkingly into my soul and I forgot how to breathe. I was pretty sure that was as close as I was going to get to a declaration of love from Nazir from a long, long time.

I WALKED into the kitchen the next morning to find it empty of everyone except a very sad, very hungover Charlie, who was eating bacon and eggs, and looking distinctly green.

He looked at me warily, the jubilant drunken Irishman of last night completely gone.

"Estrella…" he started but trailed off.

I poured myself a coffee and topped his up as well. I sat down across from him.

"It's fine, Charlie." I didn't want another awkward conversation, and I had a sneaky suspicion that he didn't remember his antics from the elevator.

"It's not okay, Rella. I'm sorry for how I treated you. It was just the circumstances. It won't happen again." He hung his head, his tone as cool and distant as I'd ever heard it. The gulf had opened back up between us, and I wondered if we were going to be able to bridge it this time.

"Just forget it, okay? We'll figure it out," I insisted.

I sipped my coffee, and a heavy silence fell over the table. "Where's Naz?" I asked to break the tension.

He stuffed some bacon into his mouth, chewing slowly as if it physically pained him. If my heart wasn't hurting so bad, I'd probably grin at his self-inflicted suffering.

"Nazir is making calls to try and get you guys an invite to the auction."

I knew where Rouen and Romanus were. They were still in my bed. They'd held me, stroking my body to completion so many times last night I felt like an instrument they knew how to play on instinct.

I smiled at the memory, but it faded as I looked at Charlie. I wanted to grab him, tell him that I loved him too and that's why we had to wait, but I knew it was useless. He needed to come to that conclusion himself.

I just hoped our friendship would survive until he did.

CHAPTER SEVENTEEN

I sat beside Naz in a sparkling black sequinned dress, the rumble of a Maserati vibrating under my ass as it navigated the winding, country road. My sexy mercenary was dressed like he'd stepped out of GQ, diamond cufflinks sparkling on a crisp white shirt. His tailored Armani suit jacket was spread over the barely existent backseat.

Naz's source had come through with an invitation, and although the loss of twenty grand would make my accountant wince, it was worth it.

Pedro the Arms Dealer hadn't been what I expected. For one, he was Dutch. I don't know why he was called Pedro, and I didn't want to ask. As if that weren't unusual enough, he looked like one of those bad Walmart pictures. He wore a hideous brown and green striped sweater that went out of fashion in the eighties and weird aviator glasses. He was short, a little soft around the middle, and had a wide friendly smile like a piranha.

But he was very respectful, even as he took my money and handed me an invitation for a midnight auction to buy abducted people.

We'd dressed like we were going to a ball and rented this giant hard-on on wheels like we had more money than morals. Like this was an event filled with paparazzi, rather than people wearing Berettas like accessories.

We pulled up in front of a beautiful estate house, ivy running up the walls like a picture straight out of glossy magazine. The Maserati proved to be the right decision, as the parking lot was like a showroom of the luxury European cars.

We pulled up in front of the valet station and I wrapped the white fox fur stole around my shoulders. Even touching something that used to be alive weirded me out. But I figured if I was playing the part of someone who would buy a person, I probably wasn't a member of PETA.

Naz's eyes were dead, and he threw the keys to the Maserati at the valets. Three huge, and definitely armed, security guards stood in front of the doors. I plastered a bored, entitled look on my face. I knew the look. I'd gone to the best private school my parents could afford, and there were quite a few entitled princesses I'd had to slap down in my time. When Hope wasn't watching, of course. She couldn't abide violence.

Naz handed the security gorillas the invitation, his own face incredulous like they should just *know* who he was. They pulled out a UV light, and I held my breath. I hadn't known there were extra security features. Pedro better not have fucked us over, otherwise we were as good as dead. We'd see how well half gargoyles stood up to a bullet in the head.

A faint purple word glowed under the UV light. *Tenebrae.* What the hell did that mean? The smaller of the muscle-bound gorillas waved us in, and I sashayed past him like he was dirt. A woman in a tight black dress and a tiny white apron handed me a glass of champagne. I took it but didn't make eye contact. My eyes were big and smoky and my lips were blood red, making my pale skin pop. It was as close to a disguise as I could get without being obvious.

"The auction is being held in the ballroom. Please feel free to go and register, then take a seat."

We didn't deign to answer and headed toward the hushed voices in the ballroom. We took a seat at the back, and I cast my eye over all the people in the room. I held back a gasp as I recognized more than a few powerful people. People who had been in Forbes magazine, or in the society pages of gossip rags. But there were more people I didn't recognize, people with greedy eyes that skimmed my body and made my skin crawl. I held onto Naz's arm tighter. Naz was just as fucking scary, and I needed these vultures to know that I was with a freaking pterodactyl, and he was a thousand times scarier than they were.

I skimmed the rest of the crowd and my eyes halted on a red-haired man. I sucked in a gasp. I didn't recognize the man, but I recognized the aura.

Archangel.

I'd only ever met one in my life, Raphael, when he'd been patching up Hope. This definitely wasn't

Raphael. He was tall and had flaming red hair that wasn't seen naturally in the human race, but you could probably pay hundreds of dollars to achieve it at a salon. His skin had a luminescence to its paleness. His eyes were cold and calculating. He scared the shit out of me, but I knew he wasn't a Fallen. I knew all the Fallen personally. Hell, they'd all come to my fifth birthday party. Now I'd focused on him, seen through the glamor he must be casting because the humans in the room didn't seem to notice him, the strength of his power almost burned against my skin. Definitely an archangel.

I gripped Naz's forearm tightly, my nails digging into his suit. "Naz…"

"What the hell?"

I looked at him. "I know rig…" But Naz wasn't looking at the Archangel. He was looking at a face that was entirely more familiar.

"What the hell?" I agreed. "What is Gus doing here?"

Gusion was a Prince of Hell, one of Luc's Fallen Angels. He also gave me a unicorn stuffy for my seventh birthday. And I still had a collection of feathers from his beautiful white and gold wings.

I stepped toward Gus, about to ask him myself, when a man appeared at the lectern, hammer in hand.

"Welcome everyone to tonight's auction. We have some real treasures for you tonight," the staid looking man intoned, as if we were at Sotheby's or something.

Naz pulled me gently to our seats. I sat down, twisting my paddle in my hand. Naz reached out and stilled the nervous gesture, his eyes holding both a warning and reassurances.

The crowd quieted down and the MC cleared his throat. "Let's get on with tonight's proceedings, shall we?" He opened his notes. "First up in lot 346. Just seventeen, and in wonderful condition…"

"You shouldn't be here," a voice sitting in the row behind us hissed. Another familiar voice. My head whipped around so fast it hurt.

"Ace? What the fuck are you doing here?" I looked at my pseudo parent, my mother's best friend. Also Fallen Angel and Lucifer's consort. I knew her face as well as I knew my own.

"That doesn't matter, you guys have to-"

She was cut off by the doors to the ballroom crashing in, and armed men in SWAT gear pouring in like a wave.

"*Policier*. This is the Police. Do not move," someone screamed from behind a helmet. Then there was pandemonium as people tried to rush the exits.

A semi-automatic weapon was pointed at my face before we could even stand. Shit.

Ace sighed and put her hands in the air too. "Too late."

PART III

CHAPTER EIGHTEEN

I'd been sitting on the cold bench inside the holding cell for so long my ass had gone numb. Both my Louboutin's and my fox fur wrap had been confiscated in case I tried to pick the cell door with a heel or something. I was freezing, shoeless and a little pissed.

Ace sat beside me, chewing her fingernails and humming a Britney Spears song, not in the least bit perturbed by the fact that we were currently in jail for attending an auction where the product was human beings.

There were eleven women in my jail cell. Three more from the auction, two women who looked like they were coming down off something hard, three angry looking hookers and a woman in her seventies with tightly rolled curls and not a single care in the world. Ace and the old lady had been having a great time. The old lady gave my Fallen Angel pseudo-parent the recipe for 'the best hash brownies on the planet'. Direct quote.

The police hadn't believed me when I said I thought

we were attending an art auction. I wouldn't believe me either. Naz sat in the cell next to me with twenty-five other men, and he looked so murderous that everyone gave him a wide berth.

A police officer came up and banged on the bars. "Estrella Jones, Arcadia Jones, Nazir Ashear, come to the front. Your lawyer has arrived."

I huffed out a sigh of relief that Gus or my guys had finally arrived to bust us out.

"Mom's going to be peeved that you used her name when you got fingerprinted," I told Ace, who had a stupidly big grin on her face. She loved to mess with my parents. But it was all in good fun. They loved one another in a way the defied human sensibilities. They were two pieces of one soul, kind of like Hope and I, but realms apart.

One of the men Nazir's cage began to yell again about who he was and how his lawyer was going to sue everyone in the city of Geneva, but I ignored him as I strode past the cop to the desk to collect my things. I'd heard his diatribe on repeat ten times already. I signed for my stuff, and turned as I placed my stoll around my shoulders.

My heart sank. The guys hadn't talked us out of our prison cell. Standing on the other side of the room, looking supremely pissed off, was Luc. He frowned in our direction, and I felt about three inches tall.

Ace swaggered up and laid a hard kiss on his lips, and then smiled up at him. "If you keep frowning like that, the wind will change and you won't be so pretty anymore."

Luc smiled down at her with so much love that I wondered how humans could be so petrified of him. Anyone who had the capacity to love another being the way Luc loved Ace couldn't be all bad.

Then he turned his eyes towards us, and they were as hard as flint. I resisted the urge to run. I retracted my earlier thoughts.

"Let's go."

I was moving before he'd even finished the word. As much as I liked to needle him sometimes, because I knew deep down he loved me too, there was a time and a place for it. The police station was not the place, and now was definitely not the time.

Romanus, Rouen, Charlie and Gus stood on the sidewalk outside the station, and my heart leapt when I saw the guys. I ran straight into Charlie's arms and wrapped myself around him before either of us got the chance to be weird.

He stiffened but eventually relaxed into an embrace that was oh so familiar to us both.

I inhaled deeply, letting his scent soothe me. Rouen came up and wrapped both Charlie and me in his arms.

"We missed you," he murmured against my hair. "Charlie was getting ready to bake you a cake with a nail file in it." I felt the vibration of Charlie's laugh against my cheek.

Someone cleared their throat. I turned to see Ace grinning and Luc looking annoyed. "Can you please leave your public displays for somewhere other than the front of the police station?" he grumbled. He looked at his watch. "I must go, but I will be back to discuss this," he waved a hand at Romanus, whose face was a stone mask, and Rouen. "Apparently, Estrella, you do not understand the concept of a loan. The souls of the *Gargoille* still belong to me."

I whirled around and faced him. "No," I growled.

He appeared in front of me, leaning down so we were nose to nose. "I am the Lord of Hell, Little Girl. Their souls are tied to me."

I stiffened my spine, leaning forward and staring him in the eye. I held myself steady, even though I wanted to run away screaming. I pointed a finger at his face. "I am the Gargoyle Queen. They belong to me. Heart and soul."

He lifted a hand and I tried not to flinch. He reached over and patted my cheek, smiling proudly then looked over his shoulder at Ace. "Kids. They say the darndest things." He shook his head with bemusement. "We will see, Child of my Beloved's Heart." With one more little cheek tap, he was gone. Just poof.

I looked at Ace. "He can't do that, right?" She raised an eyebrow. Of course. He was Lucifer, he could do whatever the hell he wanted. "He wouldn't do that, I mean."

Ace just shrugged. "I'll talk to him." With that, she disappeared too. I was left on the sidewalk with my guys and Gusion, who was attracting far too much attention. He was classically attractive. He looked like a Californian surfer and a Roman statue had a golden, ridiculously good looking child.

"Are you going to just poof out of here too, or are you going to stick around and explain why two Fallen and an Archangel were doing attending a meat market?"

Tiny creases wrinkled his perfect nose, and he looked to be considering his answer. Finally, he sighed too.

"Fine. I will meet you at your hotel." And then he was gone. Fallen Angels were not known for their social etiquette. I looked around, hoping that there wasn't security cameras in front of the building that were filming their little vanishing trick.

When Gusion disappeared, the tension left Romanus' shoulders. He wrapped an arm around my waist and ushered me to the car. "Let's get out of here before Interpol change their mind about Nazir," he said as the tail lights of our car flashed.

"Interpol?" I asked, and looked at Naz's carefully blank face.

It was Charlie who answered. "Apparently, there's a list somewhere that has Naz's prints on them as a person of interest in some undisclosed cold cases. It took Luc a lot of fast talking to get him out, and Gusion a lot of fast talking to get Luc to give enough fucks to want to make the effort."

I slid into the car beside Charlie, Naz sliding into the other side so I was sandwiched between them, our legs all tangled in the small amount of room. I looked at their thighs touching mine, and resisted the urge to run my hands up both inseams. I cast a look at Charlie under my lashes. One day soon.

I pressed myself a little closer to him. I was going to change tactics. Giving him space to sort through his issues had failed. Plan B involved a lot of temptation until he cracked.

Making sure our bodies touched as much as possible, I turned to look at Naz. A small smile tilted up the corners of his mouth. I think he was on to me.

I broke the silence in the car as we pulled away from the curb. "Well, that was a bit of a clusterfuck," I stated redundantly.

Romanus scoffed. Well, it could have been worse. I was so damn tired. Someone should have told me that being this on edge all the time was exhausting. I snuggled closer to Charlie, who hesitated but eventually lifted his arm to wrap it around my shoulders. I laid my head against his chest, appreciating the steady thump of his heart. I moved my hand to his inner thigh, and slid it upwards, just to hear the sound of his tempo quicken. He sucked in a breath, and when my fingers brushed the hardening length in his pants, he put a hand over mine to still my exploration.

"Rella." It was both pained plea and chastisement. I grinned, and stopped moving.

I closed my eyes to nap, but I didn't move my hand. I liked the fast thump, thump, thump of his heart beneath my cheek.

I WALKED into our hotel room and resisted the urge to fall face first into bed. Gus had arrived before us and was currently surrounded by silver room service trays.

"Is that to share?" I asked, sitting opposite him at the

table. I hoped so. There were twelve domed trays, and when I lifted one I saw that it contained waffles.

My mouth watered. I loved waffles.

Gusion just waved at the table, inviting us to eat, and went back to looking at his paper. It was hard to remember that he was literally as old as time itself, considering without his wings and in his jeans with holes in the knees, he looked like a model in his early twenties.

I waited until everyone had filled their plates, and I'd shoveled at least half a waffle in my mouth, to start asking questions.

"So, who was the Archangel?" I said as I chewed. Apparently it wasn't just the Fallen who lacked proper social etiquette. My parents would be horrified.

"Uriel."

Huh. I didn't know much about what happened with my parents around the time Hope and I were born, and no one really talked about it, but I gathered two things from eavesdropping on conversations as a kid. One was that everyone hated Azriel, or Azriel the Dick as he was more commonly known as in our household. The second thing was that whenever they mentioned Uriel's name, they all said it with the exact same tone; disgust with an undertone of fear. Growing up, I knew absolutely no fear. With seven dads, the Devil as a father figure and the Mob as extended family, there wasn't much I had to fear. I could list them on one hand; Hope getting injured, jumping out of the oak tree in my backyard, and squirrels. I hated squirrels.

But when my parents talked about Uriel, it was like my heart did a small record scratch at his name, every single time. The Archangel Uriel became the boogeyman under my bed.

I'd grown out of it now. How dangerous could an Archangel be? There were rules that were pretty strictly enforced. It's why Gus fell in the first place.

"You are right to fear him, Estrella," Gus said, and I narrowed my eyes at him.

"You can't read my thoughts." It sounded more like a question than a statement.

Gus laughed, his smile lighting up the room. Damn he was pretty, but I wasn't interested in him like that. "No, but your face is comically easy to read at times." He folded his paper in half and rested it on the table beside him.

"Luc asked me to watch Uriel some time ago now, and I can tell you that he is not an angel you want to cross." He stopped and thought for a moment. "Actually, I wouldn't go pissing off any angels, but least of all Uriel. He is pretty rigid in his enactment of God's law and it gives him a lot of moral leeway. Consider him very Old Testament."

Romanus growled his agreement. "What was he doing at a slave auction anyway? The laws aren't that flexible, I know that much. Somehow, I don't think he was there to smite all the wrongdoers."

Gusion shook his head sadly. "No. He wasn't. He wasn't there to buy anyone either. I can't work out what he's up to exactly, but I know that morally, it is wrong, even if he isn't breaking any laws. That's just the kind of angel Uriel is. He is poisoned with cruelty, thinly disguised as salvation."

We ate in silence as we thought over Gusion's words. If he wasn't at the auction to buy a slave, what the hell was he doing there? Could it be possible we were all on the same side?

A fork stabbed a piece of waffle off of my plate and held it to my lips. I looked over at Rouen, who was eyeing me expectantly. "You aren't eating. And I can feel your hunger."

I rolled my eyes at him and took the offered piece of food. These guys took the hunter/gatherer thing to a whole new ridiculous level.

I suddenly remembered something. "Charlie, the invitation had the word Tenebrae written in UV ink as some kind of security measure. Can you look into what it means? Also, see if we can't hack one of the SWAT guys body-cams. I saw a lot of familiar faces last night, and I wouldn't mind having a list for a later date."

Gus laughed. "When you're done, give the list to Ace. She'd like to pay them all a personal visit to express her disappointment in their choice of purchases."

I knew what that meant. I'd definitely gotten my avenging streak from Ace. She may be Fallen, but she was still an adamant crusader for the weak and vulnerable. I smiled.

"Happily." Not even Charlie had a problem with that.

Charlie was eating toast as he typed away furiously on his computer. "Huh, Tenebrae means rising darkness."

I rolled my eyes. "That's a little cliché, don't you think?" They looked at me expectantly. "Seriously? The aid foundation is named Shine, and the shady sub branch literally translates to Darkness. That's a little on the nose, even for me."

Charlie just shrugged, shaking his head a little and went back to his computer. I stuffed the remainder of my waffle into my mouth. I had a hot date with a warm bed. I was done.

SOMETHING POKED MY CHEEK. I groaned and rolled over.

"Rella, wake up." Hands shook my shoulders, but I swatted them away.

"I'm sleeping, so unless you want to get naked and sleep too, go away."

A husky laugh that I recognized as Naz's rippled through the air. "I wish, sweetheart, but we gotta go. We've been made."

I was out of bed and on my feet in an instant, the blood rushing away from my brain making me woozy. Naz steadied me.

"What?"

"Charlie's dot bots picked up Interpol surrounding the building."

"We were cleared. Are they here for you?" I said as I jammed stuff in my backpack, dragging on my clothes quickly.

"I don't think they are here officially." Naz's voice was sharp, and I stared at the flinty look on his face.

"You think Shine, or Tenebrae or whoever it is, has Interpol on their payroll?"

Naz shrugged. "It would explain a lot of things."

I strapped my swords to my back, and threw a jacket over the top to hide their bulk. "I thought it was Interpol that raided the auction last night. Why would they do that and then try and track us down today?" I walked into the living room, to see everyone was packed. Gusion was gone.

"Last night was private mercs hired by Ace, in conjunction with local cops. When Charlie hacked into the police files, he found all the body-cam footage wiped, and apparently, Interpol has had control of your sister's case all along."

My brain whirled as I tried to take all this in at once. We left the room, walking quickly to emergency stairwell.

"Up," Romanus ordered. I could feel the intensity of his eyes on the back of my head. "We'll jump across and leave through the next building over."

I whipped my head towards him. "Are you insane? It's like twelve stories in the air. We'll die."

Rouen gave a mirthless laugh. "Gargoyles. We can make a fifteen foot leap."

"We aren't all gargoyles, Rou. What about me? And Naz. What about Charlie? Besides, would a gargoyle even survive a fall like that?"

I'd seem them take some serious damage, and I thought they were immortal, but it was all conjecture. They would survive more than a normal human, of that I was sure, but if they were nothing more than a bloody stain on the pavement below, would they just come back to life? There was so much I didn't understand.

It was Romanus who answered. "We wouldn't survive a fall like that in this form. We'd be recycled back to hell as immortal souls, until Luc wanted to restore our bodies again."

I stopped, tugging my hand from his.

"Then we aren't doing it. There's another way. There's always a different way."

Romanus just picked me up and hoisted me over his shoulder in a fireman's hold, climbing the stairs again quickly.

"I've calculated the odds. This is the best way, with the least likelihood of getting caught. I wouldn't put you in any danger that wasn't absolutely necessary. Now stop wiggling."

I gritted my teeth. "Fine." I knew he was right. Romanus was super overprotective. If there was even a slither of doubt that I couldn't do this, he'd find a different way. "Put me down."

He did, but didn't slow his pace. I sprinted behind him, puffing slightly. I was pretty fit, but running up six flights of stair was making my thighs burn.

We pushed open the door that said, "Do not open." Weren't we rebels?

We walked between the huge, whirring air conditioning units, keeping low. We made it to edge of the building and my stomach did backflips. There was a huge distance between the buildings. I looked down and took ten steps away from the edge.

"Thats a hard fucking nope!"

No one even answered me. Rouen just took a long run up and jumped between the buildings with ease. He made the distance, landing on his feet. I could feel my jaw hanging open. He grinned and waved.

Romanus looked at Charlie. "Do you consent to me you throwing you across?" Charlie looked pale. Probably as pale as me.

"Fuck no. You can't throw him." I grabbed Charlie's hand, and tugged him to my side. Romanus took Charlie's metal case, filled with all his tech gear, and tossed it across like a frisbee. Rouen caught it with ease.

"She won't go until you do," Romanus said to Charlie impatiently. "Naz, go!"

Naz took a slightly longer run up, and I held my breath as his foot hit the edge of the hotel's roof, his arms and legs windmilling. Fuck, he wasn't going to make it. His foot slipped on the lip of the other building, but Rouen was there, grabbing his arm and pulling him over.

I gasped out a breath. Thank god.

"Charlie next."

Charlie sucked in a big breath and nodded. He leaned over and kissed me deeply, like it might be the last time. I didn't want to watch but I couldn't look away.

Romanus grabbed him by an arm and a leg. "Sorry, kid. This is gonna be weird." He spun, whirling around like an olympian doing hammer throw. He turned and turned and then at the last minute, let Charlie go. My heart was in my throat as he flew in slow motion across the gap. He cleared the drop and Naz and Charlie caught him mid air, all three of them going down in a heap. I huffed out a relieved breath.

They were fine.

Romanus cocked his head to the side. "I can hear them coming up the stairs. We need to jump." He stood in front of me. "Wrap your arms and legs around my body and do not let go."

My heart hammered overtime. At this rate, I was going to have a heart attack. I jumped, circling my arms around his neck and wrapping my legs around his waist like a baby koala. I hope he didn't need to breathe, because I couldn't loosen my grip.

"Do you trust me, my Queen?"

I nodded against his back. "Implicitly."

"Close your eyes, Rella. It will be over in seconds."

He took the same length run up as Naz, and leapt. I squeezed my eyes tightly shut and prayed. Prayed to every deity I could remember. He jumped and there was the weightless feeling of flying. The only other time that was comparable was when I was on Romanus' back in dragon form. But then he had wings and it was a thousand times less terrifying.

We landed with a thud that shook me loose from his back, and I fell onto my butt on the rough surface of the neighbouring roof.

"Lets not do that again anytime soon, okay?" I said as Romanus reached down and helped me to my feet. He planted a quick kiss on my lips.

"We gotta go," he said, and pulled me along the rooftop to the door. We took the stairs all the way down to the parking lot, slightly staggered apart so we didn't draw attention. The guys weren't masters of blending in at the best of times. We finally all made it to the alley beside the hotel and walked quickly toward the nearest train station.

"What now?" All our carefully laid plans flew out the window when we got busted by the cops. Our element of surprise was gone.

"We head to Calais, to the big refugee camp there. Shine will have a presence for sure, because it would have several ways to move them out of the country. It's the ideal location to snatch desperate people from an unrecognized refugee camp, where there's very little governance," Charlie said. "We go there as representatives of the NRH. The time for stealth is gone, and we will get an element of protection that way. They won't be able to just bury us all quietly."

"Sounds solid to me," I told him, looking from Romanus to Naz. They both nodded.

"Separate, and meet at the coach station ASAP," Romanus ordered, snagging my hand. "You're with me."

Shocker. I pulled my cap down lower over my face, and we walked quickly toward the train station. Everyone else peeled off in different directions. I hated them being out of my sight, but understood the reasoning behind the order.

Romanus reached out and entwined his fingers through mine, pulling me closer to his side.

"Estrella?" The sound of his voice close to my ear startled me, and I jumped a little, bumping into a man talking on his cellphone.

I resisted the urge to apologize. "What?" My eyes searched the crowd for any hint of threat, but no one seemed to be paying us any attention, most either looking at their phones or with earbuds in listening to who knows what.

"I feel a great affection for you. I am glad you chose me as Alpha."

Shock stopped my feet, but Romanus' hand in mine tugged me along, making me quick-step to catch up.

"I didn't choose you for Alpha, Rom. You won that one, fair and square. Are you okay? Did you hit your head or something when we jumped?"

A small smile curled his lips, and I loved that smile. Romanus wasn't the most smiley of guys, he was the epitome of tall, dark and broody. But when he smiled, it was like a gut punch every time. Even a tiny grin warmed my insides.

"I've been alive a long time, well of a sorts anyway. I've experienced the full tumult of emotions available to a person. I guess, what I am trying to say is that I think I may love you, Estrella."

He didn't look at me as he said it, his focus in front of him as we made our way through the late afternoon foot traffic, and I was kind of glad because he would have seen me gaping like a cod. "This is hard for me, because for the last five hundred years, the only person I've had to care for is Rouen, who is gargoyle, and not fragile human."

"I'm not human anymore either," I blurted out.

"Perhaps not, but you are still more fragile than a normal Gargoyle Queen. You are different, beautiful in your fragility and it drives my beast wild that we could lose you if you are hit by a car, or trip down the gutter wrong. I have to resist the urge to drag you into a den and worship your body so you never want to leave."

The bus station loomed in front of us, rows of buses loading and unloading passengers like cattle trucks during peak hour.

I tugged him to a stop. "What are you trying to say, Romanus?" I stepped out of the flow of pedestrians, and he followed along behind me.

"What I am trying to say is that I am sorry if I am too suffocating. I am fighting the beast, because I know you would not do well caged, but I have lost a Queen before and it is a pain I would not wish on my worst enemy. The breaking of a bond to the Queen is crippling. But I didn't love my former Queen the way I love you. I had a great respect for her, and she was safe and soft and gentle, but I did not feel for her half of what I feel for you. If anything were to happen to you, I would not survive it. Neither would Rouen."

I blinked like an idiot for what seemed like an hour. Finally, I shook my head, shaking out the shock.

I knew how I felt. I knew what he wanted me to say. But for some reason, I couldn't make my lips move. It was too much. Too soon. Rational people didn't fall in love in three weeks. Rational people did not enact deadly vendettas against international criminals either. Rational people didn't fall in love with four completely different men.

So instead of saying those three little words, I leaned forward and kissed him hard, praying he could read my emotions, that he knew I loved him too. He kissed me back equally as fervently. He poured his feelings into that kiss.

"I promise to try and be safe," I whispered. It sounded lame, but I couldn't make my lips form the right words.

He straightened his shoulders and gave me one of his rare smiles, the one that curved his cheeks, crinkled his eyes and lit up my world. Then he released my hand, turning to continue walking toward the bus station.

As I watched him walk away, this strong, proud man, I got mad at myself. Charlie's words kept rolling around in my head, how I have the emotional capacity of a frat boy. But Charlie was wrong this time.

"Romanus?" I shouted. He turned, and the people parted for him like the Red Sea. He looked back at me, but didn't move toward me. I swallowed hard. "I love you too, okay?"

The smile he gave me made my heart stutter in my chest. "I know, Red. Now come on, our pack needs us."

CHAPTER NINETEEN

I huffed out a relieved sigh when I saw the guys on the bus to Paris. From there, we would catch a connection to Calais. They were all sitting in seperate seats close to the back, and we walked straight towards them. Rouen took up a whole seat, and Naz sat along the back row, his dead eyes warning away anyone stupid enough to bypass the seats toward the front. Romanus pushed past him and took up the opposite end. I stood next to Charlie's seat.

"Is this spot taken?" I said coyly, and Charlie smiled.

"This seat is always available for you," he replied and moved his case, shifting it beneath his feet. I pushed my pack into the luggage rack and sat down beside him.

I wondered what it would be like to meet Charlie like this, two strangers on a bus, without all our baggage and back history. Just a girl meeting a cute boy on a bus. Not that I would change our past for anything. I loved Charlie so much because I knew everything about him. I knew the very fabric of his soul.

With the sun streaming in through the window, making his hair shine like rose gold in the light, my breath caught in my throat. I didn't know if it was Romanus' declaration, or the events of the last week, or the fact he made my heart race, but I didn't want to wait any longer.

"Charlie?"

He had his head resting against the window, his eyes closed. "Mhmm?"

"We should get married."

His eyes snapped open so fast I thought they'd roll back into his head.

"What?"

This was how I must have looked thirty minutes earlier.

"I wanted to know if you would marry me?"

His eyes were glued to my face, and I let the little smile I felt at his shock creep onto my face. The bus pulled out of the station, and Charlie was still silent. His eyes hadn't left my face, and his mouth kept opening and closing like he was gasping for air. My heart pounded in my chest in his silence.

"What about…?" He tilted his head towards the guys. Rouen had the stupidest big grin on his face where he sat directly behind us. He looked like he was watching the climax of a rom com or something.

I shrugged and sent them all a questioning looks. "Is this okay with you guys?"

Romanus gave a disparaging grunt. "Of course we are okay with it."

Rouen clapped his hands like someone's grandma,

all palms. "We're gonna be sister husbands, finally!" he said way too loudly. I sent him a mock stern look, and Charlie looked puzzled. He didn't remember his declarations, but apparently Rouen was never going to let it go.

I raised an eyebrow at Naz. "'Bout time," he said, sending my a grin that pulled at my heartstrings. How'd I get so damn lucky?

I smiled at them all, and turned back to Charlie. "What do you say?"

He looked between us. "Are you sure? I mean, how? When?"

I laughed. "I've never been more sure of anything ever." I leaned forward and kissed him.

"Tomorrow?" he asked.

I blinked. I didn't think you could even organize a marriage that fast, but it wouldn't matter anyway. It wouldn't be legally binding Stateside until we hit up a courthouse, so why not?

I looked at Romanus, and he gave a small nod. We might not have a wedding with a priest and our families with us, but we could have a ceremony that was far more personal, and permanent, than anything humans could make up.

I leaned my head against Charlie's shoulder. "Tomorrow it is."

Tomorrow he'd become mine, and we would all be complete.

AS WE STEPPED off the bus in Paris, the first thing I

did was contact Hope. The rush of love and warmth that came through our bond made me smile.

Rella! I was worried about you.

Of course she was. That's what Hope did, worried about everyone and everything.

I'm fine, Sis. We're making good progress.

By getting arrested? She sounded amused, and I groaned.

Did Ace tell you? Crap, my parents were going to chew me out about this. From cop to criminal in less than a month.

No, the paparazzi turned up asking Mom what she'd been arrested for in Geneva. At a foundation luncheon. She was mortified.

Laughter bubbled from my lips, and the guys gave me a strange look. I waved at them to continue walking.

She can blame Ace for that one. I did try and talk her out of it. Anyway, I just wanted you to know that we want to head to the refugee camp in Calais in an official NRH capacity. Can you set it up? We think that the traffickers might be moving them from some of the less governed camps.

I could all but hear the cogs turning in Hope's mind. *It can be done, but it might take a day or two to get in touch with the right people, go through the proper channels so you can talk to people you can trust.*

Hmm. I really wanted this to be over now, so I could go home, but we could probably all use a day or two of down time.

That'll be fine, Sis. Besides, Charlie and I are getting married tomorrow, kinda, and I'm gonna make him Pack, so a couple of days would be good.

WHAT?!

Hope's squeal, even mentally, made me wince. And then I laughed.

It's time, Hope. If this whole thing has taught me anything, it's that I should take my happiness where I can. And I love Charlie. This has to happen. I feel it deep down in my soul, you know?

I could feel the happy hum of Hope's emotions. It definitely mirrored mine and Charlie's.

Of course it's time. I just didn't imagine you, of all people, rushing into marriage. You are like the world's biggest commitment-phobe. You agonized about getting a goldfish.

I laughed again, and Charlie wrapped an arm around my waist, pulling me closer. Naz had gone into the hire car place attached to the bus depot, and the guys were keeping watch. Charlie and I just stood in the shade of the ticket office, looking like nothing more than two kids on a honeymoon, with our stupidly large grins.

I know. But it's like the Gargoyles started chipping away at the wall, and once they made a hole, all this emotion I'd been bottling up just poured out. It was true. Romanus and Rouen had been like a battering ram to my emotional defences. Very sexy battering rams.

Duh, Rella. Empath, remember. I've known you've loved Charlie since you were twelve and he let you use his new skateboard before he'd even had a turn. You just needed to get there yourself.

I rolled my eyes. Sometimes being twin to an empath had its pitfalls. *I know, Hope. I better go. I love you.*

I sent my own wave of love and appreciation down the bond. She was worth every heartache I had to suffer on this journey. *I love you too, Relly. Stay safe, okay? Kiss my new brother-in-laws for me.*

I leaned over and kissed Charlie's cheek. "Hope is happy for us."

He pushed me back against the wall and nuzzled my neck, peppering little kisses down my collarbone. "Of course she is." He pulled back and looked me in the eye, a brief flash of uncertainty on his face. "You haven't changed your mind, right?"

I kissed him softly, reverently, finally enjoying the ability to just kiss him without worrying about everything that would come with us being together. His family, mine, the rest of the guys.

"Never." Worry crept into my gut. "Are you still sure? You are taking on a lot more than you wanted. I know your dream didn't include-" he kissed my lips again, silencing my doubts.

"I'm sure. It won't be exactly what I had in mind all these years, but as long as you are there, it'll be perfect. Besides, the demons are growing on me, and Naz is Naz. We will make it work."

I tried not let the doubts take control, but it was hard. I gave him one last kiss as Naz drove up in our new SUV.

"Need a ride?"

I gave him a saucy wink. "Just say the word." He laughed, but the heat in his eyes was anything but humorous.

We all piled into the luxury SUV, and I took a moment to appreciate that new leather smell.

Once we hit the road and were on an arterial highway out of Paris, I relayed what Hope told me about our "official" visit to Calais.

"We'll need a place to lay low for a couple of days until Hope sets it all up," Naz said absently to the car. Romanus' hand twitched every time Naz swerved between cars. He wasn't a great passenger.

"Somewhere out of Calais. Somewhere away from people," Romanus added. "We'll need... space for a couple of days."

I raised my eyebrows at Rouen, who just grinned back at me, a mischievous twinkle in his eye. I went online and booked us an out of the way cabin on the banks of the Somme under a fake name, and gave Naz the address. We sat in silence for a while, and I let the sun lull me and my thoughts into a contented daze. Pressed between Charlie and Rouen, I was as close to heaven as I was ever likely to get. Rouen's hand wrapped around my thigh, his fingers teasing the seams of my jeans absently. I desperately wished I wasn't wearing pants in that moment.

Rouen's nostrils flared, and he turned to look at me, heat making his eyes molten. Such beautiful eyes. He slid his palm up further, and I held my breath as he rubbed his hand firmly against my pussy through my jeans. I let out a tiny whimper, and suddenly everyone's eyes were on me. Feeling a little self conscious under the scrutiny of every male in the car, I wiggled away, but Rouen's hand travelled with me, gently petting, coaxing me back. He looked over my head at Charlie, and some kind of unspoken guy code thing must have passed between them, because Charlie hooked his fingers under my chin and turn my face to his so I was staring into his crystalline blue eyes.

His gaze ran over my face, taking in my features. "Damn, you are just so beautiful. I kept waiting and waiting for any other woman to compare to you, and every single one was lacking." He leaned forward, kissing the corner of my mouth, then my now parted lips, running his tongue across their fullness. His hand came up to cup my cheek, and he stroked the rough pad of his thumb over my cheekbone as he deepened the kiss.

Rouen's fingers deftly unclasped the button of my jeans, and I lifted my ass so he could wiggle them down over my hips and part way down my thighs.

I wanted to turn to look at him, but I was transfixed by Charlie's eyes. They were burning with an indescribable heat, the kind that made you want to jump into their depths and burn alive. "I can't wait to make love to you, Rella Rua. I can't wait to hear you scream my name when I fuck you."

I threw myself into the kiss, even as Rouen's fingers skittered through the folds of my pussy, flicking lightly over my clit, making my body jerk towards his hand. Charlie's tongue flicked in my lips, an echo of what Rouen was doing with his hand. I moaned against his lips, plunging my tongue into his mouth, dancing with his own. I pulled back and bit his bottom lip, making him groan. He dropped his hand from my cheek to my hip, sliding his hand up under my shirt and to my lace covered breast. He sucked in a little breath as his fingers skimmed over my already taut nipples.

"I can't wait to see you riding my cock," he groaned and shifted. I ran my own hand over his hard cock, trapped beneath his denim jeans. He grabbed my wrist and moved it away, shifting hands so he could trap it up above my head.

"Just let us love you, Rella. There will be eternity to return the favor, but for now, let us worship this beautiful body and listen to your pretty moans."

Charlie's fingers pinched my nipple lightly, and Rouen used the moment to slide a finger inside my dripping wet core.

"Oh," I whispered out on a breath, but it was captured by Charlie's mouth as he rolled my nipple between his fingers, his lips still working mine like a master. Rouen slipped another finger inside me and I arched against his hand, my moan echoing around the car.

I could hear Naz cursing softly in the driver's seat, but I was too caught up in Rouen's clever fingers and Charlie's soft lips. Charlie moved from my lips, pressing kisses across my jaw and down my neck, taking my earlobe into his mouth and sucking gently. Electricity ran up and down my spine as pleasure coursed through me.

The heel of Rouen's hand pressed tight against my clit, as he thrust his big fingers in and out of my pussy, curling them to reach my g-spot, working every pleasure zone inside me to bring me higher and higher. I threw back my head, letting Charlie kiss down my neck, over my collarbone and down between the valley of my breasts exposed by the V of my shirt. He moved the soft cotton aside, and I could feel the wet warmth of his breath against my skin as he pressed soft kisses to the swell of breast. He pulled the lace down, freeing my aching nipple to the air and the view of everyone in the car. And probably passing motorists. But not for long, because he moved to suck my nipple into his mouth, a light scrape of his teeth sending me wild against him. I wrapped my fingers in his strawberry blonde curls, keeping him where I wanted him, though I didn't think he'd move for the Devil himself right now.

Rouen used the moment to add another finger, stretching me deliciously wide as I let out a small scream that echoed around the car.

"Fuck!" Naz groaned, and the car swerved to the side of the road, the sound of gravel shaking me a little from my pleasure haze. Charlie moved up my body, kissing me.

"Don't worry about that, Rella Rua. Naz was just having a hard time concentrating with all those sexy noises you are making."

He moved back down to my other breast, and I forgot everything but the sensation of their skin against mine. I opened my eyes and I could see Naz's eyes in the rear view mirror, watching me as I writhed against my guys.

I could feel their pleasure at watching me, the sensation folding into my own and making it even more intense. I could feel my climax building beneath my skin, a prickling heat that was going to consume me, but was just out of reach. I desperately moved against Rouen's hand, my fingers holding roughly onto Charlie's hair.

"Oh fuck. Oh fuck. I'm going to come," I whimpered, and Rouen upped the speed his fingers. Charlie bit down on my nipple and that was it, I flew apart, clutching Charlie to me as if he was the only thing anchoring me to earth.

I panted, trying to suck in air.

Rouen slid his fingers from me, making me whimper at their loss. He leaned forward presenting his fingers, still glistening with my cum, to Romanus.

"Alpha."

Romanus leaned back between the seats and sucked Rouen's fingers into his mouth, his eyes holding mine. I moaned involuntarily. I'd seen them do this before on the plane, but it didn't get any less hot.

Romanus let out an involuntary grunt of pleasure, then bowed his head a little.

"My Queen." There were so many things layered into those two words, a whole range of feelings that I was only just beginning to grasp. He turned and smiled at Rouen. "Good work, Beta."

He looked at Charlie, who'd lifted his mouth from my nipple but still had his head resting on my chest. He winked, and I could feel Charlie's small smile against my skin.

Guys were weird.

"You good to drive, Naz?" He asked my dark eyed merc. Naz gave a shaky nod.

"I'm good, Alpha. My cock is harder than cement, but I'm good." He sent me a hot look in the mirror as he pulled back into the freeway traffic.

My guys straightened my clothes, interspersed with kisses. I felt worshipped. Loved.

Panic tried to sneak in. I cared so much now, my soft center of my feelings exposed and vulnerable. If anything happened to them, I would be nothing but a sad, empty husk.

Rouen pressed a kiss to my temple. "Relax, my Queen. We have you."

I rested my head on his shoulder, my hand wrapped in Charlie's. There was no room for doubt. This was right.

ROUEN AND ROMANUS had spent fifteen minutes talking in hushed whispers, too low for even my ears. I was getting suspicious. That suspicion doubled as we pulled into Amiens, still thirty minutes from our destination, and everyone had disappeared from the car. Rouen had dragged Charlie out of the car and hustled him onto the street, murmuring vague excuses and telling me he'd be back in thirty minutes. Romanus, Rouen and Charlie had disappeared into the crowded streets of Amiens, leaving me alone with Naz. He climbed into the back with me, leaning in to kiss me lightly.

"What are they up to?"

Naz grinned, and shook his head. "That's classified."

I pouted, which isn't a good look on a grown woman, but made him laugh. "Stick that lip back in, Rella, or I'll be forced to kiss it."

I raised an eyebrow. "Forced?"

He laughed more and cuddled me closer until I was on his lap. I rested my head against his shoulder. "This is all going to work out, right? I'm not making a mistake, tying him to us? Damning him like Adnan said?"

Naz pressed a kiss to my hair. "If it makes him half as happy as I am, then we'll all live a long and exciting life together."

"No regrets?" I wasn't sure I actually wanted the answer.

He shook his head. "None. It'll take a bit to get used to everything, but I'm happy enough."

"Despite the fact you've been stabbed, arrested, chased by Interpol and have to share me with three other guys?"

"Well, when you put it like that," he said, miming getting out of the car.

I smacked his shoulder and kissed him, appreciating the soft, yet commanding press of his lips against mine. His hand curled around my back, holding me to his chest. We sat in the warmth of the car, both silent, but it was a comfortable silence.

Eventually, I couldn't take it any longer.

"Wanna have sex in the cargo area?" I whispered, grinning.

He groaned. "Yes. But no. We don't have time, and I'm already walking around with a massive hard on as it is. But soon, I'm going to fuck you so good you won't even remember your own name." He gave me another blistering hot kiss and shifted me off his lap. I looked past him, and saw Romanus and Charlie were walking towards the car, holding several plain boutique shopping bags.

"Close your eyes," Romanus said as he opened the

rear cargo area. Naz slipped his hand over my eyes. Where was the trust? I could hear them rustling about, then the sound of Rouen's voice, as he too placed something in the cargo area.

Romanus climbed into the driver's seat, and Rouen into the passenger side, leaving the seat to my left for Charlie, who's smile was so wide I thought his face would crack.

"Whatcha up to, Charlie?" I asked, and he just shook his head. Dammit, I hated surprises. But I couldn't help the smile that affixed itself to my face and stayed there for the whole trip to the tiny town with an unpronounceable name on the banks of the Somme where we were staying.

I picked up the key for our cabin at a post office. The elderly lady behind the counter handed over the skeleton key with much pomp, giving me a run down of the old cabins quirks. You had to bang the shower pipe twice to get hot water, don't open the kitchen window or it'll get stuck, thump the top of the door and kick the bottom at the same time to get the front door to unlock, and so on.

Charlie sat in the car, typing furiously on his laptop while he still had access to the internet, before we went off the grid. For Charlie, that would be like cutting off a limb for a few days, but I had a some ideas on how to distract him. He wanted to wrap a few things, and I knew he was trying to at least recover the deleted body-cam footage from the raid on the auction. The other guys went and got supplies from the local grocery store. I couldn't even grab a peek in the cargo area. Dammit.

As we drove along a tree lined dirt road, following the post office lady's hand drawn map, I kept catching glimpses of water. They might have been generous, calling the place 'on the banks of the Somme' as we'd been heading away from it for awhile, but I didn't mind. The more isolated, the better.

Finally, the trees opened up to show a tiny log cabin with a wrap around porch and lead-lighted windows, making it look rough by idyllic. The clearing between the trees was small, and well hidden and I hadn't seen another house in fifteen minutes. It was perfect.

Charlie pulled me from the car. I squealed as he almost dropped me, but he caught me at the last minute, lifting me into his arms, and carrying me up the porch steps. I wrapped my arms and legs around his body, kissing him deeply.

Then I yawned. I was so damn tired, my eyelids feeling like sandpaper. I'd done nothing but catnap for a week, and my body was ready to shut down. The sun was just beginning to set, and it was only 9 p.m., but I was ready for bed. For sleep. It had been an extremely long forty-eight hours.

Charlie kissed my cheek, running a hand up and down my back as he slowly slid me to my feet. "Come on Rella. Let's get you to bed."

I shook my head, but another yawn rocked me. I watched Rouen walk around the back to do a perimeter check, even out here in the middle of nowhere, and Romanus tried to open the door according to the old lady's instructions, but it didn't budge. I stifled a giggle as I watched him and Naz kick and thump and wiggle the door, each swearing under their breath. I could feel Charlie's body shaking as he held me close to his chest.

Finally, they found the right combination and the door swung open. Charlie swung me back up in his arms and walked me across the threshold, grinning down at me, his eyes promising me everything.

I slid to my feet again, and looked back at a cabin trapped in time. Everything screamed provincial. The main area was essentially one room; kitchen, living room and dining room all in one. A huge fireplace took up almost the entire right hand side wall. Big stuffed couches and hand woven rugs dotted around the room made it feel homey, and all the furniture was rough hewn wood. It was beautiful. It ran on solar power, according to the website, and I found the light switch. Framed hand pressed flowers hung on the walls, a testament to someone's time and patience.

Another yawn wracked my body, and Romanus hustled me towards the doors in the back of the room. A massive bed sat in the center of the bedroom. A gorgeous quilt lay over it and there must have been twenty throw pillows. I ran from the door, hurdled the bed end and landed on the pillows with a sigh. Bliss.

I kicked off my boots and wiggled out of my jeans, crawling beneath the quilt.

"You sure you don't need any help unloading the SUV?"

Romanus huffed out a laugh. "Sleep well, my Queen." As soon as he closed the door, I was asleep.

CHAPTER TWENTY

I woke snuggled into the too warm back of a gargoyle. As I pulled away, I realized it was Rouen. I slipped an arm around his waist and pressed myself closer to his body. I felt a happy rumble beneath my hand.

He rolled over, and we were nose to nose. I covered my mouth. "Morning breath," I explained in a muffled voice.

Rouen rolled his eyes, pulled my hand away and kissed me softly. I made a happy sound and stretch right along his body, wiggling a little against the hard prod of his morning wood. He groaned and grabbed my hip.

"Enough of that, you temptress. We have a big day."

"We do?"

He nuzzled my neck. "Mmhmm, now get this pretty butt out of bed. It's nearly ten."

I kissed him a little, and slid out from beneath the blankets. I must have been really out of it last night, because I hadn't even felt Rouen hop in beside me. I hoped I didn't snore. I watched as he stood from the bed, naked of course, and I took a minute to appreciate the smooth lines of his body. The long ropes of muscles that ran down his back, the small dimples above his perfect ass. I couldn't help but run a finger down his spine. He gave me a hot look over his shoulder, then sighed.

"Tomorrow. Today, we are busy." He gave me a quick peck on the lips, and led me out my door to the bathroom. He turned on the water, checking it was the perfect temperature, though how he'd know was beyond me.

"I'll be back in a minute," he said, and then he was gone. Something weird was going on, but bubbles of excitement fluttered in my chest. I stepped gingerly into the water, and let out a relaxed sigh, the water just right. He really was perfect. I rinsed out my hair with a fancy shampoo that smelled of violets.

He returned, not bothering to knock. I looked out, and was surprised to see Naz, not Rouen. He was smiling goofily, which was the weirdest thing I'd ever seen.

"Should I be worried?" I asked, leaning around the shower curtain. I looked down to see him holding a large box. "What's in the box?"

"Come out and see," he taunted.

I turned off the water, and he rested the box on the sink so he could hold out the fluffy white towel to me. I walked into the towel, and was surprised when he started to dry me, dabbing water from my skin.

He vigorously dried my back, down each arm, across

my chest, over the slight curve of my stomach. He dropped to a knee, and ran the towel up each leg slowly, and I sucked in a breath when he reached the apex of my thighs. He kissed my stomach, and then moved the towel down the other leg.

He stood and leaned in to kiss my cheek. "Open the box."

I noted the name of a boutique on the lid as I removed it. Buried beneath the tissue paper was a white chiffon dress, rows and rows of crystals lining the bodice. I sucked in a gasp as I pulled it out. It unfolded in swaths of diaphanous fabric. It was short at the front, probably hitting just above my knee, and slightly longer in the back.

"Naz, it's gorgeous," I whispered. It took my breath away.

"Then it's only half as beautiful as you," he answered. "I'll help you get it on. It has tiny pearl buttons on the back that are going to be a nightmare."

He held out the dress and I stepped into it gingerly. He smoothed it up my body, and I threaded my arms through the simple sleeves. It hugged my torso up the top, and flared out from my hips like a cloud. Naz started hooking the pearls into their satin loops, cursing a little under his breath making me giggle, which made it harder to thread the buttons. By the time he reached the top of the bodice, I was almost sweating trying not to laugh.

"You look like a goddess," Naz murmured, and his eyes shone with a wonder that made my own eyes mist up. He cleared his throat.

"I'll let you finish up." He gave me a tender kiss on the lips. "I'll see you soon."

He shut the bathroom door with a quiet click, and I stared at myself in the now foggy mirror. The dress made me glow, despite the burnt coffee color of my dye job, and the dark circles that seemed to have plagued me the last few weeks. I swiped on a little bit of tinted lip balm that I kept in my bag with a toothbrush, and ran my fingers through my hair. I found some underwear on the stool beside the vanity, and slipped them on. I was fairly sure that the skirt of this dress was at least a little bit see-through.

Someone knocked, and then Rouen was poking his head back around the door. He sucked in a breath.

"Beautiful. Are you done in here?" I nodded, and he opened the door all the way, grabbing my hand and leading me into the kitchen, where a beautiful wreath of flowers lay on the island bench. Wildflowers in blue, white and yellow were threaded into a crown, twined together with string. It was breathtaking. Rouen lifted it and placed it on my choppy short hair. "Every Queen needs a crown."

Another quick kiss, and he was gone. Romanus appeared from nowhere, wearing a white shirt tucked into his dark jeans, a couple of buttons open at his throat. He looked so handsome, my heart stuttered.

He looked as if someone had sucker punched him. "Wow."

My smile was so huge, my cheeks were beginning to ache. "You look very handsome, Alpha. What have you done?"

"Nothing less than you deserve, my Queen." He took my hand and kissed my knuckles. Then he tucked it into his elbow and led me out the front doors of the cabin.

What I saw made me suck in a breath and blink back tears furiously. They'd somehow converted the back yard into a wedding. There were only two guests who weren't my guys, and seeing them made the tears spill over.

Hope stood there, dressed in a beautiful dark green tea dress, her deep red hair being lifted by the soft wind. She looked ethereal. She walked toward us, her eyes already overflowing and tears streaming down her cheeks. She was such a softie.

She wrapped her arms around me and pulled me close. A tumult of emotions flowed down our bond, but it was overwhelmingly love.

"You look like a bride, Rella," she whispered.

"I feel like a bride, Sis," I choked back. I fanned my face trying to get my shit under control.

Hope looked up at Romanus and gave him her famous wide smile. "Off you go, Loverboy. Go take your place, I've got it from here."

Romanus ran his knuckles down my cheek and walked over to where my guys stood in a line, each dressed in a crisp white shirt and dark black jeans, except Charlie. Charlie looked so handsome, his light blue shirt matching his eyes. He gave me a look of such overwhelming happiness, I swore my heart would burst.

Standing off to the side of them was Memphis. He was dressed in a black button up shirt and black pants.

"Memphis is going to officiate. I mean, it won't be official, and it's probably a little unorthodox to have a Fallen Angel commit a wedding ceremony, but hey, I figure at least he's met the Big Guy, right?"

I couldn't help my bark of laughter, that kind of came out like a snort. Our celebrant was going to be Mephistopheles, literally a Prince of Hell. It made a perfect kind of sense.

"Are you ready?" Hope asked, and I could feel her rummaging around in my emotions. I didn't stop her. She wouldn't find anything but an unending pool of happiness right now.

I walked toward the guys, who were standing under a tall tree, a large swath of the same fabric as my dress creating an impromptu arbor.

Charlie stood there, waiting for me, his eyes shining with love. My heart thumped so hard I was convinced it was going to beat right out of my chest.

When I was standing beside Charlie in front of Memphis, I sucked in a deep breath. I looked at each one of my guys, so different but so right for me. Hope kissed my cheek, letting go of my hand so I could place it in Charlie's warm, soft one. Like this was a real wedding. I was really getting married right now.

Memphis cleared his throat. "Dearly beloved, we are gathered here today…" Hope scowled, and a small, secret smile twitched his lips. Or maybe I imagined it. "Estrella and Charles, I didn't have much time to prepare for this, as I was informed of this event less than an hour ago, when it was rather violently demanded of me." He shot a look at Hope, whose face was fierce beneath her tears. Was Memphis teasing her? Dark, brooding, never cracked a smile in his life, Memphis? It was a day for surprises alright.

He cleared his throat again. "So I can only give you my advice. Sure, love is patient, and love is kind. This much is true. But love is also messy, and volatile. Love is anger and tears, passion and all emotions that are wild and human. It is also the greatest force in this universe. Love is enough to redeem a man, heal a woman, and save a damned soul. If you hold love in your heart, then you will weather any storm, overcome any foe, and know untold happiness. This is the true Heaven."

Hope started to cry softly, and I smiled. Charlie held my hand and lifted it, sliding a thin wedding band onto my finger, and I let out a soft sound. It was perfect. Five strands of white gold twisted together in an endless circle. Five lives entwined. A tear trickled down my cheek.

"Rouen made it last night. It just feels right, doesn't it?" he murmured, and I could only nod. "This is pretty perfect. Just you and me, and the pack. Initially, I didn't react too well to the idea of sharing you," he said louder.

Someone let out a strangled cough, and I gave Rouen a mock stern look. Charlie just grinned. "But any doubts I might have had were erased when these three guys helped me set this up for you. They wanted it to be perfect, not just for you, but for us both. And I respect the hell out of them for that. I didn't think anyone would love you as much as I do, but I'm happy to say I was wrong. Because I love you with every fiber of my soul, Estrella Jones, and I feel that love mirrored in them. I could never deny you all the love that you deserve. I'll spend eternity loving you, and I know for certain that they will too. Will you do me the honor of being my wife, until death do us part?"

"Even after that," I murmured, and Hope leaned toward me, handing me a ring. It wasn't until then that I noticed all the guys wearing one. Even Nazir, which shocked the hell out of me.

I slid the cool weight of the ring onto Charlie's finger. "You have my heart, Charlie Mulligan. Even when I didn't know, when I thought I was happy, you held a piece of my soul with yours. I'd be honored to be your wife."

He leaned forward and kissed me then. Memphis huffed. "You are ruining my moment here, guys. By the power vested in me by the Ruler of Hell, and I can't imagine God having any problem with this union either, I pronounce you man and wife. Now you can kiss the bride. Again."

Charlie kissed me with such tenderness, I was convinced I was going to cry again. The guys, and Hope, whooped and cheered, and I smiled against his lips. This was perfect.

HOPE, in all her wisdom, had brought an entire case of champagne, and a whole spread of pastries from my favorite Manhattan bakery. I wasn't sure how Memphis managed to sift it all, as well as Hope, here at once.

The guys were messing around in the clearing, and I

was sitting on the porch with Hope, sipping champagne from glasses we found in the cabin. The guys had forgone the glasses and drank straight from the bottle. So classy. Romanus and Rouen had unbuttoned their shirts, of course, and Rouen was lying on the grass soaking up the sun. Charlie, the only one with the alcohol tolerance of a human, was starting to sway, and Naz was trying to teach him marksmanship by throwing rocks at empty champagne bottles. Actually, Naz was looking a little worse for wear too. Memphis and Romanus were having a serious discussion, about gods only knew what. It was perfectly idyllic, and I never wanted the moment to end.

"You're really lucky, you know that? Any one of them would have been perfect for you, but together you are so much more," Hope said softly from beside me.

I gave her the side eye. "What's going on with you?"

She waved a hand. "Nothing. I've got everything under control. This is your day."

"Well, what's going on with you and the bad boy of Hell then?" I nodded toward Memphis. Color flooded into Hope's cheeks, mottling her an adorable shade of red. She slammed down our connection, and I grinned. Interesting.

"Don't ask." She looked at the delicate filigree watch on her wrist. "We should go. I sense you have other things to do tonight." She wiggled her eyebrows, but little did she know. Tonight, I'd complete our pack. My skin buzzed with the need to make Charlie completely mine. Heat ran through me, and Hope cleared her throat.

"Yep, definitely time to go. Memphis?" she called, and the Fallen Angel in question turned at the sound of her voice. "We should leave these love birds to it. Ready to head home?"

He nodded and was in front of her in the blink of an eye. He wrapped her in his arms, tenderness shining in his eyes for an unguarded moment. But I saw. I wonder if she did too?

CHAPTER TWENTY-ONE

They disappeared with a pop, like the fabric of reality was snapping back into place. I walked down the steps and sat down beside Rouen.

"You guys have gotten my new husband drunk."

Rouen laughed. "You mean *our* new husband, right? He'll be fine, my Queen. He's just happy. Give him a few hours and then we can complete our pack." I laid my head against his chest. Naz and Romanus came to sit beside us, their bodies casually touching mine. Naz's put his hand on my thigh, and Romanus placed my feet on his lap.

I considered never leaving this place. We could be happy here, the four of us.

Charlie walked over, standing above me, his body silhouetted by the sun.

"Want to dance, Mrs Mulligan?" I laughed at the absurdity of me being a Mrs anything. I stood, brushing the grass from my butt, and he grabbed my hips, and pulled me up against his chest.

He started to hum, two stepping us in a circle around the lawn.

"Are you seriously humming Whitney Houston right now?"

Charlie just hummed louder, and Rouen started singing along. Rouen was fantastic at a lot of things, rending heads, and well, giving head came straight to mind, and I loved him so much, but he did not sing like an angel. He sung like a screaming goat video. It made me laugh harder, Charlie holding me up as we both broke down into hysterics. Romanus groaned and thumped Rouen's shoulder.

"Stop. That's fucking torturous."

Rouen just grinned and laid down across Romanus' lap.

"It's true, though. I will always love you," Charlie whispered against my cheek.

I tilted up my face for a kiss, which he happily provided. Then he deepened the kiss, and heat unfurled in my belly, lust mingling with happiness.

"Rella?"

"Mmm?" I murmured against his lips.

"I'd like to make love to my wife now."

Someone whooped from the peanut gallery on the lawn, and I grinned.

"I'd like that husband." I could hear Naz muttering that it was about time to the gargoyles, but I blocked them out.

Right now, it was just me and Charlie. The man in question scooped me up into his arms, probably flashing my panties to everyone else, and carried me up the stairs and inside the house.

We stumbled our way through the living room to the bedroom, and he threw me on the bed. I bounced a little on the soft mattress, and made a pathetic squeaking laugh.

"Charlie!"

Charlie was on me in an instant, lying between my knees, and kissing me deeply.

"I can't wait, Rella. I want you now. Hell, I wanted you five years ago. You were the star of every wet dream I had all through high school."

"But no pressure, right?" I teased.

"Are you kidding? It's make or break time, baby," he laughed, rolling us over so I was on top. "You look so damn amazing in that dress. I'm going to make love to you while you look like a fucking dream come true."

I leaned forward and kissed him. "You just don't want to wait until we undo all the buttons, do you?"

He grinned his panty dropping grin. "Exactly."

He tore the delicate lace of my panties away, and I gasped. I didn't think people tore off underwear anymore, but I stood corrected. He slid his hand along my slick heat, and moaned.

"I'm not going to lie. This is going to be hard and embarrassingly fast, but we have all night," he promised. I didn't care as I tore at his shirt, ripping it open and scattering buttons everywhere, to reveal the smooth, hard muscles of his chest. The light ginger curls of his chest hair were rough under my palms, and I loved it.

I unbuttoned his jeans, peeling them down his legs

with more desperation than finesse. As soon as he kicked them off his feet, his hands were back on my hips. He lifted me up, and I gripped his cock, guiding him into me, then getting my hand the hell out of the way as he slammed me down.

"Yes," he hissed, and I agreed on a moan as we began to move together, each grind hitting my clit as well as my g-spot. Charlie had had some practice, this I knew, but wow. I threw my head back and rode him, reveling in the sensations that were running through my body and down to my nerve endings. Charlie's eyes never left my face as he pressed up into me, adjusting the roll of his hips to my moans of pleasure. I reached down, rubbing my clit with my finger, and Charlie let out a strangled noise.

"Oh damn," he panted, thrusting wilder, urging me to quicken my pace. I pistoned my hips quicker, throwing my head back as the pleasure pushed me higher and higher. It was hard, and wild and fast, tinged with a feeling of desperation and I loved it.

My orgasm washed over me and I clenched my inner muscles around Charlie's dick. He let out a long groan as he jerked inside me, filling me with his seed.

"I love you, Rella, so damn much."

I collapsed forward onto his chest, panting, my hair stuck to my face and our bodies still connected on the most intimate level. "I love you too, Charlie Mulligan. Now get me out of this dress," I demanded.

He laughed, kissing me like he owned me. Or I owned him. "My pleasure."

. . .

FEATHERLIGHT KISSES BRUSHING across my cheeks woke me. I opened one eyelid lazily, expecting to see Charlie, but it was Naz's chocolate brown and mercury eyes I saw.

"Hey," I croaked out through a parched throat. "Where's Charlie?"

"He decided that you were a Bridezilla, and hotfooted it out of here." His face was smooth, completely neutral, and if it wasn't for the sparkle of mischief in his eye, I might have freaked out.

"Not funny, asshole."

He chased kisses down my temple and across to my lips.

"We are waiting for you," he whispered against them. "Again." He was openly teasing me now. I stuck my tongue out at him. It wasn't my fault they kept coming up with surprise events that were special and magical just for me.

I stood up and looked for my dress, or my jeans, or something.

"Don't worry about clothes, you won't need them." Naz hooked an arm around my waist and pulled me against his bare chest. He was wearing his jeans still, which hugged his delectable ass like a second skin. "Have you changed your mind? About changing Charlie?"

I shook my head violently. I wanted Charlie to be pack more than anything now, and no matter how much I enjoyed my moment with Charlie and his beautiful, fragile humanity, I needed him to be with me for eternity.

"I haven't. Am I doing the right thing, Naz? It feels right, but I don't know if I'm doing what's best for me or for Charlie."

He stood in front of me and ran his hands up and down my arms. "Trust your gut. And if it goes bad, we will deal with. Clary always said don't borrow tomorrow's trouble for today. Or maybe it's don't steal yesterday's trouble for today. Whatever. Just do what feels right."

I nodded. "You're right. Let's do this."

Naz let me go, and I grabbed his hand, walking out of the room naked. After all, every person in this house had seen me naked and in the throes of orgasm now. No point in being modest.

Once again, the house was empty, and Naz ushered me through the living room to the front door. The night was beautiful and still, an idyllic French summer evening. I could hear the night noises of the nocturnal animals, and as the door squeaked open, it covered my oomph of surprise. The guys had lit up the night. Fairy lights now hung where the chiffon archway had been earlier, and dozens of candles littered the ground in tiny circles, casting an eerie light around the clearing. A small brazier crackled off to one side, and that's where I saw them. My partners.

I walked toward them like my limbs were possessed, irrevocably drawn to them like a compass north. They were all dressed, or perhaps undressed, similar to Naz, bare chested in just jeans. The firelight glistened off the gargoyles as if they were dusted in real gold, or oiled. They seemed huge silhouetted against the flames.

Charlie stood with them, laughing at something one of the other guys said. My heart wanted to explode as the breath burned in my lungs. I wanted to close my eyes and burn this moment into my mind forever. Romanus spotted me first and beckoned me over. The raw lust on his face made me feel powerful, like a goddess more than a queen.

I joined them and they huddled around me.

Rouen ran a hand up my spine, and I shivered. They all eyed me expectantly, but I focused on Charlie.

"Are you sure this is what you want, Charlie?"

He laughed, leaning forward to kiss me. "For the thousandth time, yes. I want to be pack. I want to irrevocably be one of you." He brushed his fingers over my cheek, and I had hot flashback to what those clever fingers did earlier. Lust began to glow inside me, and the three men already bonded to me stiffened.

We needed to get this shit done fast, and get to the fun part.

I turned to Romanus, leaning into his wide, muscular chest.

"What's the first step?"

He kissed my eyelids, then my nose, before answering. "We are already Pack, you are already Queen. My blood will change him, your blood will tie him to pack. We'll both take his blood, then heal his wounds. Then it will be complete. I'm unsure how it will affect him. Other than Nazir, we haven't turned any humans, though it was sometimes done in the olden days by smaller packs."

I wrinkled my nose. Despite my new biting fetish, consuming blood still made me a little squeamish

It must have shown on my face because Rouen laughed. "I find that the whole thing is easier if you do it while having sex," he stated seriously.

"Does it increase the magic?" I asked. That would make sense; all sorts of rituals used sex to strengthen the magic.

"Nah, but to quote Miss Poppins, a mind blowing orgasm helps the medicine go down."

I laughed so hard my belly hurt and I was huffing out laughs like a muppet. "Thanks for destroying my childhood, asshole." I punched him in the shoulder. "What about afterwards? I remember after the Alpha fight there may have been mention of an orgy to cement the pack?"

They all laughed. "You might remember that, huh?" Rouen said, winking.

"We will see how Charlie feels. We do not need to solidate his position in the pack right now."

I resisted the urge to pout.

We were all silent then, the weight of what we were about to do was heavy on us all. The crickets sounded louder, the crackle and pop of the fire almost soothing.

Rouen let out an exaggerated sigh, though he was grinning. "A Beta's work is never done."

And then he kissed me. And boy, what a kiss.

His tongue danced along my lips, before he pushed forward to deepen the kiss. His hands slid up the naked curve of my hips. He pressed his fingers into the soft flesh of my ass, and pulled me close to his body. I could feel his cock, hard and eager. I let out a little moan as I felt someone move in behind me. A kiss was pressed to my shoulder, then to the base of my neck and I shivered.

A happy hum of appreciation whispered in my ear as another hard cock pressed against my ass, and I wiggled back against the warm body behind me, drawing Rouen with me so I was pressed between two muscular bodies. Rouen stooped to kiss my neck, and I looked behind me into the face of Naz. He held my eyes as he moved his hand over my hip, down to my inner thigh, his fingers brushing the lips of my sex, his feet nudging mine apart so he had better access.

As he dipped his fingers into the wetness of my folds, a sharp breath hissed between his teeth. His finger skimmed over my clit and I bucked against his hand.

Rouen moved his mouth back to mine, kissing me as if he were desperate to capture all my moans with his lips.

He didn't have to wait long as Naz pushed a finger into my pussy, and I let out a long, low whimper. Rouen's hand slid down my stomach to rub a thumb over my clit. As their hands worked in unison, I was sure I was going to lose my mind. I gripped Rouen's hair in my fist, pulling his head back so I could bite along his jaw, my body desperately pressing against his.

"Uh uh, my Queen."

He groaned and pulled away from me, but his body had barely left mine when Charlie was in front of me. He was naked, his hard cock pressing against my stomach, and his eyes hooded with lust.

He kissed me, and I wondered if he could taste

Rouen on my lips. Naz moved his fingers away from the aching heat of my center and I let out a growl of protest. I could feel his chest rumble out a laugh from behind me, but then his warmth was gone too, replaced by the radiant hardness of a gargoyle. Romanus.

I wrapped my arms around Charlie, leaning back into Rom like he was a solid wall of muscle. Charlie put two hands under my ass and lifted me so I could wrap my legs around his waist, my body pressed tightly between my two men. I groaned as every minor movement made my aching clit rub against the hard lines of his abdominal muscles.

He looked me in the eye as he slid his cock inside me, and it was a goddamn revelation.

My moans echoed around the darkness. I felt the hard length of Romanus' cock pressed against my back, but he made no move to do anything with it. He just held me steady as Charlie began to slide in and out of me, slowly building his pace until our moans made a symphony in the forest.

I felt Romanus' breath on my neck, as he kissed the hollow behind my ear. I moved my head to the side, giving him unfettered access to my neck and he moaned long and low. I prepared myself for the sting of his teeth piercing my flesh, but I still winced a little. He pulled away, his hands coming around to nudge Charlie's mouth to where it needed to be.

Charlie looked at the blood pooling on my neck, and I could see the sweat on his brow and his chest was heaving. I caught the brief look of panic when he saw my blood, but I also saw him straighten his shoulders in resolution. He leaned forward and captured the bleeding bite on my neck with his mouth. He sucked hard and I came on his cock on a scream. Holy shit, that was amazing. No wonder the guys went wild when I bit them. He sucked in pull after pull of blood, until Romanus tapped his cheek.

Charlie buried himself deep inside me as he came on a roar.

Romanus licked the wound on my neck, the tingling of gargoyle healing mixing with the shuddering after-shocks of my orgasm.

Charlie slipped out of me, and as soon as my feet hit the soft grass, I pushed him down, so we were both a tangle of arms and legs on the grass.

"I love you," I whispered against his lips, giving him barely a brush of a kiss before moving to his neck. I bit down on the vulnerable flesh, and he moaned. Rouen was suddenly there, pressing a finger between my lips breaking the suction seal.

"Careful my Queen, our new pack mate might not like being bitten with your cute little blunt teeth." His finger shifted to a claw, and it was almost enough to shock me out of my lust haze. Rouen dragged the nail over Charlie's stubble, and sliced the shallowest cut alongside his pulse point.

"Ready?" I whispered, and I could feel Romanus big body over mine, his cock seeking entrance. Charlie's eyes locked with mine. "I've never been more ready for anything in my life."

I raised my ass a little, pushing back into Romanus, searching for that silken hardness that I craved. As he slid into me, I lapped at the blood trickling down Charlie's throat before sealing my lips around his wound.

The energy between us all was intense, the bonds pulsing with the pounding hearts of my mates.

My mates. Not just my pack, but my mates. Something deeper than husbands and lovers. A soul deep connection.

As Charlie's blood seeped into my system, I could feel the bond to Charlie snap into existence, just an almost invisible thread that strengthened and brightened until it shone like gold inside my mind. I could feel Charlie harden against my stomach as the slow, rhythmic thrusting of Romanus created delicious friction.

Romanus thrust his wrist toward Rouen, who bit down on it, piercing the skin and sucking gently. When the blood flowed down his wrist and landed on the grass beside us, Romanus planted his hand down next to Charlie's head, which was tipped back in pleasure.

"Take my blood and become Pack for eternity, Charles Mulligan."

It was an offer with a shadow of warning. But Charlie was all in, latching onto his arm with a moan.

The magic was high in the clearing now, an almost physical force. I didn't know why it was different to Naz's turning, maybe because we weren't yet a pack, maybe because it was a life or death situation. Maybe it was because right now, we were completing our pack. But I could feel everyone's emotions and the alpha magic swirling around my skin, wrapping around my body like a third lover.

As Charlie drank from Romanus' arm, my Alpha gargoyle kept pounding me from behind, driving me into Charlie's body.

It was too much. My orgasm crushed me like a tidal wave, and I barely came up for air before Romanus reached his own climax, burying himself deep inside of me, pressing his teeth gently into my shoulder blade making me come all over again. Charlie came all over my front in hot spurts, a desperate groan pulled from his lips.

Romanus shifted away, and I rolled my heated body onto the cool dewy grass.

Romanus raised his body over Charlie's, until they were pressed together chest to chest. There was nothing sexual in the action, but Romanus leaned forward and sucked on the wound on Charlie's neck.

I felt the bond explode in my mind, all of Charlie's emotions flowing between us. Lust, happiness, confusion all battered at our barrier. Romanus slid a tongue against Charlie's wound, healing it completely like it had never been there, then rolling away so his body was pressed close to mine.

We laid there in the silence for a moment, speaking with our emotions along the bonds. I turned my head and I could see Rouen and Naz sitting beside the fire, hands resting on their thighs, cum shining in the flickering light above semi soft cocks.

I sighed happily. At least everyone had some fun.

I rolled over until I was face to face with Charlie.

I gave him a tentative smile and pushed a little love down the bond.

"Are you doing okay?"

He opened one eye, and chuffed out a happy sound. "That was, I mean this is…" he ran out of words but I knew exactly what he meant.

He came closer, staring deep into my soul. He had a direct line to it now, a shining golden thread that was lassoed around my heart.

"I love you, Rella."

I stared back, appreciating my night vision yet again so I could see the beauty of his eyes.

One the normal Mulligan blue, and the other a swirling amethyst.

CHAPTER TWENTY-TWO

I sat naked on the front porch, the suns rays kissing my skin, my completely naked Beta lying on the warm floorboards near my feet. I sipped my coffee as I listened to Romanus and Naz talking softly in the kitchen while they made breakfast. Charlie was still sound asleep on the rug in front of the fire in the living room. We'd all slept there last night, a tangle of bodies, symphony of soft breaths.

I ran my toes up and down Rouen's back, and his body was almost liquid in its relaxation.

It was perfect. I'd thought the word a lot the last couple of days, but I couldn't think of a better description for this moment in time. Tomorrow, life would restart, my vendetta would resume, and we'd go back to catching bad guys. Today was a moment for just us. Our pack.

Naz pushed through the screen door and let out a disgruntled huff. "Would it kill you to at least keep on a pair of boxers, dude?" he said to Rouen as he passed me a plate of pancakes with berries and cream. I dug in, suddenly ravenous.

Rouen didn't even lift his head from where it was resting on his arms. "Rella is naked too."

"Not the same thing. When Rella is naked, I want to ravish her body. When you are naked, staring at your wrinkly old man balls makes me puke in my mouth a little," Naz teased, walking over to rest his sexy, jean clad ass on the porch rail.

Rouen sat up and rolled over, staring down at his crotch.

"My balls are not wrinkly old man balls! They are the epitome of testicular perfection."

I laughed, sucking back a chunk of pancake. I coughed hard, and Romanus was there thumping me on the back.

"Your balls are fine, Rouen. Here, have some pancakes," he reassured his lover, handing him a plate piled high with pancakes and syrup.

I swallowed and laughed harder as Rouen took the offered plate. I gave him a mock frown. "Is that a grey hair, you know, down there?" I waggled my eyebrows suggestively.

His gaze whipped from mine to look at his balls, and then frowned at me. "I don't have pubes."

I was bent over laughing now, and even Rouen was finding it hard not to grin. Romanus leaned over and kissed the top of my head. "Don't tease our Beta, my Queen."

He moved to the chair beside me, trailing his fingers

over Rouen's short hair on the way. We hadn't confirmed Charlie's place in the pack last night. He wasn't Alpha though, and everyone seemed okay with waiting to find out.

As Rouen had said, Betas were a lot more casual about rank compared to Alphas.

Charlie had been quiet, but it could have been exhaustion. I know I'd been rung out by the time we staggered into the house.

Still, I tapped my foot anxiously, waiting for him to wake. I wanted to get a read on him now that our emotions weren't running high from the wedding and the ritual and all the sex.

I felt Hope's presence in my head only moments before she spoke. *I'm not interrupting anything, am I?*

She sounded amused and so happy that I couldn't help the grin that curled my lips.

We are having a break from all the orgies. What's up?

Hope's laughter trickled down the bond. *Just wanted to let you know that I've set everything up for you in Calais. You'll have to meet with the Mayor first, and probably have your picture taken by the press. That's booked in for the day after tomorrow at ten.*

I mentally groaned. I hated the press.

Hope made a disapproving noise, then continued. *The day after I've booked you a one o'clock meeting with John Pierre Romaine, who is as close to an overseer as you'll find at the Calais camp. It's unofficial, you know, just people hoping to jump the Channel. Anyway, John Pierre will give you a tour, along with Franco de Moines, who is the Shine Foundation representative at the camp.*

I picked up my phone and wrote down all the details in notes.

I've booked you the presidential suite at the Chateau de Clucave just outside of Calais. I hear the beds are huge, she teased.

I rolled my eyes than realized that all my guys were looking at me.

I pointed to my head. "Hope."

I'm not sure if that made me sound less insane or more, but they nodded and went back to talking softly.

So you completed the super secret Gargoyle ritual. It wasn't a question, because I could feel her rummaging around in my brain, looking at all my bonds. She was curious and I was used to it. Having an empathic sister had meant I was her favorite test subject for practicing her abilities growing up. We had rules of course, she never delved too deep and if I said stop, she pulled out immediately.

These connections are so much stronger now, since you've added Charlie. It's like you completed a circuit or something. Her mental hands prodded at the bonds in my mind, testing them. Three sets of eyes snapped back to me, and everyone looked concerned. Or weirded out. That was probably a better term.

Stop playing with the bonds, Hope. You are freaking out the guys.

She withdrew immediately. *Whoops. Sorry. I should go, anyway. Stay safe, Rella.*

I couldn't guarantee that, so I hedged around it. *You too, Hope.*

The connection disappeared, and I shrugged at the

guys. "Sorry. She gets curious. I'll warn her not to play with the bonds next time."

Naz shook his head, making the fine black strands shine almost blue in the sun. "I'll never get how you can just let her dig around in there. It's so… intrusive."

I stood and stretched, appreciating the warm sun on every inch of my skin. The guys watched the movement like hungry predators. I was tempted to take them all back to bed, but I resisted. Downtown needed a break from all the traffic or I was going to end up with friction burn. I watched as Rouen stood as well, his sculpted body uncurling from the floorboards like some sexy golden god.

Maybe only a short break then.

He leaned forward and kissed me. "I love that I put that look on your face," he purred, and it was a sound that went right to my core and made it tingle. Damn sexy gargoyles.

The door squeaked open, and Charlie stood there looking more vital and alive than I'd ever seen him. He was dressed in jeans and his white shirt, but he'd left the shirt completely unbuttoned. His hair was mussed and his eyes were still hooded from sleep. Or maybe it was from lust, considering he was now taking in my nakedness in one long, slow stare.

He leaned forward and kissed me tenderly, and I sighed against his lips.

He pulled back and looked at Rouen. "Are you always going to be naked?"

Rouen shrugged, completely unabashed. "Probably."

Naz rolled his eyes and made a disgusted noise, but Charlie just nodded.

Romanus cleared his throat. "We will give you two a moment alone. Charlie, there are pancakes if you are hungry." He hustled the other two guys into the house and Charlie sat on the chair I just vacated. He patted his lap and I sat back down. His fingers ran along my arm absently.

"How are you feeling?" I asked gently, rubbing my cheek against the soft hair on his chest.

"Good. A little disoriented, I guess. There's a lot going on up here." He tapped his head. "I've been used to one person in my head, and I mean one was enough, but now there's four other people banging around inside my brain and it just feels strange. I don't know how Naz accepted it so easily."

I suspected that Naz had deep wells of darkness in his mind, places that he shied from, which our bonds came in and filled. Like filling up mental potholes. Charlie didn't have that kind of luck, if you could call it unlucky. He'd have to make room for us all himself, and I imagine that wasn't as easy as it sounds.

"We have the rest of the day to get used to it, but tomorrow we have to head to Calais. Hope has arranged everything for us to act as delegates of our Foundation. Just gotta shake some hands and we'll be in."

Charlie sighed. "I kind of wanted to stay here forever." I kissed his chest, smiling as he echoed my own thoughts.

I felt him suck back a breath and settle himself back into work mode, tension humming through his shoulders. "I guess we have time to watch some B-Grade action footage then. I managed to hack my way into their system and retrieve the data from the SWAT body-cams. Whoever deleted them didn't know much about computers. Just because you empty the trash can, doesn't mean your garbage is gone, you know?"

I nodded, even though I had no idea, but Charlie didn't care. He'd already moved onto the next thing in that wonderful, strange brain.

"Let's get some breakfast first, and then we can all watch me and Naz get arrested."

I WAS glad I had that second cup of coffee when I got a good look at the body-cams. There were faces on there I hadn't seen on the night, but I recognized now. A US foreign correspondent. A high ranking German diplomat. A former 90s pop star. There were faces that Naz recognized too, from his other line of work. A drug smuggler from Egypt. The right hand man of an African despot. It was basically a who's who of scum bags. I wrote down every name. I'd make sure this list got to Ace somehow.

I couldn't rain down vengeance on all of these people, but there was nothing the Consort of the Devil liked more than a little karmic comeuppance. I didn't see Uriel, and neither Ace or Gusion came up in the footage. Handy trick.

However, one face looked all too familiar. "Pause that."

Charlie did as I asked, and the face stilled on the

screen. A face I recognized all right, and I wasn't too surprised to see that asshole at a sex slave auction either.

"This guy is the major stockholder for a pharmaceutical company. He's been really vocal about his opposition of the NRH supplying drugs at cost price to low income countries. Tried to lock us up in court a bunch of times." I stared at the guy, with his smarmy smile and his weak chin. My gut clenched, and I knew this guy had something to do with Hope. It was too coincidental. She has a meeting with the UN about our pharma policies, then she gets abducted. You didn't need to be a rocket scientist to know that there was something suss as fuck about that.

"Zoom in."

I racked my brain for a name. He had a real upper-crust name. Came from old, old money. Richards. Someone Richards. "Maximoff Richards."

He was dressed in a tailored suit that did nothing to hide his pudgy middle, his slick haircut hiding a receding hairline and a balding patch at the back of his head. Charlie had frozen him yelling something at the man beside him. I couldn't see the other guys face, he was turned away from the camera. His hand was pushing Maximoff towards a rear door. My eyes caught on something glittering on his shirt.

I poked at the screen, making colors go haywire beneath my finger and Charlie hissed. "Don't touch the equipment. It's sensitive."

I raised my eyebrows, and resisted the urge to run my hands up and down the screen. Because I was mature like that. Charlie was way more picky about who touched his computer than he was at who touched his dick. Well, he was before. I leaned over, and slid my hands into his unbuttoned jeans. "What about this equipment?" I purred, and he sucked in a breath. I wrapped my hand firmly around his semi hard dick and squeezed. He groaned. I removed my hand, making sure to run my fingers across the trail of hair on his lower stomach. "That's what I thought. I'll make sure not to touch your equipment again."

Rouen laughed at the stunned look on Charlie's face, and I resisted the urge to grin. "Can you please zoom in on Richards lapel pin, please, Husband?"

Charlie narrowed his eyes, but I could see the corners of his lips curl. "Of course." He zoomed in, and although the picture blurred a little, I could see it was a circle with seemingly random squiggles in it. It wasn't anything I recognized. It wasn't this years Gucci anyway.

"What's that?" I asked the guys. I could feel Romanus' hot breath on the back of my neck as he leaned closer to the screen, and I resisted the urge to turn and kiss him.

"It's a sigil," Rouen answered.

"An angelic sigil," Romanus added.

I sighed, and put my head in my hands. "Anyone want to put a hundred bucks on it being Uriel's sigil?"

Strangely, no one took me up on my bet.

"I can't check until we get back to civilization, but I think that's a pretty great working theory. What do we do from here? I mean, I'm all about avenging Hope, but Archangels are a little out of our pay grade, don't you think?" Charlie said, his eyes round. He wasn't wrong. We couldn't be more out of our depth right now.

"Catalogue the faces, and we'll see what we can do about creating a list. If you can spot anyone else with one of the pins, put them on a seperate list. We'll give what we have to Ace and Gusion."

I pointed back at Richards. "This guy we'll chase up back in the States. My gut says that if he didn't put the hit on Hope, he knows who did. But we can't just leave. We need to clean up what we can here. We can't bring down the whole organisation, but we can put a huge fucking dent in business."

CHAPTER TWENTY-THREE

I couldn't believe we were shopping again. Seriously, who knew that a blood-fuelled vendetta would come with a need for a whole new wardrobe?

But when Charlie had dragged me into the store, he'd made a good point. I couldn't meet the Mayor of Calais in bloodstained jeans or a tee that hadn't been washed in two weeks and had its own collection of suspicious stains.

Romanus and Naz were doing recon on Town Hall, and Charlie and Rouen were doing some kind of pretty woman style makeover thing with me. Rouen, however, had directed us straight to the lingerie section of the department store, and was muttering about thigh highs and demi cups. He was currently holding up a red strip of lace that was masquerading as a thong.

"No thongs."

Rouen gave me sad eyes. "Not even one little thong?"

I laughed and shook my head, starting back towards the practical business wear I was supposed to be looking at. I liked the playfulness we were all feeling after our forced timeout. I grabbed a plain black pencil skirt and frilly white blouse that dipped low enough to show the top curve of my breasts. It was an outfit that screamed pen-pusher, and didn't say part-time murderer, at least to the casual observer.

I looked at Charlie and Rouen, as they picked outfits for me, most of which I would put back as soon as they weren't looking. Rouen in particular looked completely out of place. I could dress him up in a french maid outfit, and he would still look like a predator.

Luckily, it wasn't going to be unusual for me to have four bodyguards when we went to the camp, especially since the recent attempt on my sister's life. Charlie's increased strength meant he no longer had to play backup.

I matched my chosen outfit with a pair of sensible heels, in case I needed to run or kick some ass.

At the register, I placed all the things I'd selected in front of a bored teenage shop clerk. However, Rouen dumped a handful of completely impractical lace and silk on top of my practical outfit. I raised an eyebrow at the lace garter belt and silk stockings, with matching demi bra and french cut panties.

He waggled his eyebrows suggestively. "When in the motherland, right?"

I mentally slapped my forehead. How had I forgotten so quickly? No wonder the Gargoyles had been so relaxed since our arrival in France. It was like catnip for their gargoyle souls. The clerk passed me a bag containing my purchases, and I wrapped my hand in Rouen's larger one.

"When this is all done, do you think we could come back to France, and you could show me where you guys are from? Maybe visit your namesake?"

He kissed my temple. "I'd love that. But I wasn't named after Rouen. Well, I was, but not until I died. Rouen isn't my real name."

My feet skidded to a stop.

"*What*? Why didn't you tell me that?" It came out as a high pitched screech and I winced at the noise.

He wrapped an arm around my waist, and propelled me back into motion. "Rouen has been my name for nearly fifteen hundred years. I honestly forgot."

Naz and Romanus pulled up in front of us as we approached the front of the department store, and I realized that Charlie must have called them at some point. Romanus took one look at my stormy face, and frowned at Rouen.

"What did you do now?"

Rouen crossed his arms over his chest. "What makes you think it was me and not Charlie?"

"Hey, don't throw me under the bus, dickhead," Charlie said, sliding into the car beside me and elbowing Rouen as he got in.

"Millenia of experience," Romanus said dryly. He looked at me over his shoulder as Naz pulled the car back into the traffic.

Rouen huffed. "I may have told her that Rouen wasn't my name when we were alive. That's all."

Naz made a loud oohing sound that was straight out of a daytime chat show, and Charlie let out a low chuckle.

There was a lifetime of strained patience in Romanus' sigh, and I was finding it hard to hold on to my annoyance. Fucking cute bastards.

"My name was not Romanus, either. We decided it was best to make a clean break from our mortal lives. Those last years were bloody and dark for us both."

I stared out the window, waiting for him to continue. I wasn't going to let him off that easily. I tied my life to these two, no four, beings, and the only one I really knew at all was Charlie.

"Why Romanus and Rouen?" Charlie asked. Always the curious one. I knew I could rely on him to ask the questions so I could maintain my pouty countenance. Guess who'd just rocketed up to the top of my favorite eternal life partner list?

"We were burned alive in Rouen by Saint Romanus in the 7th century. He poisoned an entire village of people, and when we came through and, uh-"

"Ate everyone," Rouen provided, and Romanus scowled.

"Yes. Well, their tainted blood was enough to knock us down." He cleared his throat, the only sign that this conversation was affecting him.

"Down, but not out. We were awake the whole time," Rouen added, shivering. Not even thousands of years could fade some memories. I crawled over Charlie's lap so I was between the two of them. I pressed my body along Rouen's, soothing him.

Romanus continued. "We signified the last of all Gargoyles. And we weren't a good example of our species at the end. Pia, our former Queen, was so gentle, so nurturing. We were a blood-fuelled nightmare come to life. The humans were right to put us down. We decided that the best way to remember how far we could fall was to take his name. Saint Romanus of Rouen."

I wanted to comfort Romanus, but it would have to wait until I could wrap him in my arms and whisper all the promises of my heart in his ear.

"Well, thats super fucking morbid," Naz muttered. "I thought my tortured backstory was bad, but it's hard to compete with 'I was burned alive by a 7th century saint.'"

Rouen buried his nose in my hair, the way he always did when he needed comfort. Romanus was harder to read, my strong, stoic alpha. "What were your names? Before, I mean," I whispered against Rouen's chest.

"Caio. But I haven't been that boy in a long time," Rouen murmured back.

Caio. It suited him somehow. The gargoyle who barely got to live before he died. I lifted my eyes to see Romanus staring at us in the side mirror. I pushed love down my bond, and the hard look in his eyes softened.

"Vercingetorix."

I couldn't hold back a giggle. "Holy shit, that's a mouthful." I gave him an exaggerated wink. "Not that I mind a mouthful." I licked my lower lip, and his eyes hooded as he sucked in a deep breath, scenting me.

The pheromones in the car ratched up a notch, and Naz let out a relieved sigh when our hotel came into sight. It was a fair way out of Calais, but it was as high class as you could get. A refurbished Chateau, it was a stupid amount of dollars a night, and everything was an antique. No cheap reproductions allowed.

I unbelted myself as we pulled into the long circular driveway. I leaned forward and nipped Romanus' earlobe. "Ever wanted to break an antique four poster bed?" I purred. His nostrils flared, and when the valet came to take the car, the sexual tension was so high that Naz practically threw the keys at the poor kids face.

We waved away the bellboy, and I went to check-in. The guys naturally formed a V formation around me, looking for threats, protecting my back. I walked up to the desk, and gave the attendant my name.

She was eye-fucking my supposed bodyguards like a starving woman, especially Naz, but I didn't want to waste time putting her in her place. Besides, they were supposed to be my guards. I couldn't help my top lip curling though. I was the least certain of Naz's feelings, and a slither of doubt crept into my heart. Charlie had loved me forever, and to the gargoyles, I was their Savior Queen and they would love me unconditionally for it. But Naz, despite his words, was thrust into the life, and did not have any prior feelings for me other than lust.

I was feeling the uncertainty of a woman who was newly dating a stupidly attractive man. When Naz slipped his tattooed hand into mine, I held back my smile.

I was fooling myself. We weren't like a new couple. We had a direct connection to each others emotions. There would never be any miscommunication.

The concierge looked down at our hands, and then at me. I couldn't resist baring my teeth at her like a feral animal this time. She expedited out check-in process and soon we were climbing the stairs as a bellboy led us to our room.

He opened the big double doors that proclaimed the room as the Presidential Suite, and stood beside the door. I slipped him a fifty and sent him on his way.

The suite was nice, done in reds and creams, every single piece of furniture expensively upholstered and incredibly spindly. The Gargoyles were going to have to sit on the floor for the entire stay. The kitchen was state of the art and three rooms led off the main sitting room. It was opulence to the extreme but I missed our little two room cabin in the middle of nowhere.

Charlie quickly set up his equipment, and visibly sagged with relief when his computer connected to the high speed internet connection. The guy had a problem. His computer was practically another appendage.

Naz hadn't released my hand, and he pulled me against his chest and kissed me hard. It was a branding kiss. The hard press of his lips moved against mine, and I slipped my free hand around his neck.

He pulled away, and bit my lower lip gently. "I only see you," he said so low, that I knew he only wanted me to hear. He lifted our twined hands to his chest, pressing my palm against his wildly thudding heart. "This beats because of you. Now it beats for you. Understand?"

I swallowed the hard lump of emotion that seemed to be choking me, and nodded once. He gave me a blindingly bright smile and then pecked me on the lips. "Good."

He released me, but not before squeezed my ass and made a happy noise. "I'm going to check the perimeter, Alpha," he said to Romanus, before letting himself out of our suite.

Rouen wrapped an arm around my shoulders. "I gotta admit, he's growing on me. I might be tempted to change my mind about him being my type." I rolled my eyes at him, and he leaned in for a kiss. "Are you hungry? I'll order room service." I could tell from the way his body was all but curled around me that I wasn't going to have to touch a fork to eat tonight. He kissed his way down my neck. "Maybe then we can have dessert?"

My body tightened at his words. If I kept up my current pace, I'd soon be walking with a permanent limp. Or like an old cowboy.

"How about we just cuddle and watch pay per view? If we keep this up, I'm going to have to walk around doing kegels 24/7."

He threw back his head and laughed. It was such a joyous sound, that it made my chest swell like his laughter was actually filling me up. "What if I promise to kiss it better?" he teased.

I pushed against his chest, grinning. "You are such a horndog. Go order us some food before your Queen withers away to nothing but a shadow." I kissed him, because it was a compulsion that I couldn't, or didn't want to, fight.

Charlie was immersed back in his virtual universe,

running a check on the faces his program had cataloged against databases in Geneva, the States and against Interpol. Also, he was running a reverse image search. The internet was a powerful tool in the hands of people like Charlie. He could find anything. Anyone.

I walked past him on my way to one of the bedrooms, and I leaned forward to kiss the top of his head. His brain was a powerful thing, and it fucking made me wet as hell. Sure, his body was hot. Beyond hot. But what was inside his head, and inside his chest, made my panties damp.

He turned and caught my lips, kissing me back, his eyes closing against the bliss. Mine did too. But then he was drifting away, back to his screen. "I love you, you know," I said, shaking my head. He was lucky I wasn't a jealous lover, because if I made him choose between me and his computer, I'm not sure I'd win.

He flashed me that classic Charlie grin. "Me too, sweetheart."

I went and hung my clothes in the wardrobe so they didn't crease. I moved to the ensuite bathroom, and appreciated the dark polished tiles and the huge three head shower. Nice. I stripped off my clothes, and ran a hand through my short hair. Fuck, I missed my hair. It was the ultimate vanity, but I loved the deep auburn of my long locks. It identified me. I was the daughter of people who literally survived Hell. A twin. A badass. An upholder of justice, until justice needed a hand. Now, I guess I was a vigilante.

I stepped into the three streams of water and let out

an audible moan. Holy crap, this was almost better than sex.

Ha. Who was I kidding? It was better than all the sex I'd had before this month, but nothing compared to my guys. They were out of this world. My body had never hummed the way it did now, like my nerves were constantly aware of them. They were a physical pull on my cells. I leaned my head against the tiles, and let the water beat down on my body.

I knew someone was in the bathroom with me, because my body perked up like the hussy it was, and when a body slid into the shower behind me, I relaxed back against the muscular chest. His scent, not something I could label, wrapped around me, and I knew it was Romanus before I even tilted my head up to look at him.

He kissed my forehead as he reached around me for the fancy little shampoos in the recess of the shower. He squirted some on his hand, and I reached back, running my hand down his body toward the hard cock pressed against my ass.

He gripped my wrist. "Not today, my Queen. Just let me take care of you." He nipped my ear, making me shiver, and then rubbed the shampoo through my hair. His fingers ran through the short strands, applying the perfect amount of pressure on my scalp as he lathered it with his fingertips. My moan bounced around the marble bathroom as his fingers stroked the muscles that ran up from my neck into my scalp, his large hands and strong thumbs applying the perfect amount of pressure. Damn.

When he was happy that my hair was clean, he stepped back into the stream of water, rinsing the suds from my hair, ensuring not a single soap sud went near my eyes. Then he moved onto the conditioner, repeating the process, but this time his thumbs rubbed tiny circles on my temples, releasing tension I didn't know I held.

He let the conditioner sit in my hair as his hands ran down my back, pressing me to his chest as he kneaded the muscles of my neck and shoulders, and the tight muscles in my back. He reached out and soaped his hands again, making sure to work every knot from my muscles.

When he was done, I felt like I was boneless, and the only thing keeping me upright was the firm press of his hand on my lower back.

"Close your eyes, love."

I did as I was told, and let him step me into the third stream of water, smelling more than feeling the perfumed soap running down my face. I stayed there, under the steady beat of hot water, pressed into the chest of my Alpha, perfectly content in this moment. Despite the throbbing hardness of his cock against my stomach, Romanus didn't try to turn the embrace sexual, just as happy to hold me as I was to be held.

Finally, when my fingers were rough and wrinkled, Romanus reached out and pressed the button to turn off the shower heads. He stepped from the cubicle, the water sliding from his body like he was some kind of sea god rising from the ocean. He made me breathless.

He held out a fluffy white towel, and I stepped into it. Large heated lights poured warmth down onto my body. His mismatched eyes shone beneath them. Fuck, he was beautiful.

"I will leave you to the rest of your nightly rituals," he murmured in a low, rumbly voice filled with emotion. I kissed him, pouring my love from my lips to his.

"Thank you."

He bowed his head low, his eyes on the floor. Deferring to me. I caught his chin, lifting his face to mine. "You shouldn't bow to me, Romanus. We are equals. All of us."

I imprinted the look on his face at that moment into my memory. He looked at me like I was a goddess, with so much love it hurt to breathe.

"What did we do?" he asked, but he wasn't talking to me. "How did we get so lucky?"

"I have a feeling in five hundred years you'll be asking that exact same question with a significantly different connotation," I laughed.

He chuckled, kissing my cheek and leaving me alone in the bathroom.

I completed the rest of my nightly routine quickly, drying my hair the best I could even though it stood on straight out and made me look like I'd been electrocuted.

I walked into the bedroom, and grabbed the first thing in my bag. I pulled on one of Romanus' shirts. It smelled of him, and hung to my knees, and I loved it. Although, there was a suspicious stain near the hem that my new super senses told me was blood. We really needed to do some laundry.

I walked out into the living room to see that they'd

completely transformed it. Or destroyed it, depending on your point of view. All the furniture in the living room had been pushed back, and someone had piled all the duvets and pillows onto the floor in front of the TV. There was a big ice bucket, filled with champagne, and several six packs of beer sitting on the coffee table, as well as several domed serving dishes filled with god-knows-what. Naz was already there, sucking back a beer, propped up on three pillows. He'd lost his shirt, and had his jeans unbuttoned. His tattoos undulated on his torso as his spoke, and looking at his body made me hungry. But not for food.

In deference to the other guys probably, Rouen was in a fluffy bathrobe that barely belted across his hips. When he moved, I got flashes of his dick, and it made me laugh. Best peep show ever.

I sat down beside Naz, and Rouen passed me a glass of champagne. Charlie was still working furiously, head-phones on, his fingers pounding the keyboard.

Romanus moved toward our wayward fourth, tapping him on the shoulder hard enough to get his attention. Charlie pushed his headphones from his ears.

"Enough for now, Charlie. Come and enjoy some time with your pack." His words were gentle, merely a suggestion to the casual listener, but I could hear the alpha power beneath the words.

Charlie pressed a few more keys and slipped his headphones from his neck. "Sure thing. This can run by itself anyway." He stood, stretching his arms above his head, and giving me a good eyeful of his hard stomach.

I had a vivid flash of running my tongue down his abs only days ago.

Heat grabbed at my core and I gave it a stern talking to. *Down girl. You need a rest day too. Chill the fuck out and just let me enjoy them.*

Charlie grabbed a beer, and tiptoed his way through the pillows to my side. I was snuggled in beside Naz, who had an arm wrapped around my shoulders, so Charlie just laid down, resting his head against my thighs.

He grinned up at me, then waggled his eyebrows as he lifted the hem of my shirt.

"Aren't you a little old to be looking up girls skirts, Charlie Mulligan?" I chastised as he groaned and flopped back against my thighs

"Never. But damn." He looked at Naz. "She's not wearing panties under there." He sounded both happy and in pain. I laughed and slapped away the hand the tried to sneak up my thigh.

"We a keeping it G rated tonight," I warned.

"G for g-spot?" Charlie suggested, curling his finger suggestively.

Rouen laughed, coming to sit beside me too, resting his legs on Charlie's abs. "G for Gargoyles-do-it-better."

Charlie's amethyst eye twinkled in the light. "Hey, I'm part gargoyle too."

Rouen held out a fist for a fist bump. "Hell yeah you are."

Romanus sat down on the other side of Rouen, closest to the door, and handed Charlie the remote. "Do whatever it is humans do to get the movies on the TV."

I laughed. I guess Hell didn't have Pay-per-view. Rouen grabbed one of the silver domed trays, and revealed tiny little pastry parcels. "Lobster puffs," he said, placing one to my lips. I bit into it, making sure my teeth scraped the tip of his finger. He did that intense thing, like watching me eat was some kind of foreplay, until I was done chewing.

"Ah ha!" Charlie yelled, and the screen changed to the opening credits of a movie. It was an old classic with Meg Ryan and Nicolas Cage. *City of Angels.*

"Very funny, Charlie," I said, running my fingers through his hair, scraping my nails across his scalp until he was all but purring.

I was happy.

CHAPTER TWENTY-FOUR

The mayor's secretary looked uncomfortable. Like her sky high heels were pinching, or she was worried she might have shit herself in public. That kind of uncomfortable. I knew the source though. It was the towering hunk of muscle beside me doing his best to look like a serial killer.

"Seriously, Rom. Stop. You are going to make the poor girl wet herself. You may mentally scar her for life if you don't stop staring at her like that."

I only felt marginally sorry for her. It was her own fault really. She'd insinuated that I was one of the Mayor's mistresses, before I'd even had a chance to introduce myself. I guess maybe I was dressed like someone's side-chick? The first button of my blouse was a lot lower than I'd initially noticed, and you saw the bow of my brand new lingerie. And if I stepped too long, you could probably see the lace trim of my thigh highs, and the decorative lace of my garter straps.

Rouen had very attentively helped me rolled on my stockings this morning. With his teeth. We'd almost run late for this appointment.

My cheeks heated at the memory of Rouen's face buried between my thighs. Romanus' nose flared at the scent of my desire, which effectively changed the object of his laser focus from the scared shitless secretary to me. I didn't mind. I liked his eyes on me. I twisted my hands in my lap, pressing my breasts up and out. Romanus' emerald and sapphire eyes followed the movement.

The secretary's phone rang, and she spoke softly into the receiver before hanging up. She cleared her throat. "Mr Trousseau will see you now."

I nodded my thanks, and Romanus gave the girl another death stare on the way through. He really didn't like the way she spoke to me. Protective bastard.

Louis Trousseau was a dapper guy, in his late forties. He was just getting a little grey along his temples, making him look distinguished and sexy, rather than old. He had on a plain white dress shirt, but the sleeves were rolled up his tanned forearms. He looked like he worked out.

He gave me a wide smile.

"Please, Miss Jones, come take a seat. Does your guard want to wait in the reception? I'm sure Cecelia will get him a coffee, maybe something to eat?" he offered.

I laughed. Romanus was more likely to eat Cecelia. And not in the fun way.

"If it is okay with you, I'd like him to stay. Don't worry about him though. You won't even notice him." I smiled pleasantly at Louis. He seemed nice enough. He had a kind face and a very genuine way of speaking that reminded me a little of Hope.

"Of course, of course. I was glad to hear from your personal assistant that you wanted to meet. I've always had a great respect for your parents foundation, and their goals. Very noble, no?" He had a heavy french accent, and it probably made him seem more charming than he was. It reminded me of Valery, one of my fathers. He had been french nobility once. Even after all these years, he had retained a little of the accent of his home country.

I made a sound of agreement, and watched appreciatively as he sat down behind his wide oak desk.

"We are very thankful that the NRH has taken an interest in Calais. As you know, the *sables mouvants* has been in Calais for nearly a decade now, as people flee the ecological disasters of their home countries. And the rate of eco-refugees is rising. We would welcome any solutions you and your foundation can provide."

I cocked my head to the side. "I'm sorry, my french is very basic. Sable…?"

"Ah, *sable mouvants*, uh, it means quicksand, no? It is what the locals call the camp. Because people come to Calais, to France to try and cross the Channel, but their laws are strict, and it is not so easy, so they become stuck here forever. No going forward, trying to cross into the UK, and no going back to where they come from."

THE UNREPENTANT   331

"Stuck," I repeated. Like fish in a barrel. I nodded. "What are you doing about the situation currently?"

Louis Trousseau let out a dramatic sigh. "We try to provide them with what we can, but every day, the camp grows. For every one that leaves, two more arrive. It has grown to over one hundred and fifty thousand in the last year. Our police force refuses to go there, for fear of being injured or worse. It is lawless place, filled with barbaric practices and desperate people."

"Are there any other organizations there now, trying to create a little order in the chaos?" I asked, trying to steer the conversation.

"They have tried, but very few remain. Shine stays with a skeleton crew. Enough to help those who want to be helped. The Red Cross provides rudimentary free healthcare to prevent the spread of disease. John Pierre Romaine is as close to an overseer that the camp has and he speaks on their behalf, coordinates the resources to those who need it most, but he is fighting a losing battle. He is a far better man than I. I would have given into despair many years ago," Louis said, shaking his head sadly.

We spoke for another thirty minutes about what the NRH could provide this Quicksand camp. A complete lack of formal education was going to hinder the next generation, so schooling was the first point of business. The Red Cross desperately needed more funding and more hands. Better housing and sanitation were necessary to prevent the current level of death and mortality in the camp.

I found myself writing notes, storing this all away, as

if I were really here as an ambassador, and not in Calais to hunt down and murder a bunch of human traffickers.

There was a knock on the door, and Cecilia the secretary poked her head around the door. "Excuse me sir, Mademoiselle. The press have arrived down in the conference room."

I stood and smoothed down my skirt, and Louis Trousseaus' eyes followed the movement. I could hear the low rumble of Romanus' growl behind me, and resisted the urge to smile. I hoped Louis thought it was a truck outside the window, or a helicopter, and not a jealous gargoyle who wanted to eat his face.

Louis grabbed his suit jacket, shrugging it over his broad shoulders and pointing out to the elevator.

"After you, Mademoiselle."

Cecilia was holding the lift open for us, either because she was an efficient secretary, or because she was eager to get rid of us. I was betting on the latter. I gave her a little finger wave as the door shut between us, and Romanus pulled me back toward his body and away from Louis. I let my fingers brush his. I would kiss every inch of him later to assure him that I had no interest in any other men outside our pack. Especially not a French politician, no matter how attractive he was.

The elevator stopped, and Louis stepped out, ushering me toward large double doors. Another efficient woman met us there.

"Mr Trousseau, Miss Jones. Just a little press conference. If you could talk about the issues you discussed, Miss Jones, and perhaps some solutions NRH is willing to provide, that will be enough. I have warned them that question time will be limited, so don't panic. This is basically a photo opportunity. Don't forget to smile," she said, giving me an exaggerated smile, showing artificially whitened teeth so bright I thought she may have injured my retinas.

"Thank you, Rebecca," Louis purred, and I looked between them. Yeah, they were definitely banging like french monkeys. Le chimps?

Louis pushed through the doors, and stood in front of the mic, greeting the journalists by name, and making a very pretty speech about improving life for all in the fair city of Calais, blah blah blah. I zoned out, my focus drawn to the press out in the crowd through the gap in the doors. Apparently, press looked the same everywhere. Like bored pitbulls.

"Please, welcome Estrella Jones, representative of the NRH Foundation."

There were a series of flashes as I walked out on stage, people snapping photos of my fake smile. This was why Hope did this shit. I was not a natural public figure, which was why I became a cop instead of going into the family business, so to speak.

I gave Louis a bright, genuine smile. His shoulders fit his suit jacket well, probably tailored. My eye caught on his lapel pin and I froze.

Uriel's Sigil.

Louis Trousseau, the Mayor of Calais, was Tenebre.

I don't know how I made it through the rest of the conference. I must have answered the questions okay, even though my mind was reeling. I hadn't picked up even a hint that Louis Trousseau was anything but concerned humanitarian. I'd liked the man. Thought he was attractive. Now I wanted to scrub out my eyeballs.

I escaped the meeting as soon as I could after the press conference was over, with assurances I was going to be in touch. Not a lie. I would see Louis Trousseau very soon, and may Lucifer have mercy on his soul.

CHAPTER TWENTY-FIVE

I was actually shaking by the time we got back to the hotel, though I wasn't sure why. I'd been in deadlier situations in my life. Hell, I'd been in deadlier situations this week. It wasn't fear that made me shake. It was this overwhelming anger, a red hot rage that was burning my gut, searing its way through my veins, demanding release.

Like a lot of cops, I'd always trusted my gut. It had been my moral compass, my safety net, my judge of character for so many years, that the fact I had been so wrong about Louis Trousseau was making me question everything.

Romanus had been quiet, his eyes hard as the gems they resembled, and Rouen and Naz seemed to intuitively know we needed silence.

When we got back to the hotel room, Charlie took one look at my shaking hands and frowned. "What happened?"

"I need to know everything there is to know about

Louis Trousseau. Everything. I want to know if he pays his taxes, what brand of toothpaste he likes, who his mistresses are and whether he sleeps on the left or right side of the bed. The fucker is Tenebre."

With that, I walked past him, running my hand over his arm so he knew I wasn't mad at him, and stomped off to the bedroom as fast as my sensible shoes could carry me. I tore open my shirt, letting the faux pearl buttons scatter all over the floor. I fumbled with the zip of my skirt, swearing when it jammed.

I sat on the edge of the bed and put my head in my hands. What the fuck was I doing here? Who the hell did I think I was, some comic book antihero, meting out justice as I felt like it? Dragging four other souls to Hell right along with me because I was a selfish asshole.

The door opened, but I didn't look up. I was having a pity party for one. A hand reached out and lifted my chin. I looked up at Naz.

"Why do you have Luc's wings tattooed on your back? Who in their right mind would permanently etch Satan's wings on their body?"

Who in their right mind would stay with me?

Naz's eyes widened a little, but he shrugged. "When I was eight, the Archangel Raphael put Adnan back together after a rocket hit our apartment building and collapsed the whole thing down on us. Memphis and Ace, these two scary ass angels with these glorious wings rescued me from Aleppo and brought me to the States. They gave me a new life. But I was so scared. And so, so angry. They dropped me off with your Dad's, these strangers. I know they were trying to fix your Mom now, but I felt abandoned." He pulled me to my feet. He reached out and worked the jammed zipper of my skirt down, holding my elbows as I stepped out of the pooled fabric.

"Then one day, I just snapped. I completely freaked, and Ace had to talk me down. But Luc was there, and I was transfixed. I wanted to piss myself, to run away, to cry and cry until I ran out of tears, just from looking at him. And I saw his huge black wings, his scary ass expression that weighed your very soul, you know the look?"

I nodded. I knew the look all right, I'd been on the receiving end of the look many, many times. He smiled, and it was a sad, bitter kind of smile. "Anyway, there I was, surrounded by people who were promising to love and protect me and Adnan, and Luc was there looking scary as fuck, and then he spoke in my head. He said 'You are mine now. None will cross me.' Even at eight I knew he was the Devil, I knew it in my very soul, but for the first time in my entire life I felt safe. Like truly safe. He gave me the first kernel of hope to fight the darkness. So I got the wings as a testament that even the bad guys can bring hope. Good. Bad. It's all subjective."

He stared down at me then, his eyes taking in my demi bra, my stockings held up with the pretty lace garter Rouen had picked, and he sucked in a gasp.

He swore reverently under his breath. His hands skimmed over the soft skin of my arms, shifting to my ribs and then down over my hips.

I stepped closer until our bodies were pressed tightly together. I tilted my head up, wetting my lower lip with my tongue. I wanted him to kiss me more than I wanted to breathe.

Naz didn't leave me hanging. He leaned down and traced my bottom lip with his tongue, sucking it into his mouth as his hands roamed lower.

He kissed me tenderly, with the careful movements of a hunter stalking its prey. Fingers brushed over my skin like whispering kisses, and I held my breath. I was in suspended animation. Waiting for him to grab me, throw me on the bed and make love to me with all the pent up passion he kept hidden behind that impenetrable wall so like my own.

But Naz had way too much patience for that. He eased a leg between my thighs and I couldn't resist the urge to rub myself on it like cat. My body bowed as he kissed me again, his mouth searching mine as if he could find the answers to the universe in the taste of my lips.

He turned me around so suddenly, a squeak escaped my lips. He pressed his lips against the column of my neck, kissing his way downwards, along the curve of my spine. He slid a hand up my ribs and across my back, pressing the palm of his hand between my shoulder blades. He pushed me forward until I was bent over the end of the bed, the straps of my garter pressing into the curve of my ass.

Naz growled long and low at the view, and the noise made my pussy pulse. He scraped his fingers along my spine, making my skin pebble beneath his touch. He pressed his body against my ass, my heels making me the perfect height to feel the hard press of his cock against my wet core. He bent forward, curving his body around mine, holding me tight against him as he kissed the line his fingers had just travelled. I ground back against him, desperate for him to loose his cock from his jeans. He just stepped away, and dropped to his knees, spreading my feet until I could feel the hot pants of his breath cooling the wetness of my panties. He hooked a finger around the edge, pulling the scrap of lace to the side.

The first lap of his tongue set my body on fire, and I moaned long and loud. Yes. His tongue made a few more lazy sweeps before he pressed it inside me. His hand slid up my thigh, moving it around to the front of my body to press against my clit.

Fuck.

I bucked against his face, and I heard the door open and close. When I looked around, they were all there. All my men, my mates.

I looked over my shoulder and watched Rouen run a hand over Naz's close cropped hair. "Allow me, Second." Naz growled against my pussy, making me bury my face into the comforter and let out a scream. Holy hell.

Whatever he saw in Rouen's face though had him shifting away from my pussy, relinquishing his spot to my Beta. He came around to kneel in front of me naked. He must have lost his pants on the short trip from behind me, and his dick sat proud along the flat expanse of his body. I lifted myself up on shaky arms and grabbed his cock, tugging him toward me so I could wrap my mouth around the hard rod of his cock.

He hissed out a breath as he slid into my mouth inch by tantalizing inch. All the while, Rouen's expert tongue was driving me crazy. His tongue had to be longer than a normal mans, because it was swirling and reaching things that were making lights flash behind my eyelids. I couldn't see Charlie and Rom, but I could feel their pleasure as they watched the other two touch and taste my body.

My orgasm swelled, and I screamed out my climax around Naz's cock. He grunted, holding my head still, thrusting into my mouth in quick shallow strokes.

He pulled away, and moved back around my body, Rouen moving away so Naz could slide his cock inside my dripping core. I arched my back and my arms shook. Romanus' hands moved to hold me up, his thumbs coming around to circle my nipples.

I threw my head back and came again, waves of pleasure wracking my body, until my arms collapsed. Romanus lowered me gently to the bed.

I rolled over, and Rouen was there, kissing me with lips that taste like my own desire. "Told you the lingerie was a winner, didn't I?" he said, grinning down at me.

I huffed out a laugh, looking around for Charlie. He was standing in the corner, naked, his hand lazily stroking his own hard cock. I looked at him with hooded eyes, appreciating the sexy dips and curves of his body.

I reached out a hand lazily, and curled my fingers at him. "Come here. That's mine."

He raised his brows, a contented grin curling his lips. "Yours? I don't know about that, Rella Rua. Seems to be attached to my body. I think that makes it mine."

Naz laughed from where he lay beside me. "I think she really wants her orgy, Charlie. Don't deny the lady."

Charlie swaggered over to me, kissing me hard on the mouth, branding me as his yet again. His fingers deftly unclipped my garter, and I had an inkling this wasn't his first time divesting a woman of her lingerie.

He hooked his fingers on my lace panties and I lifted my ass so he could tug them down my legs. As he flicked them off of my feet, he lifted my knees and pushed them to the side, baring me to every man, er gargoyle, in the room. The heavy scent of arousal thickened the air, and I could feel the caress of four sets of eyes.

He settled himself between my knees, hiding me from view, but I could feel the heavy press of the head of his cock against my entrance. But I wanted to be on top. I was Queen.

With my newfound strength, I flipped us so I was on top. From here, I could see Naz laying beside us, his eyes watching me with a look so hot it threatened to scorch my flesh. I could see Romanus at the head of the bed, his eyes running over every inch of me, and as I lowered myself onto Charlie, his lip curled in a little snarl of lust.

I was going to come just from their eyes alone. Charlie grabbed my hips and slammed me down on his cock, my eyes shooting back to the man beneath me. There was just me and Charlie for a moment as we found that timeless rhythm.

The sounds of pleasure rolled around the room. Mine, theirs, it didn't matter, it was the most beautiful sound I'd ever heard. Rouen came up behind us, and his eyes met Charlie's over my shoulder.

"Can I?" Rouen asked, and I twisted toward him, but his eyes were on Charlie.

They seemed to be having a wordless conversation, and Charlie's rhythm faltered as his face creased. But then he nodded.

Rouen pushed me forward, and Charlie wrapped his arms around my back, thrusting up into my body hard, hitting all sorts of spots that made me scream into his chest.

I felt more than heard Charlie suck in a breath as he stilled. "Holy fuck," he hissed, and I sat up a bit, confused. But then I felt Rouen's tongue slide against my slit. Holy fuck, indeed.

Charlie sped up again, whimpering with helpless pleasure at whatever Rouen was doing behind us. Then I felt the finger slip through my slick juices, and circle my ass. Oh damn.

Rouen pressed a finger inside me, and I clenched around Charlie's cock as the dual sensations meshed together. Charlie slammed into me over and over, and then he was shuddering, his hot cum emptying inside me, making my inner muscle convulse as I came. Again. I kissed Charlie hard, letting my tongue tangle with his. Then I slid off, wanting to see what Rouen was doing that made Charlie go wild like that.

Rouen was kneeling between Charlie's thighs, and I sucked in a breath. Charlie couldn't tear his eyes away from the Gargoyle who's big golden head was a hairs-breadth from his cock.

"Charlie?" Rouen said, asking permission. Asking permission to what?

But Charlie nodded again, hesitantly this time without me as a buffer. Rouen face was so flawlessly happy that I would have given anything to have him smile like that every minute of the day. "I am going to lick our Queen's cum from your dick, and I'm going to taste you both on my tongue," he explained, pausing to let Charlie protest, but my sexy irishman was silent. When Rouen slid his tongue up the semi hard cock of Charlie, I thought I'd come just at the sight. Fuck. Then he took Charlie in his mouth, and I could feel my own juices dripping down my thighs. Double fuck!

Romanus was suddenly there, picking me up and sliding me onto his already hard cock, but not obscuring my view of our Betas. Charlie had his head thrown back as Rouen moved his mouth up and down his now hard as a rock cock, his hands wrapped in the blankets in a white knuckled grip. Rouen had his hand on his own dick, stroking in time with his mouth.

Naz was pumping his cock where he rested against the wall, chasing the echoes of so much pleasure. My nails dug into Romanus' shoulders as he pounded into me like a demon. I couldn't sort the pleasure flowing through our bond anymore, it was just one huge nimbus of sensations so intense it was nearly painful.

I screamed so hard when I came again that my throat hurt, and I sent my pleasure in a bright golden wave down our bonds. I bit down hard on Romanus' shoulder, anchoring myself to my Alpha incase the pleasure blew us all to smithereens.

"Fuck!" Charlie shouted, grabbing Rouen's head and thrusting hard into his mouth. Rouen choked him down, his own cum spurting in hot waves all over the comforter.

Romanus collapsed us both back onto the bed, and I shifted off him so I could touch a little part of them all. Especially Charlie. I stroked his hair.

"I love you," I said, but I wasn't speaking just to Charlie. I loved them all so much it threatened to break me apart.

Romanus made a contented humming sound. "Guess that sorts the pack structure too."

I raised myself up on my elbows. "Seriously? How?"

Romanus pointed to Charlie. "He's Third. Rouen is still Beta."

Huh. Well, that was a hell of a lot more fun then when Romanus and Nazir had to sort out their pack rankings. There were still a lot of bodily fluids, but none of it was blood. My eyes snagged on the bite mark on Romanus' chest from my teeth. Well, almost none of it.

Naz's fingers ran through my short hair.

"Someone should leave a damn big tip for the cleaning lady," he murmured.

Laughter swelled in my chest, and mixed with happiness.

CHAPTER TWENTY-SIX

Apparently there was no better way to finish off a great demon orgy than with a little blood letting. Louis Trousseau sat cable-tied to a chair in his living room. Luckily, his wife and kids were in Paris for the night.

His security detail had been laughably easy to disable, and if I was Louis, I'd be writing a strongly worded letter to my security firm. If he lasted the night, that is.

"Come on, Mr Mayor. Please don't insult my intelligence. I know you are Tenebre. We know the Tenebre traffic humans. Do you have your own little harem of stolen women here? Girls? Boys? People you took from their families and bought like cattle. Should we check your basement?"

Louis Trousseau stared at me with absolute venom in his gaze, his unblinking stare, his hatred coming off him in almost tangible waves. But he remained stubbornly silent.

"No? Not here? Maybe in the apartment your corporation rents down by the docks. Odd place to rent a service apartment if you ask me. Rough area to put up your business colleagues for the night."

Still nothing. I sighed, and pulled one of my swords from their scabbards.

Rouen came over, leaning close. "You in lingerie is hot, but you drawing a sword from a cross scabbard…" he whispered, making a groaning noise beneath his breath. I remembered the look on his face as he sucked Charlie, and my libido went wild, making my body tingle. That one was going to be in the spank bank for eternity.

"Let's move him to the bathtub. Don't want his kids to come home and be traumatized by all the blood in their living room, right? Easier for the clean up crew as well."

I ran the sharp tip of my sword up over the Mayor's finely cut shirt, pressing the point into the hollow of his throat. In the smartest move he'd made that night, he held perfectly still.

"I didn't touch any of the people they took. What they do, it's not my thing. The apartment is for my mistress and her child," he whispered.

I raised an eyebrow. "Her child?"

He swallowed hard, his face freezing in horror as the movement made my sword nick his throat. These really were sharp. I had a whole new appreciation for Rouen's swordsmithing skills.

"Our child," he corrected, confirming my hunch.

"Well, while I don't condone you betraying the sanctity of your marriage, I'm bonded to four men. So people in glass houses, right?"

I lowered my sword a little, and he sucked in a deep breath.

"But you knew though, didn't you? Knew they were stealing people from *Sable Mouvants*. If you weren't a part of it, I know you were complicit. That makes you just as bad in my opinion."

"Mine too," Naz growled, holding his gun tight to Louis Trousseau's temple. "I was a refugee once. One of those people fleeing to a better place. I don't appreciate you treating them as expendable."

Louis Trousseau didn't cry in the face of Naz's threats, and a small part of me respected his brass balls. The bigger part of me wanted to inflict hurt on him, though. The darkness in my soul was loving this.

I put a hand on Naz's wrist. "Look, Louis, I liked you when we first met. This is why I'm just so disappointed in you right now. But I'm going to give you a chance to redeem yourself, somewhat. Now we've opened up a dialogue, and you see we can be quite reasonable, I'm going to ask you a few questions. How you answer those questions will be the indicator of whether you live or die tonight."

I leaned in close. "Don't lie to me, though. Trust me, my big scary friend back there will know if you are lying, and he'll be more than happy to tear your head from your shoulders, blood splatter be damned. Do we understand each other?" Louis looked past me to Romanus, who was indeed doing his best big and scary impression, and nodded.

I stood up and clapped my hands together. A subconscious part of my brain argued that perhaps I was becoming a little unhinged as the darkness in my soul came out to play.

I sat down opposite him, crossing my legs and threading my hands behind my head. "Let's talk about Tenebre, shall we?"

Silence again, but he gave a short nod of his head. Progress.

"Let's start basic, yeah? Who, or maybe I should say what, is Tenebre? I know it's Latin for darkness, which is a little on the nose, if you ask me." I tapped the side of the aforementioned appendage. "Give me something else. How did they recruit you?"

"They recruited me out of university. They explained it like it was some exclusive, uh, fraternity, no? But they promise to set you up in a position of power or influence. They got me in as an aide to the President straight out of university, and then into other high ranking positions until I ended up Mayor. At first, they asked for nothing…"

Naz stared hatred at Louis. "Until they asked for everything, right?" he asked.

Louis Trousseau swallowed hard, as if he could see his life flashing before his eyes.

"They came to me, said that one of the arms of Tenebre needed to operate out of *Sable Mouvants* and it was now my turn to pay back everything they had given me. Or they would take it all away."

He indicated the house, but I knew what he meant. A strong threat if you've spent your entire career on top.

"And what did they want you to do?" I asked, with a patience I wasn't feeling.

"Get the *flics*, the Police, to turn a blind eye to reports of refugee disappearances. Not to provide any assistance or resources to the camp. Tie up any offers of aid from outside sources in red tape."

"They wanted the people in the camp to remain desperate," I murmured, feeling ill. Tenebre played the long game, and that kind of insidious evil had a way of spreading like a virus.

Louis nodded, looking scared, but not overly ashamed.

"How many members does Tenebre have?"

He shrugged. "Thousands? Maybe hundreds of thousands. I could not tell you. We have networks, of about twenty-five to thirty. But they are from all over the world. Our meetings a teleconferenced."

I looked over my shoulder at Romanus. "Pass me the photo." He raised a single eyebrow. "Please," I added.

He pulled a photo out of his pocket and handed it to me. It was a slightly grainy photo of Maximoff Richards, the pharmaceutical tycoon from the auction.

"Do you know this man?" I watched Louis go grey as the blood leached from his face.

"Yes."

"Do you understand why I'm here now?"

He nodded slowly, and I could see the defeat in his eyes. He didn't think he was going to get out of this unscathed anymore. He didn't have to know we found him by pure, dumb luck. Or maybe it was fate, if you believed in that kind of thing.

I looked at him expectantly, waiting for an explanation, a last ditch effort to plead his case.

"I didn't know," he said, his voice rising an octave as desperation crept into his voice. "I mean, I knew, but I didn't know who. He just said he needed to take care of a business rival who was going to cost him millions. I didn't even make the connection until just then. If I'd known, I swear I would have had a pressing engagement anywhere else when your sister's PA called to set up today's meeting."

I laughed. Poor bastard, I was beginning to feel a little sorry for him. But it was a fleeting feeling. Regardless of the who, he'd approved the murder of an innocent person for the financial gain of a scumbag like Maximoff Richards. It was just his bad luck that it happened to be my family.

But now I had a name, someone to cross off my shitlist. And I had Louis Trousseau to thank for that.

"One last question, Louis, and then we're finished. The overseer, and the representatives for Shine out at the camp, did they know that people were being stolen to be sold to the highest bidder?"

"I don't know."

My sword whipped back up, and settled against his chest, right over his heart. "I don't believe you."

"I swear it on my children's lives. I was given my orders, but they don't give us any other Tenebre contacts in the same area. I think it's to prevent us turning on each other. My contacts are from Hong Kong, Sydney, New York," he swallowed hard, "but I don't know any other who are in France. They are here, but I wouldn't recognize them if I walked past them in the street, or shook their hand."

There was a wild fierceness in his face now, the kind of crazed truthfulness that people get before their executions or on their deathbeds.

I dropped my sword again. "I believe you. Hang tight, Louis. I have to talk to my friends. Rou, watch him."

My Beta did as he was told, and I walked over to talk to Romanus and Naz.

"I believe him, but now I'm not sure what to do. He's guilty, as guilty as a man can be, but taking out the Mayor of Calais is pretty high profile, even for us."

Naz shrugged. "We can do it. Why would anyone suspect us? We've never met the guy before today."

Romanus was silent for a moment, contemplating our current situation before he spoke. "We cannot kill them all. He said thousands. Murdering a person in cold blood does things to a man," he looked to Naz, then back at me. "Or woman. I say we let him live. But we will pass on his name to someone else. He will get his karmic returns, Rella."

I thought hard about both of their opinions, but in the end, my mother's soft heart won out. I couldn't kill an unarmed and restrained man.

I turned back to the room. "Let's take a vote. All those in favor of letting the Mayor live, raise your hand."

I got a sick sense of satisfaction out of watching Louis Trousseau struggle to raise his hand against his bindings. I was glad Hope wasn't here to see me now. I raised my hand, and so did Romanus. Surprisingly, my normally even tempered Beta's hand stayed firmly down.

I gave him a questioning look, but he just shrugged. "He's a scumbag. The world would be better without him," he said evenly, like we were talking about a cockroach rather than a human.

"Noted. Well, Trousseau, looks like you are the deciding vote. What do you say?"

The bound man looked at me like I was crazy, which probably wasn't all that wrong at this point.

"I vote to live," he said slowly, ensuring I couldn't misconstrue his answer.

"Looks like the ayes have it. Sorry boys, no bloodshed tonight." I walked up to Louis Trousseau and punched him hard in the face. The satisfying sound of his nose crunching under my fist made me smile. "Well, minimal bloodshed."

I got down closer, so he could see how serious I was about my next words.

"Mayor, I strongly suggest you retire, abandon Tenebre, move to the country and raise chickens. Because if I hear even the faintest stir that your corrupt ass is still in politics, I'm personally going to come back here and shred your flesh so finely that they'll be able to bury you in a cigar box. Are we clear?"

He nodded, his eyes watering. Ugh, he was about to cry. That was our cue to leave.

"Let's go," I said to the guys, leaving behind a sobbing Trousseau tied to the chair.

CHAPTER TWENTY-SEVEN

I lay in bed early the following morning, trying to judge the time difference between Hope and I. Ah, fuck it.

Hope?

The sensation of her surprise came back through the bond, *Shit, Rella, uh… hey, how are you?*

She sounded flustered, and I grinned.

Am I interrupting something?

What? No! I'm just in bed. Sleeping.

I grinned harder. Liar, liar. She'd never been good at lying, but I'd let it slide this time.

Can you talk? I've got some news.

What is it?

I took a deep breath. I'd agonized over whether I should tell her at all, or just get rid of the problem myself and let her continue moving on with her life. But the fact remained, I was in Europe and she was in Manhattan and until I was home, she was at risk if she was unaware of what stalked her.

I found out who ordered your kidnapping. It was Maximoff Richards.

I didn't have to explain who that was to Hope. She had an almost eidetic memory for names and faces. I could feel the shock rocketing down the bond and I wanted to wrap her in my arms and tell her there was no reason to worry.

Oh. That was all she said as she let it sink in. *Why? I mean, I know why, but what I can't understand is why bother going to those lengths to take me out. I'm a figurehead at most. The NRH would still have continued our pharmaceutical plans without me.*

I wasn't so sure about that. The NRH would continue, sure, but the disappearance and possible death of Hope would have destroyed us all for a long time. She was an integral part of the NRH, and the beating heart of our family.

Is Blue Halloran back from Boston yet? Are you protected?

Hesitation. *Yes.*

Hmmm not a lie, but she was hedging all the same. I sighed to myself. There was nothing I could do about it now. I'd be back in two days, and then I'd get to the bottom of what the hell was going on with her and the Mulligan Family's favorite enforcer.

I better go. Love you, Hope. Say hi to Memphis for me, I teased.

You can't see me, but I'm flipping you the bird right now. Love you, Rella. Be safe, she answered, and we both slid our mental shields back into place.

I rolled over in bed and wrapped my arms around Naz,

feeling Romanus at my back. I snuggled down between them, loathe to get out of bed. But we had appointments to keep, and I desperately wanted to go home already.

I heaved a sigh and wiggled my way out from between them. I shifted around on floor, looking for yesterday's skirt. I peeked over my shoulder to see Romanus' eyes heavy with lust. I gave him a little butt wiggle and he growled. Damn that sound just went straight to all my happy places.

I blew him a kiss over my shoulder and walked toward the bathroom. I turned on the shower and hopped in.

"Five," I whispered under my breath. "Four, three, two…"

The door clicked open and there was suddenly a body in the shower with me. I let out a little oomph as I was picked up and pressed between the wall and Romanus' hard chest.

I smiled against the lips devouring mine.

"One."

MY HEART ACHED as I walked past another small child with eyes that were too big and limbs that were too thin. As I spoke to the people, I came to understand why the camp was colloquially called Quicksand. It seemed the more desperately people tried to leave, the more they were dragged deeper into hopelessness until some gave up altogether. Charlie's eyes were uncharacteristically somber as he took in a level of poverty around us. I reached out and grabbed his hand, but I wasn't sure who was supporting whom.

John Pierre Romaine, the overseer of *Sable Mouvants* was a French expatriate who lived in London until five years ago, when he came over to do a university placement with an aid organization, but stayed even when the organization left. He seemed like a genuine enough guy, but I no longer trusted my gut instinct after the Louis Trousseau debacle.

He walked us through the haphazard streets of The Quicksand, tents and shanty houses put together from building waste and trash. "I couldn't leave. I tried to go back to university, back to downing beer with my mates at the pub every Friday night, but all I could see was the sad eyes of a kid who'd never known an actual bed. The place really is quicksand. You can't just walk away." We stopped outside a shed made of sheet metal. "This is the closest thing to a restaurant we have here. The people in this camp know how to make do with what little we get, and I try to ensure that the money stays in the camp, you know. We have a couple of teachers who run a school for the kids, and we try to ask the city for money to feed the them lunch every day. A guaranteed meal, even if it's just rice or beans."

The woman inside had a bright smile, but a face that was lined so deeply it told of a life that was marred by worry. She handed us a plastic cup of rice, a thick stew on top. I gave her a hundred bucks from my purse.

She protested in a language I didn't understand, attempting to hand it back, but I insisted.

"Tell her to use it for produce or use it wherever it's needed," I said to John Pierre.

JP, he insisted I should call him JP, translated what I said, but the lady let fire a rapid spill of Arabic, I think.

I leaned closer to Naz. "What's she saying?"

"She's insisting we come to lunch. JP is telling her that you might be busy."

I placed a hand on JP's elbow. "Tell her we would be honored to join her for lunch."

JP's face lit up with respect, and then explained that we would come. The bright smile made its way to the elderly lady's eyes this time.

She turned to a boy in the building behind her, and gave him an order that had him tearing out of the shanty and away down the alley between the buildings.

After eating our stew, which was amazingly tasty despite the limited ingredients, we moved along.

JP showed us the school, and the woefully under-resourced medical center. But while the strong sense of desperation permeated everything, there were also kids playing football in the streets, laughing and arguing, while old men talked in fold up chairs out the front of makeshift houses, and weathered women scrubbed linens in big tubs of water. It was its own little micro-cosm of life, irrefutable proof of the tenacity of the human race.

An hour later we stopped out the front of a house. Well, it was several rough buildings jammed together to create the idea of a house.

"This is Helena's place. She and her husband Farouk live here with their daughters and grandchildren.

Farouk is a carpenter, and spends most of his days weatherproofing the more basic shanties, getting people out of tents. Their sons-in-laws have gone to England searching for better work, but they have no status there. They are illegals. Aliens," JP explained.

He knocked on the doorframe. A man a decade older looking than Helena answered the door, but his smile was just as wide.

"Come in. John Pierre, are you staying for a meal?" he asked in heavily accented english.

"No, sorry Farouk. Too much work to do. Helena fed me earlier though," he laughed as he clapped the older man on the arm. He turned to us. "It was a pleasure meeting you all." His eyes met mine. "I hope we can work together some time in the future. We need your help."

I reached out and shook his hand. "You have my word."

I meant it too. There were always too many people in need. It was like bucketing water from a well during a monsoon. But we had to try.

Farouk showed us through to what I assumed was the communal living area. "Please sit, sit," Farouk insisted, rattling off the names of his daughters and grandchildren so fast I would never remember them as he pointed to woven mats on the floor and indicating we should sit on them.

But I did recognize the boy from earlier, who's name apparently was Sunny. I smiled and thanked them for their hospitality. The women bustled between the room and the kitchen, eyeing my four guys who took up way too much space in the little shack.

As soon as Farouk realized that Naz spoke arabic, they were engrossed in a conversation that was so rapid, I had no chance of keeping up. I had no idea that Naz still spoke the language of his childhood, but I was glad he did.

At some point, a toddler came over, and poked Romanus in the chest, her grimy little fingers reaching up to rub his stubble covered cheeks. Romanus, my big, mean looking Alpha, turned his face to the side and blew a noisy raspberry on the toddlers pudgy little hand, making the baby emit the most adorable giggling sound. The baby shuffled closer until she was sitting on Romanus' knee, poking his face again, until more raspberries were given. It went straight to my ovaries.

When another of Farouk and Helena's daughters came out and saw, she smiled, waggling her eyebrows at me in the universal female sign language for 'what a hottie, you should get you some of that.' I laughed, well, until she handed me a baby.

For the lack of son's-in-law here, there was an awful lot of tiny humans. I looked down at the little baby, who's tiny, serious eyes were searching my face, and wondered what my kids would look like. Could we even have kids, now we were all kind of half gargoyle? It was a question for Romanus, but I didn't think he would know either. Our situation was pretty unique. Maybe, I'd just get my IUD removed, and see what fate and mother nature had to say about the whole thing.

I held the baby out and away from me, worried I'd

drop it, or suffocate it on my shoulder or any of the million other ways I could break such a fragile little being.

"Can I hold?" Rouen asked from my other side, and I looked to the baby's mother. She nodded, as she dropped off a platter of food, and then walk/ran back to the kitchen.

Rouen cooed at the baby as he tucked it into the crook of his arm, making cutesie noises that sounded completely ridiculous coming out of the mouth of a gargoyle.

"Please, eat," he said, shooing the older kids away until we'd each picked up something from the tray. I chose a cabbage leaf stuffed with some kind of spiced rice, and it was amazing.

Eventually, all the food was on the floor between us, and the kids had their own little plate of food in the corner so Helena and her daughters could sit with us. We talked about life in the camp, their worries for their husbands, their worry that they would never leave The Quicksand, and neither would their kids.

I told them all the suggestions I would make to the board of the NRH. A purpose built clinic and school room, scholarships and sponsorships for teens and young adults, to help them get started in life. Better shelter against the cold seaside winters.

I hesitated. "Have there been any weird disappearances in the camp?"

Helena and Farouk looked at each other, and when Farouk spoke, he chose his words carefully. "Always, people are leaving camp, disappearing across the channel. But even if they do not tell John Pierre they are leaving, always the camp knows. Lately, people have been leaving without a word. Just vanish."

I'd suspected it was true, and Louis had said as much, but a tiny part of me was hoping I was wrong.

"I'm going to try and fix that too." I nodded, and we stood. Rouen handed the sleeping baby back to his mother. Romanus smiled at his toddling friend, who was stuffing so much rice in her mouth that it was dribbling out the sides.

Helena and Farouk showed us to the door. "Thank you for your hospitality," I said again.

Helena reached out, holding my forearms tightly. "You will do good," she said in very halted english. I didn't need to ask what she meant.

I stared at her in the eye, giving her a look that promised her I would try, even if she didn't understand my next words. "I will do everything in my power to make sure no one else vanishes."

We said our goodbyes, and I left with a sick feeling in my stomach that had nothing to do with Helena's cooking and everything to do with her confirming my suspicions.

"Let's go talk to the Shine rep," I said, and strode back the way we came.

Both JP and Franco de Moines' offices were housed in one of the few proper buildings in the camp. Our SUV was parked next to a banged up old Toyota and some kind of three wheeled utility vehicle that hardly looked roadworthy.

Franco, I found out, was a slightly pudgy older man

with worry lines an inch deep on his forehead and a lot of grey hair. He wore grandpa cardigans and spoke with a slight lisp that made his accent, which was somewhere between Spanish and French, almost unintelligible.

He gave the guys standing around me only a cursory glance before handing me a huge wad of paper and telling me everything he'd been trying to achieve in the camp, including graphs and projections. If this was a front, I had to hand it to Franco de Moines, he'd done his due diligence.

I suddenly wished I had Hope's ability to be a human lie detector. But I had a pretty good bullshit-o-meter and two gargoyles with supernatural senses, so that was going to have to do.

"Did you know that the Shine Foundation is a front for a people smuggling operation?"

If it hadn't been such a dire situation, it would have been almost comical. His jaw fell open, his eyes went so wide they almost took up half his face.

He let out a squeak, then a huff, before he said, "Pardon?"

I was kind of worried the old guy might have a stroke. But then he straightened his shoulders, an angry flush rising up his neck and into his cheeks. "How dare you? I have worked night and day crusading for this camp, trying to make this awful place something a little bit better. And you think what, that I'm here stealing people?" His voice rose higher and higher with each word until he was whisper yelling at me.

I gave him a reassuring smile. "No, Mr de Moines, I don't think you are smuggling people. But I know for a fact Shine is a front for a consortia of people who do bad things, and that someone is stealing people from right under your nose here at *Sable Mouvants*. What I'm telling you is that you have to find out who, and do not go to Interpol. I'll leave you the number for someone I trust, and they will make the problem go away. But be careful. They are dangerous and will do anything to protect their interests." I leaned forward, placing my hands on his folding table which was doubling as a desk. "But if I find out you do have anything to do with this, I will find you, and turn you inside out. Clear?"

Franco's face was still ruddy, but he nodded. "I believe you, Miss Jones. Now get the hell out of my office."

I nodded politely, standing and walking out the door of his office. Surprisingly, I did believe him. He seemed like he was genuinely crusading for the people of The Quicksand. It was that or he was a really good con artist. I wasn't sure I could tell the difference anymore.

We walked down the three steps and towards the car. I was suddenly exhausted, like I couldn't draw in enough air to fill me up.

"Let's go home," I said to them as we walked across the gravel parking lot. "Charlie, call NRH and see if we can borrow the jet. If not, let's just fly commercial."

Charlie nodded, leaning over to kiss me, already sliding his phone from his pocket. He climbed in the backseat of the SUV beside Rouen and Naz hopped in the passenger side. I wondered if they meant to split themselves into Alphas and Betas, or if it was just a happy coincidence?

Romanus hopped in the driver's seat, no surprise, and I stood at the door, taking one last look at The Quicksand. I felt like I was abandoning them already. I understood now why JP couldn't go home and I'd been here only hours.

"Miss Jones!" Sunny yelled as he raced down the street toward me, a foil wrapped package in his hand. I met him at the steps of the demountable office buildings. "My grandmother sent this for you to take home. It is the fatoush that you liked."

I took the food from Sunny. "You are a lucky boy, Sunny, to have such wonderful grandparents. You tell Helena that I will see her soon, okay?" I waved goodbye, as I walked toward the car, sad but relieved.

Tick. Tick.

The car, containing nearly every piece of my heart, exploded into a fiery ball of flames.

CHAPTER TWENTY-EIGHT

My eyes stung and the world was silent except a high pitch ringing in my ears. I staggered to my feet, weaving as my everything spun.

I needed to get to the car. They needed me. Why couldn't I feel the bonds?

I tripped over some debris, falling to my hands and knees. Blood dripped down my face, and I struggled to see. I wiped my eyes, and immediately wished I'd been blind. Rouen was on the ground, the bottom half his torso missing, his face burned and charred, his golden eye staring sightlessly.

"Rouen!" I screamed as I struggled to his side, my hands desperately trying to close the wound in his abdomen, to put everything back inside where it was supposed to be. I couldn't hear anything, not even myself, my throat aching from what I subconsciously realized were my own screams.

I crawled away from Rouen towards the flames. I

had to get to them. They needed me. The doors were already gone and I stood, my hands slick with Rouen's blood slipping when I grabbed the shell of the car.

I refused to believe what I saw. Romanus was indestructible. He was my alpha. He would survive a tank. I refused to believe the torso still strapped into the driver's seat was Romanus. He could survive a car bomb.

Naz sat in the back, asleep. His head was at a weird angle, but he would be fine, if I could just get him out of the flames. I reached in, dragging him across the backseat. Why couldn't I move him?

"Come on, Naz. I need you. Please," I sobbed, as I pulled him from the wreckage. I overbalanced, pulling Naz down on top of me, cracking my head on the gravel. His body laid over mine, and my heart knew what my brain refused to contemplate.

"No, no, no, come on, wake up." I shifted him off me, trying to do CPR. Where was everyone? "Help me!" There was no thumping of his heart, no steady rise and fall of his chest.

I felt a tug on my bond. Charlie. I crawled across the gravel, cutting up my hands and knees in my skirt, but I didn't feel it.

Charlie was on the other side of the car, blood covering his face. "Rella," he gasped, blood bubbling past his lips. I grabbed hold of his hand and pressed it to my cheek.

"I'm here, Charlie. We're gonna be okay. All of us. We're gonna be okay. I love you so much. We're going to be okay."

His body started convulsing as he coughed, the

blood from his mouth spraying over my face. I turned him on his side, desperately trying to free his airway, but his body shook with wet gasping breaths until they stopped.

"Charlie? Stay with me. Don't leave me."

I laid my head on his chest, straining to feel the beat of his heart against my cheek. Silence.

Someone grabbed my shoulder and rolled me off of Charlie. Finally, help had arrived.

My brain failed to comprehend why I was looking at Pedro the Arms Dealer. What was he doing here?

He was saying something, but I couldn't hear him over the high pitch ringing in my ears.

"What?" I shouted.

He leaned closer, until he was shouting directly into my ear. "I said, tell Naz no hard feelings. It's just business."

I felt the cold press of a gun barrel against my head. Then black.

CHAPTER TWENTY-NINE

The white light of the room threatened to blind me. I squinted, raising my hand to shade my face. Holy shit, was I in heaven?

"Hardly," a familiar voice answered my unspoken question.

I turned and looked at Luc, Ace beside him. They looked pissed.

I blinked a few times, adjusting to the light. Where the fuck was I?

The bomb. The guys. Fucking Pedro.

"Figures she wouldn't end up with soul amnesia. She's been one foot in here since high school," Ace murmured to Luc. She came over and hugged me, and that's when it all sunk in like I was being doused in acid. I was dead. And in Hell. The kind with a capital H.

I looked around the room, with its snowy white marble. "This is kind of false advertising, don't you think?"

Luc rolled his eyes. "You are in Hell, Estrella. I am

the Lord of Hell. Now would be the time to learn to be a little more respectful."

Eesh. Probably sound life, er, afterlife advice. I searched the white halls. "Where's Charlie? Where's my guys?"

"My guys," Luc corrected. "Charles Mulligan has made it just outside the doors of the palace. Nazir's soul was sorted to the first level, but I have sent someone to fetch him back."

I turned to him now, closing the distance between us. "Luc, where's Romanus and Rouen?" I didn't like the stubborn set of his jaw. "Luc?"

"They had one job, Estrella. One. And they failed and now you are dead. I'm unsure you a fully grasping the seriousness of your situation. You are dead."

"Luc…" I warned. "Where are they?"

He raised his chin. "I'm the Devil, I am true to my word. You don't get to question me, Child. I staked them in the demoness pit as promised."

"No!" I shouted.

"Yes. They let you die!" he roared back. "You are my child and they let your mortal life end at twenty-two. They needed to be punished." His voice had gotten scarily low, which made all the little hairs on my arm raise.

I took a deep breath. "It wasn't their fault. If it was anyone's fault, it was mine. Please, Luc. I need them."

He stared at me, his jaw set stubbornly in his scarily handsome face.

Ace, who'd been silent up until now, sighed heavily.

"I have to go. They've just discovered your death." Then she disappeared.

I didn't have to ask who They were. My family. I'd never see them again.

Tears spilled from my eyes to run in a huge deluge down my cheeks until they were wetting my shirt. I scrambled around for my bond to Hope, but it was gone. I couldn't imagine the pain she was feeling right now, and I couldn't soothe her, couldn't wrap her in my arms and protect her from this or any other hurt ever again.

I was suddenly pressed against a big chest, huge dark wings wrapping around me, as Luc hugged me.

The shock was enough to slow my tears. "It will be okay, Estrella, Child of my Beloved." I hadn't forgotten he called me *his* child earlier. "I promise it won't be so bad. You will be happy here at the palace with Ace and I. You will see your family again, I will make sure of it."

He patted my back awkwardly, then released me. "Let us go get the *Gargoille*. It is pancake day, and the demonesses should still be gorging themselves in the palace kitchen, so your beasts should be unmolested."

I just blinked "Pancake day?"

"Mmmhmmm. The only thing the demonesses like more than cock is pancakes."

Luc led me from the white room and down a hall-way, the marble floors getting darker and darker until they were black. Once we stepped outside the palace doors, Luc clicked his fingers and we were somewhere else.

My eyes fell on Romanus and Rouen, their naked bodies staked to the ground spread eagle.

"Romanus! Rouen!" I ran from Luc's side to Rouen who was closer. His eyes found mine, and they were a heartbreaking mixture of relief and guilt. I pulled at his bindings, until his arms were free. They came around my back, crushing me to his bare chest.

"I'm sorry. I'm sorry. I'm sorry," he repeated over and over against my ear. My tears started up again.

"It's okay. Let's get you out of here." He sat up and worked the knots around his ankles while I went to work on Romanus.

I knelt beside him, but Rom refused to meet my gaze. "Leave," he growled, shaking his wrists and making it almost impossible to untie the bindings.

"As if. Now sit still."

He continued to struggle. "You need to go. Take Rouen. I failed you both. I deserve punishment. Damnation. Your mortal body is gone, because of me."

I gripped his face, forcing him to meet my eyes. "Listen to me. This was not your fault. This was all Tenebre, and that fucker Pedro, and we are going to make sure they get their karmic punishment. But I need my Alpha. I need you to love me, and tell me it'll be okay as long as we are together. I need you."

His green and blue eyes stared at me, looking past my face and deep into my soul. He heaved out a breath that shook his whole body, and stopped struggling so I could untie his bindings. Rouen did his feet, his hand squeezing Romanus' leg in silent support.

When they were free, all three of us stood before Luc, a united front.

The King of Hell, the Devil himself, heaved an exasperated sigh. "Even when you were a tiny infant, barely weeks old, I just knew you were going to be trouble, Estrella Jones." He turned and left the demoness pit, and I averted my eyes from the other souls staked in the ground. I hadn't noticed them before, my focus totally on my guys. People being punished was a sight I would have to get used to if I was going to live in Hell.

Luc snapped his fingers, and we were back in the palace. Charlie and Nazir stood talking to Gusion, the beautiful Prince of Hell.

I let go of Romanus and Rouen's hands, tearing across the marble to throw myself into Naz's arms. I reached out for Charlie and dragged him to me. I felt the press of the gargoyles to my back, and finally I could breathe.

"You can get emotional later. Come. I'll show you to your suite. I had it prepared twenty odd years ago for your parents, and look how that turned out?" Luc strode out of the great hall, walking up a winding set of dark marble stairs.

I stepped away from the guys, pausing on the first step. This was it. The first step to the remainder of my afterlife.

I looked around the palace, and then back at my guys.

There were definitely worse ways to spend eternity.

CONTINUE ON FOR A SNEAK
PREVIEW OF THE FALLEN

HELL'S REDEMPTION BOOK 3

ABOUT THE AUTHOR

Grace McGinty is eclectic. She has worked as a choco-latier, a librarian, a forensic accountant and finally a writer. Like her professional career, the genres she writes are also eclectic. She writes romance, reverse harem romance, fantasy, contemporary young adult and new adult books.

She lives in rural Australia with her crazy family, an entire menagerie of pets, and will one day be crushed by the giant piles of books that litter every room.

Find out what happens next! Continue on to read the first chapter in Hope's novel, _The Fallen_.

THE FALLEN

CHAPTER 1

I woke to an angel standing over me, a dagger pointed at my chest. I smiled, well, at least I tried to. The searing ache in my jaw told me it was probably broken.

Azriel. I spoke into his mind and he stilled, his dagger still pressed to my chest. I took a quick inventory of my body. I was one solid mass of pain, and it felt like they'd kicked me into the room. I was chained to a bar, like a side of beef. I was naked.

Azriel, I whispered again. This time he reared back as if I'd struck him. *I guess it makes sense you're here.*

I couldn't draw breath, a rib must have broken and punctured my lung, and my heart was beginning to feel sluggish.

"Who are you?" Azriel hissed, finding his voice at last. His dagger was still pressed firmly to the space above my heart, indenting my skin. "What are you? No human should be able to speak into my mind, Witch."

I'm Hope. You know my mother and... I struggled to

define my relationship with Ace. It was part maternal, part bad influence. *And my Ace?*

Again, he pulled away as if I had struck him. He had such a beautiful face, achingly perfect even when he was gaping like a codfish.

His dagger slipped to his side. "You were one of her children. The aberrations."

Hey! I protested, but it wasn't as forceful as I'd have liked. I was dying, quickly. *Finish it. I hurt.*

He just stared at me, at the ruins of my face, the length of my bruised and broken naked body. But he didn't leer. It was like he was cataloguing me, as if I was a puzzle that looked complete, but he still had an extra piece left over.

Luckily, he didn't grant my request immediately. In the next flash, Luc, my twin Estrella and Memphis sifted in.

"Azriel, no!" Memphis shouted, lunging toward us. Azriel looked between me and the pair of Fallen angels, his face scrunched in confusion as he disappeared.

Estrella was beside me in the next breath. Blood was beginning to spill over my lips and down my chin. Estrella was pale, her beautiful blue eyes huge and wild in her face.

Rella, I whispered. I wanted to tell her that I loved her, and that she had to be strong. We were twins, but we had a connection greater than any other. My death would break her.

"Shh. I'm getting you down and then we'll get you to a hospital. I got you now. It's okay." She was fiddling with the chains and Luc came over, snapping them quickly. Memphis was there to catch me in his arms. I caught a quick glimpse of the naked rage in his eyes before a pain so intense swept over me that I screamed through my broken jaw. Everything in my body twisted, and sadness chased away the rage on Memphis' face. My empathic abilities were swamped with the depth of his pain, almost drowning out my own. He knew I was dying, that I wouldn't make it to hospital. I looked around desperately for Rella, wanting to send her one last reassurance, but my eyelids closed heavily, my body desperately trying to heal. Too late.

When I managed to open a single eye, we were no longer in dank basement that was to be my tomb. Instead, sun burned hot against my naked skin.

"Mephistopheles! What have you done?" I turned my face toward the beautiful voice that spoke. If I could have drawn enough breath, I would have gasped.

An angel stood before me, more beautiful than any I had ever seen. More beautiful than Luc or Memphis, who weren't actually beautiful so much as awe inspiring, or maybe terrifying would be more accurate. He was even more beautiful than Azriel.

"I didn't do this, Raphael." Memphis sounded hurt that the other angel had even suggested it. The cold note of vengeance had threaded its way back into his emotions. "Humans did this. You must heal her."

"Must I?" Raphael almost seemed amused, his hand reaching out to stroke my face. I turned my face into his palm. "Ah, you are one of Acerezeal's progeny." He gave me a warm smile, and it felt as if my body was healing itself from the strength of his gaze alone. That, or it no longer cared about dying.

"It is too late, old friend. She is the domain of Azriel now."

I couldn't even feel mad that this beautiful Archangel had just sentenced me to death, as long as he didn't stop stroking my cheek. His touch chased away the pain.

"Azriel came and left again. He rejected the call. Isn't that proof enough? Please, Raphael." I'd never heard any of the Fallen beg before, but I knew without a doubt that Memphis was begging for my life. Kinda gave me the warm fuzzies. Or that might have been the beginnings of my nervous system shutting down. At this point, I didn't care which.

Raphael was pondering Memphis' words. "How unusual. Well, I guess if she isn't slated for ascension by the Angel of Death, there's no harm in healing her a little. Most unprecedented, though."

He pressed a hand to my chest, inches from my exposed breast, and a healing warmth spread through my body. I grimaced as my ribs realigned, and my jaw snapped back into place, but the Archangel was buffering me from my pain. I knew this because he took it into himself. I could feel the waves of pain hitting him through my empathic senses.

My breathing became less labored, every movement no longer an agonizing torture.

"There, still broken but not beyond repair. Sometimes the human body needs to heal itself."

I tried to speak, but the pain in my jaw was still intense.

Instead I spoke into his mind. *Thank you.*

Raphael raised his brows. "You are welcome, little one." He turned to Memphis. "Does Michael know she can mindspeak?"

Memphis shrugged, jostling me a little in his arms and I grimaced.

"Sorry," he grunted at me. "I assume Michael knows. He knows all."

The Archangel Raphael laughed. "True. But he isn't as omniscient as some people wish to believe."

I summoned enough energy to look around. Wherever we were must have been somewhere in Africa, poor and rural, because out the window there was an abundance of children with big smiles but heartbreakingly thin limbs. There was a Red Cross on the door. Some kind of clinic maybe?

Where are we?

"Malawi," Raphael answered, his eyes watching me closely.

The gaunt faces broke my heart. *What do they need?*

Raphael gave me a smile that threatened to light up my world. "I see you inherited your mother's warm heart and inability to turn your back on suffering. They need what all these countries need. Food, water and infrastructure. Access to consistent healthcare services. A stable, uncorrupt government and a good influx of funds to help lift themselves above the poverty line." His emotions threatened to overwhelm me, and I mentally locked them in the box with all the other shit that needed to be processed later. Estrella had always stressed the need to keep my empathy a secret from everyone.

I gave a tiny nod. I'd make it so, or at least try my best.

"You must go now. She will still need someone to set her bones and she has lost a lot of blood." Raphael turned back towards the door. "Ah, your cavalry has arrived, Hope."

As he said the words, Luc popped into the clinic with Estrella.

Raphael smiled warmly at the devil. "Lucifer! You look well. I see having Acerezeal back has healed your wounds."

Then Luc did something that I wouldn't have believed possible if I hadn't seen it for myself. He hugged Raphael, a full blown smile on his face. "Hello, old friend."

Rella's jaw dropped open, and I wished mine could do the same. I'd never seen him hug anyone except Ace. Hell, I'd never seen him give anyone anything more than a handshake. Even as children, we would climb over him like our own personal climbing frame, but acts of tenderness were never offered, and definitely not expected. To see him being openly affectionate almost defied belief.

Luc turned to Memphis and scowled. "A little warning next time. Hand her to me."

Memphis scowled back, and held me tighter. For a moment I thought he might refuse and then they'd have a tug'o'war over my battered body, but eventually Memphis shifted me to Luc.

Luc held me safe in his arms, his large onyx wings curling around me protectively.

"Ace would have my balls if anything happened to you," he said, then sifted. I knew what he really meant. It was hard to hide your emotions from an empath. He'd been worried. He felt an affection for us that stemmed from his love of Ace, at least in the beginning. Now, I think he cared for us because we became the surrogate children that they would never have. Though neither of them would ever admit that.

Luc sifted us back to my apartment, Memphis and Rella seconds behind.

I could read Raphael, I told Rella as soon as she regained her land legs, and her eyebrows rose.

As she processed my thought, her forehead crinkled deeply. *Secrecy is more important than ever now. You'd be a threat to them all. Even if they aren't Fallen, it doesn't make them the good guys.*

I didn't respond. My body throbbed and it was a lecture she'd given me once a week since we were three. It was an issue for another day. Today, I just needed to heal from near death.

Minutes after we arrived, and Luc had laid me on my bed, Ace sifted in. She took one look at me, a little less broken but I'm sure I still looked like crap, and sifted back out again.

I curled into a ball and Estrella came over and pulled a sheet over my body, covering my nakedness. Probably too late for modesty. She laid on the bed and curled herself around me. We'd slept like this often since we were babies. I was always smaller and weaker, and

Rella was always my fierce protector. I petted her hand. She would have been terrified.

I'm okay now, I said soothingly. She let out a shuddering breath, and tension slowly seeped from her muscles.

Ace returned less than a minute later with Mom and Eli.

"Hope!" Mom raced to my bedside, stopping with a horrified look on her face when she took in my broken face, the bruises on my neck and chest. The blood drained from her cheeks and I thought she was going to pass out. Ace must have thought so too, because she shifted a few feet closer.

Eli stood beside me. "What happened?" He'd gone into doctor mode. Although he'd retired from being a neurosurgeon a few years ago, centuries of habit died hard.

I couldn't answer him, the pain in my jaw was intense. Estrella filled them in as Eli began to do triage, checking the severity of my injuries.

"She was jumped outside the Summit. Abducted. JJ is dead, executed professionally. Luc and I only found one guard, but he was just protecting the door. A grunt. He told us who paid him and that was it before Luc…" she made a tearing action with her hands, and I winced, as did Mom. Ace just looked satisfied.

Estrella recounted the whole thing without emotion, her own training kicking in. She'd become a cop for the Boston P.D. A damn fine one at that. She'd assessed the scene with cool efficiency. "I felt her go down. I called for Luc. We got there just as Azriel was going to…" This time her voice hitched, a single crack in her professional facade.

Ace let out a hiss. "I'm going to kick his fucking ass."

Not Azriel's fault. He was just doing his job, I defended to Estrella, who begrudgingly passed it on. Ace scoffed, and so did Memphis.

I hadn't realized Memphis was still here. He'd drifted into the shadows in the corner of my room. I tried to get a read on him, and flinched back. His emotions were still a torrent of darkness that scared me. I didn't know why he'd come for me. Memphis, or Mephistopheles as he'd never invited us to call him by Ace's nickname, didn't leave Hell often. Ace called him a Hellbody. She had a weird sense of humor.

Estrella must have picked up my loud thoughts. *He was with Luc when I called. Luc brought him for back up. Overkill, in my opinion. Nothing on the human plane could take on Luc, let alone Luc and Memphis together.*

I could only agree. Luc was petrifying on his own. With Mephistopheles in tow, they were your worst nightmare made flesh. And they'd come for me.

I looked at the dark Fallen angel, his almost midnight black skin making the startling blue color of his eyes all the more intense. His wings sucked up the light in the room, casting him in shadow. His face was perfectly smooth, but it was so hard it may have been marble.

Thank you, I whispered. He inclined his head, and I tried to shift past the anger in his emotions, delving deeper. I was rewarded with the hint of something softer, though I couldn't quite reach out fast enough to grab the emotion. It was like a scent on the breeze, barely a hint before it was swirling away beneath the churning rage.

I was pulled from my analysis by Eli's growl of frustration. "She needed to go straight to a hospital. She's going to need surgery to pin some of those fractures, and she has lost far too much blood. I'm calling an ambulance." He whirled away, a phone to his ear.

Estrella looked guiltily at Mom. "I didn't know how I could explain us sifting into an American hospital with her naked and bleeding. The tabloids would have been all over it, considering she was very publicly in Geneva a few hours ago."

Mom stroked Estrella's hair. "I know, love. It's okay. You did what you thought was right. Eli is just worried. He loves you two."

We knew. We might have seven fathers, but each of them loved us unconditionally.

Eli must have still had some serious clout at the hospital, because the paramedics were there in minutes. Or maybe it only seemed like minutes, because Raphael's healing was starting to wear off and my thoughts were getting slower and slower.

The Fallen went invisible as the paramedics walked through the door. "We'll go collect the rest of your seven," Ace said to Mom. "Lux must be going nuts." She sounded amused. "Memphis will help."

The large angel scowled. "I'm not a taxi service," he grumbled, but he threw me another inscrutable look and nodded. Luc, still invisible, leaned close despite the fact the paramedics were loading me onto a stretcher. "You didn't call me." He sounded hurt.

"There wasn't time." I wanted to reach out and touch his cheek, but that would look super strange.

Luc just growled. "You will call me if you have need." His tone brooked no argument and I smiled.

The Devil had my back. Always.